Mean Tide
by
Sam North

...Oliver began to shake. Grandma was possessed! Any moment now something utterly gross was going to crawl out his Grandma's mouth and try to attack him. Or worse her head was going to spin all the way around! She was Grandma Swivelhead. Run, he told his legs, but nothing happened.

Sam is the Course Leader for the Masters in Creative Writing Programme at the University of Portsmouth. He divides his time between the UK and Canada. Sam is the founding editor of www.hackwriters.com – an award winning international writers' magazine and he is a member of the Writer's Guild of Great Britain.

Also by Sam North

(Fiction)
209 Thriller Road
Ramapo
Diamonds – The Rush of '72
Eeny Meeny Miny Mole* *as Marcel d'Agneau*
The Curse of the Nibelung – A Sherlock Holmes Mystery
(a new 2005 edition of the title originally written under Marcel d'Agneau nom de plume)
Another Place to Die

(Radio Dramas)
The Devil's Dog
Final Accounts
Adventures with Randolph Stafford
Copycats
The War in Drab Nebula
History Man
Tales Dead Men Tell

(Screenplays)
The Pushover
Got it Bad

Acknowledgements
For my mother, Joanna North and her special friend Quon with thanks for their guidance, advice, love and affection over the years. For Kit and her encouragement to write Oliver's story and bringing this edition to life.

Mean Tide

Kids can survive anything, they say. Oliver, aged twelve, has a missing father somewhere in Africa, his mother is confined to a clinic and he is recovering from chemo. There is no choice but to send him to live with his only relative.

   So on a foggy day, one bald boy, with his cat, Flop, arrives at his Grandma's house at the water's edge in Greenwich. Oliver discovers to his horror that his Grandma Otis, a famous psychic, hates cats. Her housekeeper Lena, loathes kids, and then there's silent Justine, who seems to hate everyone. And why does the man next door have 100 carved wooden owls pointing at Grandma's house? Oliver quickly realises that he is living in one of London's weirdest crumbling homes, right next door to a crunching scrap yard and a towering power station. Add crazy Harriet, who has seen every fortune teller in London; Aura, a mysterious, aspiring actress and Bullet, the homeless kid with a very mean streak, trouble can't be far behind. When Oliver and Justine find a dog with it's throat cut washed up on the riverbank, Oliver feels a strange connection to this dead animal and so begins his own induction into a psychic world...

Praise for Mean Tide:

"Mean Tide gripped me completely: quirky characters, humour, wonderfully drawn setting, so satisfyingly laced with mystery and darkness and the surreal. An engaging, unusual and completely engrossing read."

Beverley Birch, author of RIFT.

ISBN: 978-1-4092-0354-4

This novel is a work of fiction. Names and characters are the product of the author's imagination and any resemblance to actual persons, living or dead, is entirely coincidental.

First published in the UK & USA 2008.

1 3 5 7 9 10 8 6 4 2

Font: StoneSans LT.
Additional handwritten font *James Fajardo* by James Paul Fajardo available via www.dafont.com/james-paul-fajardo.d856

1. A difficult boy... and one cat

The train came to a gradual halt at Newark station and almost immediately a mainline train rocketed through the station on another set of tracks, buffeting the Sprinter train. From Oliver's perspective, it looked to have been doing 200 miles an hour at least. He'd felt the power, the incredible rush of air. Oliver felt a surge of optimism, he was going to get on a train like that, going so fast you could hardly see it when it flashed by and it was going to London – his new home.

Abruptly Oliver was jolted from behind. People were anxious to get off.

"Oi, move it," someone shouted at him.

"Move it, boy."

Oliver grabbed his shoulder bag and jumped down to the platform, slipping on the wet surface and almost falling. It was only then he remembered Flop.

"Flop," he shouted and instantly scrambled to get back on board the train again.

"Move out, mind out," he was shouting as other passengers tried to get off, reluctant to let him by.

"This yours?" Someone was asking him as Oliver managed to squeeze back onto the carriage.

"Is it dead?"

Oliver came up abruptly as the train guard stood before him with a large cat box in his hands.

"What do you want to carry a dead cat around for anyway?"

Oliver's heart had already stopped. Flop was dead? How could this be? Flop dead? His only friend. Flop had seen him through everything. He seized the cat box from the guard and although he nearly dropped it, he struggled with the box through the doorway and onto the platform below. Oliver ignored everyone as he set down the cat box and squatted down beside it to peer at his cat. Flop wasn't dead, he couldn't be. He studied the ginger tom very intently, calling his name softly.

"Flop, Flop, it's me, you're alright aren't you?" Flop said nothing, but after a while of staring hard, Oliver could see his little stomach rise and fall in a regular rhythm. He could make out his little pink tongue slightly protruding out of his mouth. Flop was really zonked out. The nurse had said he'd sleep, she'd given him something in his milk that morning. She'd liked Flop, she couldn't have done anything bad to his cat, not her. There were people who had hated Flop and wanted to get rid of him, but not her.

"It's okay Flop, we're going to London, you'll wake up and you'll have a whole new life."

A bitter chill wind swept over the whole platform. Oliver looked up and saw people picking up their cases and bags, he guessed another train was approaching.

"We have to go Flop," he announced as he scrambled to his feet, noticing for the first time that his knees were wet now. He shouldn't have knelt on the wet ground. He hated having cold wet knees.

Oliver swung his bag over one shoulder then bent down to pick up the cat box again. Flop was most certainly not dead. But he certainly didn't look well. The London train was pulling in on the other platform and somehow Oliver got the impression that it was impatient, as if it didn't really want to stop at Newark, it only really liked to stop at big cities.

He lugged his cat box towards the train, his shoulder bag swaying annoyingly at his hips where something sharp was digging in.

"Over here." A passenger called out to him. Oliver saw it was the woman who'd sat next to him on the train.

"You have to get on here, it won't wait for you, y'know."

Oliver ran over towards her as she waited by the door for him. The cat box seemed to be heavier than he remembered and it didn't smell so good. Flop had obviously peed when he was put in there, he'd been so scared.

A sea of hostile faces stared at him as he struggled down the aisle, noticing that the train was already pulling out of the station. He saw no vacant seats, just a hundred crowded eyes fixed upon him. He felt his hands and armpits getting sweaty, so many people... he kept his eyes firmly fixed on the sliding door ahead, aware that someone with a large suitcase was coming towards him. Oliver was just about to stop and start walking backwards when the man swung the suitcase up in the air, trying to place it on the overhead rack. He swore loudly when he discovered the rack was too small. Oliver quickly moved past him before he lowered the case and blocked the aisle.

"Bloody stinky animals, they'll let anything on these trains," he heard someone remark as he reached the sliding door. One more carriage to go. He felt his legs shaking, why were all these people so angry?

There wasn't anywhere to sit except on the floor between carriages. He was happier now he was with Flop, even if he was a bit cold. Flop stirred, a faint bleat came from his dry mouth, whatever the Nurse had given him, it had worked almost too well. Flop was probably having nightmares. Oliver leaned in and pressed his lips to the metal cage.

"We'll be in London soon, Flop, I promise. We'll have a new life. Grandma will love you, there'll be new fields, everything will be new. You'll see the river an' everything, we'll have a great time."

The train began to pick up speed.

About an hour later he wondered if anyone would come and check his ticket, but no one did. He was wondering what Peterborough looked like, when, quite without warning, he began to think about his mother and school.

He remembered having this stabbing headache in old Stonesy's class, the Maths teacher, who had at least noticed when he'd slid unconscious under the desk. Mr Stones had quickly grabbed him and taken him to hospital himself because Oliver had looked so bad, especially when he'd begun to cough up blood. Back came the stench of the hospital, the surgeon who'd come in wearing a rugby shirt and made terrible jokes about all the blood pouring out of Oliver's nose. And later, how he'd shown Oliver the picture of the hole he'd made in his head and the tumour he'd cut out of it, the size of a tennis ball. Then they made him have chemotherapy and told him his hair would grow back, that he'd never have headaches again. They'd lied to him of course. They'd lied a lot. Didn't tell him about his Ma. Didn't tell him anything. He'd lain in bed, bored, unable to read because of the headaches and often having to put the pillow over his head because he couldn't bear the noise of the other kids laughter and their constant talking. Then their jeers when no one came to visit him.

At first he'd thought no one had told his Ma where he was, that somehow she'd not noticed he hadn't come home. He had the notion that perhaps she'd gone looking for him and there had been some sort of mix-up, they'd gotten his name wrong at the hospital desk, or confused him with someone else. After a week had passed and she still hadn't appeared, he began to fear the worst. He began having dreams about his mother lying dead at home, and his father in some prison somewhere. He awoke from sweaty nightmares, a dead scream on his lips. The other kids complained about him. But still no one told him what was going on. His Ma was weird, he knew that. He knew she got hysterical at the slightest thing, she'd just freak out if he said or did something she didn't like, then be all friendly and cuddly to try and make him

3

forget her shrieking at him, or throwing things at him. Once she'd thrown him against a wall and he'd been bruised for a month. She disliked Louth, she detested being trapped in a tiny market town where nothing ever happened. For some reason she hated the Cornmarket and would hurriedly walk by the Victorian buildings and avoided the whole town on market days. But she loved the local poet Tennyson and was always pressing people to build a statue for him in the town square. She must have written a hundred letters to people about it.

She was always cursing his absent father, Stephan, perhaps as much as ten, twenty times a day. His Dad had been working on the local newspaper as a photographer, doing the usual births, weddings, jubilees and prize-cows, then, suddenly, he'd decided to go to Zimbabwe and help people and catalogue what he'd called '*a human disaster in the making*'. Oliver had been ten years old then. More than two years had gone by since and he had a muddled memory of it all, filled with TV pictures of African homes being bulldozed and pictures of women crying over hungry children.

Stephan wanted glory, he had a London publisher interested in a photographic book and was determined to bring his unique eye to the situation.

Oliver remembered him leaving. It had been sudden, just after he'd returned from school one afternoon. Charlotte, his Mother, had thundered at them both and locked herself in her bedroom, thrown a lot of things at the door. He remembered watching a silver alarm clock sailing through the air towards the taxi that had come for his father. He recalled being hugged, his father's rasping day-old beard on his face, the pain of a father's kiss, wiping his mouth with embarrassment. But that's all. Try as he might, he couldn't conjure up his father's face, not a single detail. His mother had destroyed almost all the photographs of him that night, burned them in the garden and, most of his clothes. Oliver had managed to hide one photo, but lived in fear she would ever find it.

No one ever came to see him. Hospital was like a prison. The summer was hot and the double-glazed windows wouldn't open. As soon as he made a friend, they'd go and they wouldn't come back. Everyone said his mother had taken his illness badly, but they never said exactly what this meant, even when he asked to see her, they just ignored him. They'd say 'You can see her soon. When she's better.' That was the only clue he'd had that she was ill.

Oliver began to hate the hospital, he was worried about Flop. Who was feeding him? A month had gone by since he'd entered the hospital. He missed Flop, and dreamt about him. It took some persuading, but he made

Nurse Swaine go to his house and look for Flop. She'd brought back this emaciated ginger rag with big green eyes. Flop had been locked in the empty house for a month, living on flies and drinking water from a dripping tap. Oliver had cried for a day when he'd seen how thin and sick Flop looked, but Flop came right to him and clung on. He wasn't ever going to let Oliver leave him alone again in a hurry.

The hospital had rules against cats, but Oliver had determination. Nurse Swaine helped him find a hiding place for Flop in the old shed in the grounds, and although Flop wasn't keen, they fed him on hospital food. Neither one of them got fat on it. Neither one of them could abide the smell of the plastic warmers they put over the food that seemed to permeate everything.

The Doctor noticed how quickly Oliver began to recover once he knew his cat was found and, sensibly, he began to encourage Oliver to play with Flop in the hospital gardens, as long as he kept his head covered. Nothing would have persuaded Oliver to remove his woolly hat, not even when one freaky day the temperature reached 90 degrees. It was his personal horror that he would be bald forever, with this big red scar on his head. He didn't appreciate it when the Doctor kept calling him 'lucky'. He didn't feel lucky. His Pa never wrote, his Ma had disappeared, his cat had nearly died, they'd taken all his hair...

He remembered the day they said he could finally see his mother. She was having a 'good day', they told him. Standing in the doorway of the psychiatric ward he'd seen his mother, sat on a chair in the sun... She was wearing a white dress and looked as beautiful as he could ever remember. At first he thought she was just lost in thought. He crossed the room and went out through the French doors to the honeysuckle scented stoop. He particularly recalled the heat, and how his mother sat with her hands holding onto the chair very tightly, as if she thought she might fly away at any moment and wanted to be sure she had anchored herself.

"Ma, it's me, Oliver. Ma, it's me." Then he saw her eyes, her blue empty unseeing eyes, and he knew she'd gone, long gone. This is what they hadn't wanted to tell him; this woman, his mother, wasn't going to visit anyone, ever again.

Oliver realised that he was crying. He hadn't cried once, not since Flop had been found. Not even when he felt the dent in his head after the operation, or he got the letter from the newspaper his father had worked for, saying they'd heard from the Red Cross. No one had seen his father for almost eighteen months now. He hadn't even cried when he'd taken hold of his mother's hand and she hadn't even tried to squeeze it back, but now, in the floor of the London train he was bawling his eyes out.

Life had to get better, it just had to.

Lena Thomas stood anxiously at the barrier entrance watching the passengers streaming off the Newcastle to Kings Cross train. She felt overheated in her Burberry coat, but too lazy to remove or loosen it. The station was dense with people at 5pm and she was concerned that she might miss Oliver. She swayed a little as people brushed by her. She felt a tad delicate, perhaps just one too many sherries in the station bar. Her eyes were momentarily diverted from the scene by a sign that read *Beware of Pickpockets* and she clutched her little Ralph Lauren leather strap purse closer to her, her bloodless knuckles a clue to the vaguely anorexic frame under the coat. At forty-two, Lena still had the traces of the 'unusual beauty' she'd once been considered when young and beginning her career on the stage. For a brief while she'd been in demand enough to feature in *Harpers* and *Cosmo* as an up and coming star of the future, but somehow the breaks had never come. She'd ended up playing what the *Daily Mail* described as '*the unfortunate girl who gets murdered in the first ten minutes*' of many Detective series on TV; or briefly, for a year had been the 'Lux girl' in a series of commercials. She might have made more, done more, but sadly the bottle intervened. That, and a brief celebrity week on *Countdown* where she made an utter fool of herself. Whether it was the sherry that finished her career, or, that her looks simply went out of vogue, at thirty she found she couldn't get a decent part in TV and at thirty-five even theatre didn't want her, or her agent, (who'd publicly dumped her in Soho House when she'd insulted his manhood rather too loudly.)

Somehow, after that, she'd ended up as housekeeper to Grandma Otis, unmarried and resigned to a less than thrilling future. She kept telling herself that an opportunity would knock soon. Grandma Otis was always promising something would happen to her, but she knew in her heart that it would be hard to leave Grandma Otis and the strange life they led. Very hard.

The train had been in the station ten minutes now and although the passengers were still approaching her from the furthest reaches of the platform, it was thinning out. There was no sign of a bald young boy. Lena had been surprised that Grandma Otis hadn't mentioned Oliver before, never mind contemplated taking him in. Certainly there was no photograph of the boy in the house. She had photographs of kids from all over the world in the house, kids who'd grown up now and still sent her letters and flowers – and even though they weren't related to her, all called her Grandma Otis; but of her own kith and kin, hardly anything. All Lena knew was that Oliver was fresh out of hospital, bald from the chemotherapy and sickly. Lena was irritated at the thought of having to look after another child *and* the old woman, even though she was going to get an extra ten quid a week for it. A boy was bound to cause a lot of trouble, they always did. It was bad enough they had Justine living there, easily the strangest girl she'd ever met. Lena had been confident in her choice of being childless. She'd once had a choice, but she couldn't go through with it, too much bother, too many heartaches. She hadn't wanted to be like her mother, shouting all the time, wheedling, begging, crying, and trying to restore order in a house where no one actually gave a shit. Lena sighed, a bloody child, a sick child at that. Did Grandma Otis know what she was taking on? At sixty-six she was too old to take on these kids, it was sheer folly, and she knew it.

Where was the child? Did he even get on the train? She approached a child lugging a big plastic bag with 'Tesco' printed on it, but he passed by her into the arms of a man who lifted him up and swung him around, both their faces full of smiles. Lena studied them, making a judgement, divorced husband, weekend child, the usual.

Where the hell *was* that boy? It had been twenty minutes now. The last passengers were approaching, two old women in button down coats accompanied by a porter trundling their huge suitcases. Lena didn't think people still travelled like that any more. That was it. The train was empty. The boy had vanished, missed the train, or run off, with a bit of luck, embarrassing, awkward. Oh hell, where was he?

She began to walk down alongside the train. Perhaps the boy had fallen asleep, and no one had thought to wake him.

Oliver was far from asleep. He'd gotten off the train only moments after it had arrived, carried the cat box to the platform and, although Flop was now awake and desperate for a pee, he hadn't quite known what to do about it. He didn't want Flop to stink up his box anymore than he had to and create a bad impression at Grandma's. Flop was hungry, angry and desperate to bite his way out of the cage. A female passenger, clearly disconcerted by what she saw, stopped to watch the scene.

Oliver shrugged.

"He's pretty pissed off. Flop's never been in a cat-box before."

The woman frowned. "He looks distraught. He needs water."

"I know," Oliver replied, "I'll get some, I've got a dish in my bag."

"You do that, remember this animal loves you, he's relying on you to look after him."

The woman sped away then, leaving Oliver feeling pretty guilty about his cat. He spotted some string on the platform and got a good idea.

"It's OK Flop, we can get you some water together."

When Lena reached the last carriage, she found Oliver stood at the edge of the platform with a skinny ginger tom-cat, a string tied around its neck, a dish of water before it, as it peed generously up against the carriage wheels. No one had mentioned a cat, not once. The boy looked small for his age, the woolly hat was nothing but a rag with the wool ends trailing down his neck.

"Oliver?"

Oliver looked around at this tall woman who had approached him and he studied her, her pale blue eyes, the grey streaks in her hair. Her clothes looked expensive and she was wearing black suede men's boots. Weird. This had to be Lena.

"Flop had to pee again, he's been twice since we got here. He's starving, he didn't get any breakfast."

Lena's lips curled, unfortunately this *was* the boy. How disappointing. He wasn't even cute. So pale, looked like he might die. They'd said he was better. They'd no business sending such a sick child to them. That's what was so disgusting about the National Health Service, not taking care of the really sick, they'd no business foisting the undead on Grandma Otis, how could they?

"Your Grandma doesn't like cats. I'm Lena, your Grandma's housekeeper."

Oliver immediately felt a shiver of apprehension. The idea of anyone not liking cats, especially his own Grandma, wasn't conceivable.

"She'll like Flop, he's a terrific climber and he catches rats and eats them."

Oliver saw Lena momentarily shudder, the image of a cat tearing a rat to pieces lay between them like undigested lunch. Flop broke the spell as he began to miaow again and tug against the string.

"You're going to strangle that cat," Lena informed him. Oliver quickly grabbed Flop and loosened the string, simultaneously shoving him back into the box, a move much resisted by the dazed animal. Flop placed his paws either side of the box and dug in. Oliver bundled him in anyway, getting a scratch for his trouble. Flop growled inside as the door shut on him.

"We haven't got any rats." Lena told him. "She won't have any cat in the house, I'm telling you."

Lena walked back up the platform leaving Oliver to struggle with the cat box alone. She didn't look back, not once. Oliver didn't mind, he was used to people ignoring him. Even before his Ma was sick, she'd often not speak to him for week at a time. He'd have to cook some days 'cause she'd forget to, or she'd been shopping at Somerfields and just bought tuna. She often just ate tuna, almost everyday. Oliver used to gag at the sight of a can, but Flop didn't mind.

Lena paused in the main hall, irritated that the kid was taking so long. She looked back, finally, and saw him struggling with the cat box. She was doubly irritated; no one had mentioned a bloody cat, not once.

"Hurry up!" She insisted, but Oliver didn't hear, the tannoy was announcing delays to trains from Edinburgh due to crew shortages.

It was with some relief that Oliver approached the taxi and climbed in, wedging the cat box between himself and a horrified Lena. She pulled a disgusted face at the stench and clasped a handkerchief to her face.

"Oh it stinks, it stinks, your cat stinks."

Oliver looked at the city, in a constant state of astonishment, even if they were hardly moving in the rush hour traffic. He'd never seen so many cars or such tall buildings. He'd no idea that there could be so many people in one place at one time. You could see a city on TV, but it never conveyed the noise, the all enveloping sound of a city, or the smell. He looked at Lena in wonder.

"It's so huge. You can walk around Louth in ten minutes. How many people live here?"

Lena allowed herself a smile. She too recalled arriving in London for the first time from Lyme Regis. She'd thought Lyme Regis big enough, busy enough in summer, but nothing had prepared her for the city, the sheer volume and size of it.

"Millions", she replied, "seven or eight, I forget. So many new people now."

Oliver nodded his head. "I knew it, millions. Do we live near a park? Do we live near a forest? Flop loves trees, he's always hunting in the trees, brought home a crow once."

"Do you see any forests?" Lena asked him, her voice spiked with sarcasm.

Oliver had to admit he didn't see any forests, just four lanes deep of cars going nowhere.

Five minutes later he was looking up at a huge tower when he saw a road sign that said *'Tower Bridge, car traffic only.'* Immediately he was excited all over again.

"Tower Bridge, will we see it? Will there be a ship waiting to go under it? You hear that, Flop, we're going to cross the Thames." Oliver looked back at Lena and smiled.

"We've got a list of places we want to see – Tower Bridge is number one. Thanks."

Lena shrugged, she had no idea which way the taxi was going, but if he thought she'd planned it, so be it. Kids – nothing but trouble and pain. It was a familiar refrain echoing through her brain: nothing but trouble and pain. Grandma Otis was going to throw a fit when she saw this urchin and his cat. She'd throw the cat out, she hated cats.

"Oh my God," Oliver shouted suddenly, "did you ever see anything so beautiful."

Lena looked, but all she could see was yet another glass building with *To-Let: 190,000 square feet* emblazoned across it.

"I can see the bridge," Oliver exclaimed, unable to contain his excitement.

Oliver was stunned into silence as the taxi rumbled over Tower Bridge. He just couldn't believe all the places he'd seen pictures of and really desperately wanted to see, were all in one area; the Tower where Raleigh had been prisoner, as well as the two murdered little Princes; the river, even a Navy battleship moored alongside illuminated wharf buildings. There was the Tate Modern in an old power station and the Millennium bridge shining across the river. Seeing it all, at night, for the first time, it was just so stunning, so beautiful, everything glistened and everywhere tourists photographed everything. Oliver still had stars in his eyes from the Japanese girl who had rushed over to the taxi and flashed her camera at them. This was London alright, this was the place trains went to, this was a huge city and it was his home now, and Flop's. He wasn't ever going back to Lincolnshire. He was going to live in the city where people used the streets at night and shone lights on buildings just because they wanted to, not because they had to keep things bright to stop the kids breaking all the glass windows.

"Do we live here?" Oliver asked, thinking they'd gone far enough now. Flop was making distress noises again, he didn't like the swaying motion of the taxi.

"No, we live in Greenwich," she informed him, pointedly, "you might as well get used to it." Lena was dying for a smoke. One couldn't smoke anywhere now.

Oliver didn't pick up on the sour tone in her voice, he was much too much in love with London and everything he saw. So many people, so many buildings, so many lives. Suddenly he remembered his head, his bald head. Would people laugh at him here? Would kids pick on him, call him 'Baldy', throw stones at him? He vividly remembered Jason Bennett when he'd contracted something, a muscle problem in his leg and he'd limped for a term. Everyone had called him a spaz and shunned him. Would kids here call him names? Would there be gangs? Would he have to join one – get a knife?

Lena noticed the change in mood, but misunderstood.

"Greenwich isn't so bad, it's by the river. You like boats don't you?"

Oliver wasn't listening anymore, his head was filled with a rash of doubts and imagined terrors. Just how would kids in Greenwich treat a bald boy? Would they kick the shit out of him? What were Greenwich kids like? Oliver began to register his surroundings and began to worry as they sped through Deptford. The tower blocks looked ugly, the metal shuttered shops shabby. Kids were gathered in knots doing nothing in particular. Litter and graffiti were everywhere. He'd built a fantasy about his Grandma's house. His mother had always talked about this big house with a view of the city from her bedroom. Would he be able to see the Dome from there? He'd never seen a picture of the house, but he remembered her tale of the huge rooms and the open fire in the living room and the kitchen garden where a huge old grapevine grew. Had Grandma moved? Worse, had his mother made it all up, like Sara Nix's mother, who pretended they lived in a house, when they really lived in a caravan in a farmer's field. Just where was Greenwich anyway? Just how far from London was it?

The cab plunged into even more depressing territory, the road widened momentarily. A small bridge caused a small rise in the road and as Oliver looked out he glimpsed a huge scrap yard, an empty muddy narrow river and even more blocks of flats, with burned out cars lying at the side of the road. The cab slowed by a pub where a crowd of dread-locked kids were shouting at someone who was carrying a baseball bat. Oliver had a distinct uneasy feeling, who were these people? Everyone looked so different to the people in Louth.

"Are we there yet?" Oliver asked, his voice betraying his anxiety.

"Not far now," came the worrying reply, "You look scared."

Oliver said nothing but it *did* look kind of scary out there to him.

The cab turned a sharp corner and the transformation was immediate. Greenwich. Old buildings, cafés, bars, people enjoying themselves.

"This place is nothing but a museum," Lena drawled. "Feels like one too."

Oliver was reviving now. Gone were the tower blocks, it looked like a small town, a lot like the town he'd just left, if anything, a bit shabbier. Here were things to see. The cab swung right, then left again. The National Maritime Museum came into view. Oliver had read about this. Nelson, Queen Elizabeth the First had lived here, history was made here. He felt giddy, this was where they lived? It wasn't going to be so bad after all.

"I know this place," Oliver told Flop, who was making noises again. "It's right by the river. This is where the Royal Observatory is. We studied it in school. Can you see the Dome from Grandma's house? Is it near?"

"Well I hope they told you how damp Greenwich is." Lena muttered as she rooted in her bag for her purse.

"We're nearly there. Don't go shouting, your Grandma gets headaches, you go in quietly and I'll show you to your room."

"But where is it?" Oliver asked as the cab turned yet another corner and entered a narrow cobbled street, its tyres rumbling on the uneven surface. It was getting misty now, a strange fog that seemed to concentrate only in one area, the place they were heading. Out of the gloom another scrap yard appeared on the left and opposite narrow, one-up and one-down brick homes. This is where his Grandma lived? She was poor? These houses didn't look big enough for two people, never mind himself too. He felt the bitter, heartfelt disappointment that only a child knows. His mother had lied to him.

"Ma said she lived by the river."

"This is the river, can't you smell it?" Lena answered, proffering the cab driver thirty pounds. Oliver noticed he didn't give her any change. They had stopped by a corrugated metal fence. *'Price and Fahd Scrap'*, a sign read. Another sign, dark blue and hard to see in the mist read *'The Lord Nelson – Freehouse'*. A pub and a scrap yard. Oliver began to steel himself for the worst. He had read a Charles Dickens novel and this place had all the hallmarks of the worst in them. Scary people lived here. Smugglers, murderers and... His Grandma. It didn't seem right somehow.

Lena immediately took out a cigarette and lit up, using an elegant gold lighter that closed with a heavy *clunk*. She blew smoke over Oliver, enjoying watching him wince and cough.

The cab had gone. Oliver was standing in the bitter cold damp mist, carrying his cat-box, Flop still protesting inside it. Lena pulled up her coat collar and took in a deep breath.

"Always stinks like this when the river mist comes up," she told him. "Follow me." She flicked her hand in a non-specific direction.

Oliver watched her walk towards an opening in the metal fence and he had to force his legs into action. The mist was creepy. It almost felt like it was coating him in some alien fluid, the smell of diesel was quite distinct now. He went after her, nearly stumbling over the uneven bricks that made up the road.

Lena led him through a heavily barbed wired alleyway, that seemed to pass right through the scrap yard. A ship was moored at the wharf, its mooring lights shining dimly through the river fog, more dense here. There seemed to be a kind of overhead crane, and he could hear the sound of a train in the distance, and from the river, the sound of a low mournful fog horn. Grandma lived here? It just didn't seem possible.

12

"Here," Lena called out, pausing by a gate. "In here," she motioned.

Lena saw Oliver hesitate. "It looks better in the day." She tried to reassure him, not that Oliver believed her. Not that she believed it herself. Then Flop began to cry out loudly from his box. He was hungry, Oliver knew that miaow. Once started there was no stopping him 'till he was fed.

Lena looked at the cat box and pursed her lips before saying, "She won't have that smelly thing in the house y'know."

Oliver clutched the cat box to himself more fiercely. "I'm not going in without him."

"Suit yourself," she answered, opening the gate with a nudge of her skinny hips. "Bitch of a fog tonight, always wrecks my throat," she complained.

Oliver watched her go up the pathway and become swallowed up by the mist. He looked down at the cat box and made soothing noises to Flop, who at least stopped biting the wire grill to listen for a moment.

"If she says you can't stay, we're going, we'll find a forest to live in, a big forest where no one can find us."

With that promise made, he walked up the uneven path towards Grandma Otis's house. The mist pretty well hid most of it. One single porch light pointed the way, but only lit up the surrounding moisture laden air in a halo. Oliver couldn't tell if the house was big or small, all he knew so far was that it was next to a scrap yard. Behind it, looming in the dark like a huge shadow, within a shadow, was another building. Oliver could dimly make out a red light at the top of it blinking. What was it? A tower block? Whenever Oliver had envisioned London and the river he'd always imagined this big house with lots of trees. Not this home squeezed in between scrapyards and tower blocks.

"Come on, you're letting the heat out," Lena complained, the edge in her voice cutting precisely through the mist and chilling his heart. Even Flop stopped his protests.

Oliver emerged from the darkness. It seemed to him that Lena had almost reeled him indoors, closing the door after him with a swoosh and a definitive click.

"We're finally back," Lena remarked, hanging up her coat and sitting down to remove her boots. She rubbed her sore feet a moment.

"I hate going uptown now. All those crowds." She looked at Oliver.

"Take off your coat and shoes, set that cat box down and get washed up, the downstairs loo is just over there. Make sure you look clean for Grandma Otis, she's upset enough without wanting to see you looking like a scruff. And if you see Justine, she doesn't talk. So don't expect a reply."

"Who's Justine?"

"She's staying here until her mother gets out of prison. Don't even mention it, alright. She keeps to herself and you will do well to learn from her example."

Oliver did as he was instructed. He noted that the passageway was narrow, but warm at least. Still, this appeared to be an odd way to come into a house. Lena could see he was puzzled.

"This is the back way. Grandma only uses the front for her visitors."

Oliver did sort of think he was a visitor, but he didn't say anything. He just sat on the floor beside Flop and took off his boots. Flop looked at him from inside the cat-box confused and anxious.

"We didn't get Flop anything to eat," Oliver remembered.

"Does he eat pilchards? I've got some pilchards."

This reassured Oliver, at least they were contemplating feeding his cat. He'd hate for Flop to have to run away to the forest without eating first.

"You wash and I'll go and see to Grandma Otis, don't let that cat out, you hear? I don't want it getting used to this place."

Lena left them and walked up the stairs in her stocking feet.

Oliver immediately opened the cat-box door. Flop sniffed the air and surprisingly elected to stay in his box, scared and unsure of where he was.

"It's OK." Oliver reassured him, but this probably didn't sound convincing as he was far from sure everything was okay. He found the bathroom and dutifully peed and washed his face and hands, genuinely amazed at the amount of dirt in the bowl. He sniffed the Pears soap and memories of his father flooded in. He had always used Pears. He wondered if Grandma knew where he was, or if she even cared.

"You can come up now." He heard Lena call from upstairs. Oliver hesitated, he'd never met his Grandma before. What if she didn't like him? What if she really wouldn't let Flop stay? He'd have to leave, he'd promised Flop. A promise had to be kept, even ones you made to yourself.

Oliver walked towards the stairs, noticing for the first time the red carpet held in place by brass stair rods, the lip of each stair threadbare, so that you could see the wood beneath. As he mounted the stairs he heard each one creak, each in a different way. He stepped back a moment to the previous stair and experimented with his weight on it... Yes, one could almost detect a tune, a stairway of tunes – ridiculous.

"Oliver?" A voice enquired, imperiously.

Oliver remembered that he was supposed to be going upstairs; simultaneously he recalled that when he was younger, he'd once found his bear on the stairs at home with a broken arm, and the sudden memory of that and *the scary voice* at the top of the stairs had totally transfixed him. He just couldn't move up or down.

"Oliver!" The same voice commanded.

"Oliver," Lena's voice added to the confusion, "don't keep her waiting."

Lena came to the top of the stairs and looked down. She could see him poised mid-way, as if trapped by some unseen force.

"She won't eat you," Lena told him, her tone softer now. "She's as scared to meet you as you are her. Go on."

Oliver ordered his legs to move and they did make some effort, but it was awfully slow, one step at a time, both socks in line, toes to the edge, then one more step, socks in line, toes to the edge.

"In my lifetime, please," Lena demanded, an edge of irritation in her voice.

"The sooner you get up here, the sooner I can go down and make your supper."

Oliver registered nothing. He was an automaton now, he was going to meet his Grandma and she was going to hate him. He knew it. It was just a matter of making the inevitable happen as slowly as possible. *'She'll hate me and I'll be unhappy for the rest of my life,'* was one of the thoughts that passed through his head.

Lena reappeared at the top of the stairs wearing a lime green dressing gown and fluffy carpet slippers. She was holding a newly lit cigarette in one hand and narrowed her eyes at him.

"I don't think you appreciate just what a lucky thing it is for you that your Grandma's taking you in, Oliver. She could have let you go to the orphanage; you could have been fostered to serial killers. Who knows what could have happened to you if your Grandma hadn't intervened."

Oliver continued to stare at Lena, the still burning cigarette in her hand and her wan drawn out face, he thought of something to say, something rude, but decided against it. He did wonder if perhaps Lena might be a secret serial killer herself, she certainly looked scary enough.

He mounted another step and sighed. Yes, perhaps being adopted by your Grandma was probably better than being taken in by killers, but would they live next to a scrap yard? Did Grandma's house have to be so spooky? And then there was the scary silent Justine, who's *Mother* was in prison! He'd never heard of anyone's mother sent to prison. What terrible thing did she do?

"I'm coming now," he said, making the last four steps in quick succession.

"That's better. You go in, you talk to her. I'll make your supper."

Lena gave him a little push towards the furthest door on the landing and Oliver immediately slid on the Persian rug situated on the highly polished floor.

"Arrggh", Oliver yelled, falling hard on his backside. He heard Lena's cruel laugh as she descended the stairs.

Oliver finally got the message. Lena didn't want him here.

"Oliver? Is that you?" He heard his Grandma call. "Come on, I've got some chocolate for you."

Oliver picked himself up and moved towards her room. Chocolate sounded acceptable to him.

The first thing he noticed was that Grandma Otis had double doors opening out into her bedroom, with thick Victorian stained glass panes. The room was huge and warm, lit by many lamps covered with silk scarves to diffuse the light. There, sat in a large bed, was Grandma Otis, smiling at him from behind pearl framed glasses. A real flame gas fire was burning in a genuine marble fireplace and everywhere there were photographs of people and children and views of places from all over the world. The whole room was filled with books and knickknacks. Three burning candles stood on a bureau, in front of a mirror, and flickering shadows jumped across the walls. Oliver noticed a collection of dolls and bears in one corner of the room and he couldn't help but instantly fall in love with this room. The thick carpet, the mixture of reds and maroons and some flowering fuchsias in front of the window, the whole room was bigger than the house he'd left behind. How was it possible such a grand room, in such a small house, and all this next to a scrap yard? It was so strange.

Grandma Otis was examining Oliver critically, pulling her shawl closer around her shoulders. She was thinking that her grandson was so small and sickly. Her initial reaction was one of disappointment and then pity as she saw the holes in his socks and just how neglected he looked. Oliver was standing at the end of the bed now, looking anxious, chewing on his bottom lip, just like his mother had when she was expecting a hiding. He even clenched and unclenched his fists like Charlotte. She hoped this wasn't a bad sign.

"You don't look a bit like Charlotte. You must look like him. We don't wear our hats indoors here."

Oliver wasn't about to remove his hat and was endeavouring to try and stare his Grandma out when he felt something soft brush against his legs. Flop. He looked down and simultaneously Flop and Grandma caught sight of one another.

"A cat! A cat in my house!" She shrieked.

Flop arched, hissed and dashed from the room, just as if he'd been shot at. Oliver was astonished. He'd never seen Flop do that before.

Grandma sat up in bed, her face quite ashen. "What is that? Whose cat is that? Lena? Lena. Come up here now."

Oliver began to back away from the bed. Clearly Grandma Otis was not a cat lover.

"It's my cat, Flop. He's never done that before."

"I don't like cats," came the reply. "Lena. There's a cat in my house." She looked at Oliver with glaring eyes and raised a finger to him. "It can't stay! No cats in this house!" She said with a hiss.

Oliver felt his own anger rising. "Then *I'm* leaving."

Oliver turned and ran from the room, almost flying as he reached the stairs, all the while calling out Flop's name.

"Suit yourself boy," she roared. "I'm not having a cat in my house, you hear me?"

Oliver almost collided with Lena at the bottom of the stairs. She tried to grab him, her fingers closing around his thin arms, she shook him hard.

"What did you do to her, what did you do?"

Oliver prised himself free and dived into another room where sheets were draped over much of the furniture.

"Flop, we've got to go, we've got to go now."

Lena rushed upstairs, convinced that Grandma Otis had been attacked, at the very least.

Oliver was busy looking for Flop, and rushed in to every room, becoming increasingly desperate, calling out Flop's name.

"Flop, come on, we've got to go!" He caught sight of his tail under an old oak cabinet and he crawled under it to join him, knowing he risked being mauled by a very angry animal. Flop was hunched up, staring at him, panting, all his hair fluffed out, his mouth was slightly open, his tongue moving in and out as if he was finding it hard to breathe.

"What scared you, Flop, what scared you? You can tell me."

Thirty minutes later Oliver was once again wrapped in his coat, his bag packed and standing outside the house in the cold fog. It was eerie out there with fog horns sounding on the river. The cat box was at his feet, Flop stood beside it licking his paws and although Oliver was determined to leave, he was a bit unsure about where to go, or how. He didn't have a penny to his name and both he and Flop would need to eat.

"We could find a forest, Flop. We could live there, you could chase squirrels, I could build a home in a tree or something."

Flop continued to wash his paws, seemingly quite unconcerned now. This was puzzling, his cat was behaving in a very strange manner, also it was bloody cold and the fog seemed to penetrate every fibre of his clothing.

Oliver suddenly looked up at a lighted window. A small face peered at him, hard to see in the mist, but instinctively Oliver knew it was her, Justine. She just stared at him. It spooked Oliver a little. He turned away, he didn't like being stared at.

The front door opened a few moments later and Lena appeared, clutching her dressing gown around her. She stepped out a little way to see more clearly. Flop pricked up his ears, but didn't run. Unexpectedly she didn't scold him.

"Your supper's ready. That cat of yours can eat. Two cans of pilchards! Didn't you ever feed it?"

"Flop's very particular," Oliver answered, rather regretting his rash decision to leave. He badly needed to eat something himself.

"He's neglected, that is what he is. You're neglected. You get your skinny bones in here Oliver and eat. Then we can talk about the cat."

Lena saw he was not moving. She sighed again, stepping out further, to see him better.

"It's spaghetti and meatballs, I've never known a boy to refuse it."

Oliver tried to be resolute, tried to persuade himself that taking Flop to a forest was the right thing to do, but it *was* cold and damp and he was *very* tired. He sighed and picked up his bag again, moving towards Lena. Flop didn't hesitate, he dashed for the front door, he wasn't going to be left outside in the cold fog. Not this cat.

"That's one hungry cat," Lena remarked as Oliver moved past her back inside. "Get those boots off and go into the kitchen, you need a hot meal inside you."

The click of the lock in the door behind Oliver felt like the shutting of a cage. This was to be his new home, an old, cat-hating woman upstairs, as well as a spooky silent staring girl and a very scary woman down. He thought... *'Daddy, where are you, come home, come and get me now!'*

Oliver was just starting his meal in the warm kitchen when the girl quietly entered. She didn't look at him directly, hiding behind her jet black hair. Oliver could see that she was about his age and she was wearing a blue track-suit and old slippers, her toes poking out of both shoes. She went to a corner and sat down beside the central heating boiler. She said nothing. Lena totally ignored her, as if she wasn't there. There wasn't even an introduction. Flop wasn't bothered though and he at least went to inspect her and sat cleaning himself right beside her, so Oliver knew she wasn't a danger.

Lena was watching him eat, the boy lost in thought as he chewed his food, at least he chewed his food. She felt her eyes being drawn to his head and couldn't help herself.

"Does it hurt?"

Oliver looked up at her, confused by her remark.

"Hurt?"

"Your head, does it hurt?"

Oliver took some bread and dipped it into the tomato sauce, thinking about the question as he did so. Then, almost as if a switch had been thrown he turned back to Lena and smiled, running a hand over his head as if he had a full head of hair, then suddenly groaning, as if in real pain. He watched Lena's astonished reaction with delight, then laughed.

"Doesn't hurt now, did when they first cut me open," he grinned at her. "You should have seen the growth. Doctor Vanich gave it to me. It was the size of a tennis ball. Really! I'm not kidding, right inside my brain."

Lena screwed up her face, she felt a touch queasy, then, deciding upon decisive action she leant forward and snatched the decrepit wool mess off his head.

"This hat is going," she declared firmly, standing up.

Oliver couldn't believe it, he was in shock, no one had ever dare touched his hat before. He was instantly devastated. And very bald. He hated anyone looking at his head. Lena grimaced at the red weals on his head and the white scar tissue. It looked nasty.

"Are you going to be bald forever?"

Oliver found it difficult to speak. Almost as if she'd stolen his voice. He looked down at the table.

"It might grow back," he muttered.

Lena felt sorry for him now, and even a little guilty that she'd snatched his precious hat, and although she was tempted to let him have it, she looked down at it and it was so disgusting she could hardly bear to touch it. It had to be burned.

"I'll be back, don't forget there's pudding."

"But... My hat..." Oliver protested, as she quickly sped out of the kitchen. Oliver looked at the door with total disbelief. He knew she was going to burn it, he just knew it. He looked back at his plate and angrily pushed the remainder of his food away; hatless, he had no appetite. The girl in the corner suddenly stood up. She was watching him with wide eyes now. Oliver knew she wanted to ask him something but just couldn't bring herself to speak. He drew comfort from the fact that she said nothing. No sarcastic comments. Nothing. He *hated* anyone seeing his head exposed.

He reached over the table and grabbed a paper napkin, quickly unravelling it and plonking it on top of his head. He sighed, he knew it looked stupid, but it was his head, she had no right to take his hat, no right at all.

The girl just walked out of the kitchen and ran up the back stairs. Oliver heard a door slam. He looked back at Flop. Flop opened his mouth and gave him a strangled meow, as if to say, yes this is all very weird, before jumping up on the warm seat and curling up to sleep.

In the next room Lena was watching the old hat burning in the fireplace, taking some satisfaction in how brightly it burned on the hot coals. She imagined a million mites dying and drew some pleasure from it. It was obvious to her that no one had been looking after that boy for a long time. Two freaks to look after now. Two neglected kids. Parents just didn't know how to raise kids anymore.

Ten minutes later, Oliver was washing his dish in the sink when Lena returned, one hand hidden behind her back.

"I'll wash up," she said, acting all friendly now, so that he was immediately suspicious.

"You go back to the table Oliver and I'll bring you your pudding."

Oliver was about to say that he didn't feel like pudding now, when Lena came up really close to him and snatched the paper napkin from the top of his head.

"This should suit you better," she said, placing a black leather baseball cap on his head.

"This cap has been waiting for you, a kid from Chicago left this behind."

Oliver felt the hat, saw it had ear flaps tucked onto the sides for the cold winters in Chicago. It was all soft and comfortable against his skin. It felt good, but he didn't really want to say so. He was still upset she'd snatched his old one. He turned to see himself in a reflection, anywhere, and had to be content with his dim reflection in the window. He liked what he saw, even if it did look something like Jim Carrey would wear to get a laugh, the ear flaps were really warm; he'd always hated his ears getting cold in winter.

"I can keep this?"

"Can't have kids laughing at you."

Oliver shrugged. "They'll laugh anyway." Then, as if he remembered something positive he moved over to his bag and removed a plastic jar and smiled at her.

"But I can really make them sick when I go to school and show them this."

Lena looked at the pickled tumour in a jar and a wave of nausea washed over her. It was huge. He hadn't made it up.

"Oh, put it away, it's horrible. Didn't you have massive headaches?"

Oliver nodded, then put the jar away, moving back to the sink to wipe his hands. Lena went over to the fridge and opened it up, taking out some green jelly in a white porcelain bowl. Oliver studied her as he went back to his seat.

"You think my Dad's dead?"

Lena paused momentarily, then continued to spoon out the jelly into a Thai wooden bowl. She could see Oliver was waiting for an answer, but what could she say? *'Yes'*. For that is what she thought. Instead she put the bowl in front of him and smiled.

"I'm sure he'd be very proud of you if he knew you'd been so sick and survived. Do you think he's..." She sought for a less final word. "Gone?"

Oliver lifted his spoon and slid it into the jelly, quite thoughtful now.

"I think he's trapped somewhere. Maybe in a secret Harare prison camp. I wrote to lots of people. My Doctor posted the letters."

"Did you get any replies?"

"No. They told me that letters don't get delivered in Zimbabwe anymore. The British Consul told me they'd put Dad on some kind of 'missing' list, but that was a year ago. I know he would have written to me, if he was able to. He wrote to me when we had to leave him behind before."

"You lost him before?" Lena asked, surprised.

"We had to come back from Brazil. My Dad was working on a documentary about global warming and the rain forest. It's dying, you know. Animals are becoming extinct and they're burning all the trees. You can see the smoke from space, y'know? I went into the forest with him. It really does rain when it gets hot.

"Anyway Ma hated it there and made us go home. She said I was missing school. I didn't want to come back, but Ma said we had to.

"Dad came back when they finished the filming. Got a job on the local paper, but he hated being there. He was bored. Ma just didn't like to go anywhere I guess. I wanted to go with Dad to Zimbabwe, but he said it was dangerous."

"He was right. It is dangerous. Those poor people have enough to worry about without having you causing trouble." Lena was curious as to how matter of fact Oliver was about his life. So much had happened to him and yet he was so untouched by it all. Brazil! How did one even begin to get a job there, let alone drag along a wife and child? She watched Oliver eat his jelly.

"I'm sure you'll hear from your father when he's able to write. I think you should speak to Grandma about him. She wants to see you now. Your cat won't disturb her, I don't think he's going to leave that chair, do you?"

Oliver grinned. Flop must have known they were talking about him because his ears were twitching. He stretched one arm out to touch the warm gas boiler alongside the chair with his little pink pads. Oliver frowned.

"Do I have to see Grandma tonight?"

"Of course. Don't be scared. She won't bite, I promise."

Oliver wasn't so sure. He tended to trust Flop's instincts better than his own and if Flop thought she was scary, then she was scary.

"No one is like your Grandma Otis. You'll discover she's almost famous. People come from all over the world to see her. She's strange, but she'll always tell you the truth. That's rare."

Oliver took one last look at Flop and sighed. He had to do it.

Lena watched him go and quickly she went to the door and shut it after him, noticing Flop had already woken and was keenly aware that Oliver had left the room. Lena already understood just how close these two were. She was beginning to accept the situation now. The question was, why had his family disintegrated? Why hadn't his father written, (assuming he was alive). It was cruelty for the sake of it in her opinion.

Grandma Otis sat up in her bed totally rigid, her eyes were open, but unseeing. There was a hint of a green glow in the room, but Oliver couldn't see where it was coming from exactly. All he did know was that this was the spookiest situation he'd ever been in. Grandma Otis seemed to be in some kind of trance. He'd come into the room and she'd told him to stand still. Oliver could see himself reflected in a mirror, his big toe protruding from his left sock. Grandma Otis suddenly seemed to take in a deep breath and she began to speak, but her voice was now entirely different, almost as if she was pretending to be a man. Oliver felt the skin on his head crawl and the green light seemed to spread all over the room.

"You want to know if your father has passed over to the other side?" The strange voice asked him.

Oliver began to shake. Grandma was possessed. Any moment now something utterly gross was going to crawl out of his Grandma's mouth and try to attack him. Or worse her head was going to spin *all the way around!* She was Grandma Swivelhead. Run, he told his legs, but nothing happend. Some part of him was hoping it was just a trick, something to scare him, see what he would do.

"You OK, Grandma?" he asked weakly.

"Be quiet, boy," came the immediate response.

"Your father is still alive. He cannot write to you. He wants to, but he cannot. Something or someone prevents this."

Oliver realised that he had seen this kind of thing before, on TV. Someone was speaking through Grandma Otis. Accepting this, he was able to deal with the situation. He decided he wouldn't be scared. This was his Grandma, nothing was going to hurt him. They wouldn't do that, not on his first night. Would they?

"Who are you? How do you know this? Where's Grandma?" Oliver whispered.

"My name is Quon, be a good boy Oliver and I will tell you many secrets. There is no need to be scared, I am your Grandmother's friend."

Oliver was still shaking, but curious now, almost enjoying the sensation and the green light that seemed to make everything sparkle in the room.

"Where's Grandma? What have you done with her?"

"She is here. She says, *'be calm'*. I am her guide, I am here to help you as well. I know the question you want to ask me. It is... *'Will my hair grow again?'*

Oliver began to feel weak at the knees. That was the exact question he'd wanted to ask. He was seriously spooked now.

"The answer is yes Oliver, but not the same as before and not for some time yet."

Oliver began to shake. His voice just a scratch.

"My mother, what will happen to her?"

"That is something that only time can answer. Some things are beyond knowing. I can promise nothing."

Oliver stared at his Grandma and although he was scared, he was kind of reassured that whoever was really speaking didn't know the answer to that. Then he saw his Grandma let out an enormous sigh and the green light began to dim as Grandma Otis's eyes and breathing seemed to return to normal. They slowly began to focus on Oliver who was now squashed up against the far wall staring at her with complete astonishment on his face. She could quickly see that he had been scared and she smiled at him.

"So, you had a talk with Quon? Don't be scared, he's old and wise. You weren't actually afraid were you?"

Oliver realised that he had forgotten to breathe and he sucked in a huge amount of air, trying to re-adjust to the new situation. His Grandma was watching him, a genuine look of concern on her face.

"He said..." Oliver took another deep breath. "He said my father was still alive, that he couldn't write to me. He said Ma might not get better, not for a while."

Grandma Otis sighed, then reached back to her bedside table and grabbed a little packet of something. She held it out for Oliver, beckoning for him to come closer.

Oliver did not feel like going closer, but he could recognise a packet of Maltesers from a hundred yards away and he was seriously tempted.

"Come on, I know you like them. Quon told me they were your favourites."

"How could he know that?" Oliver asked, puzzled. "How could he know?"

Grandma Otis shrugged. "I never ask how he knows, he just does. He told me a long time ago that your mother, my Charlotte, was ill, but she wouldn't answer my letters. Y'know how many years I have waited to see you? I've not seen you since you were a child. She wouldn't visit, not once. And that father of yours, him going off like that, leaving you with her. Stupid man, fancy going to Zimbabwe. Doesn't he read the news? People are starving there."

Oliver advanced a little closer and she pressed the Maltesers into his hands.

"Don't let them melt."

He opened the packet with his teeth, remembering something his mother had told him about this woman.

"Ma told me you threw her out when she was pregnant with me."

Grandma Otis immediately looked pained, she reached under her pillow and withdrew some photographs. She laid them out before her for Oliver to see. He sucked on a Malteser letting the chocolate melt slowly in his mouth. He saw his mother as a young woman, she was so pretty. He laughed with surprise and delight.

"That's Ma, and there's you. Is the baby me?"

Grandma Otis settled back against her pillow and smiled.

"Aye, see the hair? You were born with such a fine head of hair. You were born right here. You squawked night and day, young man. Wouldn't sleep, worried us to death. You and your mother lived here for two years. I cried for a week when you left, but she had to go. Your father came for her."

"You didn't throw her out?"

"Oh yes. He wanted her back and she didn't want to go. She was content to let me cook and clean for her, but your father loved her and wanted her. I should have known then that Charlotte wasn't right." She sighed, helping herself to a couple of Maltesers. He rather resented that, but she *had* given them to him.

"God knows how to test a mother, he really does. He can test, test, test, and then laugh when you come back for more. I threw her out, made her go and live with the man who loved her and she never forgave me for it."

Oliver took another look at one of the photographs. He had never seen a photograph of his mother laughing before. It occurred to him that he'd never seen his mother laugh. She'd looked so pretty then. He frowned and looked at Grandma Otis.

"But who is Quon, exactly?"

Lena stood at the bottom of the stairs listening, but not hearing. She looked happier, there were no shouts, they were getting on. She was pleased about that. She took a sip from her sherry glass and headed on back towards the kitchen.

Grandma Otis had more photographs on the bed, showing her dressed in safari clothes and holding a huge fly swatter. Oliver examined the shots with growing interest, impressed when he saw elephants or lions in any of the photos.

"How long were you in Africa?" Oliver asked.

"Oh, nearly twenty-five years, went out there in '67 with my husband. It was still an adventure then. I was teaching. My husband was teaching also. We lived out in the bush. Nicolas, that's my husband, your grandfather, he took sick and died. It was so sudden, I hardly had time to register it before I also fell ill. Such a fever it was too. I was burning up. The village natives were quite ready for me to die and I was waiting for the moment, when quite suddenly I felt a cool hand stroking my face and a voice saying, *"Everything is fine, I'm here now, I'll take care of you."* That was the first time Quon came to me. He died a long time ago y'know, but he found me and told me I would be saved."

Oliver looked at her with a new found fascination. Africa, voices, saved from death. He knew these things happened on television, but in real life, to his own Grandma? It was amazing to think of how adventurous she had been.

"Quon had always wanted to travel, you see. He knew I'd be travelling."

Oliver ate some more Maltesers as he filtered this information through his brain.

"But how can he know anything, if he's dead? How can he know about my father?"

Grandma Otis sighed and clasped her old, slightly puffy, hand over Oliver's.

"Quon would know if he was dead, Oliver. He wants to help you, you'll see, you'll see."

There was an awkward silence between them then, Oliver not sure what to say next.

"You'll discover many surprises in my garden tomorrow. We've got a special climate here, caused by the power station. It's so high you see, keeps it sheltered from the cold. I've got plants growing here that normally only grow in Africa. I use the herbs for healing. It's wild, but special. Same the other side in Trinity Hospital gardens. You'll hear the birds tomorrow. Hundreds of them live in the Ivy growing up the power station walls on the other side. Sometimes on a quiet night when the birds are excited I almost find myself back in Africa. London is full of such surprises."

Oliver didn't doubt it, not at all.

"Did you meet Justine? You be nice to her. She's a strange girl, but she's been through hell and we're taking care of her until her mother gets back. She probably won't speak much, but she's bright. Gets 'A's all the time at school. But she's a worry. I hope you can be a friend to her."

Oliver left the room soon after and as he was coming out onto the landing, he saw her. Her door was slightly ajar and he saw her eyes reflected in the light. But she said nothing and Oliver was still a little scared of her. He ran downstairs to make sure Flop was okay.

A while later, sat in his mother's old bedroom, he pondered the change in his life. On the wall was pinned a Rod Stewart poster, yellowing with age. All around him were records and tapes and magazines from his mother's past. It was so weird. It was as if Grandma Otis had never once set foot in this room since his mother had left all those years before. On his bed lay hairy gonks, and an abandoned teddy bear with just one eye. He listened to his mother's old vinyl L.P.s that crackled, but he was quite impressed by David Bowie singing about *Spiders From Mars*. It dawned on him that his mother must have been a completely different person when she was young. He turned over and stared at the row of shoes on a rack. Then laughed out loud when he saw the huge platforms attached to bright yellow plastic shoes. He noticed pictures on the wall of his mother when she was young, dressed like a hippy, wearing beads and standing next to a horse.

Grandma Otis nudged open the door and smiled, happy to see him laughing. She looked at the rack of shoes and laughed herself.

"Your mother always suffered from an excess of bad taste."

"I never knew she was a Duran Duran fan. She used to dance too. See the picture on the wall?" He laughed, then, somewhat wistfully. "She never even told me she'd lived in Africa".

Grandma Otis shook her head in the sad memory of it all. A rash of ugly memories crowding through her brain: the drugs, the arguments, the attempted suicides, the screaming and slamming of doors. She shut her eyes.

"She was born in Durban. I was planning to come home to have her, but she came early. She loved Durban, loved to swim and ride horses. She didn't want to come back to live here. But..." Grandma Otis sighed.

"I wonder why she stopped smiling," Oliver was saying, but Grandma Otis was leaving, she couldn't bear to look into this, the memories just never went away. Never.

Downstairs, a few minutes later, Grandma Otis sat with Lena in the living room. They both stared at the dying coal fire in the grate. Grandma Otis was wearing a huge quilted silk dressing gown and she sipped a mug of hot Horlicks. Lena topped her mug up with a dash of brandy. Upstairs the sound of Davie Bowie was coming through, loud and clear, from Oliver's room.

"It's funny." Grandma Otis said, after a while. "I used to hate Charlotte's music, but now it doesn't seem so bad."

Lena smiled and huddled her dressing gown closer to her neck.

"I met William, my ex, at a Bowie concert in Reading. Gives me goosebumps to hear it now."

Past midnight, Oliver lay asleep in his bed, the music long since ended. His door began to creak a little, opening an inch, then two inches, finally four. Flop slinked in and jumped up on his bed, purring and settling down beside him. Almost asleep, Oliver instinctively put out a hand to cuddle the cat and Flop licked his fingers. Flop had decided. It was warm, they had food, they'd stay.

In Grandma Otis's room, she lay awake, troubled, watching the full moon through her window. She was worried. Something strange about the boy. A different strange to little Justine, who been through so much when they took her mother away. Oliver was so tightly wired. Like he'd snap in two. But she knew right away, the moment she had clapped eyes on him, that he had a good heart and a good heart was hard to find.

2. Harriet

Everything smelled like porridge. That was the one thing Oliver's father had liked in the morning, and although Oliver had been entirely sceptical about eating it at first, once he had smothered it in milk and honey, it was edible. Flop had gone out, but the indentation of the missing cat was clear to see on the bed cover. Oliver swung his legs out of the bed and examined his mother's bedroom again. It was so strange to be in a room full of old posters and faded hippy clothes, but he had mixed feelings about his new situation. He knew his mother wouldn't ever again appreciate what she had, probably didn't care, but the scariest thing was the unspoken fear he had about whether he too might be like her one day. Add that to the list of things he was scared of: eating rissoles, AIDS, aliens, mushrooms, spiders, frogs (or was that toads?), smelly cheese, monkeys – but only because they smelled bad – and then there was the Dentist. He'd just looked scary, right from the beginning. His toxic breath that smothered Oliver when he lay squirming in his slippery red chair with a stupid picture of a frog on the ceiling. Yes, going mad really was scary, there was a lot of it in the family, he could see that now. Grandma was clearly crazy, kind of nice with it, but living with a dead person wasn't exactly normal. His mother had gone over the edge completely and his father had never really had much sense (according to his Ma and she should know.) There was no hope for him, none at all, it was all just a matter of time.

The smell of porridge wafted into his room again and reminded him that he was hungry and needed to pee. Time to get up, start his new life. His eye caught a poster he hadn't noticed before, half-curled up on the rear wall, partially faded from where the sun had touched it over the years. Oliver stood up and placed the palm of his hand on it, to flatten it out, so he could read it. *We are not alone* it proclaimed. *Close Encounters of the Third Kind*.

"Wow, Ma was a science fiction freak!" Oliver exclaimed aloud. He grinned. He'd seen the movie on TV and been scared to death – OK, confession – he'd watched most of it from behind the sofa. It was strange, but somehow just the existence of this poster brought him closer to his Mother than all the other things in the room.

Lena was making coffee in the kitchen, stirring boiling water into the cafetière. Harriet was reading her stars in the *Daily Mail* as she nibbled on a piece of brown toast.

"It says, *Big decisions today. The eclipse of the new moon will alter everything, but ask yourself, are you ready for such changes?*"

Lena smiled. "The last big change in my life was when my hair turned grey."

Harriet looked surprised, frowning as she examined Lena's hair.

"You're grey?"

"Not since my date last night with Harmony. Grey is social death. I mean, a man goes grey and we're all supposed to say how distinguished he looks. I go grey and they ask me if I would play Miss Marple in *Murder at the Gallop* or something dire, it's like you died overnight."

Harriet brushed back her own genuine ash blonde L'Oreal hair tossing it to one side, giving it the once over, as if to make sure it was still there.

"I'm never going grey. I'm going to stay blonde until they arrest me for bringing old age into disrepute."

Lena brought the cafetière to the table and set it down, noticing the cat patiently sitting by the door.

"I've got to get that boy up."

"Does Grandma Otis know there's a cat in her kitchen? Doesn't she have a 'thing' about cats?"

Lena smiled, sitting down at the table and pulling the sugar towards her. "She and the cat met, I don't know who was the most frightened, you should have been here last night, quite some scenes. But it's a nice cat, I could do with the company. You think I should let it out?"

Harriet shook her head.

"First day? Is it safe to let a cat out here? I wouldn't let my cat out in this neighbourhood – correction – I wouldn't let my cat live in this place. Every time I come here I'm surprised I still have wheels on my car when I get back."

Lena pulled a face to let Harriet know that she was exaggerating.

"No one steals anything around here, everyone knows Grandma Otis. It looks bad, but I think it's one of the safest places in London, it's a real community."

"That's because there's nothing worth stealing around here, except scrap metal. She's not poor, why doesn't she move? She could live up on Maze Hill by the park."

Lena pushed the plunger down on the cafetière and shrugged.

"Memories. It was her father's place. He was the power station manager. Her father was God around here in the war, and after. He got a medal from the King for his services to the nation *and* made a pile on the black market too, from what other folk tell me. Grandma Otis holds that he was the straightest man in London and he never profited once."

Harriet frowned. "Growing up here, in all those sulphur fumes – yuk – it must have been disgusting. Coal fires, smog, London must have been ghastly."

Lena nodded in agreement. "Yes, but everyone had a job back then. You couldn't breathe, but everyone had a bit of pride."

"I heard that someone sold their one bedroom council flat for £390,000 around the corner. Grandma Otis could get a fortune for this place, it's freehold isn't it? They could fit twenty homes on this site. I can't believe she doesn't just sell."

"She's had offers. They want to build a block of flats on this land. She's refused everyone so far."

Just then Justine appeared, like a wraith from the dining room. She was dressed in her school uniform, grey pleated skirt and tumble down socks over her scuffed brown shoes. She was putting on her coat and she stopped when she saw Harriet. She seemed surprised to see her.

"You remember Harriet?" Lena asked her. "You ate your breakfast, Justine? You'll be late if you don't go soon."

Justine didn't answer any questions, of course. She grabbed her rucksack off the back of a kitchen chair and headed towards the backdoor. Flop immediately began to wail to be let out, stretching his body up towards the door handle. Justine opened it up and Flop shot out.

"I don't think..." Harriet began but Justine was out of the door and gone.

The kitchen door opened and Oliver appeared dressed in jeans and a faded red sweatshirt, his head covered with his new cap. It seemed to Lena he looked more pale and woefully undernourished than the night before, if that was possible. She stood up, flustered, not exactly sure what to do or say, she just wasn't used to having him here yet.

"I can smell porridge," Oliver said, matter of factly. "Where's Flop?'

Lena looked at the door, as if hoping the cat would come back in on its own accord.

"Just went out. He looked a bit desperate."

Oliver thought about it. At home they had had a flap and Flop just came and went as he pleased. He'd have to remember to let him in and out here.

Just one more little problem to think about.

"He won't go far. The cat will be scared." Harriet told him, hoping she sounded calm about it.

Oliver quickly opened the door, looking for his cat. It was cold now. Definitely colder than the day before. He could see Flop at the edge of the garden.

"Don't go far, you don't know where you are, OK?" Oliver turned back to the kitchen. "Did he eat anything yet?"

Lena shook her head. "Not yet. Got nothing for him until I get to Sainsburys."

"Good," Oliver declared. "He won't go far if he's hungry."

He returned his gaze to the cat and the scrap yard behind him. In Louth they had trees. Not many trees for Flop out here that he could see. "I'm going to have some porridge, Flop, you can have some milk when you finish, OK?"

He shivered momentarily and came back inside, closing the door behind him.

Lena was at the stove pouring out the porridge into a large ceramic bowl, adding milk and treacle to it. Oliver and Harriet watched as she scooped the treacle out of a glass jar and held it suspended over the bowl from two feet, letting the thick treacle fall in slow motion from the spoon to the waiting grey matter below.

Lena suddenly remembered Harriet.

"Oliver, this is Harriet, she's a regular with your Grandma, she's going to take you out today – show you around."

Oliver looked at Harriet with narrowed eyes, as if making a decision as to whether he approved of this scheme, or Harriet. He got up off the floor and went to sit at the table where Lena slapped down the bowl of porridge before him. Oliver continued to stare at Harriet, taking in her blonde shoulder length hair and her meticulously made-up face, her heavy gold bangles wrapped around her slim wrists and he wondered what type of woman she was. She was pretty, but looked tightly wound up, she reminded him of someone's mother at school who'd once been a model and couldn't forget it. He ate his porridge, savouring the rush as the sweet treacle slid down the back of his throat.

"Not going to say anything?" Lena asked him, as both she and Harriet watched Oliver eat his porridge with the etiquette of a starved refugee.

"Is there any more?"

Harriet laughed. "Didn't anyone ever take care of you at home?"

Oliver regarded her with a frown, but then quickly realised that she didn't know anything about him.

"You ever have to eat hospital food for four months?"

Harriet was genuinely appalled. "Four months and you're still alive? You poor kid! Lena get this boy some more porridge, he's starved."

Oliver laughed and finished what he had in the bowl.

"Four months and six days, some people died, they got poisoned, but I couldn't eat the meat, it smelled like plastic. I used to visit the old people and eat their fruit."

Lena smiled. "Kids know how to survive."

Harriet put out a hand towards Oliver's head but he instinctively shrank back.

"Don't you worry Oliver, we're going to take good care of you here. Did it hurt? The operation, I mean."

Oliver shrugged, leaning back to allow Lena to place another steaming bowl of porridge before him, the milk slopping about over the top of it, revealing a black treacle hole just visible beneath.

"Eat it slowly, it's hot. Your stomach might explode."

Oliver just grinned and ate his porridge just as quickly as before, a frown on his face as he considered how to reply to Harriet's question.

"The chemo didn't hurt, but it makes you sick, a lot. I used to puke every time I ran or when I had to climb the stairs." Oliver grinned remembering something.

"One time I puked, stood up and slipped in it and rolled down the stairs and when the nurse ran after me, she slipped in it too and she fell the whole way down. She was really pissed off with me. Doctor Anderson said that they'd given me too big a dose and that's why I was sick. I didn't have to have any more treatment then, except for when they did something to the burns on my skin."

Harriet stared at Oliver with a mixture of disgust and respect. She recognised that this boy had been through hell. It was remarkable he was so cheerful, so calm about his experiences.

"Did you ever think you were going to die?" Harriet asked. Lena gave her a sharp look and Harriet realised, too late, that this was a dumb question to ask a boy who'd been through so much.

"I'm sorry, I didn't mean to ask that Oliver, it was stupid of me, I'm..."

Oliver shrugged, he was used to this question. It was something he'd discussed with all the kids on the cancer ward. Death was like a lottery ticket. That was what Dr Vanich had told him. He was as likely to die as winning a million on the lottery and that was really difficult.

"I knew I could die, but..." He frowned again, putting his spoon down and looking at Lena and Harriet very carefully, as if making his mind up about whether to tell them something important.

"Promise you won't tell Grandma this...?"

Harriet looked at Lena and both of them exchanged worried glances. It was good to feel he trusted them, but what was he going to say? It was worrying.

"Your secret is safe with us," Lena reassured him.

Oliver pushed his half-finished bowl of porridge towards the centre of the table as he considered how to express what he had to say.

"Is it about your operation?" Harriet asked. "Because if it is too gross, don't tell me. I'm scared enough of catching something. I swear my mobile phone is going to fry my brain. But how do you live without one?"

Oliver looked at her with a puzzled look. Harriet was forced to explain.

"They use similar frequencies as microwave ovens, so if you spend too long talking on one, your brain gets cooked. Or so they say."

Oliver pulled a face. "Eewe... that's gross!"

"Harriet's brains were cooked a long time ago – and not by any phone," Lena remarked dryly.

"What were you about to tell us, Oliver?"

Oliver watched her cross the kitchen to a pile of washing in a basket and proceed to fold the bundled clothes and towels.

"When they were operating on me," he began, "I could see everything. I could see them cut open my head and the Doctor lean right over and look into my head. At first I thought it was strange because his face was all blue, then I realised that the blue light was shining out of my head. The Doctor was pointing at it and I remember a nurse looked away, as if she was scared. Then the Doctor got a pair of things, I mean tongs and he went right into my head and pulled out this blue box. The Doctor was really surprised, he showed it to everyone. Everyone was looking at it as he held it up to the light, it was really pretty. The light shone out of it and it was a brilliant blue, you could see the blue light touch everything in the room."

Lena and Harriet exchanged worried glances again. A blue box in his head? How weird; how extraordinarily weird.

"Then they closed me up again," Oliver continued. "It was amazing. They didn't give me the box later. I asked for it. He gave me the tumour to keep, but I know it came out of a blue box. They never told me what happened to it." He sighed. "I never told anyone about that box before."

"A blue box, you say?" Harriet asked, looking at Lena again, uncertainty in her face.

"How did you see this? Didn't they put you out?" Lena asked.

"Put me out?" Oliver asked, confused.

"Put you to sleep," Harriet explained.

"Yes, but I still saw everything."

Lena shook her head. He had imagined it, of course, but still, what did it mean? She looked at Harriet who seem to nod with her, agree with her unspoken thoughts that Oliver was a lot more strange and complex than your average young boy.

"Got to go to the bathroom." Oliver announced abruptly, a note of alarm in his voice.

Lena laughed. "I told you not to eat your porridge too quickly."

Oliver got up from the table and ran from the room, embarrassed as well as desperate.

Harriet smiled, "Poor kid."

"Weird kid... A blue box, in his head? He actually saw it?" Lena retorted.

Harriet poured herself some coffee and added milk.

"Not so mad. Perhaps it is just his way of dealing with it, y'know. It's his way of explaining what went on. He had something bad in his head and they cut it out. He thinks it was a blue box. It's cute. I think it's kind of special."

Lena thought about that.

"Why brilliant blue? I mean, how did he see it? I suppose it could have been a vivid dream he had under the anaesthetic. That would explain it."

Harriet sipped her coffee. "Let him believe it was a box. Don't try to disillusion him Lena. Let him keep the box."

Lena looked at Harriet and saw that she was serious. She shrugged. It was none of her business anyway.

"What happened to that bloke you were seeing?" Harriet asked suddenly as she closed the door.

"What happened to yours? Steve wasn't it?"

Harriet pretended to stick her fingers down her throat and gag. "That bastard? Don't even mention his name!"

Oliver sat on the loo and sighed. The hot porridge was still sitting in his stomach like he'd swallowed a hot-water bottle. He wished he hadn't been so greedy. He had been hungry, but not that hungry. He got up and flushed, then washed his hands. He noticed a picture on the wall of Grandma Otis and his mother when she was just a kid. There was an ostrich in the background and they were both smiling out of the picture, looking happy. His mother had a big bandage on her leg. Oliver wondered what had happened to her.

He went back downstairs, drying his hands on his jeans as he went. He could hear Harriet talking, her voice was much higher than Lena's. He didn't know what to make of Harriet. She was different to anyone else he had ever met. She was going to take him out – why? She looked friendly, but it was too soon, he was still a bit nervous about being in London. Oliver didn't like to leave Flop on his own. He stopped outside the kitchen door. He could hear Harriet getting worked up about something.

"I'm not kidding Lena, he grabbed me by my hair and threw me out. I mean, shit, you'd figure a normal man would want you to spend the night once he's shagged you, but no, he just threw me out and tossed my clothes out of the window. My green Versace tube, for God's sake! That cost me a fortune. Doesn't he know, you just don't do that to a Versace dress?"

Oliver pushed open the kitchen door and entered. Harriet immediately realised that he'd heard her and pulled a face. Lena shook her head, hoping Oliver hadn't heard.

"The boy's only twelve Harriet, watch that mouth of yours."

"Twelve? He looks older."

"But not old enough for you, thank God," Lena remarked, narrowing her eyes at her.

Harriet giggled as Oliver did his best to ignore both of them and strolled to the back door to open it and call Flop back in. He didn't have to say a word. The moment the door was wide enough Flop shot back in and practically hugged the boiler, plonking himself down beside it with a brief half-cry, as if to say; *it's bloody cold out there, where were you?*

"That cat's never going to leave this place," Harriet remarked.

"He needs some milk." Oliver declared, closing the back door and walking towards the fridge.

"I've got some warm milk for him here," Lena told him. "You sit down. Do you have to take any pills? I forgot to ask."

Oliver looked back at her and nodded. "Just one, at night." He rejoined the table and poured himself some milk as he watched Lena take the milk saucer to his cat. Flop ignored it and just licked his paws.

"Probably likes cream." Harriet suggested.

"He only likes me to feed him, usually." Oliver told her.

"Well, I fed him last night and he nearly bit my hand off," Lena told him, returning to fold her laundry.

Oliver drank some milk, then fixed his eyes on Harriet, asking, "Did he really throw you out on the street, naked?"

Harriet swallowed hard. She looked at Lena but Lena just mouthed at her,

'You're on your own' and fixed a mean stare on Oliver, noticing for the first time just how piercing, how brilliant blue, his eyes were.

"He was a real pig, Oliver. Don't you ever get like that. Of course, I go for the pigs every time. If there is a choice between the devil and a saint, I pick the devil. I can show you the bruises, they're huge."

"Harriet," Lena drawled, a distinct warning note in her voice.

Oliver was still curious however. "But why? Why pick someone who'd do that to you?"

"Because Harriet is doomed Oliver." Lena intervened. "You'll find out, some women are just born losers with men. Harriet is a prize specimen, an Olympic champion loser."

Harriet glared at Lena a moment and thought of something really bitchy to say but Oliver got in his question first.

"But why don't you just say no?"

The concept of this approach was just so startling Harriet and Lena both instantly broke out with laughter, which built, with every moment, into a hysterical wave of astonishment.

"No?" Harriet repeated, coming up for air. "You want me to start saying 'No'? Sweetie, you start saying 'No' in this town, you might as well be dead."

Lena steadied herself and tried to regain her former composure.

"You're giving him the wrong idea about things, Harriet. I don't think he's safe in your hands."

Harriet made an attempt to look innocent, fluttering her eyes, "Me? Rubbish. Right, we have to go. Are you ready? You better have a coat on, it's chilly today. Did you see the Dome yet?"

Oliver looked out of the window and saw the wind bending the top of the one tree. "I can see the top of the Dome from the landing window. Do you think I'll get to go on the London Eye?"

"I can get tickets. We'll do it at night. London always looks best at night."

Oliver smiled, he could tell Harriet would keep her word. He was good at sensing that kind of thing. "I'll get my coat. Where are we going now?"

Harriet stood up, finished her coffee and smiled. "My shop first, then Mr McTeal."

Lena looked very interested all of a sudden. "McTeal, the psychic? You've got bored with Grandma Otis?"

"He's supposed to be the best. The Royals use him all the time. Anyway, Grandma Otis never says anything different, she's always seeing disaster around me. I want a second opinion."

"Is he a Doctor?" Oliver asked.

"He's a fortune teller," Lena remarked. "He only pretends to be a psychic. He won't tell you anything different to what Grandma Otis says, and if he does you know he's making it up."

Harriet stuck her tongue out. "Well, I'm still going. He's expensive and Dorothy Minner says he's brilliant. He did total immersion with her and told her she had to get a divorce. He even told her which one of her friends her husband was sleeping with. She swears by him."

Lena snorted. She didn't think much of McTeal at all.

"What's immersion?" Oliver asked as he went to get his jacket from the corridor.

"It's when you go naked into the hot tub and he pours all kinds of herbs into the water to make you relaxed and he taps into your inner senses."

Lena smirked. "He should be paying *you* for that. He's a perv, Harriet, just a bloody perv!"

Oliver returned with his jacket on and looked embarrassed. "Are you going to get into the hot tub with him today?"

Harriet grinned at his embarrassment. "Don't panic. We're just going for the reading. The hot-tub treatment costs a fortune. Besides, I wrinkle easily."

Oliver looked pensive for a moment. "A gypsy came to our door once and read Ma's hand. Ma was really angry with her. I don't know what she said. She cried for hours after it. Why do you go? I'd be scared to know what's going to happen to me."

Harriet shrugged as she put on her thin orange cotton coat. "Look Oliver, all I want is just one decent man in my life. It shouldn't be so hard. Actually, preferably hard, he should definitely be hard."

Lena laughed, but it was stopped short when a bell rang out surprising them all. Lena reacted instantly by switching on the electric kettle. "That's your Grandma. Come on, let's get you out of here, before she thinks of something for you to do."

Oliver looked at Flop and quickly went over to his cat, squatting down to hug him. "Be good, drink your milk. I'll bring back something to eat, I promise."

He stood up again and Flop looked up at him, perhaps uncertain as to whether Oliver was coming back. Oliver picked up the uncertainty in Flop's eyes. "I'll be back, I promise."

"Enrol him at the library, Harriet. I think a boy should read. Justine can take him when she goes. She loves the library."

"Boys only read dirty books or computer magazines," Harriet remarked cynically. "Did you ever read a book, a real story, Oliver?"

Oliver knew she was just trying to provoke him. "I read *Harry Potter*, all of them. But I read some old science fiction in hospital by Philip K Dick and he's my favourite writer now."

Lena looked surprised. "Oh, I used to read his stuff when I was young. It was all so depressing. Everything turned out just as bad as he predicted it would."

Harriet wasn't impressed. "Just typical of you, anything with a 'Dick' on the cover."

With that Harriet was out of the door, dragging Oliver with her, leaving Lena to prepare Grandma Otis's breakfast, a lingering smile upon her lips. Harriet would sort Oliver out. Let him know what was right, what was not. Harriet would sort him out.

Oliver emerged into his Grandma's walled garden and was impressed. He'd not really seen anything the night before, what with the fog and everything, but this was an amazing place. He was happy to see that there were trees on this side of the house and the wild bushes went right up to a huge brick wall and beyond that loomed the power station with it's four huge brick chimneys he'd mistaken for Tower blocks the night before. There was a door in the wall covered by overgrown roses and a cobbled car parking area where a double garage stood, also covered by climbing wild roses and clematis, as well as huge foxgloves that poked in through the broken glass windows.

"It's like the secret garden," Harriet explained. "God knows why she lives here. Scrap yard one side, river the other. The house needs at least eighty thousand spending on it. When she's gone they'll knock it down for sure. She could get over a million for it, she's mad to stay here."

"I love it!" Oliver exclaimed, looking back at the old brick house and its blue slate roof. He was astonished to see a crane moving at the back of the house with a big black car clutched in its jaws. Suddenly there was the sound of crunching as something grabbed the car and began to crush it. Scrap yards, cranes, walls, a river and a secret garden, it was weird, but great. He was sure he was going to like it, so would Flop, eventually.

"Do you like Flop? My cat?" he asked Harriet as she came to a halt by her ice-blue Mini Cooper S. "He's really good at catching rats."

Harriet smiled as she unlocked her car. "He is? Then maybe I should take him on my next date." She grinned at Oliver and indicated he should get into the car. Oliver laughed, thinking that perhaps Harriet would be OK after all.

Grandma Otis was standing at her window watching Oliver with Harriet, wondering how it was he was so at ease with her, but grateful for it nevertheless.

Having a boy around would be a handful and Harriet would be useful to be his 'aunt', give him advice when he needed it. She hoped he would make friends with Justine, but that was a long shot. Justine was so full of fear and anger and she had put up a impenetrable wall around her, it would take a very special person to break through.

Lena entered the room with breakfast and Grandma Otis shuffled back to her bed. Lena brought the breakfast to her bed, set it down, then plumped up the pillows behind her.

"Of course, he's got the gift, y'know," Grandma Otis declared, as she reached for her tea. "He doesn't know it yet, but he's going to be a magnet for trouble."

Lena sat with her own mug of coffee and thought about it, suddenly remembering that story he'd told about the blue box.

"He's very sweet, very trusting. You don't think he'll be a problem surely?"

Grandma Otis dipped a piece of toast into her tea and turned to face Lena, her face stern now, as if she'd seen the future and it was all bad.

"Oliver is going to change our lives. Harriet will sense it. She's got the most developed nose for trouble I know. She can find it where none ever existed. Believe me..."

Lena nodded and stuck her face close in to her coffee mug so that the steam covered her face and made her sweat.

"Did Quon tell you that? He's a good boy, I hope you haven't taken against him."

"No, no, I like him. I'm just saying he's got a trusting nature and that'll invite trouble. You have to take him shopping. He needs new clothes. He looks like a refugee."

"Tomorrow. Let him have some time with Harriet and she'll tell me what suits him. Though God knows he'll want what all the other kids have and it will cost a fortune."

"Well, he can have what he likes. That boy hasn't been spoiled for a long time. It's not as if I'm short."

"I just hope his hair grows back. The kids will give him a hard time around here if it doesn't."

Grandma Otis sighed. "You can't grow grass on barren rock. Now... have you got the book? How many appointments today?"

Lena set down her coffee and flipped open a large diary. "Got someone from Eltham first, new woman, never been before. Then the Mayor, he's bringing a VIP, he says, someone in the Government. He's a bit nervous, we've already had someone to look the place over to make sure it's safe."

Grandma Otis shook her head. "I don't like these sort of people, they've always got so many problems and they never believe you if it isn't what they want to hear. Sometimes, Lena, I think I should just give up. We could sell, move to Devon."

"Devon? Things are depressing enough without going there. Couldn't we go somewhere more exotic, say Seville or Florence? Or Bayonne? I know you'd like Bayonne."

Grandma Otis just smiled as she sipped her tea. "I've told you before Lena, you'd miss England... Sooner than you think."

3. Hands of Fortune

Harriet swore as she noticed the time on her watch. "Stay here," she instructed Oliver, as she immediately got out of the car, ran around in front of it and dashed across the road, narrowly being missed by an annoyed van driver.

Oliver watched her disappear through an archway, into Greenwich marketplace. He noticed the shop she had went past sold maps and paintings. One huge print seemed to show the river and how it ran in a horseshoe. Oliver itched to examine the map and the old sailing ship models in the windows and made a mental note to return to this place.

The traffic was the worst he had ever seen. Greenwich was choked with cars and trucks and he was sure Harriet had parked illegally on these double yellow lines because people would blast him with their horns as they went by. He wondered what Harriet was doing. He knew she was going to be late for her appointment. Oliver was fascinated by how busy this area was, quite different to Louth, even busier than his town on a Saturday morning.

He spotted Harriet again. She'd changed her coat to a bright yellow one with a black velvet collar. She waved to Oliver, but then, quite without warning it began to rain and he saw Harriet dash back through the archway again.

Oliver was puzzled. Where had she gone? The rain bucketed down, making everything virtually disappear. The sound of the rain on the car roof was deafening and traffic almost came to a stop all around him. It was darker and the rain was bouncing high off the road forming little pools around the drains that couldn't cope with the sudden rush of water. Oliver was just getting worried (he'd seen a traffic warden hurriedly crossing the road heading towards them) when Harriet reappeared at the driver's side of the car frantically opening the door as fast as she could and climbing in, slamming the door after her. Oliver noticed she was now wearing a sensible black waterproof coat with an enormous hood inlaid with some tartan material. Harriet said nothing. Just started the engine and almost without a glance at the traffic surrounding them, drove out into it, blasting her horn, weaving her way around dithering motorists, splashing the traffic warden as she crunched through a pothole.

Oliver looked back and saw that the warden was drenched. He smiled. His father would have loved that. He hated traffic wardens.

"Dad could predict the weather by watching how the animals behave. Used to do it in Brazil all the time. He told me that a sloth could predict rain down to the second."

Harriet smiled. "Sloths huh. I've dated some of those too." She smiled at him making sure he was belted up. "So, what do you make of the madhouse you've come to? You like Grandma Otis or do you think she's crazy? What about Justine, the quietest girl in the world."

Oliver had to think about it a while, watching the windscreen wipers frantically trying to keep their view clear of the road ahead.

"Justine is scared. I don't know how I know that, but I know she's scared. Grandma Otis is just like something in a fairy tale. I love her bedroom. It's weird."

Harriet smiled. "She's a good woman. You're very lucky she wanted you to come and live with her. It's a madhouse, but it's your family and they all have good intentions."

Oliver nodded, tensing up as Harriet began to tailgate a Lexus.

"My doctor thinks there's no such thing as seeing the future," Harriet mused. "He thinks your Grandma is making it all up. When she told me four years ago that I have to have an operation, my doctor said no. But Grandma Otis insisted. So I went to another doctor and he had me in hospital the next week and fixed the problem. Doctors don't like amateurs, y'see."

Oliver pondered this as Harriet negotiated the traffic, beginning to climb a steep hill beside Greenwich Park, passing enormous grand homes.

"I'll take you through the park on a sunny day," Harriet told him. "You'll love the park. There's some deer up by the far wall. I don't know why they don't let them wander, it would be much prettier. They do in Richmond. This is where the Royal Observatory is. GMT, y'know? Greenwich Mean Time and all that."

Oliver knew about 'all that' and was keen to see it, but Harriet just drove on up the hill, towards the heath. He longed to walk in the park, discover what was there. He looked back, but the sweeping rain obscured his view.

"Do you live near here?"

"Of course. I've got a little place in Blackheath. You'll see. You'll like the village. It's cute. Really cute. Bought it before the prices went crazy, thank God."

Oliver was puzzled now. Somehow, all his life he'd thought of London as one huge city, but so far all he'd heard about were villages. It was so much like home, but just so much more of it. He didn't know if he was disappointed or pleased. Both, he supposed. He wondered where Richmond was, and whether he'd ever get to see the deer.

Harriet turned off the main road onto a narrower road, crossing the flat, treeless heath, slowly finding their way to the Cator Estate on the other side. As they entered, Oliver noted two gateposts that seemed to signify that they were entering a more exclusive area. They passed expensive, mansion style homes and although Oliver didn't much care for the speed bumps, he thought the homes and the wide avenues would be a pretty good place for his Grandma to live.

"We're here," Harriet suddenly announced, slowing down to look for a parking space. The only clue that Mr McTeal's grand house was different to any other in the estate, was a not so discrete sign in the lower ground floor window, of a large human hand hung up by two chains. It was sort of creepy, like a disembodied giant's hand.

Harriet must have sensed Oliver's nervousness and she put out a hand to his head and rested it on his new baseball cap.

"It's OK, he's just going to tell me how wonderful the rest of my life is going to be and then we'll go for an ice-cream or, something."

Oliver looked at her, wondering if she was thinking he was five and could be so easily reassured with a bribe of an ice-cream. When he looked at her face, however, he realised that it was she who was nervous and wanted him to say something to reassure her.

"I bet he'll tell you you'll meet a handsome prince." Oliver told her, attempting sarcasm.

Harriet laughed and made to get out of her car. "I hope so, I've been through enough frogs already."

Walking to the house Oliver noticed there was a large, silver Celtic cross in one of the bedroom windows. He took this as a good sign. Harriet stood at the door as Oliver waited at the top of the steps, looking at the giant's hand. Harriet was looking at it too.

"If you look at the lines, they all have names: love-lines, life-lines. That's how he reads the hands. He can tell what kind of person you are and what kind of life you'll lead." She saw Oliver's sceptical look and smiled, "you'll see."

"I believe you. My mother said it was just a Gypsy trick, but the Gypsy scared her, so I know what she said was true."

"Gypsy?" Harriet asked, but the door was being unlocked inside and the question died on her lips.

Oliver was watching Harriet nervously adjusting her clothes and licking her fingers to smooth down her hair. She sighed. "This rain makes my hair go crazy," she said, but to no one in particular.

The door opened, at last and there stood a young girl, no more than sixteen and astonishingly thin. She was dressed completely in black, from her glossy braided raven hair, to her painted toe-nails. Oliver just stared at her with wonderment as he walked down the steps and into the reception room. Harriet seemed all smiles and was talking to her as if she knew the girl.

"Nice dress, is it Moschino?"

The girl nodded.

"Thought so. Black makes you look so mysterious, but I'd add a blue contrast or a shade of purple in your eyes, give you a lift, y'know?"

The girl looked at Harriet as if she were going to say something rude, then smiled, revealing perfect white teeth. The spell was cast. Oliver was in complete awe of her, her smile had completely charmed him. He immediately wished he was older and that she would notice him.

"I tried white, but my father sort of freaked out about it," she was telling Harriet.

"White is for the theatre. You need a warmer tone to compliment the black." Harriet reaffirmed. "I'm sure I've seen you before."

The girl went to the corner of the room and opened a fridge. She looked at Oliver.

"Would you like some Coke? I'm afraid I've run out of everything else."

Oliver nodded, but Harriet declined and the girl threw him a cold can which he only just caught. Harriet was still looking at the girl.

"Ophelia. You were Ophelia at the High School production last term. It was a disaster, but you were excellent. My boutique donated some of the costumes. Doing our bit for the community, y'know."

The girl seemed completely astonished. "You saw that? I was supposed to be the understudy. Oh shit, you actually saw that?" Clearly the girl had not been as impressed with her performance as Harriet. "I was terrible."

Oliver opened his Coke and watched Harriet and the girl. They seemed so at ease, yet they didn't know each other. He wondered if he'd ever be able to do that, just talk to people, not worry about asking their names or anything.

"I remember you forgot your lines at one point, but I thought you covered it so well by crying and running off-stage. It was quite dramatic."

The girl smiled. "It was fright. I really was crying. They spun me around and sent me back on stage. All I needed was one word, but it just wouldn't come and blocked everything else. God, I'll never be an actress unless I can learn lines. Denis tried hypnosis on me, but I still can't remember a whole play. Well I can, but not necessarily in the right order."

Harriet smiled. "It will come. You should definitely continue, everyone was so taken with you. I had no idea you were Mr McTeal's daughter."

"No one does, thank God. I'd have people plaguing me to read their fortunes all day. Denis can do it, but I'd go crazy." She smiled at Harriet, then shrugged. "I hope he tells you what you want to know."

Oliver watched her go, caught a glimpse of her long thin hands. Somehow he knew she was the one who had the silver Celtic cross in her window.

Harriet turned to smile at him as the girl left the room.

"You were scared of her when we came in, weren't you?"

Oliver was about to protest, but Harriet cut him off. "Anyway, I think she's going to be very famous one day. She's someone you can just watch and they have a kind of magic. You'll see. She'll be famous."

Oliver thought about that, about how everyone he knew now were always talking about the 'future', making predictions. Just about everyone was different to the people he knew back in Louth.

"Why do you want to know the future anyway?" he asked.

Harriet stole a sip of his Coke to freshen her mouth and then looked at him with surprise on her face.

"Don't be foolish. Don't you want to know if your hair will grow back? Or if you meet a beautiful girl one day who will love you? Or if you'll write a piece of software that'll make you rich."

Oliver was about to reply that computers gave him headaches and he already knew that the chances of his hair coming back were near zero, when a door at the end of the room opened. Both he and Harriet stared with mouths agape as an obese man exited the inner room sideways to get through the doorway. The very floor shook as he lumbered past them to the outer door with an audible asthmatic wheeze. Harriet caught Oliver's eye and they both shook their heads in wonder that anyone so large could walk, let alone would want to see a fortune-teller.

"What do you think he wanted to know?" Oliver whispered as the door closed again.

Harriet shrugged. "The usual, probably. Y'know, will he ever find the perfect sandwich."

Oliver pulled a face then laughed. "You're mean."

Harriet gave him a piteous look. "People never give up hope. You'll see. And stop pulling those faces. Try to act civilised. You don't know what kind of problems that poor man has."

Oliver buried his face into his Coke can and sighed. Everyone was so strange. He looked up again and saw a man staring at him. Mr McTeal was standing in the inner doorway mopping his brow. He was short, only five foot or so, and wearing a flamboyant blue silk shirt opened at the top revealing a gold chain. He wore red rimmed glasses and a small toupee which sat on his head like a dead squirrel and made him look like a TV presenter of some naff quiz-show where they gave away really stupid prizes.

"Oh my God!" He heard Harriet whisper under her breath as she caught sight of him. Oliver sensed this wasn't necessarily a good sign. He couldn't take his eyes off the man's toupee. He wondered how much further it could slip, before it would leap off his head and run for cover. He found himself having to bite his bottom lip to stop himself from laughing.

"You must be Harriet." McTeal said, smiling, his voice softly Irish. "You met my daughter? She looked after you, I hope. Is this your boy? You didn't tell me you were bringing your son."

Harriet regarded McTeal with some surprise. Oliver looked at her and realised that she was quite flummoxed. He smiled, thinking about how he could tease her about this later.

"This is my Aunt Harriet. I'm afraid she's stuck with me today."

McTeal nodded, accepting this reasonable explanation, although Oliver sensed that he didn't entirely like the situation.

Harriet stood up and dragged Oliver up with her, squeezing his shoulder, thankful for Oliver's common sense.

"This is Oliver, my nephew, Mr McTeal, he's here to make sure you don't drug me and pack me off to whiteslavers."

McTeal allowed himself a momentary smile, revealing pure white, elegant, but very false teeth, that made Oliver feel quite queasy.

"I only supply slavers on Thursdays, so I'm afraid you're out of luck, Oliver."

Oliver kept his mouth shut and did his best to avert his eyes from the toupee that now seemed to have slipped another inch or two and wriggled when McTeal spoke. Harriet was walking towards McTeal as he backed himself into his inner room.

"I saw your daughter play Ophelia," Harriet informed him, "it was very moving."

McTeal shrugged. "She died well, but I'm afraid she was utterly traumatised by the event, it will be difficult to get her back on the boards now."

Oliver reluctantly followed Harriet into the room and sniffed the air. Incense. He recognised it instantly. His mother had burned incense for as long as he could remember and he felt almost comforted by the cinnamon scent. He was too scared to say anything. The room was moody, made moodier by the blue grey walls. There was a long, maple-wood floor and a Japanese-style low slung table centred within it surrounded by large silk over stuffed cushions. He could hear his shoes squeak on the wooden floor and he saw that Harriet was removing hers, so he followed suit, almost falling over in the process. As he kicked off his first shoe, it landed by a large electric machine parked near a wall. He saw that McTeal was frowning at him.

"Careful, that machine is very sensitive. It charges the air with positive ions and lifts the atmosphere. Can you sense it? It should make you feel more energetic."

Harriet made some kind of noise that indicated that she agreed with him, but Oliver didn't really comprehend. How could an electric machine change the atmosphere? Well actually, he did feel like he was standing on the edge of a steep cliff with a whoosh of wind coming up at him from the sea below, but he often felt like that when he was nervous.

Harriet was examining the masks on the wall, huge Japanese face masks with lurid paintings on them. McTeal sat beside the table and squatted on one of the cushions, indicating to Harriet to join him. He saw she was looking at his masks.

"Japanese Noh theatre masks. I collect them. I have eighty upstairs. It's my only indulgence".

Harriet was impressed. "I had no idea fortune telling was so profitable."

McTeal smiled. "My financial astrology column is syndicated in hundreds of magazines worldwide. You would be surprised just how closely one can predict the stock-market using astrology. A lot of people rely on my stock tips. I told the Minister to buy euros before they bounced. In fact," he leaned forward and lowered his voice. "I'm at Number 11 tomorrow. He likes to know what fortune favours him, before he makes his moves. He's a long term player that one." McTeal tapped his lips with an index finger to indicate that this was confidential.

Harriet sat down before him and regarded the little man with his crooked toupee with a little more respect. He had built himself quite an empire. She'd heard the rumours about him advising senior government figures, but she'd no idea it had gone so far up the ladder. She wondered if this was a good thing or not. As a specimen of manhood McTeal was a big disappointment. She sighed. Why was it that all the good looking ones never had any money?

"You can sit here," McTeal pointed to a spare cushion. "But remember this is your aunt's reading not yours, so please, just observe."

Oliver complied. He wasn't going to say a word, this was all too spooky. What was McTeal going to say? He looked back at the window again, his eyes catching sight of a crystal hanging by a thread, one strand of sunlight catching it and being bounced to the far wall as a streak of rainbow. Just as quickly a cloud covered the sun outside again and the rainbow vanished.

Harriet smiled at McTeal noticing that he wasn't very comfortable on his cushion. He was trying to fold his legs under him and sweating a little with pain. He noticed her look.

"I'm fifty now, take a tip from me, keep your legs supple when you're young and they'll look after you when you're older. Wish someone had told me that when I was twenty."

Harriet just thought about all her broken promises to work out and join the gym, and lift weights. Sex was the only workout she got and that wasn't as regular as she liked these days.

McTeal reached for her left hand and Harriet watched him quite intently as he studied her palm. She could see him sweating under his toupee and Oliver was watching a droplet trickle down his neck under his shirt collar. Both Oliver and Harriet made brief eye contact and quickly looked away lest they broke out into hysterical laughter. Oliver only just held it in.

McTeal was oblivious to their observations and concentrated hard upon Harriet's palm.

"There is much pain in your hands, such trauma. I can understand why you came to see me, my dear. Your love-life..." He momentarily shook his head as if he'd seen real trouble.

"It must be hell... A real emotional roller-coaster. Such passion one moment, such coolness the next... Such terrible risks... Such miscalculations... So many foolish decisions..."

McTeal shrugged and arched his back, as if in pain, all the time searching for the appropriate words.

"To be frank, my dear, I can't see anything that might make you happy. There have been betrayals, there is violence... Someone you trusted has betrayed you... Someone you like *will* betray you...." McTeal let go of her hand and stared hard at Harriet.

"Tell me, didn't you ever consider becoming a nun?"

Harriet swallowed hard and looked back at him with a mixture of horror and despair. She involuntarily crossed herself, breaking into hysterical laughter, water welling up in her eyes.

Oliver watched this with absolute fascination. Harriet didn't seem to be taking it very well so far. McTeal reached out and grabbed her other hand, quickly upturning it and tracing her love line with a sharp pencil.

"Let me look at your right hand, my dear, perhaps there is *some* hope."

Harriet winced as the pencil tickled her palm, but she already had that sinking feeling, the man didn't even have the grace to lie to her. She snatched a look at Oliver who was now examining his own hands and trying to compare them to a wall-chart hanging behind him.

McTeal continued to shake his head as he traced her life-line. Harriet began to bite her bottom lip, rather regretting the £200 this was costing her.

"Let's face it," McTeal told her at last, "I'm afraid you'll never be lucky in love. Your mound of Venus is all wrong. Your love-line is so faint and pitted. You know that it has been one tragedy after another, or else you wouldn't have come to see me. You just can't choose men and somehow they know you can't commit and take advantage of you. You have been engaged more than once, I guess."

"Six times," Harriet admitted guiltily.

McTeal nodded. "And each time you broke it off... Each time you convinced yourself there was a good reason."

Harriet looked at him with rising anger. "If you call breaking my arm the night before the wedding a 'good reason', if you call finding another girl in bed with my fiancé 'good reason'. Actually I didn't break off the last one, he broke off with me when I wrote off his new Alfa." She shrugged. "Hell, it was only a car, but he thought more of that car than me. I swear."

McTeal sighed and clutched at both her hands again. "On the upside you're going to live a long life and there's money... Not a fortune... But enough and... I'm sorry... But..."

Harriet frowned. "What? What now? Any children?" As soon as she said it she realised that she'd said it with more passion than she'd intended. McTeal heard the anxiety in her voice and made a note to tread carefully.

"I think that perhaps this would be unwise. My dear, it is rare to see such an unlucky hand, truly. Tell me honestly, are men that important to you?"

Oliver rolled his eyes, he couldn't believe he'd ask that! Harriet let loose a sudden loud snort of derision. McTeal was taken aback. He let go of Harriet's hand and watched impatiently as Harriet tried to compose herself, perhaps thinking of the money she was paying him. Harriet sobered up and took a deep breath as she considered for a moment what she might say, snatching a look at Oliver who was all wide eyed, also nervously wondering what she was going to say next.

"So, let me get this right," Harriet began, holding up one hand and looking at it with an exaggerated impression of McTeal's manner, "the bottom line is that I'm going to be an old, borderline, poverty-stricken bloody spinster with no grandchildren." She pinned her eyes to McTeal who was now sitting up straight, looking very defensive. "Is that about right?"

McTeal smiled back at her like some salesman who'd already got your name on the contract and knew you couldn't back out. "Well, I wouldn't put it so negatively myself. You could always take up sculpture. You might find it very soothing. Even yoga, or art might save you, help channel your energy."

Harriet ignored him, and showed Oliver her palms, putting them up right close to his face so that he couldn't exactly avoid them.

"What do you think, Oliver?" She looked at McTeal before Oliver could answer. "I mean, I'm paying for half an hour right? Might as well read the kid's hands as well."

Oliver immediately sat on his hands, looking at Harriet with imploring eyes. McTeal understood Oliver's reluctance and looked at his watch. He sighed. Perhaps he hadn't earned his £200 yet. He had only talked for ten minutes. He reached out and grabbed Oliver's cap off his head before Oliver could do anything about it. Oliver protested but McTeal had already pulled him towards him and placed his fingers on his head.

"Sit still boy, this won't hurt you."

Oliver froze, the last person to say that to him had drilled a hole into his skull. "Harriet, my head..." he wailed.

Harriet was speechless with silent horror as she stared at the keloid scars on Oliver's still raw head, but McTeal seemed unfazed as he felt for the bumps and traced his fingertips over Oliver's skull, seemingly covering every inch.

"This boy has suffered a great deal, but I needn't dwell on that. You are a brave boy Oliver, I can see that. You have great tenacity and strength of will. You have survived a major test and now can plan a way forward in your life. Often it is said that reading a child's hand reveals nothing, because the real tests of life have not yet been made. However, the head has already been formed and can reveal a great deal. Phrenology is much underrated in this country, but in Turkey they have a great respect for it. Feel this bump here, Oliver?"

Oliver nodded. He wasn't actually in pain, he just hated anyone looking at or touching his head; this was a very sensitive area for him.

"You may not realise this, but you are a very lucky kid, this bump is your patron saint of luck. Take good care of your head Oliver and it will take good care of you. Might even become a good writer. I see a strong artistic bent here, definitely something creative, working with people a lot, helping people shape their lives. Perhaps you will write something that reaches lots of people, a computer game or a book? Who knows? You have a strong sense of loyalty and hate to let anyone down. People like you and you will always have friends, I see an affinity for animals. They trust you."

Oliver was about to say something when McTeal turned his head the other way.

"You have been having very vivid dreams, am I right?"

"Yes," Oliver admitted. It was true. Sometimes they were so real it was hard to believe that they hadn't happened.

"So real you think they may be true, yes?"

Oliver nodded. He wondered how McTeal knew that. McTeal was rubbing a bump on the side of Oliver's head now. He looked up and caught McTeal's expression, much more serious than before.

"What?" Oliver asked, worried now. "Am I going to get sick again?"

McTeal shook his head. He suddenly seemed flustered. "No, no... nothing like that. Your hair might come back one day, but... There's something else. It's a feeling I get. I don't really like to say."

"What?" Harriet asked, a concerned note in her voice. "You can't leave him hanging in the air like that, he'll fret."

McTeal looked sharply at Harriet and she immediately understood that he didn't really want to say, but she insisted.

"Tell him; he's been through enough, he's stronger than you think."

McTeal shrugged, as if to say *'if that's what she wanted, let her have it'*.

"OK, there's a specific warning to Oliver here... A danger. You mustn't climb trees, mountains, anything high. You understand me? I want to be specific here. This particular configuration is a warning signal. It stands out. Take no risks where heights are concerned. Perhaps even flying would be a risk for you. Stay close to the ground. You need not be worried about the tumour coming back, but climbing, flying, that is out of the question. You must heed this boy. I am deadly serious. You are at serious risk if you fly or climb."

McTeal rested his hands and sat back on his cushion, mopping his brow. He was done.

Oliver didn't know what to make of it at all. He had no intention of flying or climbing anywhere. He looked at Harriet and made a face.

Harriet looked at her watch. There was still fifteen minutes to go, it seemed churlish to complain too much, but she felt she had to, this man was not offering value for money.

"That's it? Two hundred quid and we get fifteen minutes for the two of us?"

McTeal was growing annoyed now. "You want me to tell you how bad your love life is for thirty minutes? Or would you prefer me to tell you lies?" He sighed, watching Oliver replacing his cap on his head with determined precision.

"OK. I tell you what. You send me one new client and I'll give you a free crystal reading next time."

Harriet made a sour face as she handed over the cash. McTeal took it and stashed it in a small wooden box without even checking to see if it was right. He began to unfurl his body and try to stand up, not without revealing some evidence of pain.

"Just don't go into relationships expecting so much, my dear, perhaps they will last longer than usual."

Harriet stood up and staggered a little as a sudden blood-rush caught her off-guard. She didn't say another word and Oliver took his cue from her, tagging along behind her.

McTeal watched them go with a frozen smile on his face.

Oliver looked for McTeal's daughter as they left, but she was nowhere to be seen. For some reason he'd wanted to say goodbye to her.

Outside in the cool, damp air, Harriet slammed the door behind her and stomped towards her Mini. Oliver could tell she was in a black mood that was growing blacker by the minute. He said nothing. He judged it wasn't safe to. He'd seen his mother in moods like this and knew when to keep his mouth shut.

Harriet remained in a bad mood as she tried to join the crawling traffic through Blackheath. She squeezed back into the flow and lit a cigarette.

"What an asshole. Thank you, Cupid. Thank you, Mr 'Fortune Teller to the stars', Mr McBastard-Teal. No love life, no kids," she mimicked McTeal's limp voice: *"Have you ever thought of becoming a nun."* Hah... The cheek of it. The absolute bloody nerve!... And I paid him £200 quid." Harriet let out a shriek that could have cracked the windscreen. Oliver sank down into his seat, trying to disappear, as people turned to look in their car.

"I'll show him. I'll marry the next wimp who bloody looks at me and give him poxy twins."

Oliver was thinking that that wasn't too good an idea when Harriet took out a CD from her glove-box and slammed it into the CD-player. Mozart's *Requiem* filled the car with music so loud Oliver thought his head would explode, but at least it seemed to calm Harriet, who blasted her horn and carved herself a space out of nowhere to break out of the stalled traffic. Oliver began to suspect that perhaps not everyone was quite normal in London.

4. Diamond Dogs

"Tide's on the turn, smells bad." Harriet remarked, as she led Oliver towards the riverside pathway. She pointed towards the nearest pub. "We can get lunch there. God, I need a drink."

"Can we go down to the beach?" Oliver pleaded.

Harriet looked down at the pebbles, stones and mud left behind by the tide and was amazed to see there was a thin strip of quite respectable beach. She was surprised. She had no idea that there was a beach in Greenwich.

"Oh God, I guess. I forgot, you're a boy, you need to do these sort of things." She threw up her hands in surrender, calmer now.

"I just want to walk on it, we could skim. I'm good at skimming."

Harriet suddenly smiled. "Skim? You're good at skimming? You are talking to a champion skimmer here. My father taught me and he was taught in Scotland, lived by Loch Ness when he was a boy. Never challenge someone to a skimming contest until you know something about them, kid. My hands are hot."

Oliver laughed and ran for the stone steps that led to the beach below.

"Watch out for the slime," Harriet shouted out after him, but too late. Oliver was already on the steps and she heard him *'Whoo-oops'*, as his feet slid out from under him and sent him flying to the beach below. He fell towards the stony beach with a half turn and landed solidly on his back. Ominously for Harriet, he made no sound. Her heart began to race. She began to panic. She ran towards the steps and almost fell herself on the green slime before checking herself on the railings.

"Oliver!" she shrieked. "For God's sake, Oliver, say something."

Oliver opened his eyes and looked at the sky. How quiet the world seemed. He watched with momentary astonishment as the clouds in the sky appeared to fall towards him, almost as if they were coming in to cover him, like a blanket. He began to register the sounds of seagulls and somewhere, further back, a woman shouting his name. Abruptly sound flooded in, loud, almost explosive in his ears.

"Oliver?" Harriet appeared in the sky above him, her face filled with worry. "Say something, say something."

Oliver took a deep breath, nothing seemed to be broken. He was fine really, he was sure of it. Harriet knelt down beside him, staring with silent horror at the debris scattered all around him and the amount of broken glass.

"My God, another inch to the left and your head would have hit this." Harriet pointed to up-ended jagged broken wine bottle from the sand. Oliver sat up and saw broken glass lying all around him and realised that he had been lucky.

"People shouldn't throw bottles into the river, they're supposed to recycle them." Oliver remarked, rubbing his head.

"Tell that to *them*." Harriet remarked, helping him up. "How's your balance?" Oliver nodded his head from side to side. "OK."

Harriet pulled a face as she tried to get the wet sand off her coat.

"This isn't a real beach. It's dirty, too. Let's go eat."

Oliver frowned. "You were going to beat me at skimming."

Harriet's worried expression melted away as quickly as it came and she shook her head.

"You'll regret this. My record is twenty-five, at least"

Oliver laughed, disbelieving and began looking for flat, well rounded stones. Harriet immediately began doing the same, amazed that she was actually standing on the beach and wearing her new Gazelles. She'd expected Oliver to cry, or something. It was clear that he had hurt himself, but he was tough. She found herself thinking that she liked him. He was different to all the other children she'd come into contact with. Unspoiled.

Oliver was standing by the water's edge, looking for stones, occasionally stooping down and clutching one, then just as quickly rejecting it, tossing it back into the river. A barge was sailing by, pulled by a ramshackle tug. Oliver looked up and stared beyond it to where the Canary Wharf towers stood towering over everything. It looked so close from his position at the side of the river. Oliver abruptly looked back at Harriet who was closely examining a stone.

"Do you believe everything he told you?"

Harriet looked at him with surprise. "Why? You think I should lie down here and wait for the tide to come in? That might solve my problems, don't you think?"

Oliver shook his head. "But do you believe him?"

Harriet laughed, but Oliver could tell from the way she tossed her hair and stared out across the river, that she did believe.

"I guess part of me does... But why should I? Why is my love life so screwed up? What did I do so wrong? That's what I want to know." Harriet shrugged, then suddenly took a firm stand in the sand, bent her knees, flipped her arm back, got her eye on the water and with a flick of her wrist sent her stone flying across the river.

"Wow." Oliver exclaimed as the stone skimmed seven... Eight... Nine times before hitting a little wave.

Harriet grinned, suddenly remembering the pleasure to be found in skimming. "Nine. Beat that Sonny Jim."

Oliver drew a deep breath, hunkered his feet down in the sand and with all his force swung back and flung his stone towards the river. It plunged immediately into a small wave and was lost.

"You call that skimming? You lose."

"Wait!" Oliver demanded urgently. "Wait." He placed his second stone in his fingers and drew his hand back, urging himself to keep control, keep balance, keep his knees bent, keep the stance... He let go. The stone kissed the water and skipped four times before hitting a floating log.

Harriet laughed, but not as harshly as before. "That would have been good, but you've got waves from the barge, you have to wait for the water to be flat, be patient."

Oliver quickly hunted for more stones, Harriet likewise, enjoying herself now. Oliver was still thinking about what McTeal had said to Harriet.

"If your luck is so bad, why don't you change it?"

Harriet sighed, examining her palms with mock despair. "How? I was born with these hands. That's it, bad karma. I've got a lousy loveline, shitty mound of Venus. I should be a zombie. They don't have to worry about feelings."

Oliver laughed and looked quite animated about the subject. "They can't be killed either. You can run a sword through them and they keep on coming at you. I saw *Sean of the Dead*. Zombies are real hard to kill, it's a problem."

Harriet grinned at how serious Oliver sounded. She began looking for stones again. "That's me. 'Harriet the Greenwich Zombie'. I get hit, I keep on going. I get hit again, sure enough I crawl back for more. It's pitiful and all because of lousy hands."

Oliver looked at his own hands and then at Harriet again. "So why don't you change them? Get new hands. People change their noses, don't they?"

Harriet was about to make a sarcastic comment, when it suddenly hit her. She shrieked and rushed over to Oliver, embracing him, lifting him off his feet and swinging him around her, whooping and laughing. Oliver joined in with the laughter, but he wasn't sure why. Also, he was scared to death he was going to lose his hat to the river.

"That's it, that's it." Harriet was shouting at him, real joy in her face. "If people don't like their faces they change them. No one thinks that's crazy. I can change my hands. I can change my bloody hands!"

She set Oliver down on the sand and he looked at her askance.

"You mean you'd really cut your hands off and get new ones? That's *gross*."

Harriet laughed. "No, stupid, I'd have surgery. Look, see my palms? They can change my love line, my life line – everything. They can cut out the bad luck and groove in good luck. God, I need to find out what a perfect lucky hand is like. I can't believe I didn't think of doing this before."

"But isn't that cheating?"

Harriet looked at Oliver with despair. "Don't they teach you anything at school anymore? Cheating is how you win. Besides, you weren't born with nun's hands. I'll do anything to change my luck. Shit, I can get my palms fixed. Then let's see what that bloody fortune teller McTeal says, huh? Hah-bloody-hah!"

"Won't it hurt to cut new lines on your hands? I mean, how will you know what a lucky love-line is?"

Harriet picked up a stone from the sand and skimmed it across the water, watching it skip the water six times.

"I could have Liv Tyler's hands, I bet she's got lucky hands. Of course I could have Jennifer Lopez's hands, but then I don't think she is exactly lucky in love."

"It sounds too weird."

"What about Sienna Miller's?" Harriet asked, lost in thought. "Maybe Keira Knightley, she's beautiful and she's got exquisite hands. I wonder if she's happy? Maybe Claudia Schiffer's hands... God, I wonder how much a palm-job costs."

"You'll get toxaemia," a small voice declared.

Both Oliver and Harriet turned and were surprised to discover Justine standing there in her school uniform, blood dribbling down her cheek from a wound.

"My God, Justine! What happened to you?" Harriet babbled as she went to comfort her. Justine seemed reluctant, but Harriet wasn't easy to brush off.

"I don't know if I am more shocked by you fighting or that you spoke. What's happened to you girl? Aren't you supposed to be in school? How did you get this cut?"

Oliver knew instantly what had happened. He wasn't sure how he knew but he had a vision of a knife and Justine ducking just in time.

"It was a knife. Girl at school." Oliver remarked.

Harriet looked back at Oliver, unsure of what to make of that and Justine looked more carefully at Oliver too.

"She said I was a freak and..." Justine mumbled, her anger controlled. "Just a scratch. It's nothing."

"You're *not* a freak. You've been through hell Justine. We're all proud of you." Harriet insisted. "All the things that have happened to you, you don't need this shit."

Harriet took something out of her purse and began to dab it on Justine's cut.

"Don't flinch, it's just witch hazel and hopefully it will stop any infection. Shall I take you home? You reported this attack to the teachers, I hope?"

"No." Justine was emphatic. "They won't do anything and I don't want to go home."

Harriet's phone rang and she answered quickly. "Oh hello Clare. It did? But it was supposed to come tomorrow. OK. I'll be there in five. Tell him to wait. There's a cheque under the till for him, but I have to sign it."

She looked at Justine and Oliver apologetically. "Got to go. You sure you'll be alright? Oliver, stay with Justine. She'll show you how to get home. It isn't far from here. I have to go." She turned to Justine again. "Justine, you can't ignore this. You were attacked. *You have to report it.* Talk to Lena about it. Promise me, OK?"

Oliver was left with Justine, whom, he knew just wanted to be alone. She was full of anger and pain and he wondered why she had come to the river.

"I'm sorry," Oliver told her. "I can go if you point me in the right direction."

Justine just looked at him, then shrugged, shaking her head. "Stay."

Oliver began to look for another stone to skim but couldn't see anything useful at all. He walked a little way along the beach away from Justine to give her some space. Above him tourists ambled by ignoring them. On the river a boat was slowly going downstream loaded with what looked like paper bales – scrap newspapers most likely.

Justine followed him at a distance, sighing, still unable to come to terms with what had happened at school.

Oliver walked further along the water's edge to look at something floating towards the mud. He didn't know why exactly, but it seemed important that he discover what it was.

"Don't..." Justine was calling behind him when he suddenly waded in and began to pull whatever it was out of the water.

Oliver hauled the dog out of the water and pulled it onto the coal black sand. He couldn't believe it. A beautiful chocolate coloured dog drowned in the river. He felt a surge of sorrow for the dog. It must have happened recently, the dog wasn't bloated or anything. It was a terrible sight.

Justine was suddenly beside him. They were staring at the dog. There didn't seem to be a mark on it. Oliver bent down and examined it more closely.

"It could only have happened today. I mean, it's not decomposed at all. It's as if it could wake up at any moment."

"Weimaraner. It's expensive. No collar. A dog like this costs a lot." Justine declared.

Oliver lifted up the dog's head and immediately they could both see why the dog was dead. The throat had been cut. Someone had deliberately murdered the dog and thrown it in the river. This was a dreadful horrible crime. No accident.

Oliver felt pain and sorrow. He hated cruelty to animals and to kill this beautiful dog, it was just disgusting.

"We have to tell someone," Oliver declared. "Someone loved this dog. They will be waiting for it to come home."

Justine was suddenly crying. She squatted beside Oliver, fat tears rolling down her cheeks. All the horrors of school, the pain she felt for her mother, the stupid bitch who picked on her, the whole crappy school, and the fact that here was this bald kid who had his own troubles who felt sorrow for a dead dog.

"We'll find the owner," Oliver was saying. "We have to."

"Chip," Justine told him wiping away her tears. "Chip under the skin. All expensive dogs have them."

"You got a phone?"

Justine nodded.

"Then we should call the RSPCA. They'll know what to do."

Justine got her phone out, checking for a signal.

"Take a photo," Oliver told her. "We can send it to the RSPCA when we get a number."

Half an hour later, Justine and Oliver were watching the RSPCA woman bagging the dog. The tide was turning and the beach would disappear in a moment. They had been surprised when the police had turned up as well.

Oliver was watching the activity on the beach when a young RSPCA woman in a blue anorak approached them.

"I'd just like to thank you for making the call. Someone will be very glad you found it. People get very stressed when a pet goes missing."

"You think you could find the owner? Was there a chip in his neck?"

"Sadly not. No collar either. But owners report pets missing pretty quickly, so there's probably something back at the office already."

The wind caught Oliver's hat suddenly and nearly blew it away. He grabbed it and snapped it back on his head, but the woman had seen his scars.

"My cousin had chemotherapy. He was bald as a coot for a couple of years, then suddenly..."

Oliver looked at her with hope. "He grew hair?"

She shook her head, a sad expression on her face. "No, he was hit by a cement lorry. Died instantly. It was a terrible waste."

Oliver looked back at the river, a sudden feeling of doom spreading over him. Oliver watched her go, then looked at Justine.

"Will they look for him?"

"Look for who?"

"The owner?"

"You don't know it's a him. But why cut's the dog's throat? They don't like being separated from their owners either."

"You know a lot about dogs." Oliver said.

"Not really, but I like Weimaraners. Wanted one, but my mother refused. She's afraid of dogs. It was probably a gang thing. Maybe someone didn't pay a ransom. People kidnap dogs you know."

Oliver had an overwhelming urge to run off and tell his mother what he'd seen and just as quickly, a jolting reminder that she wasn't around, wouldn't be interested, would never be interested. He was on his own now.

"I'd like to go now," he said quietly and Justine nodded. It was time. She didn't know why, but she took his hand and he let her, feeling comforted. They slowly walked back together along the river walk, holding hands, saying nothing, each disturbed by the events of the afternoon.

5. Aura

Sometimes you are caught a little off guard. Just because you have made the big discovery, it doesn't necessarily mean that anyone else will be impressed. When they got home Oliver told everyone about the dead dog. Lena was so deep into a bottle of sherry, all they got out of her was a, "That's nice dear."

Grandma Otis had crossed herself many times over and said, "I knew you'd bring trouble. It's written as clear as the wind."

Then she told him it was time for her afternoon nap and they were instructed, "Not to make any noise." Neither of them even noticed Justine was back from school early.

In short, Oliver's afternoon was turning out to be somewhat anti-climactic. Justine had homework to do – so she went to her room. Flop was out, probably hunting mice. So Oliver decided it was time to explore the outer limits of Grandma's house.

The garden was overgrown, full of trees and flowering shrubs and brambles, but what was behind the house? There was something peculiar about the whole building to his way of thinking. The way the door was positioned and how everything seemed to be at the back. Of course, having a scrap yard on one side probably would have something to do with it, and the huge wall that led to the old power station. Oliver found a side passage filled with overgrown weeds and a doll's pram, rusting, covered with ivy. When Oliver finally threaded his way to the back of the house, he realised that his bedroom actually overlooked the neighbours' house, and this house, it was more of a shack, really, came between Grandma's place and the actual scrap yard.

Now he was at the back he realised something else. Grandma's house was the wrong way around. Or more precisely, the front door was at the back, as were the bay windows. There was even a short driveway that stopped where a metal fence had been built across it, and the neighbours' shack was sort of occupying the front lawn. It was very strange. On the other hand, living in a house that overlooked the scrap yard and cut off the view of the river couldn't be so good either. It was no wonder Grandma had sort of turned it around to face the garden at the back.

A shower of sparks arose from behind an overgrown lilac bush. Oliver pushed his way through and found himself at the back of a makeshift garage alongside the shack and, through a broken wooden door he could make out a small man in goggles and a pair of oily overalls, welding some metal bits together. There was another shower of sparks and the snap of electrical power. The man suddenly looked up and started as he laid eyes on Oliver.

"Hey... Private property. This is private property. You go."

Oliver immediately realised that the man was Chinese, or at least from the Far East.

"What are you doing?" Oliver asked, ignoring the man's aggressive manner. "What is that?"

The man was still angry that Oliver was standing there.

"This place not yours, go! I call the police."

Oliver decided to stand his ground.

"This is my place. My Grandma's place. I can stand here if I want."

This did not seem to pacify the man in goggles at all.

"You live there? With the witches? Go away. You evil. You witch too." He seemed very serious about this and quite agitated that Oliver was standing his ground. For his part, Oliver found the idea of him being a witch funny.

The man was waving his acetylene torch in the air and ran a great risk of setting fire to something. The flame brushed his hair and Oliver was about to shout out, when at the very same moment an oily rag caught fire on the work bench. The man quickly tried to switch off his torch but in the process knocked various bottles over, some of which spilled their guts and the rag began to burn more intensely. He finally got the torch closed off, but the burning rag had fallen to the ground and set fire to a puddle of liquid on the floor. The man began swearing and stamping on the rag, but then the fire jumped from the rag to the trouser legs of his overalls. Oliver watched in horror as the man was being transformed into a live bonfire. The man began to yell and curse in a language he didn't know, but Oliver knew that if he didn't act quickly, the whole garage would burn and the man could die. He kicked the door open with all the force he could muster and created a gap wide enough for him to jump through. Oliver grabbed a blanket that was lying over an old car in the garage and flung it over the man who was still jumping up and down as the flames ran up his overalls.

"Lie down, you have to roll, put the flames out." Oliver shouted. He spotted a bucket of sand hanging on a wall and he ran over to it. It was way too heavy to lift, but he could scoop the sand out with his hands and throw it.

This he did, throwing it, first at the burning puddle of oil, then at the man, who had the sense to fall to the ground and begin rolling to extinguish the flames. He was still shouting, but at least he was covered up and the flames were smothered. Oliver put out the last of the flames with the sand and it was over.

The man angrily flung off the blanket. He was black from the smoke and fumes, coughing and spitting as he tried to grab some air. He looked at Oliver with pure anger and Oliver stepped back.

"I didn't do anything," he protested, "are you alright?"

The man was still cursing, examining his hands and overalls for damage.

Oliver was worried. Perhaps it was a bit his fault. He *had* distracted the man, he *had* chosen not to go away when the man asked.

"You'd better go and see a doctor."

"No doctor," the man said with quite some force. "You made the flame grow. You witch. I saw you make the flame grow."

Oliver didn't take too kindly to that. He was most definitely not a witch and he most certainly hadn't made the flame grow. The man wasn't going to thank him for saving his life. He could see that. Something else he could see too was that the garage was full of owls. Huge models of owls, all facing towards Grandma's house. He was just about to say something before leaving when the man tried to get up, then, silently, passed out, falling back loudly against the garage floor, scattering some empty cans.

Oliver ran over to him and felt his pulse. The man had fainted, that was all. The fumes from oil and gas were still incredibly strong here and Oliver realised what the problem was. Some incredibly strong liquid had spilled in the fire and was dripping from the workbench down onto the floor beside the man. Already Oliver's own eyes were sore and he could feel his breathing getting difficult.

With some effort he pulled the man clear of the area, then went back to the work bench and put a cap back on the bottle of liquid. He thought it might be hydrochloric acid, but it wasn't labelled – definitely a strong acid of some kind. Then, remembering a doctor was needed, he went into the man's house to look for a phone.

The kitchen adjoined the garage and was filled with packets of dried food and hundreds of cans of bean sprouts. Oliver moved on into the first room and was again surprised to discover it too was full of owls, all pointing towards Grandma's house. In the next downstairs room, he found one big owl in the process of being carved from driftwood, all the tools lying where they had been left on the floor. But no phone. He realised that he wasn't going to find a phone, and the man probably needed water more than anything else.

Oliver rushed back to the kitchen, found a cloth, made it damp and filled a glass of water from the tap. He noticed that there was a newspaper cutting of the man in the garage, stuck on the fridge door, in it he was standing by a huge owl and smiling.

Back in the garage, the man was still lying there unconscious. Oliver knelt beside him, wiped his face and waited. At last he began to stir. Oliver bent his head, slid the goggles from his face and gave him a sip of water. The man drank it, then, quite without warning opened his eyes, fixing them on Oliver. Even though still dazed, the animosity was still there.

"You!"

But he didn't attempt to move.

"You spilled some acid. The fumes made you faint." Oliver informed him, making him drink some more water, "do you feel better now?"

The man didn't say anything. Oliver could see he was going to recover, so he stood up and began to walk towards the back door. He'd wanted to ask about the owls, but he didn't think the man would tell him.

"Wait," the man growled.

Oliver turned and watched him struggle up, watched him wince as he discovered raw, burned skin on his hands.

"What's your name?" he asked finally.

"Oliver."

The man nodded and began to walk towards his kitchen door, seeming to ignore Oliver. Then, at the door, without turning his head, he muttered, "thank you."

Oliver needed to get out of the garage. The fumes were deadly. He shrugged and made for the door. As he entered the bushes again he began to think, *Was it my fault? Had I really caused it?* But he had done his best to save the man. He'd done all the right things. Done all the things school had taught to him to do if there was an emergency.

Flop was there to greet him in the garden, nervously following his trail. So glad was the cat to see him, it allowed itself to be picked up and hugged although it didn't at all like the smell that was on Oliver and soon forced him to put him down.

"There was a fire, Flop. And acid. There's a weird man in there, he makes owls."

Flop had already decided that everything around here was weird, including houses that were the wrong way around and loud noises coming from the scrap yard every five minutes that were calculated to make cats have heart attacks. He let Oliver fight the way back through the wilderness to the other side for him. He didn't know what had happened to Oliver, but he wasn't about to let him escape for so long again.

"Got to wash, then join the library. You want to join the library Flop?"

Flop wanted to lie down and think of supper. That's what cats were good at. Still, Oliver was in a funny mood. He couldn't help thinking that the accident in the garage had been his fault and he felt very guilty.

Libraries held no mystery for Oliver. He'd been a regular at Louth library since he was a kid – and he hadn't just stuck to the kid's fiction either. He liked to explore, read different things – history, mystery, adventures. He'd once tried a sexy book but some of the stuff in that had made him want to throw up, all that tongue kissing and licking the rude bits. When it came down to it this boy preferred the kind of book where some guy kicked a door down and stood there with a gun in his hand... If he absolutely had to be nice to a girl, he'd just give her a quick hug before going back to killing the bad guys.

That, and discovering the world. At school he'd explored thousands of pages on the Internet, he'd loved mining all the details from differing parts of the world, talking to kids on *Bebo* in places like Singapore and Seattle, but today he wanted to find out about a particular place. He was still feeling the effects of the afternoon's fire.

He was trying to ease a huge atlas from the top shelf, one of many fat books about worlds, space and oceans, when the whole top row came crashing down upon him, knocking his hat flying and sending him sprawling.

Oliver sat there in the pile of books, dazed and not a little sore from the blow to his head. He was embarrassed and knew people were looking at him and mocking him. Confused, his eyes a tad out of focus, he looked up and saw a boy in a tatty faded T-shirt studying him and an old man bitterly muttering, "Bloody kids" as he turned away back to his local newspaper.

Suddenly, a young girl crouched down beside him asking, "Are you alright? Hello? Can you hear me? Are you alright?"

Oliver abruptly realised that he'd lost his hat and quickly scrabbled amongst the fallen books for it, locating it and hastily clamping it back on his head.

The young girl was still there and Oliver didn't want to make eye-contact, he felt so embarrassed. She put a hand on his shoulder, she was trying to be nice to him.

"Perhaps you should ask for help before taking the books from the top shelf. They're a bit heavy. Are you sure you're alright? You got quite a knock on your head."

Oliver frowned. He knew that voice. How could he? He was in London now. How could he know anyone's voice? He looked up and saw he was looking at a Celtic cross and Mr McTeal's daughter. She was still dressed completely in black, but her long black hair was tied back now and she was smiling at him, not at all angry with him. She too had a moment of recognition, but had difficulty in placing him.

"I've seen you before today, haven't I?

"You're..." Oliver realised that he didn't know her name.

"Aura McTeal." She reached down and began to pick up the books.

"You work here?" Oliver asked getting up off the floor. He realised that his legs were shaky.

"I'm a library volunteer, well sort of volunteer. I'm helping with the literacy programme here for all the incomers."

Oliver bent down to help her with the books but just dropped to his knees, clutching his head. He had a sudden shooting pain and stars in his eyes. Although he hadn't made a sound, Aura McTeal had noticed the pain in his face and she steadied him, held him close to her.

"It's OK, you've had a blow to your head. You're dizzy, that's all. Your head must be very sensitive."

Oliver felt her arms around him, felt her warmth, sensed the genuine concern she had. He was like two people suddenly. This one, with a headache, being held tight, and the other, standing beside them saying, *'Wimp! Get up, be strong. You think she really cares?'* But it was so long since he had been held, it was hard to pull back.

"Your face is really white. You want me to take you to the hospital?" Aura was whispering in his ear. "What did they do to you? Was it a tumour?"

"I'll be fine." Oliver told her, pulling back, but very reluctant to do so. It felt good to be held when he was feeling bad.

"You only just got out of hospital, right?" Aura asked him.

Oliver nodded. "I'm feeling better now. I'm sorry. I didn't mean to be so..."

"Come on," Aura said. "Let's go and get a Coke. There's a place next door."

"I'll be OK really," Oliver declared. "Thanks."

Aura smiled at him, releasing him, picking up and replacing the books. "What were you looking for anyway?"

"Map of Zimbabwe."

"You should use Googlemaps. Lighter." She said, smiling.

"I get headaches when I look at the computer now."

Aura nodded. She could understand that. The kid in the T-shirt was still watching and Oliver felt uncomfortable about that. Why didn't he just go away.

"Zimbabwe, you said?" Aura was asking, as she opened the atlas for him.

"My father... He went there." Oliver told her. Then in a smaller voice. "He never came back."

Aura looked at this bald kid in his funny cap and pensive face and her heart skipped a beat. Not only had he had a tumour, he'd lost his father too. She wondered how it was that some people got all the bad luck. She took his hand and squeezed it, noticing a fresh burn mark. He smelt strangely of fire and chemicals.

"What happened to your father?"

"He's a photographer. He went there to work." Oliver coughed, then continued. "It's been nearly two years now."

"Two years?" Aura exclaimed. "He's been missing two years?"

"He didn't even write. He should have come back and..."

Aura squeezed his hand again. "I think you should wear a shamrock or something. Your head *and* your Dad – you couldn't be much more unlucky."

Oliver smiled at her and shrugged. "My doctor, that's Dr Campbell, he said, attempting the doctor's Yorkshire accent. *'Oliver, you're very lucky, that's all that's keeping you alive.'*

Aura nodded. She understood that. "What scares you most?" She asked. "Never hearing from your father again?"

Oliver considered the question quite seriously and shook his head. "Never having hair again."

Aura regarded him with surprise, then laughed, revealing her sharp, ultra white teeth, squeezing his hand again. "Want to know a secret?"

Oliver nodded, not really understanding why she was being so friendly to him. He wanted her to be friendly, but he wasn't used to people taking him seriously.

Aura leaned in close to him and whispered, "I was like you not so long ago. When I was thirteen. It's my secret."

Oliver pulled back from her, confused. He looked at her. She was teasing him, he knew it. No way she had ever been like him.

Aura shook her head. "Serious. I had chemo and everything. See this?"

She guided Oliver's hand under her hair and at touch, everything came clear. The long black hair was a wig. Under it was hair, but short and spiky. Aura smiled. This was to be a confidence between them. Oliver's heart beat a little faster. She had hair under there. It had grown back. It had grown back!

"I wore a hat for three years. Slept with it on." Aura confessed, her eyes a little glazed with emotion as she recalled those sad days.

Oliver felt like crying. Too many shocks in one day. Aura could sense he was disturbed.

"Come on, I'm taking you home. That bang on your head won't have done you any good. You live close?"

Oliver nodded. Somehow, embarrassment notwithstanding, he allowed her to lead him down from the mezzanine and out of the library into the late afternoon air. He wasn't going to say 'no'. He didn't know why exactly, but the moment he'd seen her at the McTeal house, he'd somehow sensed she would be a friend of his – why, he didn't know – but he knew, as she walked beside him, that she would be his friend.

"God, I need a smoke," she declared wistfully.

"You smoke?" Oliver asked, horrified. She'd had cancer and she smoked?

"Don't look at me with such accusing eyes kid, I didn't say I was going to smoke, I just said I needed a smoke. A girls got to have some vices, y'know."

Oliver understood that. The doctors had all told him no sugar, no chocolate, absolutely no sweet stuff for the first three months after the operation, and every day he'd fought a burning desire to eat a giant sized bar of Cadbury's chocolate. He'd weakened one day, eaten the whole bar and then lay in darkness waiting for something terrible to happen. Nothing. Not a single reaction. He awoke the next morning feeling pretty pleased with himself and then promptly threw up. Lesson learned.

They walked to Aura's scooter, a battered red Honda with tape holding most of it together. She climbed on and Oliver clambered up behind her. "Hold on. Was that your mother you came with today?"

Oliver sighed. Did he have to tell her about his mother too?

"No, my aunt. I live with my Grandma now. Do you like living with your Dad?"

Aura waited until she'd started the engine before replying. "He's not my real father, my *real* father lives in Newcastle. My mother left him for Denis, that's my stepfather's name. He was telling fortunes at Gosforth races and she fell for him. She'd have left me behind too – if my real Dad hadn't shipped us down to her. We had to change our names to McTeal too. I'm going to move out when I finish school. Roll on that day."

"He's a bit strange."

Aura laughed. "He's a bloody nut case, that is what he is, but when my mother ran off with someone else he was very good to us. I have a stepmother now who's only eight years older than me, but she's fun. Don't know why she married Denis McTeal, but a lot of women seem to like him.

God knows why anyone would like man with a dead squirrel on his head."

Oliver laughed, it *had* looked like a dead squirrel.

"Now, where am I going?" Aura asked.

Oliver looked ahead and signalled left. "It's near a pub by the river. By the power station."

"I know it. It's not far at all."

Oliver was glad of that. He'd meant to remember the road and everything, but somehow what had happened to him this afternoon made him forget.

"You know what I found in the river today?" Oliver asked.

"What?

Oliver looked at her as she turned towards the power-station. "A dog with its throat cut. It was a Weimaraner, really beautiful. It's horrible what people do."

Aura looked at him suddenly, then looked away, disbelieving. "Is that true?"

"Yep. Justine was with me, she's a girl who lives in my Grandma's house. She had an argument at school and got knifed. I can't believe anyone would murder a dog."

Aura shuddered. It made her feel strange. "It's scary. All kinds of things turn up in the river now. You be careful. You've come from up North somewhere, haven't you?"

"Lincolnshire."

"Thought so. Things are different here. Don't trust people. Be careful."

She drove fast, weaving in and out of traffic as she wended her way towards the river. Aura dropped him off right outside the house and gave him a big smile.

"I have to do the library thing three days a week, or else Denis won't give me my allowance. Come in tomorrow, OK? Bring some identification so I can register you. We'll find a Zimbabwe map and speak to Old Joe."

"Who's Joe?"

"He's a refugee. From Chechnya, I think. He knows how to find people. Or he knows people who know how to find people. Perhaps he'll talk to you? He's pretty old, but his brain is still going."

Oliver smiled a goodbye. Her words, *"he knows people who know how to find people..."* ringing in his ears. He watched Aura drive off, then ran into Grandma Otis's house, a glimmer of hope in his soul for the first time since his father left.

He opened the back door. The smell of dinner cooking greeted his nostrils and Flop ran to him with a loud "miaow". All was well.

Lena looked at him without smiling. "Mr Ng was looking for you."

"Mr Ng?" Oliver didn't know anyone called Ng.

"Our neighbour. The Chinaman who's always writing letters to the council about your Grandma. He came by and left you something. He looked pretty neglected. His wife left him, y'know. Went back to China. She came to see Grandma Otis and told her she had to go. She didn't like it here and he's been holding a grudge against us ever since. You watch out what he's put in that box. I don't trust him. How he even knows you're here beats me. I mean, you've only been here one day. Bloody neighbours watch this place sharper than council tax officers."

"Where's the box?" Oliver asked, looking around the kitchen.

"In your room. Don't disturb your Grandma. She's got a client in. Still got ten minutes. Dinner in half an hour. I hope you're hungry. Run and tell Justine. She always comes late to supper."

Oliver gave Flop a hug then ran up to his room. There, on Oliver's bed, sat a shoe box. Oliver quickly opened it, forcing the lid off. A beautiful painted tawny owl lay there in a bed of green tissue. Oliver smiled and lifted it out of the box. A note lay underneath. On yellow paper, all it said was: *'For your protection.'*

Oliver stared at the owl and wondered for a moment what the message meant. The door opened behind him and Flop dashed in, skidding to a stop when he sniffed the painted owl in Oliver's hand.

"It's for our protection," Oliver told him. "I think it's sort of like a rabbit's foot or something." Flop didn't like the sound of that. He disappeared under the bed and Oliver heard him going a little crazy under there, clawing at the canvas lining. "Rabbit's foot, not cat's foot," Oliver reassured him. But Flop wasn't having it, he was staying put.

"You're honoured." Grandma Otis declared, from behind Oliver.

Oliver turned and there she was, wearing a mauve shawl and black dress. She smiled at him. "Mr Ng came to the house and delivered it personally. I don't know what you did, but he was very keen for you to have this box. He prizes his owls a great deal. He believes they protect him from evil spirits."

Oliver nodded. "They're all over his house and they're pointing at your room."

Grandma smiled, a look in her face that seemed to say, *'I thought so.'*

"Why?" Oliver asked. "Why?"

"In his culture, owls protect. He thinks I'm a witch. He's written to the council to complain about me, many times. Lena writes to the council to complain about his chanting and the lack of maintenance on his house.

Fortunately, the council leader is one of my regular customers and just to save face, I made him buy one of Mr Ng's owls. Does that explain everything?"

Oliver shook his head. "What about this owl?"

Grandma smiled. "Put it in the window, aim it at *his* owls. Fight fire with fire, I say. Now, tell me more about this dog you found. Quon tells me that there's more trouble to come and I want to know what it is before it gets out of hand."

"Trouble?" Oliver asked, as he placed his new owl in the window, carefully aiming it at the room full of owls. The idea of his owl facing all of Mr Ng's amused him.

Grandma Otis had already left his room. "Trouble follows you. You're a magnet for it, Oliver, it's hovering, waiting, looking for an opportunity. It's one of the hazards of the trade."

Oliver frowned. Certainly a lot had happened since he'd arrived, but how was it possible it was connected with him? Surely the dog would have been at the beach, even if he hadn't gone there? Maybe Mr Ng would have burned himself anyway today? And what about Aura? He'd already met her twice and made her his friend. Was that a good thing or a bad thing? Things didn't happen this fast in Louth, that was for sure.

"Come on," Grandma Otis called him from her room. "I want to talk to you."

For a moment, Oliver contemplated joining Flop under his bed, but one look at the six inches of space there and he knew that Flop was on his own. It was time to face the firing squad. He turned and left his room.

He crossed the landing to Grandma's room and she was sitting there, at her dressing table, with a crystal in her hand. She looked up at him as he cautiously approached.

"I'm going to take a look at your aura. I want to see just what it is I have invited into my house."

"I met a girl called Aura, today. She's beautiful and she's adopted by the fortune teller and she had..."

"Hush," Grandma Otis told him, "hush... Let me work. Come closer. You smell of fire. Give your clothes to Lena after this and put on some clean ones. I don't want you playing with fire. Understand?"

Oliver nodded and did as he was bidden. He gingerly approached her. Ridiculous to be scared of a crystal, but he was. What was it going to say? What did it do exactly? Grandma Otis was scanning his whole body with it, watching the crystal, and the air between him and the crystal, very intently.

Oliver caught sight of himself in the mirror and was surprised to see a green glow with a tinge of crimson all around him. It was more intense wherever the crystal passed over him. He was going to remark on it, but thought better of it, just in case he was the only one who could see it. He'd made a fool of himself enough times for one day.

Grandma sighed and let the crystal fall to her lap. "You've a long way to go before you're healed, but I can say one thing for a green boy, there's not a mean bone in your body. You're more your father than your mother, that's for sure. I don't like the crimson emanations, but they're there and we'll have to deal with them. Now get you to a bath. Why do you stink of chemicals? What have you been doing? Get going now. Get a bath in before dinner."

Oliver walked to the door and looked back at her briefly. "Did you actually see a colour?"

Grandma Otis looked at him with her pale, puffy, blue eyes. "I saw exactly the same as you in the mirror. Green and crimson. The colours combined like that always mean trouble to come. Don't worry. It's not you, but watch out for your trusting nature. Don't always believe everything people say."

Oliver left for the bathroom. Grandma had seen the colours too. How was it possible that one could see his aura? Why had he never seen them before? In the bathroom mirror he looked again, but he could see nothing except his dirty hands and face. He ran the bath and puzzled over all of this.

In her bedroom, Grandma Otis puzzled over it all too. Oliver's aura was powerful. He had the gift, alright, but what was happening? What had she invited into her house? Why was he green and crimson? She'd seen this before, on a man – an evil man, a condemned man – but what did it mean when it surrounded a child? How would she correct it? What could she do to make him safe? That he was in danger, she was absolutely certain, but what could it be? How would it come? These were the real questions. When trouble came, how would Oliver defend himself?

Grandma Otis looked up beyond her bedroom door momentarily. She caught a glimpse of Flop, slinking out of Oliver's room and dashing into the bathroom. She smiled. As much as she didn't like cats, she knew that Flop was good for Oliver. The one certain thing in his life, the one thing from his past that he could be sure of. Grandma Otis was jealous of that. If only she'd had someone love her as much as that cat loved Oliver. But... She sighed... best to forget all that. She'd had her turn.

It took some time for Oliver to realise what was missing from his Grandma's house. Later that evening he realised exactly what it was – no TV. There was no TV in his room or the living room or in Grandma's room, though he suspected Lena might have one in hers.

It was quite a shock. Flop and himself wondered from room to room and confirmed it. This was probably the only house in London without a TV.

Oliver wasn't entirely devastated. He had discovered a huge floor to ceiling bookcase in the dining room filled with detective books that would come in handy for desperate rainy days. There were also tons of books on Africa that looked really old, but had illustrations, and that too would be good for a stand-by.

He sat on the stairs and thought about his situation. There were positives to consider. One: he wasn't in the hospital, two: he had an old record player with a whole stack of LPs with all the classics there. Pink Floyd, Bowie, Sergeant Pepper, Talking Heads and three albums by someone called Donovan. It would come in handy if he ever took up an A-level in rock history. He had an owl and Flop to keep him amused. It was enough, for now.

As he sat there, head in hands, wondering what to do, he slowly became aware of a pair of eyes fixed upon him. A door was open and he knew it was Justine staring. Flop was aware of it too and he wondered off to investigate. Where Flop went, Oliver had to follow and he came to her door and she stared at him with her customary silence. She suddenly turned and walked back up her stairs. She hadn't closed the door so Flop and Oliver took it as an invitation to go up.

The attic room was severely impressive. It was huge and all they way up to the rafters. There was even ivy growing inside, coming through from the outer walls. In the corner, there was a small double bed with six stuffed toy cats of different shapes and sizes lined up at the base of it. There was one tall cupboard for her clothes and she had just one movie poster on the wall of *City of Lost Children* which had a spooky image of a man rowing a child out to what looked like a fortress and there were floating mines in the water.

Justine sat on a cushion hugging her legs, as Oliver took it all in. Flop was already on the bed inspecting the cuddly cats, not entirely sure about them, his tail swishing back and forth as if expecting some kind of challenge. None came.

"Weimaraners cost nearly five hundred pounds y'know. More if they are show dogs."

Oliver immediately understood and felt guilty. "I meant to call the RSPCA."

"I called," Justine told him, pointing at her bed. "You can sit there. Got no chairs."

Oliver sat on the floor with his back to the bed. He didn't want to disturb Flop when he was settling, he didn't like that. "What did they say?"

"No one reported the dog missing."

"No one?"

"No one. It's unusual. It was obviously well looked after."

"What do you think it means?"

"Maybe they went away and left it with a friend and it got away."

"But then why would it's throat get cut?" Oliver asked.

"Someone who doesn't like dogs maybe?"

Oliver frowned. "Maybe they'd shout at it, or throw a stone or something to scare it off but cut its throat? That's evil."

"Maybe you were right about the kidnapping, Oliver. Perhaps they wouldn't pay up?" Justine thought about what she'd just said. "I'd pay. If it was my dog I'd pay."

They were silent then – the dead dog lying between them, as it were.

"Do you go to St. Saviours?"

"Yeah. How...?"

"Met a girl from there. Aura. She's older than us. She said that you should talk to her about the girl who attacked you."

Justine looked at Oliver with astonishment. "You know her? Aura McTeal? She's practically famous. She was in that Dickens TV serial they made near here. Before she got ill. How could you know her, you've only been here like a day."

Oliver had no idea about the TV serial. "She says that the school had a strict no knives policy and the girl could be expelled."

Justine pulled a face. "You don't understand. It's not like that. If I say anything her friends will pick on me. It never ends. Never tell anyone anything about yourself or your family when you go to school. You hear me? Say nothing. They'll use anything against you." She looked at Oliver more intently. "You'll have it rough anyway, being bald. They'll pick on you, they'll pick on anything."

Oliver was already dreading this. He knew exactly how cruel kids could be.

"Do they know about your mother?"

Justine sighed. "Yes. I was stupid. It was in the paper. Simone laughed. She said it was funny that someone had the same name as me and then she twigged. She put it in her blog and it went around the school like wildfire. Then I'd find stuff all over the web about how my Mum was in for murder and she was a serial killer. How I was white-trash and was violent. I had death threats and..." Justine shivered. It was something that haunted her everyday.

"I hate computers." Oliver remarked.

"It's not just on Facebook and stuff. They send text messages, pictures too. Horrid, hateful disgusting stuff. I changed my number – twice. Now I never talk to anyone – ever. I'd change schools, but they'd try to find me. Once they have something to beat you with, they never give up, and the teachers do nothing."

Oliver had been listening but he suddenly felt lighter and he had a flash image come to him and it was dark and choking, he felt water closing over him and short of breath. He looked up at Justine with abrupt extreme clarity. He knew why she was at the river the day before, after she had been attacked. She had planned to kill herself. He had no idea how he knew this, but he believed it to be true and couldn't say anything to her. Instead he looked at her and said.

"I'll be a friend. We can be two freaks together."

Justine offered him a weak smile. "Great. Two freaks better than one I suppose."

Oliver jerked his head involuntarily. He had had another flash. How the hell these came to him he didn't know, but he had seen something as clear as day.

"The owner *is* looking for his dog, Justine. He hasn't reported it, but he is looking, but there is something strange about him. Something really strange."

Justine was studying him quite intently. "You're like her, aren't you. Your eyes flutter, just like your Grandma."

Oliver didn't know what she meant.

"You Grandma, when she sees stuff – her eyes flutter. You went somewhere then. You're just as crazy as her."

Oliver didn't know what to say. He sensed Justine was getting angry with him.

"You did it yesterday, when you knew it was a girl who had knifed me."

"I don't know how..."

"It's OK. I'm not pissed. I know what Mrs Otis does. That's why I'm here. My mother used to come and see her all the time. She helped my mother. It was my Dad. He defrauded the Government. I never understood what he did. He disappeared and my mother was thrown into jail. Two years. They took our house and everything. She was devastated. She won't even let me visit she's so upset."

"And your father?"

"God knows where he is. I don't care."

Oliver frowned. This he could understand. "My father disappeared too. In Africa."

"I know. Lena told me. But he didn't do anything wrong. He might be lost or something. My Dad is a crook and he didn't give a damn about me or my Mum. Now I live here."

Oliver suddenly felt very tired. Flop put out a paw to his neck and he abruptly found himself staring out of a different window, heavy rain battering the glass. He was in a small, plain room with a tiny bed, an old computer on a shabby table in one corner and there was the stench of whiskey. Oliver could see the bottle on the table and one glass and he had a terrible overwhelming feeling of loneliness.

Oliver opened his eyes. He was lying on the floor by the bed. Justine was holding his hand and Flop was breathing hard, staring at him from the top of the bed, a worried expression in his eyes.

"Jesus, you freaked me out Oliver."

"What?" Oliver felt as though he had swallowed smoke and his chest was tight.

"You just rolled your eyes and keeled over. God, Oliver, you really are a freak. What did you see? You saw something, *I know*. Was it the dog?"

Oliver sat up rubbing his head where he'd fallen. He felt slightly nauseous from the experience.

"Does your dad drink whiskey?"

Justine steadied him, worried now he'd grown quite pale. She was scared Oliver had seen something. She was scared of the pain in this kid's head and, this she had never admitted to anyone, her long held wish that her father was dead. She had almost come to believe he was dead and understood that this was just her way of dealing with him abandoning her. Now she realised that Oliver was going to tell her something different.

"Perhaps it wasn't him. Perhaps..." Oliver drifted off for a moment.

"What did you see, Oliver? Justine whispered. "You saw something."

"A man, he's in a small room. It's white, it's raining. He's got an old computer and I saw a bottle of whiskey, Bells, I think. I saw the label. He's lonely. He's very lonely."

Justine said nothing. Her father definitely drank Bells whiskey. She was glad he was lonely. He deserved to be lonely. Lonely was the very least he could be.

"I'm sorry," Oliver told her.

"Don't be." Justine looked at him carefully. She could see he was dizzy now.

"Have you always been able to do this? See things, I mean."

Oliver shook his head. Then nodded. "I didn't know it was weird at first. I thought everyone could do it. It was just between me and Flop. Flop can predict the weather. He knows exactly when there's a storm coming, he goes crazy. But I can read letters."

Justine felt the hairs on her neck rise. "Read letters?"

"I can somehow see what's inside a letter before you open it. Not always but sometimes. Not all the words. I can see them writing it."

"Wow."

"But that's all. I never told anyone before. No one."

"Not even your mother?"

"No."

"Wow. You kept it a secret all this time. Impressive."

Oliver was suddenly serious. "I think it was your father, Justine. I think he's living, a long way away."

Justine nodded with a sigh. "I know."

"I think..."

"I think you'd better go to bed. You look drained. Are you taking pills for your...?"

Oliver nodded.

"Be careful Oliver. Don't let anyone outside of this house know what you can do. They really will call you a freak and make your life a misery. Believe me."

Oliver understood only too well.

"If you need advice, speak to me, OK?"

"Yeah."

Oliver hauled himself up and made his way to the stairs, Flop quickly joining him. He turned to say goodnight but Justine was turned away from him, her shoulders hunched. He had the feeling that she was crying.

As Oliver went down the stairs he wondered if he had been right to tell her about her father. He wondered how it was he had seen anything at all. Everything seemed to have changed since he'd arrived at this house. Everything was so much more intense.

He was confused, but he sensed the loneliness that man experienced in his room was just as strong as the loneliness Justine felt in her attic. It seemed to him that loneliness had a shape, much like a cold underground cavern with dripping water falling on your head. That was what loneliness was.

6. Bullet

There was a letter for Oliver on the breakfast table. He'd been referred to the Royal Marsden Hospital in Chelsea. His new specialist would be a Professor Imai, and he had an appointment with him in two months time. Lena seemed impressed by the hospital's name. Well, as impressed as someone with a sherry hangover could be in the morning but she was thinking practically, too.

"Now you've got a letter addressed to you, you can join the library. Take it along and get yourself enrolled. Just because you aren't at school yet, doesn't mean you can't read. I'm all for keeping you out of trouble."

Oliver had fully intended to go back to the library. He wanted to see Aura again and find that man who, perhaps, could help him find his father. Lena was a tad suspicious of a boy who actually wanted to read, but glad he'd be out of her hair all the same – especially the way she was feeling this morning.

"Your Grandma has a busy day today, so it's good you're out. Be back for tea, mind. Tomorrow we'll go shopping, get you some clothes."

Oliver nodded. Some clothes would be good. So far, living at Grandma's wasn't so bad. He got fed and had his own room and school wasn't really a factor until September (and that was the whole summer away.) Perhaps his hair would have grown a bit by then. He wasn't counting on it though. In addition, there was Justine and she needed a friend, even if it was only him.

"Flop come down yet? He was gone when I woke up."

Lena made a face at him. "He was waiting for his breakfast when I came down at seven. Made a bloody racket too. I hope he hasn't got worms. He eats like a dog! Justine let him out again. She's a worry. I don't know what gets into her. She vexes me so. Never tells me anything. Do you know how she got that cut on her face?"

"Er... No. But I like her. She's very honest."

"Blunt, rude, spiteful and arrogant are some other words I could call her, but I suppose you are right. She is honest and that's something."

Oliver grabbed some toast and dipped the edge of it into the marmalade as he rose from the table.

"I have to go. Do I have to pay anything? Will I need money in the library?"

Lena frowned, remembering. "That's something else we have to discuss – pocket money. Grandma Otis says you're to have ten pounds a week and you must keep to a strict budget. She wants to see a proper accounting. She wants you to learn the proper value of money."

Oliver couldn't believe his luck. Ten pounds! His mother used to give him just one pound, if she remembered. He never had any money.

"I used to get five shillings." Lena added, thinking back. "Of course, five bob used to get me into the cinema and buy me all my sweets for the week. Couldn't ask a tenner to do that now. Now, don't forget your coat, and take care. Remember, this is London and you mustn't believe everything people tell you. And watch out for Mr Ng, he's a weird one, that man. Nearly gave me a heart attack, yesterday, when he appeared from the bushes."

Oliver had absolutely no intention of going anywhere near Mr Ng, ever again. Still, he had given him one of his owls and that was nice of him.

"Going now." Oliver declared, grabbing his coat from the corridor.

"Don't forget your envelope, the library will ask for it." Lena called after him.

Oliver quickly went back for it and then escaped. He was free for another day. Greenwich was for exploring.

It was raining. A newspaper hoarding outside the newsagent announced – *'Olympic Stadium Bankruptcy Scandal – A Billion Goes Missing'*

Oliver realised the Olympics would be taking place just across the river. He wondered if he'd get to see something when it happened. So much history here in this part of London and it was still happening.

He arrived at the library, dripping wet. Old-age pensioner faces stared at him as he turned aside and dodged behind a screen so he could wring the water out of his sopping hat. Oliver wasn't down however, he was back in the warmth of a library and if no one was smiling at him now, at least someone would, soon. He resolved to find Aura quickly, but a quick walk around the building soon revealed the truth: she wasn't there. Perhaps he'd come too early? Perhaps she was sick? Or the rain had put her off? Within five minutes of arriving, he was as depressed as all the other sad sacks in their grey mackintoshes and black cracked leather shoes. Oliver went up to the mezzanine where the atlases were, and sat at a table, resting his head in his hands. It was his own fault, he shouldn't have got his hopes up of seeing Aura. She didn't have to be there, just because he wanted her to be there.

"She ain't here." A voice told him.

Oliver looked up and discovered he was looking at the same boy as the day before. He didn't look healthy and was way too thin. His jeans had holes in the knees and his fingernails were black. He looked like he didn't give a damn about himself.

"Don't worry, she'll be here. She's a volunteer. Comes and goes when she likes. It was Aura you was waiting for?"

Oliver nodded. Why was this boy taking an interest in him? Oliver guessed he was about fifteen. His teeth were yellow and neglected. Didn't he know you had to look after your teeth?

"I'm Bullet." The boy told him. "Got shot in the neck." He pulled out a bullet affixed to a shoelace he had tied around his neck. "This is the bullet, another centimetre to the right and I'd be dead." Bullet pulled a face. "Sometimes I wish I was. Fuckin' rain, makes me depressed."

Oliver was sort of impressed. "Who shot you? Why?"

Bullet laughed, revealing more of his bad teeth and a pasty, white tongue.

"I was sleeping in a doorway, right, in Lewisham, 'cause I got thrown out by my old woman, right. These punks drive by, and – wham – I got shot. This woman sees it and she calls an ambulance, right, they saved my fuckin' life. They could have left me, I bloody would have."

Oliver was transfixed. He could see the scars for himself, there was no way Bullet was lying. "You didn't want to live?"

Bullet made a face. "You try spending a bloody year sleeping in doorways, you don't give a shit what happens to you, do you? What would you know, anyway? Bet you got a nice warm bed and someone to tuck you in at nights. "Night-night sweetie."

Oliver ignored the taunting. "You quit school?"

Bullet laughed, sitting on the table. "Chucked me out after I burned the gym down. Served them right, wouldn't let me play volleyball in my D.Ms. Didn't even ask me if I could afford trainers. Just said no. So I burned it down. I was sniffing glue then, makes you a bit crazy." Bullet made big eyes at Oliver and laughed again.

"I'm the original fuck-up. My Granddad's in jail, my father's a drunk, my mother's out off her face most of the time. It's a sort of family tradition. I turned fifteen last month and forgot about it, 'till the cops stopped me and pinned me up against a fuckin' wall and beat me."

Oliver looked at him in wonder. His own life wasn't great, but this boy's life was a complete mess. Bullet shifted position again. Oliver noticed that he had problems sitting still, as if he was on edge all the time, expecting trouble to come from any direction.

"What you in here for anyway?" Bullet asked him.

"I wanted to look at the atlas...."

"How come you're in here?" Oliver asked.

Bullet shrugged. "It's warm, it's free, it isn't raining in here."

"He giving you trouble?"

Oliver turned around and there was Aura, standing right beside him, still wearing her red rain coat, her nose dripping with rain-water.

"Can't believe this bloody weather. Heard on the radio that's there's still a drought order on, can you believe it?" She smiled at Oliver and removed her coat. "You still here, Bullet?" Aura was not so easily impressed by Bullet. She gave him a sharp look.

"Leave this boy alone, Bullet. He's a kid and he's been sick, OK? Come with me, Oliver. Got someone you might want to talk to. Got to get you a library card. Did you remember to bring something to identify yourself with?"

Aura walked away and Oliver stood up to follow. Bullet held him back a moment as he watched her go.

"She thinks she runs this place. You watch out for her, she's always giving orders. She'll have you as a slave before you know it. People like her are all alike." He gave Aura the finger behind her back.

Oliver shook Bullet off and followed after Aura. Bullet was wrong. She was OK, it was Bullet who scared him. He wondered if he really did sleep in doorways. He looked as though he did, but every day? What about winter? How many other kids slept rough? London was scary.

Aura took him aside as she walked him downstairs.

"Stay away from Bullet, OK? He's seriously wrong in the head. There are two hundred and fifty-seven gangs in this city, Oliver and none of them want him to join them. He's really bad news, Oliver. Understand?"

Oliver nodded. Bullet bad news. Avoid. He found himself being steered towards Joe, an old man, who looked so tired and frayed he resembled a ghost, a living ghost reading a newspaper in a library. His skin was so creased and his suit so crumpled, with shiny elbows in his faded pin-stripe jacket, he was almost like a scarecrow.

Aura sensed Oliver's reluctance to meet with the man.

"It's OK, he's a Croatian refugee, he speaks good English. He was a school teacher until he had to flee the fighting a few years ago. He's exactly the person you need to speak to. He knows how to find people."

Oliver looked up at Aura and was about to protest further, when he saw a red weal on her face. It was so fresh he could see the imprint of a hand. He was so shocked that someone had hit her, he said nothing at all. She noticed he had seen her mark and quickly spun him around towards Joe.

"Go fix your own problems, I've got enough already." With that, she was gone and Oliver was left on his own, just feet away from Joe, the old Croatian.

Joe saw him staring and he nodded at Oliver, smiling to reveal a brand new set of totally white teeth. Opening his mouth was like cracking open an egg, it completely transformed him.

"You're the boy with the missing father?"

Oliver was surprised to discover that Old Joe spoke perfect English, with just a slight accent. He wasn't scary at all. Oliver moved towards him and Joe indicated for him to sit opposite him at the table. Oliver moved cautiously forward and pulled out a chair to sit on.

"How old are you?" He asked.

Joe shrugged and turned his palms up on the table revealing huge lumpy scars.

"Not as old as you think, then again, sometimes I feel older than the stars."

Oliver was looking at the man's hands, his eyes growing wide, Joe noticed his stares and quickly turned them over again.

"Sometimes people can be very cruel. Sometimes people you think are your friends, can be evil. I survived. I am here. The British Government has found me a place to live, they have given me clothes, some money and yet..." he sighed. "I am alone. My wife, daughter and my son are dead. My niece Greta, it is possible she survived and I would like to go back to find her. But..." he shrugged again. "Many years go by..."

"All your family were killed?" Oliver asked.

Joe brought his fist down on the table with a loud bang, his eyes suddenly aflame.

"Burned in their home. I was teaching when they came and set fire to the school. I was trying to put out the flames, when they came to my home and killed everyone. *Everyone.* Cut their throats, left them to bleed to death. All my family."

Oliver stared at him in astonishment, a vision of horror in his head. All of them dead. He tried to think of how he would have felt if he had come home to find everyone murdered, but the thought was so alien to him he just couldn't.

Joe was watching him, letting his words sink in. But what Oliver was thinking was, if there were people like that, killing children and everything, perhaps his father had been dead all this time. All Oliver's hopes that his father would return were for nothing.

"A dog got its throat cut yesterday. Found it down by the river." Oliver told him.

Joe frowned. "Not a good sign. That's how the trouble began in my county. They cut the throats of the dogs, so they don't warn us they are coming... No, not a good sign at all."

Grandma Otis was in her garden, dressed for Antarctica, even though the weather was quite mild. She'd seen from the window that her roses needed attention. Black spot had got in amongst them and it would be hard to eradicate. Spraying each rose bush quite methodically, a sudden twinge of pain stabbed her left shoulder. She let escape a cry of distress and stood up as straight as possible, but the biting pain seized her shoulder again. Gritting her teeth she let the spray canister drop to the ground. Grandma Otis knew what this was; bad news. Bad news was coming and it was close. She'd experienced this kind of pain before and she concentrated very hard on trying to blot it out. She turned towards the house and with a heavy sigh began to walk towards it, her gaze distracted by the sight of an old station wagon being crushed in the scrap yard. The squeal and crunch of metal seemed to echo her own grinding bones.

Lena was coming out of the door with a mug of hot tea. She saw her and stopped short.

"What is it? What's wrong?"

"Pain. Trouble's coming. Find me the tiger balm, it's my shoulder again."

Lena hurried back indoors all wide eyed and panicked, as Grandma Otis reached the back porch, where she picked up the hot tea mug and pressed it against her shoulder to ease the pain. Something bad was going to happen and she knew, although she couldn't be certain, it would concern Oliver. Worse, there was nothing she could do about it.

Oliver sat before a computer screen and stared at the web pages of the International Red Cross. Joe was pointing to names on the screen as Oliver was scrolling the pages and noting down email addresses.

"Now you try Amnesty International. You will have to email them all, if you want to find your father. Everyone; not just once, but many times. You have to annoy them, work at it, so that in the end they will help you, just to make you go away."

Oliver turned to Joe. "How come you know how to do this Joe?"

Joe shrugged. "I didn't know. First I wrote letters that got ignored, then I discovered email. They read it. I know my niece is alive and I want her to join me here. I wrote to everyone. The Prime Minister, presidents. You can't just ask them to help you because your father is missing or you're unhappy."

Oliver frowned. "I can't?" It seemed pretty reasonable to him.

Joe shook his head quite emphatically and rubbed his face a moment, to help his concentration.

"No, I can tell you, they *aren't* interested. You have to let them know how much profit there is in it for them."

Oliver was really confused now. "Profit?"

"Ja, it's true. These are important people, politicians and bureaucrats, and where I come from, politicians will only listen to you if they think by helping you they will get on television when your father steps off the airplane. That is how you get their attention Oliver. Is like playing the piano; no? Play the right tune and people listen?"

Oliver was beginning to see the light.

"Make it sad? I could tell them my mother is sick and they just took a lump out of my head the size of a tennis ball."

Joe nodded wisely. "Yes, oh la-la-la, I can hear the tune already. I think we begin to write the letter."

Oliver smiled and opened up email on the computer. He'd never met anyone so old before who could use a computer as well as Old Joe. He was smart, even if he couldn't see the screen so well.

"I'm going to make a website for all the people like me, so they can find each other," Joe told him. "There are thousands of us now".

"Like Facebook?" Oliver remarked.

"Exactly."

It was gone five o'clock before Oliver was finished with Joe, and the library was emptying. Aura was finishing up a literacy class with some immigrant children from Romania and Bullet was asleep at a reading table. Joe was pretty tired himself, but they'd got a letter written and emailed it to all kinds of people and places in Southern Africa. Aura came over to them both and rested her hands on Oliver's shoulders.

"We're closing early today. Short-staffed. Has Joe been helpful Oliver?"

Oliver gave her and Joe a brilliant smile.

"Joe's been fantastic. He really knows how to use the web. He knows how to find people's email addresses and we've sent letters to everyone, newspapers and magazines, even the Presidents of South Africa and Malawi."

"And Namibia and Botswana," Joe added. "Someone will know him. He's a photographer, Oliver tells me. He must sell his pictures to someone, or else he could not exist. Someone always knows."

"Look, got my own page now." Oliver said excitedly. "We've already got the first section done." Aura was impressed as she watched Oliver open up

Sam North

the pages, but she could also see how tired Joe looked.

"Great. You've been very busy. I'll check the email for you on Friday, perhaps someone will reply."

Old Joe smiled, wiping his eyes. "If I had had this technology when I was Oliver's age, I think I could have been President by now."

"Go home now Oliver. You've done well today."

She turned to Old Joe and gave him a quick peck on his cheek.

"Joe, that was really sweet of you to help him."

Joe shrugged. "He wants his father back. We shall find him. Now, I must go home. My eyes, they give me so much trouble when I look at the screen for so long."

Aura looked over to where Bullet was still sleeping.

"Hey Bullet, wake up. We're closing. Doss somewhere else."

Bullet opened one eye. "Who cares?"

But Aura had already moved on and out of the building.

Oliver was busy making sure he had noted down the names and addresses of all of the people he'd written to and, when he looked up, was surprised to discover that Old Joe had already gone. Indeed, he was passing by the library windows as Oliver looked up, giving him a little wave. Oliver waved back, suddenly aware that Bullet had come up beside him, yawning.

"You're in pretty tight with the Princess."

"She's nice." Oliver declared, defensively.

"You think? She's rich. She goes home to her big house and her big bed. She's just down here to make herself look good. That's all these people ever do; come here, smile at us peasants, then go home and wash themselves with fuckin' TCP."

Oliver shook his head, but didn't say anything. He didn't want to get into a fight over this. Aura wasn't like this. Bullet was wrong.

"I gotta go to work." Bullet abruptly announced.

"Work?" Oliver asked, unable to hide the doubt in his voice.

Bullet smiled. "Wanna see? You can come."

"Got to go home," Oliver told him, hoping that would end things. Bullet scared him with his shaky probing eyes.

"Come on, you ain't seen nothin' yet, mate, and I know you want to."

"I have to get back to my Grandma's soon, she'll worry."

Bullet grinned. "You'll get back. Grandma's do too much fuckin' worrying. You'll get back. I promise, I'll protect you."

Oliver didn't really know how to say no, so he nodded, feeling stupid, knowing it was wrong. Bullet grabbed his arm and pulled him away from the computer desk.

84

"Come on then. I'll show you how to make money."

Oliver sensed he'd just made a terrible mistake going with Bullet, but that was the way with fate. You had to go all the way with it, then see where it takes you.

Outside on the street, Bullet lit up, inhaling deeply. He offered a drag to Oliver, but Oliver shook his head 'no'.

Bullet shrugged. "Anyway, who the fuck wants to live forever? I've already been shot and that didn't kill me. Anything that helps you die when you're young can't be all bad." Bullet stated, laughing. "Come on, got places to go, people to see."

Bullet walked off like he owned Church Street. They passed the Dance Agency and made their way past the Greenwich Picturehouse, with Oliver trotting alongside him, Oliver's head practically spinning as he tried to take everything in. He was thinking that Bullet probably wasn't so bad a friend to have and he was probably going to have some fun.

"Where are we going?" Oliver asked, noting a crowd of people outside the bar by the cinema.

"You'll see."

Oliver noted that Bullet certainly had a strong effect wherever they went. People seemed to veer off to one side as he came towards them. Oliver didn't know where they were going, but Bullet seemed to be quite purposeful.

"What kind of work do you do?" Oliver asked, as they crossed the road, narrowly avoiding a taxi that blasted them with its horn.

"You think I go to an office or something?"

Oliver frowned. "No, but..."

"How the fuck do you think I live? No one to tuck me up at night, kid. I'm fifteen, they don't give kids any bloody money and if you want somewhere to live they stick you in a foster home with a lot of junkies and some fat creep who wants to cruise your arse every night, for free. I live on the streets, got to make a living best you can. Come on, I got to pick a place. Which do you fancy?" Bullet adopted an Italian accent for a moment. "La Cucina di Soteri. Like Italian do you?" Then in his normal voice. "How about the North Pole? Place is a bit posh, even for you I'd think, besides it's back the other way."

Oliver was definitely worried now. He had a strong sense Bullet was about to do something illegal. What if they were on CCTV? He cast his eyes skywards for the cameras, couldn't see one, but he knew they would be there. They were everywhere. He was suddenly regretting tagging along with Bullet.

A cool blast of wind grabbed them and Oliver noticed the weather was changing; clouds were building over the city.

"Besides," Bullet suddenly told him, "didn't I tell you I'd give you a good time? Can't do that without money, now, can you?" He'd made a decision. "Fish tonight. Follow me. We're off to Thames Street."

There was logic to this, but Oliver knew now that he was running with trouble. Something bad would definitely happen. Sooner or later

"You hungry?" Bullet asked in a slightly mocking tone.

Oliver nodded and he was about to tell Bullet that he hadn't got any money when Bullet clapped a hand on his shoulders and gave him a quick friendly squeeze.

"We get money, then we eat." Bullet declared.

Oliver frowned as Bullet steered him along the pavement.

"What exactly do you do there?" Oliver asked.

"Come on, you'll like it. You don't have to do anything, just watch and learn."

Oliver was curious. Bullet was being quite mysterious. He ran alongside him. Bullet was striding out with a sense of purpose now, navigating the streets with confidence.

Lena was knocking on Justine's door, opening it a little way to call upstairs.

"Justine? It's seven. Dinner's nearly ready. Is Oliver up there with you?"

A moment later Justine appeared at the top of the stairs and shook her head.

Lena frowned. "I told him to come right back after the library was closed. Must have closed at least an hour ago. Think he could have got lost?"

Justine shrugged. She wasn't in charge of Oliver, Lena was.

"Well, after you've eaten, will you go and look for him? I know you've got homework, but he's new here and he might be lost."

Justine sighed. She disappeared a moment and then reappeared with her jacket and scarf.

"I'll go now. Keep my dinner warm."

Lena blinked. Couldn't remember the last time she'd heard Justine speak.

"Thank you. That's really good of you. I've got a busy night. Grandma Otis is booked solid. I'll keep your dinner warm. I don't know what a boy can do around here at night, but get into trouble. His Grandma is worried about him."

Justine clumped down the stairs. It was a bother, but the kid was OK, besides she needed some fresh air. There was only so much you could read about climate change without wanting to scream at somebody. She wondered if Oliver might have gone to the river again. He'd seemed pretty upset about the dog.

Bullet had stopped momentarily in a shop doorway to look at his face. From his back pocket he took out a little plastic bag and extracted something that looked like human hair. He pulled it really tight over his head and attached it by a slim hook over his ear. He smoothed it over his right cheek, and then turned to Oliver. Oliver immediately jumped back with revulsion. Bullet looked hideous. He had a fierce scar running down beside his eye and his upper lip was drawn back to reveal some teeth. He looked as though he had been slashed with a knife and he had never had it treated properly. It utterly transformed his face and Bullet seemed really pleased with himself as he placed a finger under the hair and made some final adjustments. He narrowed his eyes and hunched his shoulders forward.

"Look great, don't I?"

Oliver nodded, but he was thinking something else.

"Now I'm ready for work," Bullet declared, moving off again, expecting Oliver to catch him up.

They came to a halt outside a fish restaurant that looked very expensive to Oliver's eyes. Inside, rich tourists were eating at candle-lit tables covered with white tablecloths. One thing was for sure; they wouldn't want Bullet in there. Bullet winked at Oliver and produced a grubby hat from inside his expansive sweater.

"Wait across the road and watch," Bullet hissed at him.

Oliver backed away and left Bullet to position himself right outside the window where the diners were eating. He didn't face the street, like a normal beggar, but the window, so that the diners just couldn't miss him. Every time they would look out or look up from their meals, Bullet would be standing there looking at them, his hideous face and hunched shoulders, slobber dribble from his up-turned lip. He was a truly ghastly apparition. Even from his position across the road Oliver could sense that the diners were repulsed by Bullet. A gust of wind took his spittle and sprayed it against the window. Oliver watched the diners' reactions; a woman nearly gagged and angrily stood up, calling for a waiter or the manager's attention. Some potential customers came to the restaurant entrance and took one look at Bullet then immediately turned away.

Inside, Oliver could see that the receptionist had seen the incident and called someone to deal with it. Any minute now someone was going to come out of the place and beat Bullet up, he was sure of it. They wouldn't stand for it. Oliver couldn't but help feel a little bit sorry for the diners. All he knew was, that he wouldn't be able to sit there and eat if someone as hideous as Bullet was dribbling outside the window. Bullet didn't budge however. He wasn't even looking at anyone. Just standing there, drooling, making himself look as unpleasant as possible.

A group of four businesswomen arrived in their stylish suits, all of them animated, laughing, and ready to dine. They caught sight of Bullet and one woman nearly retched right there on the spot.

"Oh my God." Oliver heard her cry out. She turned away, but another of the women put her hand into her shoulder bag and produced a five-pound note, crushing it into Bullet's hat. Then, she too ran off to join her friend as they began to search for another place to eat.

Oliver was beginning to understand just how smart Bullet was. Six customers turned away in less than ten minutes. This restaurant was losing money because of him. Oliver could now see some reaction within the restaurant. The manager had finally been summoned by the diners nearest the windows and they were being quite vocal in their distress, pointing at Bullet. Any moment now Bullet was going to be in big trouble. The manager began to walk towards the front entrance, stopping a moment to talk to the receptionist. He then headed on outside, aiming towards Bullet. Oliver would have liked to have heard what the manager was going to say, but a motorbike started up nearby which distracted him and when he looked back, Bullet was gone, the manager was walking back inside and the situation was over. But where was Bullet? Oliver was about to walk back across the road when he felt a hand on his arm. He looked around and Bullet was standing there, his fake scarring gone, only the red marks of the tight hairline still remaining. There was a wet stain on his sweater from all the spittle, yet he looked pretty pleased with himself, he couldn't stop grinning.

"£55 quid. Not bad for twenty minutes work, eh? It's fuckin' ace. Did you see their faces? Practically puked on their lobsters, works every time."

Proud of himself, Bullet led Oliver away from the area, back up Norway Street.

"Of course, you can't do this outside the same place again, but there's plenty of restaurants here and Blackheath, all over. It's really quick money. I mean, some people beg down in the tube for hours an' only make sixty quid. You got to use ingenuity to make money in this game."

"How did you get the idea to make yourself so ugly?" Oliver asked.

"Read this book about beggars in India and how they deliberately cripple themselves and their kids, 'cause they reckon begging is their career, y'know? I mean, is that totally fucked up or what? People cutting their limbs off, breaking their hands, slicing their ears off... So I got this idea of making myself look like shit the easy way." He rubbed his face. "Leaves a scar though, takes time to go. Wouldn't want to do it too often. Shit, I'm hungry, let's get a burger."

Oliver was starving, but he didn't have any money and kind of felt guilty because Bullet had gone out and 'earned' his.

"I haven't got any money."

"I told you I'm paying. It's your first time here. My treat."

One thing was still bugging him. "Why don't the police arrest you when you do that stuff outside the restaurant windows?"

"Too much bother. Wouldn't want to fuck with my human rights now, would they?" He grinned. "Cops never do anything if they can help it. Too much paperwork."

Oliver digested that, it seemed reasonable, but what if they found out Bullet was faking it?

Bullet was grinning again. "Did you see the face on that woman who came to eat at the restaurant? She nearly had a heart attack when she saw my face. Bet she has nightmares for months. People just hate people who look like crap. They think all the people who look weird should be locked up."

Oliver thought about all the people who looked strangely at him, even now, and knew that Bullet was probably speaking the truth. People didn't like other people to look different to them, it unnerved them.

"You do this every day?"

"Most days. I have to make at least a hundred quid a day or I'm not really operating. I go up to the city on weekends. You should see what they pay to get rid of me in Soho."

Oliver didn't think he'd heard that right. Bullet, the kid who sleeps rough earned a hundred a day?

"I thought you just sat around the library."

"Yeah, I'm just hiding out right now. It's warm. I'm telling you kid, you can make a career out of this. You'd be good. You've got a cute girly face and you're bald, you wouldn't have to do anything, just sit in the square and tourists would cram money into your fist, really."

Oliver's head was still full of this concept of him sitting in the square begging for a living. He resented the remark about his 'cute girly face' too. There was no way on Earth he was going to beg. Maybe Bullet didn't know it was wrong. In fact, Oliver had begun to comprehend that Bullet didn't have any idea of what was right and wrong at all. He just did whatever he wanted. There were things he said that didn't quite match up, however. Did he really make a hundred pounds a day? What did he do with it? Why didn't he live somewhere? They arrived at a burger stand. There was a strong smell of onions frying.

"So, what you gonna eat?" Bullet asked nodding towards Oliver.

Sam North

Thirty minutes on, their food eaten, their stomachs filled with Coca-Cola, Oliver sensed he was enjoying this. He liked listening to street musicians, all of them trying to earn money from tourists and locals. Greenwich was a busy place and everywhere they went Bullet always seemed to know someone.

When Bullet wasn't looking, Oliver had stashed half his burger in his coat pocket. A 12-ounce burger was just too much for him and he didn't want to offend Bullet by throwing it away.

Bullet wasn't watching anyway, he was too busy talking about himself. About his great plans on how rich he was going to be, what car he was going to drive (a Maserati) and then there was a long list of people he was going to get even with. Oliver wasn't really listening, just absorbing the sights and sounds of Greenwich at night.

They were walking towards Lewisham, to see a mate of Bullet's who'd called him. He had some 'stuff' to get rid of. Oliver didn't know what it was and he could tell Bullet didn't really want him around anymore. Oliver realised he needed to pee. It was suddenly *very* urgent. He remembered, too late, that he wasn't allowed coke or lemonade for just this reason. He couldn't get into the pubs and there didn't seem to be anywhere to go and he was a bit shy about going behind a tree, not that there were a whole lot of trees.

Irritated, Bullet took him down the back of a residential street and checking they couldn't be observed, he shoved open the garden gate of a private house and roughly pushed him in.

"They can't see you, just piss and get out. OK. Do it."

Oliver had felt nervous trespassing, but he had no choice, worse, it took ages to come out, but the relief was great. He felt very guilty, but he was pissing on the grass and they probably wouldn't notice.

Suddenly a light came on. The back door was opening. Oliver hadn't finished. "No..." he wailed. He stopped. It wasn't a comfortable situation and he quickly zipped up again. He backed into the shadows.

A huge dog came bolting out of the house. Oliver couldn't see it too well in the dark, but the dog could see him, and immediately it began to bark and growl. Oliver ran for the garden door, but the dog was already there, not inclined to let him pass.

"What's there boy?" A scared woman's voice was asking.

Oliver said nothing, but he was aware that he was in real trouble now. Heart pumping wildly now, he wondered what to do. Bullet should have distracted the dog by now. Why wasn't he doing anything?

"Call him?" Oliver hissed, but Bullet said nothing.

The dog make a step towards him, he could see it more clearly now, it was

90

big and the teeth were bared. This could get bad, he knew. He tried to remember what to do, recall what his father had told him about dangerous dogs when they were living in Brazil. There had been so many wild dogs in Brazil and he'd been afraid of them. Oliver tried to make himself invisible. It was pure instinct. *'Face down the dog,'* his father's voice sounded in his head. *'Remember they're scared too.'*

His hands thrust into his pockets; suddenly he found the half burger he hadn't wanted. Yes! He took it out, showed it to the dog, which at least indicated some interest, sniffing the air and then he tossed it towards the house. The dog looked at him for a moment, unsure of what to do, but couldn't resist the idea of inspecting what he had thrown and ran back towards the meat.

Oliver seized his moment and quickly dashed for the doorway and fell out into the street, grabbing his hat on the way, which had snagged on a bush.

He was safe, but his heart was beating loudly. The garden door suddenly slammed shut behind him and he heard a bolt being slid into place.

It started to rain. Absolutely chucking it down. Sat on the pavement, Oliver was soaked in an instant. He groaned, his heart still racing.

"Shit," Oliver swore and immediately felt guilty for doing so. He looked around for Bullet, but Bullet had gone. It was only then he saw the sign on the gate, *'Beware of the Dog'*. Bullet's little joke? If so, it was a mean, bad thing to do. He could have been mauled. That had been a bloody big dog. Oliver picked himself up and started to run. He didn't care which way.

Aura sat in the back of the car beside her stepmother. Mr McTeal, her stepfather was driving the Jag with impatience. They'd been to dinner with friends and Aura had been forced to attend as the friends were rich and they had a son whom Mr McTeal though would be perfect for Aura. She wasn't even seventeen yet and they were thinking of marrying her off. It was practically medieval. The boy, who was nearly eighteen, with thick curly black hair and staring eyes, was finishing his A-Levels at Eton and planning to help his father run the largest hotel in Kuwait afterwards. Naturally his Daddy owned it. Mr McTeal was his advisor in all things astral. Marrying off Aura to a billionaire was just one of his main ambitions in life. Of course, he had not consulted Aura on these things. He had informed her that the stars had ordained it. As if.

Aura had been bored stiff. She hated the boy on sight and almost certainly he had hated her. He was opinionated, had racist views about everyone and clearly his opinion about girls was that they were only good for one thing.

They ought not to have any ideas about the world, or politics, certainly not ecology, about which Aura was passionate. She knew the planet was dying and it was people like him who were going to kill it.

They were heading home now and Aura was doing her best to keep control of her emotions. Of course, Mr McTeal and his lovely child bride Charmaine had adored the boy in question, thought him perfect in every way. Didn't think he was rude or arrogant at all. Money blinded everyone in Aura's experience.

She was staring out of the window as they crawled through the traffic from Lewisham and she was astonished to see Oliver. It had to be him, running like a scared cat along the pavement. He was miles from home, heading away from Greenwich up Blackheath Hill.

She wanted to lower her window and shout out, but Mr McTeal had them firmly locked. Even though they had slowed down behind a queue of buses she couldn't get Oliver's attention. He looked so pale, scared even. She couldn't believe that he was out here on his own.

"Bloody kids," Charmaine was saying, seeing what Aura was staring at.

"Bet he stole something. No one runs like that unless they've stolen something."

"I know him," Aura remarked. "He's not a thief."

"You couldn't possibly know him," Charmaine declared. "Really Aura, it's time you kept better company."

"We should stop. He shouldn't be here. I'm sure of it."

Mr McTeal pretended not to hear and accelerated around a bus. Aura twisted her neck to look back but Oliver had disappeared. She didn't know why but she sensed that that boy was destined for trouble. A lot of trouble.

"Can't believe it," Mr McTeal exploded. "They've dug up this road again."

Oliver was angry now. He'd got himself lost twice. How it was possible, he didn't know. But he was wet, the sky had closed in and he still hadn't remembered to ask what street he lived in, or how the street layout worked.

He'd gone miles in the wrong direction, gone all the way up to the Heath before he'd found a way down again on Crooms Hill. Oliver felt stupid, but now he was sure he was back in Greenwich, he was searching for the signs of the power station chimneys. Everything looked so different at night.

He felt guilty and stupid for going along with Bullet. He felt resentment and anger and it wasn't as if Aura hadn't told him to stay clear of him. Bullet was mean. He'd meant for him to get hurt. He knew that now. He saw a clock in an illuminated shop window. It had gone ten o'clock already.

Grandma Otis would be seething. She'd want to beat him and it was all his own fault. He'd known in his heart that Bullet was going to be bad news.

He glimpsed what he hoped were the towers in the distance. His heart beat a little faster. Home. He knew where he was going at last.

Justine had gone beyond angry now. She'd been out twice already looking for the little shithead, eaten a lukewarm dinner and endured being soaked and seen nothing. Oliver was just nowhere to be seen. There were some kids hanging about on the main road, but she walked all the way to both stations, the river and there was just no sign of him. She had grown nervous for her own safety then, there were altogether for too many people out there.

It was ten thirty. Grandma Otis was still busy with clients, it was a session that had been going on forever. Lena was passed out in the kitchen – she'd drunk a whole bottle of sherry worrying about Oliver and Justine was thinking they'd have to call the police. She was convinced something bad had happened to him.

Flop was anxious too, sat by the back door listening for his master. Justine desperately wanted to go to bed; she had French first thing and History to follow. She needed her sleep to cope with that.

Someone else was also fretting about the boy. Aura lay on her bed wondering about Oliver. That look of panic on his face as he ran through the streets. She'd hoped he'd made it back. She wondered why they even let a sick boy like that out on his own at night. It wasn't right, not right at all.

7. Body Double

Oliver had to find the road which headed down towards the river. As he approached Trafalgar Road, the main route that took all the through traffic to Woolwich or back to town, he could hear the thunder of trucks rumbling on through and the hiss of their brakes. He also saw, in the shadows, kids, bored kids, kicking bottles and cans, looking for trouble, looking for one bald kid who'd be good for a laugh.

Oliver willed himself invisible, but he knew eyes were on him as he approached from the opposite side of the street. He knew he had to get across the busy road, he knew he mustn't make eye contact. Louth might have been a backwater, but it had its fair share of bored kids who liked to smash windows at night and terrorise each other.

A huge articulated truck was wading through the street, so large it seemed like an ocean liner. Oliver could see three boys and a girl detach themselves from the group, begin to walk towards him as he waited to cross the road. Oliver just knew he had to ignore them, couldn't let them begin talking to him. They'd kick the shit out of him for sure, they'd know he was a country boy. The truck was getting closer, it's engine roaring as it accelerated and changed gear. The other side looked clear of traffic... Oliver ran for it. Right in front of the truck. There was a hiss of brakes, tyres skidding and screaming, a blast of a horn as the whole truck jinked, then shot forward again as the driver gunned the engine. The driver swore in German out of his window. But Oliver had made it to the other side, and as the truck rolled on by, he didn't break his stride, just kept on running, turning only once he'd reached the shadows to make sure he wasn't being pursued. They had given up. He was safe.

He made one false move, mistakenly turning off Hoskins Street and finding himself in a dead end street. Miserable and cold, he retraced his steps, looking up into the orange light of the street lamps for the familiar power station chimneys that overshadowed his new home.

"Oh that way," he told himself.

"The river is over there." He wasn't used to streets that went off at all kinds of angles.

It was getting later and later. He began to worry that Grandma Otis would have called the police, that they'd be looking for him. He began to grow very uneasy and noticed it was getting damp and misty again. He knew now that this was a good sign, it should be cooler by the river. Truth was, it couldn't get cool enough. Grandma Otis would make sure of that. He speculated on how she'd punish him, if she'd try to beat him... No, she'd get Lena to do it, Lena would like to beat him, he was sure. A dog barked as he passed by an enclosed front yard and a light came on. Oliver hurried on, concentrating only on getting home and curling up with Flop.

He finally found the right road, with its uneven cobbles and was approaching Grandma Otis's house when he noticed a number of cars were parked in the road and inside her yard. New cars. One was a Jaguar, another a black Mercedes. Why were they there? What was going on?

As he drew closer he noticed that all the rooms at the bottom of the house were illuminated, and a curious glow seemed to light up Grandma's window. Was Grandma Otis having a party? If so, it was very quiet. Either way, it was spooky and the fuzz hair on Oliver's neck seemed to bristle.

He took a cautious approach and aimed for the back door. Someone was waiting for him, however. From out of the shadows two arms grabbed his foot, then dashed away. Flop!

"Flop, Flop", Oliver whispered. "Come here, tell me what's going on?"

Flop came back to him, let out a hesitant cry and allowed himself to be picked up and cuddled. Flop had known Oliver would come back. For more than an hour he'd been waiting, knowing Oliver was trying to find his way home...

"Can we go in? What's happening? Is Grandma mad at me?"

Flop purred. He was happy. He felt safe now.

Oliver opened the back door and peered in. The light was on, the kitchen looked a mess and, as he inched it open some more, he could see Lena, asleep and sprawled out across the table top, snoring. Oliver's heart soared. He could get in. With luck he and Flop could get all the way to his room without anyone noticing. He could even pretend he'd been there for hours.

"Let's get in, come on," he told Flop.

Oliver entered and set Flop down who made a dash for his bowl, diving into a plate of prawn flavoured biscuits. Oliver shut the door and locked it behind him. As quiet as he could, he removed his shoes and took off his jacket, hanging it up behind the door. It was warm in the kitchen, and aside from Lena's snoring, a friendly place to be. He stood up again and accidentally knocked into a bottle on the floor. It seemed to him to make a terrible crash, but it didn't disturb Lena. When he picked the bottle up, he knew why. Sherry. It smelled real bad too.

Flop took a sip of his water then came back to Oliver, wanting to be carried again. Oliver picked him up and snuggled him. "Come on, let's go to bed."

Flop miaowed as if to say, *'At last...'*

Oliver could hear footsteps upstairs and he wondered what was going on. The quietest party on earth, that was what. He wondered if he should go up at all, but decided it would be OK, Grandma Otis was busy, she wouldn't want to be bothered. He'd sneak up and slide into his room. He walked over to the stairs speaking softly to Flop.

"Nearly got biten by a dog, Flop. You would have been really scared."

Grandma's own room was tight with people, the only light, a soft green glow that seemed to emanate from Grandma Otis herself. She sat up in bed with a shawl wrapped tight around her as she concentrated hard on the job in hand. The people in the room sat around her with intent gazes, barely breathing. Two tall men in expensive suits leaned back against the outer walls with bored expressions on their faces, only mildly interested in the proceedings, probably only there to accompany their wives or girlfriends. At the end of the bed sat a woman with stooped shoulders, dressed in an orange cotton dress, with a skimpy woollen cardigan barely disguising her anorexic figure. As she sat, silently sobbing, two of her female companions tried to comfort her. There was an overwhelming element of sorrow in the room and altogether too many people for comfort. The atmosphere was close, humid and electric.

Grandma Otis let out a sigh, then released a disembodied voice that came from her mouth, but was most definitely not her own or Quon's. It was the voice of a child, a male child, a boy aged ten or younger.

"Mummy? It's me, Steve. Mummy? Can you hear me? It's me, Steve."

The woman in orange sat bolt upright. It was clear from her total astonishment that she clearly recognised the voice calling her. The transformation in her face was instantaneous. She immediately became animated.

"It's Steven, it's Steve," she cried out to everyone. "It's his voice, it's him. Steven? It's me, Mummy!"

"It's dark, Mummy, why is it so dark? Where are you? When are coming to get me?"

The young child's voice was pitiable and realistic. Even the two men who had been acting so bored earlier were now listening with interest and keenly watching Susan and Grandma Otis.

Susan was shaking her head violently now. "Why didn't you wait for me? I told you to wait. I told you not to swim alone, there's under-currents. Oh, Steve, if you'd only waited."

There was a sudden creak on the stairs and everyone jumped as they strained to see out onto the landing. The green glow surrounding Grandma Otis flickered and began to fade, yet simultaneously, an apparition appeared at the top of the stairs: a vision in yellow, a young boy, glowing in the reflected light from Grandma's room, revealing his startled face.

Susan leapt up from the end of the bed and cried out: "It's Steven, it's Steve, he's come back to me, he's come back." She ran forward and wrapped her arms around the apparition she thought to be Steve. Immediately there was a hissing and a loud cry of pain as a cat landed clumsily onto the floor. A struggle had begun between Susan and the apparition. The more she squeezed, the more violent the struggle became.

"Steve?" wailed Susan.

The others in the room began to rise, spooked and not a little concerned for Susan's safety. The atmosphere was one of nervous expectancy tinged with growing scepticism.

"Steven!" Susan cried out once again and this time there was an immediate response as the child in question managed to get his head out from under her crushing figure.

"Leave me alone, leave me alone, I'm not bloody Steve!"

Everyone froze to the spot. The last fragment of light surrounding Grandma Otis died and Oliver broke free of Susan's grip. Susan, however, still did not realise what had happened.

"Steve, you came back to me, you..."

"I AM NOT STEVE!" Oliver shouted angrily, evading Susan's hysterical clutches.

Oliver found himself facing a room full of adults who were all experiencing a rising tide of anger. Behind them Grandma Otis lay slumped in her bed only slowly coming back to herself.

One of the men came to Susan's side and took her by the arm.

"Come on Susan, obviously you've been victim to some terrible, malicious fraud. It's *not* Steven, darling, it's not *Steven*."

Grandma Otis finally found her own voice, though it croaked and sounded frail when she finally uttered:

"Oliver? Are you there? What's happened? Are you there?"

Susan broke free of her escort and turned on Grandma Otis, her nostrils flaring, her eyes mad with grief and anger.

"You wicked witch, you cruel woman. I came to you and you did *this*, you..." She spat as she spoke, she was so angry.

"What kind of trick is this? You stole my Steve. He was coming back. He was ready. You stole him."

Oliver rocked back on his feet, standing right on the edge of the top step, not at all sure what had been going on, or what was happening now. He recognised that the atmosphere had turned very ugly and, somehow he was involved.

Grandma Otis sat up in her bed, tight lipped and flushed, unaccustomed to being called a cheat. She lifted her stick into the air and pointed it at Susan.

"Mrs Ford," she snapped, "you can think what you like, but no one ever comes back, not in the flesh, never." She turned to Oliver and tried to rein in her anger a little.

"Oliver get to your room, you've no part in this." She turned back to Mrs Ford and her anger returned. "That's my grandson and he's got enough troubles without you adding to them."

"Steven was *here*." Susan hissed at her. "You let him go."

Susan's escort put an arm around her and pulled her towards the stairs, but she wasn't finished yet. "I'll sue you. He was here, he was here!"

Grandma Otis slammed her stick down on her bed, startling the other two women who had remained still and tight lipped until this moment, completely confused by the evenings' events. The women stood up and grabbed their coats. "He was here." They confirmed in unison.

"They can't come back," Grandma Otis insisted, her own anger rising once more. "Anyone who says so is a fool, anyone who believes it is a bigger fool. You can sue me all you like, but it was you who came to me to hear your son one more time. If you heard him, you heard him, but I'm no magician. If you want to raise the dead, get yourself a bloody witch doctor!"

Oliver took this opportunity to duck into his room, quickly closing the door behind him. To his relief, a cross looking Flop was sat on the bed, frantically licking his paws, looking up momentarily, as if to say, *'About bloody time, lock the doors, pack the bags, they're all mad.'*

Oliver joined him on the bed and discovered that he was shaking. His back hurt where the woman's hands had gripped him. Just what had been going on? Was Grandma Otis really trying to bring people back from the dead? Like Frankenstein? He didn't know whether to be frightened or impressed. 'Granny Frankenstein' would be pretty amazing really, but he knew he'd probably gotten the wrong end of the stick.

He heard them talking outside and going downstairs. The front door slammed and soon after he heard car engines being started. Flop and Oliver listened as the last car drove away leaving just the silence of an old house and the sounds of a distant foghorn on the river. Flop leaned into Oliver and Oliver tickled the top of his head. Both of them were confused and anxious. Oliver whispered into Flop's pink ears. "It's pretty scary Flop. I think everyone in this city is seriously weird."

Suddenly his door creaked open. Flop leapt into the air and dived under the covers. Oliver's heart stopped.

"Where were you?" Justine hissed, sneaking into his room. "What did you do just now?"

"Nothing."

"You must have done something. People were swearing, doors slamming, I heard shouts about getting a lawyer. Where have you been?"

Oliver didn't know what to say. Everything was wrong. He was utterly stupid for going anywhere with Bullet and now he'd upset everyone in the house. He deserved to be punished.

"You're lucky Lena passed out. You just can't go off like that. Anything could happen to you – anything."

"I was lost."

"Where? I was out everywhere looking for you... In the rain."

"It went bad. Bullet tricked me, I nearly got bitten and he was begging and..."

Justine put her hands up in the air. "Way too much information. Bullet? You know a boy called Bullet? What's with you? Have you got no sense at all? Anyone called Bullet or Pistol or whatever is going to be trouble..."

Oliver sighed, this was a lot like talking to his mother, before she got ill.

"I'm sorry."

"You don't have to apologise to me, well you do, if I get a cold for going out in the rain I will make sure I sneeze in your direction, Oliver."

"I won't do it again."

Justine narrowed her eyes. "I hope not, Oliver. There are too many weirdos out there. Get some sleep and next time you go anywhere, tell me first. OK? Nasty things happen at night. Remember that."

With that remark hanging in the air she was gone. Oliver felt doubly guilty now. A moment later he heard her door shut and her heavy footsteps up her stairs to the attic.

Flop stayed put under the covers, not sure it was safe to come out yet.

Half an hour later the pipes were rumbling after Grandma Otis's bath and although she was more calm now, inside she still seethed. Her reputation would survive this, there had been moments like this before. Her regulars would come, they knew she was the real thing. She'd never wanted to see these people in the first place. She'd instinctively known that these people would be trouble. They'd been referred. Well, she'd not do a favour for that quarter again, that was for sure. People missed the dead all the time, but it was unhealthy to obsess about it. That woman Susan was driven by guilt. She knew that she'd let her attention wander and her child had drowned. That was all this was, a saga, a charade to deflect her guilt, to avoid the blame for her carelessness.

Downstairs she heard Lena coughing and dragging her body off to bed. There had to be a way to wean her off the sherry, it was going to do the woman in one day. Grandma Otis sighed as she shuffled from the bathroom to her bedroom, plonking her aching bones down in front of her dressing table mirror.

She let down her long, grey hair and began to brush it out. A nightly ritual in front of her mirror. For her, no matter how late the day ended, it wasn't finished off properly unless she gave her tresses fifty hard brushes. That's the way it had always been, since she'd been a child. Always fifty brushes with her mother-of-pearl brush. She looked up into the mirror and started... it was not herself looking back but a young boy, a leering, sullen, wild young boy. He looked directly at her and mouthed *"Oliver."* Then winked at her.

Grandma Otis was so shocked, she was so completely taken aback she dropped her hair brush onto the carpet, her hands instinctively shooting to her neck, clasping the small gold cross she had there holding it tight. The vision disappeared, it had only lasted a second, less if it had ever existed at all – but it left Grandma Otis thoroughly spooked, there was no other word for it. Oliver was in danger, whoever the boy was, he had nothing but evil intentions upon her grandson.

She was up on her shaky legs as fast as she could rise and walking towards Oliver's room. She pushed open his door and the light fell upon his bed. He was lying, still fully clothed across his bed, with the cat curled up in his arms. Flop looked up at Grandma Otis and let out a tiny warning cry to Oliver. He awoke instantly and blinked as his eyes adjusted to the light from the landing. He knew immediately that he was about to be punished for his adventures that night, and for causing trouble when he got home.

"I didn't mean to cause trouble," he began. "I was just coming up the stairs and..."

Grandma Otis waved the remark. "Who's the boy, Oliver? Who is he? A thin boy with a mean look, a permanent sneer on his face, looks bitter and he's got a scar..."

Oliver blinked at Grandma Otis with utter confusion. How was it possible she could describe Bullet so accurately? It was impossible she could know Bullet, impossible.

"You know Bullet?" Oliver was totally caught off guard.

Grandma Otis steadied herself by holding onto the door. She knew she'd hit a mark. He had met this boy.

"He's evil, Oliver. He isn't your friend, even if he pretends to be. He means to harm you. I don't know why, but I have had a warning. Do you understand me? A warning. He wants to harm you."

Oliver nodded his head. A warning. Well he'd had one too! Bullet was no friend, he knew that well enough. He couldn't tell Grandma about Bullet without telling her where he had been or what he'd done and he wasn't going to makes things worse than they already were. He tried to change the subject.

"I'm sorry I upset everything here tonight. Will you get into trouble? Will she really sue you?"

Grandma Otis pulled a face. "She could try, but she won't. They aren't my regulars, friends of a friend."

"What did they want?"

"The impossible. Some people can't live with their guilt and they want to talk to the dead... Some people just want to make sure their loved ones are safely over and others..." She sighed with a heavy heart. "Well, they just want advice. I couldn't help them tonight, they wanted more than I can give them. If they think I'm a fraud, then I've survived worse. No one likes you if you won't give them what they want."

Oliver digested this. "Bullet isn't my friend, he's..."

"He's mean, that's what he is and he wants to get you into trouble."

Oliver frowned. "Well he can't. I don't ever want to see him again."

But Grandma Otis knew otherwise, it wasn't something Oliver could choose. "You know, your mother made a friend once. She was called Alison. She was the nicest girl you could ever want your daughter to be friends with. Then Alison discovered boys and pills and she'd steal money to pay for everything. She stole from everyone, but she was very clever, because she made everyone believe that it was your mother, my Charlotte, who was the thief. She even had *me* convinced, I am ashamed to say. I thought it was my own daughter taking money from my bag and others' pockets. When Alison pointed out that your grandfather's gold watch had gone we all accused Charlotte of taking it, and she had a new record player that I hadn't paid for. Well, we all liked Alison and no matter what Charlotte said, we just didn't believe she was innocent."

"Is that when my Mother ran away from you?" Oliver asked, familiar with this story, but interested to hear it from Grandma's side.

Grandma Otis looked away for a moment, a tear welling up in one eye as she recalled the terrible incident so long ago.

"Yes, but of course, that is when we discovered Charlotte was innocent, because Alison went on stealing from us and although she tried to blame it on all sorts of people, we knew better."

"When Charlotte came back, we tried to make friends again, but..." Grandma Otis rubbed her eyes and sighed. "She never forgave me, never."

She looked at Oliver's face and saw how tired and pensive he looked. She knew right then that something bad had already happened to him. Perhaps he'd tell her in time. She hoped so. She hoped he'd learn to trust her.

"This new friend you have made. He's a lot worse than Alison. He seems friendly, but..." she searched her mind for the right thing to say. "He wants you to be as unhappy as he is, he's jealous of you."

Oliver looked up at her with surprise. "Jealous?"

Grandma Otis smiled at him, a moment's genuine affection showing. "You have something he hasn't got Oliver. People like you. Did I tell you Harriet has fallen for you?"

Grandma Otis registered his embarrassment and turned away, adding as an afterthought as she pulled the door to: "Do you know how happy I am you came to live here? I always wanted to see you, y'know, but Charlotte refused to bring you to me. I once came to Louth, but she wouldn't let me see you. I waited, but she wouldn't even let you out of the house that day." Grandma Otis sighed. "This is your home now, Oliver, you will be safe here."

With that said, she was gone and Oliver was left sitting up in bed in darkness. Flop lay across his lap, solidly asleep, only the fading luminosity of the new owl on his window ledge was there to keep him company. He'd expected a telling off. He wasn't sure how to deal with what Grandma Otis had actually said. He was happy to know she wanted him to stay, but he was still unnerved by her description of Bullet. She was right, no matter how she'd known about him. He was definitely going to avoid him, big time. He lay back down on his bed and snuggled up to Flop who put out a paw to his face again and left it there. Sleep wanted him and he was ready.

8. Head Count

Lena was making breakfast, nursing a severe hangover as she made the scrambled eggs. A glass of bubbling Andrew's Liver Salts sat fizzing on the table with a small stack of paracetamols beside it. She turned from the pan and picked up the glass, knocking it back and swallowing four of the pills, as Oliver wandered in, lobster-red from the hot shower towelling his wet hair dry. He could see Lena looked as though she was really suffering.

"Did you see Flop yet? Did he eat?"

Lena stirred the scrambled eggs some more as the toaster flipped up, exposing the over-done toast. "Get the toast won't you. Your breakfast is nearly ready. Your cat already ate and went out. I dropped a raw egg and he was all for scoffing it down."

Oliver pulled a face. "Yuk, he never ate an egg before, but once he ate my mother's corn on the cob. He stole it off the table and wouldn't give it up. He ate all the corn off it too."

Lena screwed up her face with pain as she shovelled out the scrambled eggs from the pan onto a warm plate.

"That's a strange cat alright."

Oliver could see that she was having a hard time looking at and smelling the food. He busied himself with buttering the toast. Lena was clutching her head as she lowered the pan into the washing up basin.

"I don't know what they put in the sherry these days, but it sure isn't what it used to be. Never used to get a head like this. Never."

As Oliver put his toast on the table and sat down to eat Lena sat down and buried her head on her arms, groaning loudly.

Oliver began to eat, he pondered what it must be like to make yourself drink so much you would wake up with a headache, and why people did it.

"Lena? When you were young, did you ever think about the future?"

Lena didn't reply immediately, or stir from her position on the table. Oliver thought she was probably too ill to answer, so he started eating, enjoying his hot food.

"We didn't think much about the future when we were young." Lena remarked eventually, her fingers going out in the space directly before them as they searched for her pack of cigarettes. They found the pack and Oliver pushed the pink lighter into her hand with his toast.

As if in slow motion, she sat up and with one sweeping action lit a cigarette. She sat perfectly still, blowing smoke towards the ceiling with her eyes tightly closed.

"We all thought the bloody world was going to end any day soon; so we didn't make any plans. All of us were the same. We didn't need to get a mortgage, we didn't need to do anything boring. We could be actors, or artists, or singers and it didn't matter if you didn't make any money, because the Russians or the Americans were going to blow up the planet, sooner or later. I knew the world was going to end when I was five years old and even when I was thirty, I was still waiting." She opened her eyes and looked at Oliver, studied him, making Oliver feel uncomfortable. "You don't know what it's like to grow up in a world that could end at any time. I used to laugh at people who made plans for the future. I told them, 'Why bother? You'll be dead. Spend your money, don't save. When the bomb drops, you'll regret not having a good time.'"

She laughed, but it was bitter and painful for her, for she soon stopped and clamped a hand to her temple again.

"I was wrong, of course. Stupid. The world's still here and I'm broke, got no future, no life. I suppose my world did end after all. I suppose all the bloody optimists were right. Everything did come right in the end."

Oliver swallowed the last of his scrambled eggs and went to the counter to switch the kettle on, checking to see if it had water in it first. It had. He flipped the switch. "I dreamt about the world ending once. Big explosions and people vaporised onto the pavements. I saw this anime *Graveyard of the Fireflies* from Japan. It's the saddest film I ever saw, the kids are starving, their town got firebombed they have to go live in a cave..."

Lena held up one hand for him to stop. "Quieter, my head hurts."

Oliver began to whisper. "My doctor told me that the reason I'm still alive is because I have a destiny and God wants me to stay alive long enough to meet it."

Lena looked up briefly at Oliver and frowned. "I used to think I had a destiny. I used to think I would be discovered one day, that I'd be wanted, loved, but I always knew that the day it happened, that's the day all hell would break loose and the world would end."

Oliver smiled. "Maybe that's why you didn't become famous."

Lena scowled at him. "What do you mean?" Then, as an afterthought, "if you're making tea, I'll have a cup too. The tea bags are in the jar marked salt."

Oliver busied himself with the cups and tea-bags as he considered his reply. "I mean, maybe God couldn't let you become famous because if you had been, then the world would have ended."

Lena blew a smoke ring at him and fell back on the table, burying her head into her arms again. "Well, I still think the world's going to end..."

"Do you like milk and sugar?"

"...and I hope I die first. Milk, no sugar."

"I went to the library yesterday and I met Aura there. She introduced me to Old Joe and we sent messages all over Africa to see if anyone will help me find my father."

Lena just groaned. "Make the tea. Make sure you wear a coat today, it's windy, might rain."

Oliver looked out of the window and saw she was right, it was blowing the trees really hard. He wondered if there would be any waves on the river. He wanted to take a look.

Lena took a final drag of her cigarette and tossed the butt end into the sink. "I suppose we'll have to think about a school for you soon."

Oliver spun around and made an unpleasant noise. "Next term, not now. When my hair grows back."

Lena opened her eyes and was about to say something sarcastic but stopped herself. She hadn't really thought about what it would be like to go to a new school and have kids taunt you for being bald. Kids were cruel, she knew that and they'd sooner pick on you for being different, than not.

"Well, it had better start growing soon if it is going to be ready for next term. Besides, you'll be cold in winter without it."

Lena slumped back onto her arms and groaned again. "Pass the tea, I need the tea."

Oliver pushed the cup over towards her. Lena suddenly remembered why she had a hangover. Why she had sat in the kitchen, waiting for him to return.

"Where were you last night Oliver? Never go out again without telling us where you are and if you can't get back in good time, call us. That's what phones are for."

"I'm sorry. But... I don't know the number."

"Write it down, memorise it. It's on the wall, by the calendar. Something else too. Justine says you got caught up in something strange last night.

Don't talk about what Grandma does, OK? Some people don't like fortune telling and... Well just keep quiet, alright?" Lena grasped her tea, desperate to concentrate.

"Grandma Otis doesn't like publicity. She's very private."

"Did anyone call about the dead dog we found?"

Lena was tired now. "Why don't you ask Grandma Otis to see if Quon knows about the dog. He knows a lot of things."

Oliver nodded. Yes, it was a good idea. Somehow Grandma had known about Bullet, so it was very likely she'd know about this dog. "I'll ask her to ask him. I still don't know how he knows things, but I'll certainly ask."

"Now if you'd be so good as to finish your cup of tea in perfect silence I would appreciate it. You're not going to get into the habit of roaming at night are you?"

Oliver was about to launch into an excuse when Grandma Otis rang her bell and Lena groaned very loudly. "Oh God, she's awake already. You can tell me later, I have to make her breakfast. Are you going out?"

"I like the wind."

"Wrap up, alright? And make sure you're back for tea. Five o'clock sharp. Not a minute past."

Oliver nodded and sipped his tea, glancing out of the window a moment to examine the weather more closely. Yes, the river, he wanted to explore the river today, see where it went, what was sailing.

Lena got up from the table and put more bread in the toaster. She looked very pale, very sick and suddenly very old. Oliver knew for certain that he'd never, ever, want to drink sherry.

The back door opened abruptly and Justine was standing there in her school uniform. She looked flushed and quite pleased with herself.

"Now what?" Lena moaned. "Didn't I just send you off to school?"

"One day strike. Wish they'd go on strike more often."

Oliver smiled at her. "Want some toast?"

Justine nodded. "Yeah. And a cup of tea. I missed breakfast." Flop snuck in between her legs as she closed the door. "Want me to show you around today? If you know what's here, you might stick a bit closer."

Oliver grinned. "Thanks. That's great. Sugar?"

"No. Just milk." She looked at Lena struggling to get out of her chair.

"You look terrible Lena. I told you to drink milk before you went to bed. You should be in bed."

"Got to make Grandma's breakfast."

'I'll do it. Go to bed."

Lena looked at Justine, unsure, but saw that she was being genuine and shrugged.

"You're right. I have to go to bed. Can't drink like I used to anymore. Can't do anything like I used to anymore."

Oliver kept quiet and made the toast for Justine. Justine took off her coat and got to work. She winked at Oliver and he grinned. He was glad he didn't have a headache like that. Never wanted to have a headache ever again.

The river was half way out and half way in, mean tide, and there was a large mud bank below the river walkway. Virtually nothing was sailing on the river, which left him feeling a little bit disappointed. Oliver and Justine were walking upriver with coats on and hoods up to keep out the unseasonable biting cold wind. Oliver was keen to discover what lay the other side of the defunct power station and Justine showed him the old Trinity hospital that had been in use in the seventeenth century, long before the ugly power station had been plonked next door to it. He knew from history that back in Queen Elizabeth the First's time Greenwich had been the most important place in England. Nelson had lived nearby somewhere. He tried to think what it must have been like to live in Greenwich in Elizabethan times. He couldn't see much of the white plastered hospital building, but had glimpsed a little courtyard through an open door and it looked very inviting with trees and bushes, another secret garden like grandma's. He looked up as something moved and was suddenly aware of the chatter of birds. Hundreds of birds screeching high in the ivy on the power station walls. Grandma Otis's Africa.

"Hear the birds?"

Justine listened and smiled. She couldn't see them but she knew they were there. "I wondered what that noise was. My god, it's amazing, Oliver."

It was kind of annoying he noticed *everything* and she'd been here months and saw and heard nothing.

"I saw a wild parakeet at school the other day," she remarked, remembering. "Climates' changing. Parakeets living here are a sign, y'know. I saw a whole tree full of them in Hyde Park last summer. They squark and squabble all the time. Scare the other birds I should think." She looked out over the river a moment. "I can't believe the river froze over. It did you know, in the 15th century. No ships could move for weeks. Wonder what that looked like? They skated and roasted beef on it, which kind of sounds stupid to me, as wouldn't the heat melt the ice?"

Oliver looked at the river and realised he would have given anything to see the river frozen over and be able to walk on it.

"You think global warming means it could dry up instead?"

Justine shook her head. "Just means we'll get more rain and floods. Your Grandma should sell the house. This part of Greenwich will probably be underwater soon. If a parakeet ever sets up home in the garden, I'd panic if I were you."

Oliver laughed. "People might come here for their summers. London might be tropical. Think what life would be like here it if it was hot all the time?"

Justine pulled a face. "Stinky, probably, very stinky. Come on, lets go."

Oliver knew there was a lot to discover around here and wondered if there were pictures of Greenwich back in those times. Had Grandma's house been standing then? Were there secret passages, smuggler's tunnels? If there were, he intended to find them.

"I sometimes like it here and sometimes everything being so old does my head in," Justine remarked. "So many people and students."

"Where did you live before?" Oliver asked.

"In Blackheath. Big house overlooking a pond. I can't believe we lost everything. They even took my clothes. Mum was crying and then she went crazy when she discovered Dad had forged her signature on all the loans. It meant she was liable for all of his debts. Everything I have now Grandma Otis gave me."

"I don't understand how tax works."

"Me neither, but when I get older, I'm going to leave."

"Leave?"

"England. I want to go to France. That's why I'm learning French. I want to live in France and make jewellery, live by the ocean or something like that."

"Wish I knew what I wanted to do. Six months ago I didn't think I had a future at all."

Justine looked at him and took his arm, squeezing it a little. Yeah, things had gone bad for her, but never as bad as Oliver. She'd seen those scars. He must have been really sick.

They walked towards the new expensive apartment buildings and the old pubs that overlooked the river, where squeezed in the middle, was Crane Street, a narrow passage between the river buildings and a row of small terrace houses on one side. Oliver was fascinated by the area now. He'd read about the foot tunnel that ran under the river somewhere up ahead which he knew he wanted to explore. He suddenly noticed a gap between buildings. The wooden floodgate was open to the river and someone had left a double scull rowing boat on the pebbles.

"Come on. Let's explore."

"I don't think..." Justine was saying, but Oliver had already run ahead and she had to follow.

Oliver walked out onto the pebble beach, Justine hurrying to catch him up.

Behind them, they could see people drinking in the pub, staring at them through the windows. As they approached the river, they noticed just how squishy the mud was and Justine hung back.

"No further. I only just got these shoes."

Oliver looked across the river at the other side. A four man crew was rowing upstream, struggling in the wind as the water spray engulfed them. In the distance lay a tug, seemingly drifting on the water, it's crew lolling about on deck. He turned, nothing very interesting today. He noticed an overturned old rowing boat in the distance resting on a slim sliver of beach and broke into a run towards it. Behind him Justine was calling on him to be careful on the pebbles, when he stumbled and fell headlong onto the beach. He ended up in a heap by the upturned boat. He swore, slipping again as he tried to rise, and slid back a couple of feet. He was covered in mud now and he'd only been out of the house fifteen minutes.

Justine was beside him now, looking down with an *'I told you so...'* expression.

Oliver sighed thinking irritatedly that he just couldn't go anywhere without getting into a mess of some kind. He turned his head and instantly received a jolt. He had discovered he was looking at a hand protruding from under the boat – a decomposing human hand.

"Shiiit!' Oliver yelled.

Justine saw it too and caught her breath. "Oh – my – God."

Oliver tried to lift the boat, but couldn't get a grip on the slippery surface under his feet and Justine came to help.

"We shouldn't," Justine was saying. "I can't look."

The boat lifted half way and stuck, its stern still partly buried in the sand and mud. A rotting stench rose up and nearly made Justine gag. The hand was attached to an arm and a whole body and suddenly his head flopped into view. Justine shrieked. They both nearly dropped the boat in fright.

"He's handcuffed." Justine exclaimed with a squeal. "He's naked and handcuffed to the seat. God it stinks Oliver."

"How come no one noticed?" Oliver was looking back at the pub. Surely they could see the old boat from there.

Oliver looked at the pulpy, pasty, bloodless head again when a black eel slithered out of an eye socket and slipped back into the half-open mouth.

"Eeyuk!" Oliver cried out, dropping his end and scrabbling up on his two feet.

Justine let her end drop too, she'd seen enough already. She got out her phone. "Got to call the police."

Oliver lifted his end of the boat again and looked down at the head again with disgust and fascination. Now he could see it more clearly, there were all kinds of slug-like things attached to it as well. He nearly tasted his breakfast again, but managed to keep it down. Greenwich was suddenly the scariest place on earth.

"Don't touch anything, you might disturb the evidence." Justine told him firmly.

But Oliver was looking at something else that they had disturbed, something that triggered something sharp in his head. He reached down with one hand and tugged at the leather strap half buried in the sand and it came away easily. A dog lead. A very expensive wet leather dog lead and Oliver knew, in an instant, whose lead this was.

"It's his dog, Justine. It was his dog we found on the beach. I know it. He was out looking for it."

"In handcuffs? You can't possibly know..." But Justine had noticed the colour drain out of Oliver's face and she knew something was happening to him again.

"I don't know how that happened, but he was looking for his dog when..."

And suddenly Oliver was lying on the sand unconscious – his eyes fluttering, his legs twitching.

Justine dropped her phone and wanted to scream.

It took nearly forty minutes, but the police finally arrived and were none too pleased to discover the tide was coming in. But it was they who'd wasted time not believing anything Justine had said. They had both waited at the beach for ages before they'd sent one bored cop along to take a statement. He'd shown more interest when Oliver had finally persuaded him to venture out onto the beach and look under the boat. He then turned very pale and spectacularly spewed over the pebbles. Justine and Oliver couldn't help but laugh. They got their mirth under control by the time he got back to them still white as a sheet.

"Did you see those things crawl out of his eyes?" He asked. Oliver and Justine nodded. "Awful. Just awful." He added. "I'm sorry you both had to see that. I really am." He called it in then. This was most definitely murder.

Now, almost another hour later still, they sat in a police car, safely out of the bitter cold wind at the end of Park Row, overlooking the river. They were watching policemen in muddy shoes and boots going over the pebbles and the surrounding area to see if there was any evidence before the tide took it away.

Oliver was interested to watch how methodical the police were. They didn't seem to have any of the equipment the forensics people had on *CSI*. He was a bit disappointed. He wondered who the man was and how he got separated from his dog. He'd recovered from his little episode on the beach and was totally convinced the dog's name was JJ. He didn't remember much, just Justine stroking his head as he came around and her worried look as she told him, "You're very weird."

"I think the dog was with him," Oliver told Justine after a while.

"On the boat? Dog's hate boats."

"Before. Oh, I don't know. But it's connected."

Justine sighed. Oliver provided all too much excitement in her life right now. She should be at home doing homework. Exams were only four weeks away.

A policewoman, Detective Kray, opened the driver's door and climbed in. She turned to Justine as she strapped herself in.

"Other kids go around smashing up windows or stealing cars around here. You people turn up dead bodies. I have a report from the RSPCA that you both reported a dog with it's throat cut – what, just a day ago?"

"It's his dog. The man we found today. He had a dog lead." Oliver said emphatically. Justine squeezed his arm, meaning for him to keep quiet.

Detective Kray smiled. "Yes well, leave the detective work to us, OK? You have both found quite enough for one week."

Oliver smiled and shrugged. "We were only going for a walk on the beach."

Detective Kray nodded and put her head to one side. "You wouldn't be playing detective would you? Not that I'm criticising you, but there's dangers in finding stuff. Lots of people don't like anyone poking their noses into things and they'd just as soon throw you both into the river as anyone else. A man has most likely been murdered here."

Oliver frowned, he was confused. "We were just taking a walk. Shouldn't we have called the police?"

Detective Kray shook her head. "No, you did right." She turned to Justine. "You were right to insist. I have no idea why they didn't respond more quickly and I'll take that up with them. I'm taking you both home. I don't want you telling anyone about this. I don't want anyone knowing it's you two who found it. Just in case this gets ugly. No need for anyone to know. You understand?"

Oliver understood. She was giving him a message: stay out of it. He was disappointed. Obviously something was going on here that they didn't have any business knowing about. It made him want to know more, of course, but he wasn't going to tell her that.

Sam North

"You'd be surprised at just how many bodies do end up in the water every year. Most people think that it's an easy way to get rid of someone."

She started up the Range-Rover and made a three point turn.

"The tide is a funny thing. Things go down the river and they come back. And sometimes we find them. Found a torso ten miles down river last year, no head, or legs or hands, but forensics discovered he'd eaten a curry just before he died and they tracked that curry right down to Lambeth *and* the restaurant that sold it. Got the credit card number of the man who ate it and within ten days we knew who had been murdered and probably why."

"Did you catch the murderer?"

Detective Kray drove off up the street towards Trafalgar Road.

"Well, that's usually the hard part. Take this man you found – that's great. A head's got teeth, at least this one has. The man will have a dentist somewhere and that will definitely identify him, but even if we didn't have teeth to go on, he might have a scar or a mark, we'd get a name that way."

"But it doesn't tell you who killed him, or why."

"No, it doesn't. But when we know *who* he was, we might find out the *why*."

Justine leant back in the seat, catching the detective's eye in the mirror.

"Why was he naked?"

"To slow down identification, Justine. Someone most likely put him in the boat and hoped it would sink in deeper water. It's a common mistake. The tide is our friend. You'd be surprised what washes up everyday."

"It might be the Mafia," Oliver told her.

Detective Kray shook her head. "Not their style. If they want someone to disappear, they disappear. You think you'd make a good detective?"

Oliver thought about this for moment as Detective Kray negotiated her way into the traffic.

"My teacher said that being a policeman, or a teacher, was a bad idea, you never make any money and no one ever says thanks."

Detective Kray snatched a look at Oliver's serious face and knew immediately that he wasn't being sarcastic. "Well, I suppose your teacher is right. It's down here, right? I've heard about your Grandma. She's the one who tells peoples' fortunes isn't she?"

"She gives people advice," Oliver corrected her, remembering what Lena had told him to say if asked.

"Take *my* advice kids, you stay home on a cold day like this and stay out of trouble. There's a lot of mean people out there these days."

Oliver nodded. Yes. A lot of mean people, he knew one in particular.

"Nice neighbourhood your Grandma lives in. I bet half the hot cars in London end up here at night. Your Grandma doesn't sell car spares by any chance does she?"

Oliver didn't get the joke, but detected the mocking tone in her voice. Detective Kray was amused by her own remark, however and continued to smile to herself as she brought her car to a halt outside Grandma's house.

"Come on, I'd better meet your Grandma."

Grandma Otis wasn't very pleased when they were brought back by a policewoman, a detective no less. She was even less charmed to discover that Oliver had found yet another body on the beach, a dead man, less than 200 yards from her house. They were talking in her hallway. Grandma Otis had felt obliged to come down the stairs for this.

"Detective Kray, this boy has only been here three days and he's already done more than I have in ten years. Justine was supposed to keep him out of trouble."

"I..." Justine protested, but caught Grandma Otis's wink just in time.

Oliver thought this was a criticism, but wasn't sure.

"Well they have done all the right things, but I think they should keep it to themselves for the moment. Don't want people to think that they know more than they do, do we?"

Grandma Otis understood, even if Oliver didn't.

"I was thinking Quon could help," Oliver remarked to Grandma Otis. Grandma Otis gave Oliver a very black look and he didn't pursue it.

Detective Kray looked interested, "Quon?"

Grandma Otis just smiled. "A friend. He likes to play amateur sleuth."

Detective Kray shook her head and smiled. "I knew as soon as I saw this old place that Miss Marple might live here. But leave the investigating to us. We'll know who it is soon enough. And," she turned to Oliver, and Justine. "You call me if you ever get into any trouble alright? Here's my card. Don't go looking for trouble, but if it finds you, call me."

Oliver had to go to the bathroom. Perhaps it was the cold wind or something, but he had a pain. It was embarrassing, but he had to run. Justine took the opportunity to make her escape as well.

When they had gone, Detective Kray walked to the front door, pausing a moment, looking back down the passage where Oliver had just quickly disappeared.

"He's been sick, I can see that. Will he get better? He's very thin."

Grandma Otis smiled. "Thank you for taking an interest, but Oliver's stronger than he looks. His father was tough and is quite a survivor, I believe.

He's a good boy. He's curious though and it's going to get him into trouble."

Detective Kray shrugged. "He's bright. Keep him away from some of the kids who hang around the streets, if you can. There's some kids out there that just live for trouble."

Grandma Otis nodded. She knew that well enough, didn't she see mother after mother looking for guidance on how to deal with that very problem?

"But you can't keep them a prisoner in the home."

Detective Kray nodded. "More's the pity. Good day, Mrs Otis."

Grandma Otis stayed in the hallway for several minutes after the policewoman had gone. Three days and Oliver had turned her life upside down. God wanted her to wake up or send her to an early grave. She didn't know which. Dead dogs and naked men washing up on her riverfront. It was getting to be like the violent London of old. A hundred years of civilising forgotten in one generation.

"Lena?" She called out. "Are you up yet? Let's have some tea."

Oliver found himself trapped by his own success now. Grandma Otis had insisted that he had to get cleaned up after his river escapade and then discovered that she'd decided he couldn't leave the house for the rest of the day. Her heart couldn't take it apparently. She asked him at lunch to contemplate what he'd seen and learnt from it. Well, as far as he could see, he'd found a body and that was that. Grandma Otis didn't see it that way, of course. The fact that he'd found the dead man was fate alright, but bad fate. She understood the connection to the dog and was convinced that Oliver was right on that. Especially since he'd come up with a name. Nevertheless, she was keen for him to break this bond between him and the dead man. She didn't know how it had happened, but it had and some might argue that since he had just arrived from the North, there was something to this fate, that he'd been sent to London for a reason. Grandma Otis didn't think so. She didn't like it one bit. She knew things didn't happen by accident, but she didn't want Oliver overwhelmed, didn't want him put in the way of forces he didn't understand.

Oliver was bored. Grandma Otis might be used to contemplating in her room in an afternoon, but he was not. What was more, he couldn't stay indoors. He just couldn't. He had to beg Lena to let him out into the garden and even then had to swear on Flop's life that he wouldn't leave it. She tried to mollify him with a promise to take him to see the Tate Modern up by London Bridge – sometime. "Why they couldn't have built the gallery in our Power Station beats me, they should do something with it, bloody eyesore."

Oliver learned that this was a sore point with the folks in Greenwich. Well, with Lena anyway.

Justine hid in her room practising her French. He'd tried to get her to come outside with him, but she wouldn't even come to her door.

"Non. Je suis occupé." She had shouted down the stairs and that was that. It was the garden with Flop. At least it had stopped raining.

"Hey, you, you help me?" A voice announced.

Oliver looked up and Flop made a break for it to the bushes. Mr Ng was on the roof of his garage fixing a hole. He didn't look so frightening anymore. He was wearing overalls and a funny hat with purple stripes.

"You unhappy?" He asked Oliver.

"I liked your owl," Oliver remembered to say. "It's keeping my room safe."

"Need more than one," Mr Ng declared, but didn't specify how many would do.

"You help me?" Mr Ng asked. "I need tools."

Oliver leapt up. Grandma Otis couldn't complain if he helped a neighbour. Anything had to be better than trying to contemplate in his room.

"What do you want?"

Mr Ng nodded. "Tools on workbench. Pass them up."

Oliver dove in through the bushes and entered Mr Ng's garage. It was quite changed from his last visit. Gone was the fire damage and all the things that he'd been making there. In its place was a huge fibreglass horse astride a trailer. Mr Ng was working on horses now.

"The sealer. Pass seal-gun. That's what I need," Mr Ng called down.

Oliver found what looked to be a seal-gun and took it up the ladder with the sealant. The wind was howling around the ladder, but Oliver enjoyed being up there and getting a look at the breaker's yard beyond. They were crushing another car and it was making a terrible din.

Mr Ng took the sealant from him and Oliver stayed up in the hole through the roof watching him fixing the gaps in his old roof.

"Why did you come to live here?" Oliver asked.

Mr Ng didn't reply straight away as he was trying to get the liquid to come out of the seal gun in a smooth action. He placed a tile on the roof and ran the sealant around it, smoothing the seal with his thumb.

"Why you come here?" he asked Oliver.

"I had to come and live with my Grandmother."

"I came to study." Mr Ng declared earnestly.

"Study?"

"Yes. I was to be doctor, but I make mistake. I get sick. I fall in love. I did not study. I marry. I have to make animals for people to sell. My wife, she dress windows. My animals go into windows. My wife, she gets sad, she wants to leave. She goes. I still make animals."

Oliver realised that he'd just heard Mr Ng's whole life story. It was quite sad. It explained the horse downstairs too.

"I like your animals. Don't you?"

Mr Ng took another tile and filled another gap, sealing it with the same practised expertise. He looked at Oliver.

"I wanted to be doctor. A man should do what he should do. What do you want?"

Oliver was sort of hoping he wasn't going to ask this question but he had an answer ready. "I want to live in the mountains with the trees and animals. I don't want to have to get a job. I just want to live in the forest and listen to the trees, swim in the rivers, explore things."

Mr Ng smiled as he took the last tile and slotted it into place. "You must go live in China. You will find many forests, many animals." He laughed revealing his stained teeth. "Yes, live in China. You replace me. That's good, very good. I like that."

Oliver smiled. He hadn't planned to live in China, but he was glad he had made Mr Ng smile. Now he really did have something to contemplate. Poor Mr Ng. Wanted to be a doctor all his life and ended up making models of animals for window displays. He wondered if he would ever get to visit a mountain, or live in a forest. But at least he was thinking now.

"I have to go now," Oliver told Mr Ng.

"Thank you. You help good."

Oliver smiled and descended the ladder. In the distance a police siren reminded him that the rest of the world was still out there. Somehow, Grandma was right... It did feel safer at her house. Almost like he was already living in the past. He could blink and instead of breakers yards, there might be fields, trees, sailing ships, sailors and many horses. What would it sound like then. No cars, no electricity, how did people know what was going on?

"That's what I want to be," he told himself as he emerged from the bush between Mr Ng's house and Grandma's garden. "I want to be a time traveller." It seemed a perfectly reasonable idea. Someone was bound to invent a way of going back or forward in time in the 21st Century. He wondered if they already had and how old you had to be to apply. Time travelling was probably going to be a good career choice one day. He made a note to make sure that he continued to study history in school in case they asked awkward questions when he applied for the job. In fact, the more he thought about it, you'd have to know so much about history, you'd have to know everything, all the politics, all about money and religion and... Oliver suddenly realised that he needed to know a million things and that was just from one second of contemplation. What had Grandma Otis started? Still, history seemed a very good thing to study.

With that settled he went back inside to make himself some tea.

9. Awakening

The sky was darkening and the wind was getting stronger. Somewhere outside, a church clock struck ten and a car horn sounded for an unnecessarily long time in the next street. Suddenly, a face appeared at Oliver's window. The face was calling to him. He looked again by the light of a car's headlights and immediately took an involuntary sharp intake of breath. Bullet was staring at him with his mean piggy eyes.

"Ha! Open up stupid. Open up."

But Oliver was transfixed. Bullet was nothing more than a severed head with worms crawling over it. Blood seemed to drip from his neck and his eyes bulged.

"No, no." Oliver shouted loudly. "Go away."

There was a crack of lightning, his window swung open. Bullet was laughing crazily, his head suspended in mid-air outside his window. "Let me in arsehole. Let me in."

Oliver scrabbled forward to close the window, aware that it was raining hard now and he was getting wet. Behind him he could hear Flop hissing and spitting. Oliver reached for the window to close it, but Bullet was in his face again, mocking him.

"Think you're so fuckin' smart, don't you? Think you're better than me. Well you are nothin', worm. You're less than nothin'."

"Fuck off!" Oliver yelled at Bullet. "You're not my friend. You're never going to be my friend."

Bullet laughed at him and Oliver lashed out at his head. Only when he touched it, it was his own head he was staring at. Dead, mute, bleeding, a huge swelling on one side.

Oliver drew in his breath again and felt hot tears on his cheeks. He was crying. Not out of fear, but because he knew he was dead. The tumour had come back, it had come back!

He reached for the window again and managed to grasp it, but he wasn't strong enough to shut it against the wind. He looked out again, his head was gone, but now he could see Mr Ng was still on the roof of his garage, waving and pointing at something behind Oliver. Oliver glanced behind him – his owl was glowing. That's what Mr Ng meant: the owl, grab the owl. Oliver lunged for the owl and held on tight...

All was calm. The window had shut all by itself, the rain stopped outside and there was no longer any scary head looking at him through the glass. Flop jumped up beside him and put out a paw to the owl. The owl glowed and Oliver could feel his breathing returning to normal...

Lena appeared. "There you are. Why are sitting out here? It's cold. Come on in. Grandma Otis wants to see you before you go to bed."

Oliver looked about him. He was on the stoop, sat on the old swing chair. Flop was nowhere to be seen and there was no owl, no head. Not even a window. He had been dreaming. But what a nightmare. He could still see the two heads in his mind's eye. What did it mean?

"Are you alright? You didn't eat much of your supper. Oliver? You look very sweaty. You haven't gone and got a fever have you?"

Oliver looked up into Lena's eyes and saw her genuine concern. He smiled. "Had a nightmare, I think. It was scary."

Lena put out a hand to his shoulder and gave him a squeeze. "I have them all the time. God, you are sweaty. You really did have a nightmare. Let me guess. Was there a dead body in it?"

Oliver nodded. Lena smiled knowingly. "Go up and see Grandma Otis. She's in a better mood now. Might as well make the best of it."

As Lena left him Oliver decided to go to the bathroom. He wasn't ready for Grandma yet. He needed to wash and change. The dream clung on and had left him feeling strange and apprehensive.

In the bathroom the hot steam in the basin sort of helped a little and he sponged himself down thoroughly. He hardly dared look in the mirror in case he saw anything strange, but when he cleaned his teeth, nothing frightening occurred, so he began to regain his equilibrium. He could explain Bullet's head appearing in his nightmare, that was because Bullet had tricked him and he was thinking about him a lot. And he could easily explain about the severed head, it was just the man's head from the body they had found on the beach, and the shock of the eel sliding out of its eye. But then seeing his own head suspended outside the window, that was what had unnerved him. Why was he dead? Why the swelling and the blood? Was something bad going to happen to him? Was he going to get sick again?

A few minutes later, he appeared in his pyjamas outside his Grandma's bedroom and she beckoned him in with a friendly smile. Justine was asleep curled up in a chair in the corner and seemed oblivious to them talking.

"Sit on the end of my bed. Mind my toes. Don't know what you did to Justine today but she is exhausted. We were talking and then poof, never seen her fall asleep so soundly."

Oliver did as he was told and moved into the room. Almost immediately Grandma Otis noticed he was troubled by something. "Lena told me that you looked feverish. You're not sick are you?"

Oliver shook his head. "I had a weird dream, that's all."

Grandma Otis pursed her lips. "I'm not surprised. You've been a very busy boy since you got here and everything must be so different to Louth. Not many bodies washing up in your little river there I suspect. Do you miss it?"

"Louth?"

"Yes. It was your home, after all. Where did you go, what did you like to do?"

Oliver thought about that for a moment. Everything he did was always before he got sick. He hadn't really done anything for so long. "I used to go to the canal a lot. I don't think it's a river... But then... There's a place you can ride your bike. A big ditch alongside the water where someone has tied a rope to a huge branch of a tree and you can swing out across the ditch and back to the canal bank. James Hadley has got some horses and he was going to teach me to ride last year, but now I won't be allowed to ride. When my Dad was there, he'd sometimes take me to Cadwell Park to watch the motor-racing. He's got a friend who races his old MG and a Lotus. He never wins, but I like going to the pits and," he grinned, "there's always lots of crashes."

Grandma Otis smiled. She could see Oliver visibly relaxing before her, calming down as he remembered Louth. She knew from her first glance at him that he'd had more than just a dream. She recalled the terrible nightmares she'd had as others' thoughts had first invaded *her* dreams. Was that what was haunting him now? Justine had told her about how he'd collapsed by the river and about his fluttering eyes. Was it beginning for him? This is how it had begun for her. If so, how could she tell him not to be afraid? Would the knowledge of what would happen to him and to others scare him? Would he close his mind to it? He was naturally curious, but when it had happened to her she was so young, it had become part of her life so quickly... Would it be good for him to get involved at all?

Oliver was still talking about Louth.

"When it snowed two years ago, I went tobogganing on Hubbard's Hills. That's just on the edge of town and it's a kind of valley that was formed by ice during the last ice age. Anyway, we were having a great time and getting really wet, when Michael Couth got out of control and crashed into the river and broke his arm. I had to walk him all the way to the hospital on the other side of town in the snow and he kept saying the same thing over and over.

'They're going to cut my arm off, they're going to cut my arm off'. Oliver laughed. "They didn't, but Michael was called Bandit from then on. Y'know, one-armed-Bandit."

Grandma Otis smiled. It was good to hear him tell a story, see his face and eyes come alive. He was so different to his mother in so many ways.

Oliver sighed and looked at his Grandma with a curious expression.

"Do you ever see anything about yourself? Does Quon ever tell you things about yourself? Warn you, or something?"

Grandma Otis nodded. "Just little things. He would never tell me if I was going to have a heart attack, or anything. I'd probably worry myself into my grave just thinking about it. No, he just tells me little things. Perhaps warn me about people, or once, when I was younger, he told me not to go to a dinner they were having at Lady Fenster's. There was a terrible fire and three people died of smoke inhalation. Quon wouldn't have known how they were to die, or why, but he knew there'd be trouble and I listened to him. One should always listen to warnings, no matter how they come to you."

She could see Oliver digesting this. She knew he had another question too.

"You think Quon could help me find out who the man was who died on the beach?"

Grandma Otis shrugged. "Perhaps, but why?"

"Shouldn't we help the police?"

Grandma Otis pulled a face and reached for her inhaler, always kept ready by her bed to help with her breathing. "I tried offering my help once. They didn't respect Quon, or his help. They'd rather not solve a crime than admit they had to use a clairvoyant. It's not like on TV. The police are very sceptical."

"Yes, but was Quon right?" Oliver asked, very interested now.

Grandma Otis sat up in her bed a little higher and pulled some pictures from a pile beside her. She began to sort through them as she spoke.

"Quon is rarely wrong. He told them where to look for a missing child once, but they didn't listen, or didn't believe him. Quon insisted the child was in an abandoned car, standing no more than fifty yards from her home, and she was still alive."

Oliver looked at Grandma Otis with rapt attention. "And was the girl in the car?"

"The police said there was no abandoned car, the newspapers laughed at me and one even printed an article saying that I was exploiting the misery of the young mother who had lost her child and I should be prosecuted. This made me very angry, but Quon was both angry and insistent. He made me send Lena to look for the girl herself."

"She found her? She found her, didn't she?"

"Indeed she did. She was right where Quon said she'd be. Trapped inside a car in someone's yard. The police had been looking for an abandoned car on the street, not an old car dumped in someone's yard."

Oliver's brow furrowed. "They found her alive didn't they? She was still alive?"

"Well, it wasn't as easy as that. Lena found the car, but it was locked and the owner was away. Lena called me in tears and I called the Police Commissioners wife. She comes to see me from time to time, you see. She made the Commissioner himself go and rescue the child. There were some red faces I can tell you, but yes, the child lived. In fact..." Grandma Otis handed Oliver a photocopy of some A-level certificates with a photo attached.

"The child sent me these only last year. She knows Quon saved her life and every year she sends me a card to say thank you. It's been eight years now. She knows how precious life is... Like you."

Oliver was glad the child lived. Happy for Grandma that someone still knew how to say thanks. He took a deep breath. He wanted to ask about his dream, about how he saw himself dead, but couldn't bring himself to ask. Instead he thought again about the dead man on the beach by the river.

"Well, maybe Quon does know who the dead man is and I could tell Detective Kray without telling her who told me? Maybe his family don't know he's dead? Maybe they're thinking he's gone away and..."

Grandma Otis raised her hand and made as if to tell him off, then smiled.

"Curiosity killed the cat, don't you remember? Didn't the policewoman specifically say that you shouldn't get involved?"

"Yes, but if Quon knows, then we could tell his family, at least. We don't need to know why he died. And then there's his dog. It's called JJ."

Grandma Otis frowned. "Quon isn't a detective, y'know. He shouldn't be used for such things either. But, if you want, I will ask him, but I can't guarantee he'll help you, or the dead man. He might not know. Sometimes if someone hasn't passed over or... Well anyway, I'll try. No talking, you listen and be still."

"Shouldn't we wake Justine?"

"She'll wake when she is ready." Grandma Otis told him. "She needs her sleep."

Oliver jumped up off the bed, excited now. Grandma Otis took off her glasses and prepared herself for the session by taking deep breaths and muttering her usual prayer for God's protection.

Oliver watched as Grandma Otis gathered her 'energies'. He sat at the end of the bed once again, trying desperately hard to be quiet and still, the two things he'd never been particularly good at. In the silence of the house he could hear many sounds. Lena's clacking knitting needles downstairs and the clock striking the half hour in the dining room, the rumble of the wind in the fireplace where Grandma Otis kept her dried flowers and the sound of his own heart, thumping hard in his chest, the blood banging in his ears.

Imperceptibly at first, the light began to change in the room and he recognised that the familiar green glow was beginning to shine around Grandma Otis. She was getting to that place where Quon was waiting for her.

Oliver began to gently rock himself from side to side, just like he'd always done when a small child. It was soothing, even if it did make the bed creak a little. As the green light was spreading around Grandma Otis, Oliver fell to thinking about the dead man on the riverside. He could see him now with immense clarity, almost as if he could speak to him. It wasn't at all scary. He could see things now, things that he hadn't noticed when he fell. The shape of the man's nose, the tiny diamond stud situated in one nostril. The dog. JJ was suddenly there, wagging his stumpy tail, jumping up, wanting a stick to be thrown. It was the chocolate Weimaraner he'd found with Justine. Oliver desperately wanted to tell Grandma Otis, but he couldn't say anything. It was like he'd gone – he was at the beach and the dog was looking at him, its head to one side as if he could actually see him now. It came forward and looked right into Oliver's eyes. Something else stirred. The hand, the dead hand, moved!

"Fetch JJ. Fetch." A voice shouted.

A stick was thrown, the dog ran off, Oliver couldn't turn his head, dare not...

The dog ran back, pleased with itself and the man took the stick from him. He was dressed now. He looked quite normal. He was standing on the beach and suddenly he turned, looked directly at Oliver!

Grandma Otis opened her eyes. Quon was with her and ready to speak, but neither one could, for they were both watching Oliver at the end of her bed, his mesmeric rocking from side to side, him thinking, totally oblivious to his surroundings now and there, spreading softly all around him, a diffused indigo light. Oliver was the one making the connection, not her, not Quon.

Here was the confirmation she needed that Oliver had the gift. He was the genuine article and glowed *indigo*, no less, one of the strongest. Of course, he wouldn't be conscious of it yet, but it was there, whether he wanted it or not, to be nurtured, to guide him through his life or... She didn't want to think about the alternative.

Oliver started abruptly and, in doing so, fell backwards, sliding off the bed and landing hard on the carpet below. "Waah," he shouted, as if waking from a nightmare. "Waah."

He lay there, on the carpet, completely motionless, unable to speak coherently, or move. Justine opened her eyes. Instantly she could see with her own eyes what was going on and she knew better than to intervene.

Grandma Otis hauled herself to the end of the bed to look down over the end of it at Oliver. She had expected something like this. Quon was still with her, he watched and waited. Grandma Otis took a deep breath and leaned on the edge of her bed, closing her eyes to let Quon through.

"Stay calm, Oliver." Quon told him. "We're here. You're safe. Tell me, you saw something didn't you?"

Oliver could feel salt on his tongue, it was such a strange sensation. He could see Justine watching and studying him, he in turn studying the room from his horizontal position. He remained mute a few moments more. Something was happening to him, everything felt so strange, almost as if he were floating on a cloud, yet, a part of him knew he was lying on the floor in Grandma's room.

"The dog. JJ." he whispered, at last. "He looked at me."

"The dog?" Quon asked carefully.

"He threw a stick. The dog ran after it."

Grandma Otis had been completely taken over by Quon now.

Justine was transfixed. Two of them, there were two of them like this, in the same room. She felt the hairs on her neck rise and she could just see sparks of colour between them, green, indigo, a flash of yellow... Like electrical pulses.

"He there now?" Quon was asking Oliver.

Oliver tried to remember. He suddenly felt a gripping pain in his heart and lungs. He felt agony, fear, surprise and suddenly, he realised that it wasn't his own pain he was feeling, but the dead man's pain.

"He doesn't know he is dead. I'm sure he doesn't know."

"This is normal, he hasn't had time to pass over yet." Quon told him.

"He's caught. He was surprised. Is he still there, Oliver? Is he still there?"

Oliver closed his eyes again. Yes, the man was still there. The man was looking at him with curiosity and confusion in his face.

"What is your name?" Oliver asked.

The face looked back at him with genuine surprise and somehow, he didn't know how, Oliver instantly knew that the man's reaction was something to do with television. Oliver was supposed to know the man, he was famous, he was on TV.

"He's on TV," Oliver whispered. "He's famous."

Justine felt scared suddenly and her cardigan accidentally dropped to the floor crackling in the electric atmosphere down there, sending sparks of multi-coloured light everywhere.

Quon pushed harder, enjoying the intensity of the moment, Oliver's strength, and the diamond bright curiosity. It was so different to Grandma Otis's, strong, but well defined and controlled powers. Grandma Otis had capacity, but Oliver had raw and uncontrolled energy peaking at such an incandescence Quon could see with immense clarity, almost like his first time with the young Grandma Otis.

"Make him talk." Quon urged Oliver. "Make him talk."

"I can't."

"You can."

"I can't. I..." Oliver closed his eyes once more and found himself not back at the riverside, but in a room, a huge white room. He was inside the man's head and the man was alive! It was a studio, a TV studio. There were chairs, cameras, and people walking to and fro. A girl in tight jeans came up to him and smiled as she fixed her blonde hair up into a pony-tail.

"Good-morning, Mr Michaels. Great show last night. Shall I do your face now?"

The room changed. Oliver was looking at a long table. Many men were playing cards, someone glanced up at him then nodded in recognition.

"Twenty-five grand. Think you can play with the big boys now?"

A beautiful red-headed woman with brilliant white teeth leant over and kissed him on the cheek, the smell of her body scent was almost overwhelming.

"Go home, Mitch. I'll join you later. Go home. I'll tell Robin I've got a headache."

Oliver experienced a weird kind of feeling, one of intense expectation and pleasure. Then, quite abruptly the room changed again and he found himself in an apartment, high up, overlooking London, it was night, the city glowed below him, in the distance lay St Paul's dome. He was entering a room, taking off his jacket, he felt tired and grumpy. The dog was wanting to be fed. It was nervous. There was someone else there it was afraid of.

"Mitch?" A woman's voice called out with a tinge of anger in it.

"Where the hell have you been?" A hand came out of nowhere and slapped him on his face, hard.

Oliver opened his eyes. He blinked, rubbing the side of his face where he had just been slapped. Slowly it became clear. *He had been the man.* He had been inside the dead man as he went about his life.

Justine was holding him in her arms, softly calling his name. She looked very worried.

"Oliver? Can you hear me? Oliver?"

Grandma Otis appeared at the end of the bed once again and looked down at him, handing a glass of something to Justine to give him. Oliver could see all this, but he felt that if Justine wasn't holding him he would float up to the ceiling, he felt so light-headed. Justine lowered the glass to Oliver's lips and he sipped. He swallowed and a red hot glow slipped down his throat, setting fire to his stomach.

"God, yuk , what was that?" Oliver cried out, trying to push away the glass.

He sat up and heard the downstairs clock striking midnight. He looked at Grandma and she smiled at him, putting out a hand to stroke his head.

"Welcome back. You've been gone over an hour."

"Are you feeling OK?" Justine asked him, giving him a quick squeeze.

Oliver struggled free. He didn't need a squeeze now, he was fine. His mouth was still on fire from the alcohol.

"Mitch Michaels." Oliver told her. "His name is Mitch Michaels."

Justine knew the name immediately. "He's got that TV show on Channel 4. He exposes all kinds of people on TV. If it's him that's dead, you would think it would be on the news."

Grandma Otis sighed. She didn't care about TV, just that Oliver had got through his first time in one piece. "You did very well, Oliver. Do you feel alright? Do you feel light-headed? Do you feel as though you could fly?"

Oliver smiled. That was exactly how he felt. "You know? What happened? I was looking at him, and then I was inside him, walking with him. No..." Oliver suddenly realised the truth. *"I was him."*

Oliver looked at Grandma Otis and Justine. He could see they had been worried, but he could also see Grandma was excited, there was something very different about her now.

"How could I be someone else Grandma? How could I be him?"

She smiled and sat down in Justine's chair. "It used to happen to me all the time. Remember the story I told you about the little girl trapped in the car?

I was inside there with her. I was as breathless as she was. I felt her desperation. I knew her panic. I knew she felt she was going to die. I felt as if I would never get out of that car alive and it was every bit as real as the real thing. I can tell you, it took more than a sip of brandy to get me right after that. Welcome to the family, Oliver. You're one of *'The Clan'* alright, and I think you're going to be someone very special."

Justine was still worried about the dead man.

"He doesn't know he's dead then?"

Grandma Otis pursed her lips. She was thinking the very same thing.

"I doubt he'll know anything about it. He'll perhaps never realise what has happened to him, or else be traumatised. His whole psychic karma will be in shock. It will take some time to make a connection. I have been in contact with murder victims before and it's a terrible thing. The whole experience haunts them in the afterlife. Your man will be looking for the door back to consciousness and he's not going to find it."

Oliver frowned. "Isn't there anyway we can help him? I can still see the dog. It's devoted to him, but doesn't get much attention. I don't understand why they had to kill the dog." Oliver closed his eyes and yes, the dog's imploring eyes were still fixed upon him.

Grandma Otis shook her head and began to settle back into her bed.

"No, and don't try. You hear me? There's enough warning signs around you without you trying anything foolish. You might have a gift, but it is going to take years to learn how to use it responsibly. You get off to bed now."

Justine rubbed her neck, spooked by everything, but glad she'd seen it.

"Come on, I'll get you some milk and biscuits. Can you walk OK?"

Oliver stood up and found that he was steady enough. And he was hungry.

He got up and headed for the landing, announcing, "I'm going to the library again tomorrow. I'm going to study all this stuff. What section do you think it's under?"

"You'll find 'stuff' under 'S'," Grandma Otis replied with a smile. "Try looking under occult or perhaps 'P' for 'psychic'. But you have a gift my boy and you won't find it in any book, not there anyway. It's not something you can talk about either. You understand me, Oliver? People will think you're strange enough because of your head, don't give them a chance to mock you."

Oliver turned around, his feet sliding on the polished landing floor. He was about to say something, but one glance at his Grandma and he knew she was right. There were some things you just didn't tell people. Nevertheless, he was puzzled by one thing. "What happened when you first started to glow green like that Grandma? Didn't people say anything?"

Grandma Otis smiled knowingly. "There's only so few who can see the light, Oliver. Justine can see, like her mother could. That's how you know, that's how you know it's real."

Oliver was confused. "You mean, no one else can see it?"

"It's like the whole room is filled with electricity. I can tell something weird is going on – it's like seeing an electric storm," Justine admitted. "Never seen it so bright before. I told you that you were weird." She smiled, still excited.

"Not even your mother could see them," Grandma Otis confirmed. "Now go and have your milk and biscuits and mind you brush your teeth afterwards. You have to look after your teeth."

"I already brushed my teeth." Oliver protested.

"You do them again after. No one in this house earns enough to pay what the dentist charges these days."

Reluctantly Oliver allowed Justine to lead him out of the room, his head still spinning with all the things that had happened to him. They went downstairs together. He certainly had a lot to tell Flop, but whether Flop would believe him or not was another matter.

10. Curiosity and the Cat

Flop woke him the next morning after returning from his breakfast downstairs. He'd already been outside. He jumped up on Oliver's bed and began to lick himself clean. Oliver could hear Flop's tongue combing his fur, when he opened one eye he could see Flop had positioned himself just below his chest.

"Flop?"

Oliver looked up at his beside clock. It was eight. Used to be Flop would wait for him to get up and they'd have breakfast together, but he supposed he was getting fed by Lena or Justine now. He felt guilty he wasn't up, but then again, at least he didn't have to go to school. That dreaded day would come soon enough. "What's going on Flop?"

Oliver was about to stroke his cat when he noticed a piece of paper tucked under his new collar. "What's this?"

Flop let him take it, licked Oliver's hand, then dashed off the bed again. As Oliver unravelled the paper he could hear Flop thundering down the stairs again and seconds later Lena's voice calling up. "Breakfast."

"Coming." He answered, a bit puzzled that everything was so early today. He stretched and climbed out of bed. Then remembered the note again and stopped to read it. It was a computer print-out of some emails.

At first he was completely baffled, then he realised what it was. Old Joe from the library had sent the note. He must have seen Flop and stuffed it under his collar. Oliver was impressed. There were few people that he'd let touch him, let alone put something under his collar. He studied the sheet of paper and realised that he was looking at some replies to his email queries.

> » Sorry we cannot help, no record of this man's
>   name on our lists. Try Red Cross.

> » We regret there is no record of this name on
>   our records.

» No record. Cannot help. Not a listed resident in Zimbabwe.
  Try Botswana.

» Suggest you try UN relief agency for area.

All four of the replies were negative. No one had heard of his father. Oliver's heart sank. How was it possible he could have disappeared so completely? He noticed a scrawl on the back of the paper from Joe... *'Come Friday to the library. We will try other people. I have ideas. Joe.'*

Oliver stood up and pinned the note to the wall. He resolved to meet with Joe. There had to be some way of finding his father. If he was dead, surely someone must have found his body? Someone must know what happened to him. Then, thinking of another body he'd seen just the day before handcuffed to the boat, he shuddered. He shook his head, stating aloud, quite firmly.

"No, he's still alive. I know it. He's still alive. They'll find him and he'll come home."

Oliver went to the bathroom, still feeling down, but resolute. If you wanted something to be, you had to keep your hope alive. He knew that. He'd stayed alive to prove to his father that he could beat the tumour. Well, now he knew he had to keep his hope alive that one day they'd find out what happened to him.

"He's still alive." Oliver repeated as he looked into the bathroom mirror. As if just saying it kept his father safe.

At breakfast Oliver remained quiet and thoughtful as Lena read her *Daily Mail* with meagre attention.

"You alright?" Lena asked eventually.

Oliver nodded as he sipped his tea.

"Who was the old man I saw talking to your cat? He put a note under Flop's collar. The cat just sat there and let him do it."

"That was Old Joe. He's helping me look for my father."

Lena didn't even look up from her paper. She just pulled a face and shook her head. "He's gone, dear. Probably got himself another woman and living the life of Reilly in Durban or someplace."

Oliver looked at Lena in horror. It was almost as if time had stopped. The whole kitchen was frozen around him, the air solid. How could she have said that? How could she say his father would just start up with some other woman and not ever write to him. There was no way his father wouldn't write to him, if he was able.

Lena seemed quite oblivious to the effect her remark had made on Oliver. She yawned and stretched in her chair, clearly bored by her newspaper.

"You're going to the library today?" she asked.

Oliver could hardly bring himself to reply. He merely nodded and Lena seemed to be happy with that.

"Well, don't do anything crazy. Your Grandma is only just getting over the dead man incident. I have never known anyone who could let so many things happen to him in such a short time. Justine told me what you saw. That poor man, not knowing he's dead, still makes me feel queer. It was bad enough they killed his dog."

Oliver finished his toast and looked out of the window to see what sort of day it was. It was cloudy, but there was at least a patch of blue. Right then and there he decided to find out where Mitch Michaels lived and go to his home. He'd find out for sure that he was dead. It was one thing to dream you saw a dead man but quite another to prove it.

He didn't know what he would do exactly, but he'd find out where he lived, go there and try to prove he hadn't imagined the whole thing.

"Looks like a nice day for once." Lena was saying to no one in particular.

Oliver got up from the table and went to put on his jacket. "I'll be going then. I'll be back for tea."

Lena looked up at him and smiled. "You have some money?"

Oliver shook his head. Lena pointed to the window ledge by the door.

"Take the coins from the ledge. Can't have you out there without anything."

Oliver took the few pound coins he found there and pocketed them. Lena stood up and adjusted her hair in the kitchen mirror. "Grandma Otis has got an important visitor this morning, so no shocks, alright?"

Oliver nodded, tying up his shoelaces.

Lena thought of something else. "If you really want to find your father, you should send a photograph to the newspaper in Johannesburg. Be a nice human interest story for them. Of course, he might not thank you for it. Who knows, you might have a little brother by now."

Moments later, stood outside the house, Oliver was angry and upset. Lena had no call to mock his father like that. Now she was even suggesting he'd started a new family. *"A little brother?* Did Lena know something about his father that she wasn't telling him? Could it really be that his father had abandoned him? No matter what, he resolved, there was no way his father would do that without writing to him, to let him know what was happening. He looked back up at Justine's attic window, wishing she was home. He'd left her a note, just as she'd made him promise. He didn't want to get into trouble with her again. Flop ran out from under a bush and brushed against his legs. Oliver crouched down to hug him. "You wouldn't run off and live with someone else without telling me, would you, Flop?"

Flop just fell over onto his side and invited Oliver to tickle his tummy.

"I'm going to find the dead man's house today Flop. I'm going to just see the place where he lives and ask if anyone has seen him. I want to know if my dream was right or not. Do you think I could have seen him in my dreams?"

Flop placed his teeth over one of Oliver's fingers, but didn't bite. Just held his fingers with his teeth, not biting down hard. He didn't let go either.

"Ow, let go."

Flop let go, sensing that Oliver was troubled.

"It's a weird day Flop. No one has seen Dad, I don't know what's going on, I'm having visions – everything's so spooky.

Flop sat up and began to lick Oliver's hand. Oliver rubbed his head in return. "I'll be back later. Take care."

Oliver stood up and looked back at the house. He had an odd feeling, those fuzzy hairs on the back of his neck stood up again, but he couldn't exactly say why. He turned and walked towards the road.

It was at that precise moment that Grandma Otis abruptly opened her eyes.

"Lena? Lena?" She called out as she struggled to sit up. "Oliver?" She called. "Lena? Don't let him go! Don't let him climb. Don't let him go near any tall buildings."

She fell back against her pillow again, exhausted and confused. Lena had rushed up the stairs and appeared at her doorway, slightly out of breath. "What? What is it?"

Grandma Otis opened her eyes again focussing upon Lena.

"Where's Oliver? I had another dream. He mustn't climb today. He is in danger. Great danger."

"He's gone." Lena informed her. "He said something about the library."

Grandma Otis frowned and shook her head. "The library?"

"He got some sort of message about his father. No trace of him yet, not that I'm surprised."

Grandma Otis succeeded in sitting up this time. "He's not going to the library." She declared emphatically. "He's not. Oh, I just know something is going to happen to him today. I just know..."

Lena sat on the bed and took Grandma Otis's hand. "He's gone to the library. I'll go up there after breakfast to make sure, alright?"

Grandma Otis nodded. Yes, best to be sure, but there was that emptiness in her heart.

Three heavy construction trucks drove out of the University of Greenwich grounds, loaded with rubble. Oliver had taken the Maritime Museum route along Romney Road for his walk, which lay opposite the site of the University, situated in the old Naval College buildings. He briefly speculated whether he would be able to attend there when he was older. He was certain he would go to University one day and he wondered when it was you were supposed to decide what it was you should study. Perhaps studying the curious things that his Grandma did would be the thing to do. He wondered if that was the kind of thing you did at University, study people, fantastic things. He remembered he wanted to be a time-traveller, so of course he'd have to study history, but useful to study the future as well of course. No point in being able to travel through time if you didn't know where you've been or where you were going.

At the corner, he saw a newspaper hoarding headline.

'Hurricane in Devon – thousands seek refuge from storms.'

Oliver stood waiting for the traffic to slow so he could cross. Justine had been right. Global warming was coming along fast. He could see someone was reading about it as they waited. He picked out the sub-headlines about the *'Thames may flood during Olympics expert warns.'*

"I always said it was cursed," a woman was saying as she looked at the hoarding. Oliver gathered she was talking to him. "The moment we won the Olympics I knew we could expect trouble and now we're going to drown in it. Should have let Paris have it."

The traffic came to a brief halt and Oliver took the opportunity to hurry across the road. Oliver had another thought. Why were all these cars here? What about the traffic choking Greenwich? How could they have all these historic buildings and all these cars and trucks constantly going by? But that was the extent of his thoughts, because now he found the passage to the covered market. He wanted advice, and possibly a hug. Lena's unkind remarks about his father were still stinging. He knew there would be one person he could talk to.

"Excuse me." Oliver asked a young woman dressed in a mediaeval costume advertising a local store. "Do you know which is Frock Lobster?"

He need not have asked. Before the woman could answer there was a shriek from inside a shop two doors down and Harriet herself came rushing out towards him. She grabbed him, scooped him up and hugged him as if he were her long lost son. "Oliver, my little prince, my baby."

Oliver was acutely embarrassed by this, but happy to be welcomed, nevertheless. Harriet dragged him towards her shop and he saw the pink logo of Frock Lobster on the striped awning. Her shop looked warm and inviting and he quickly found himself plonked onto a stool by the cash counter being introduced to the two girls dressed in black inside. They were smiling at him and laughing at Harriet as she prattled on and made a big fuss.

"This is Clare and Roxanne, they help me here. They're students. Clare's at Greenwich University studying Media and Roxanne is studying to be a fashion designer so that she can steal all my clients when she opens her own place. Girls, this is Oliver, my new boyfriend and we are going to teach him to respect women and treat them right, aren't we girls?"

Clare and Roxanne laughed and Oliver could immediately see that Harriet had been talking about him. But although he was embarrassed, he didn't mind. At least he was welcome here and Harriet looked happy.

"I was going to call Grandma Otis to invite you out next Sunday. I've got some tickets for Alton Towers. Clare and Roxanne are coming. We thought it would be fun."

Oliver nodded, finding himself grinning like mad. Walking into Harriet's life was like wading into a pool of sunshine on a cold day. "Will I be allowed?" Oliver asked. "I don't think I'm supposed to go on some rides."

Harriet suddenly remembered. "Oh shit, that's right. Well I'm sure there are things you can go on. You could wear my old scooter helmet. That would keep you safe."

Oliver laughed, agreeing that that would work. "OK."

"Good that's settled. Now come into the back room and see what I've done. I've had it with fortune tellers. I'm going to take charge of my life and change things. You're going to think I've gone completely mad. Did you want a Coke? Clare get him a Coke, or did you want coffee? We have genuine Starbucks coffee."

"I'm not allowed coffee, my mother said it was bad for you."

Harriet looked at him in amazement. "She did? What did she want you to do? Go straight onto hard drugs?"

Oliver thought about it for a moment, giving the question more serious consideration than was intended. "Well, I like tea, but not with sugar, and I like Coke, but it's got sugar in it and I don't like Diet Coke, because I read somewhere that it's bad for you, too."

Clare laughed now. "You didn't say he was so serious. I'll get him a Coke. You're teeth can survive one Coke."

Harriet wagged her finger. "Your mother must have been so strict, but she wasn't wrong, believe me dentists are no fun, I've screwed enough to know."

Oliver found himself in the back room of the shop where racks of frocks were stored and all around the plain white walls Harriet had pinned up photocopies of palm prints. Each print had names and short biographies attached to them and Oliver understood immediately what they were. Harriet stood beside him and waved her hands in the air saying, "Ta-da!"

Clare came in and shook her head at Harriet and Oliver. "She's mad, y'know."

Oliver grinned. He knew that. That's why he liked her.

"These are Elizabeth Taylor's hands, see they're all puffy. These are Reese Witherspoon's hands, but I don't know, they are so too cute. It's amazing what you can find on the web these days. Who would have thought celebrity palm prints were on there?" She walked to another pair and peered at the name. "Oh yes, these are Scarlett Johannson's, she's got no problem in getting men to fall in love with her, but I'm never going to have such lovely hands anyway, so I don't know why she's on the wall at all. These, here, are Kate Moss's hands, but I'm not sure I'd like her taste in men. Oh, and these are Natalie Portman's, but altogether too sensible I feel. Bet you like her."

Oliver blushed. Actually she was someone he liked. He looked at another print with very serious intent to avoid any further comment. He was enjoying watching Harriet being so excited about these palm prints.

Harriet sighed as she moved over to the far wall. "I didn't like Audrey Tautou's hands at all, but I really like Emily Watson's hands. I'm told men are intrigued by her, but then, so they should be. She was on the cover of *She* last month and looked absolutely gorgeous. Clare got me a copy of Sienna Miller's hands, but will the man stay faithful? I am a specialist in unfaithful men. I wouldn't need to change an inch of my hands to attract them. All these women have really emotional lives... I mean, all I want is one perfect love life."

Oliver heard one of the girls snigger at the front of the shop.

"I heard that!" Harriet said loudly.

Oliver went closer to a pair of hands and compared his own palms to the picture. "What about these?"

"Those are Kate Bosworth's. Do you know how expensive it is to get hold of these palm prints? I had to pay a fortune to get them. Look, she's happy, but maybe too happy. I don't think I could cope with that."

Oliver sighed. Perhaps Harriet was being a bit too picky. "Well, I like these hands. You should choose beautiful hands, maybe someone will fall in love with you anyway?"

Harriet looked at Oliver more carefully, then held up her own hands for him to see. She had big hands, her fingers covered with many gaudy rings. "You see my problem? She's got small hands. Everyone famous seems to have small hands, or long thin elegant hands. I am wearing tennis racquets at the end of my arms."

Oliver smiled and turned to see Clare coming back with a Coke for him.

"Is she on about her hands again? I've told her, it's not the size of the hands, it's the fingers. Men love long slender fingers."

Harriet made a rude noise. "It's all very well for her. She's got hands a man would die for. I've got bloody pancake hands."

"But, it's not the hands." Oliver questioned. "Is it? It's the lines on the hands."

Clare grinned. "He's as bad as you. I've told her, Oliver, it won't work. You can't change your life by changing your love lines. If you could, everyone would do it."

"They just haven't thought of it." Harriet asserted, somewhat defensively.

"Well, what will you do to your hands, exactly?" Oliver asked, as he opened the Coke can, which fizzed loudly and began spurting its contents everywhere. Oliver took a quick gulp from the can and burped loudly, causing Clare to laugh as she left the room.

"This boy's alright." She told Roxanne, who was serving someone in the front.

Harriet leaned back against the wall and sighed, looking at the palm of one of her hands. "Well, first, they erase the lines on my hands, the ones I'm born with, then they cut new lines into my palms."

Oliver pulled a face, it sounded so harsh. "Well, what if you chose this hand, right." He pointed to a pair of hands on the wall. "What if these hands are from someone who is really happy and everyone loves them, then they get cancer, or run over and squashed? Would that mean you'd get cancer or run over too?"

Harriet scowled, looking at the pair of hands Oliver had chosen. She shook her head.

"With those hands I could develop problems they haven't invented yet. Oh God, you're right! I've got to make sure there aren't any fault lines in these hands. They could be happy then – Wham! – two years from now there's a huge truck just waiting for them to cross the road."

Oliver sipped some more of his Coke. "But how will you know that? How can you stop that?"

Harriet smiled. "I'll get these palms read, just like I got mine done. It's a kind of insurance, y'see? I'll get them read, but I won't let them know whose hands they are reading, that way I'll know it's true."

Oliver looked at more hands. "I like these."

Harriet examined them and nodded her approval. "Katherine Hepburn. She used to be a famous actress. People used to talk about her romance with her lover. 'Tracy and Hepburn', big romance, only he dies early. Of course she's heartbroken, but she got to write his memoirs for big money. Hmm, you're on the right track, kid. Lot of happiness, some nice memories, he dies early so you don't have to worry about alzheimers... yeah, everyone loves a tragic ending."

Oliver thought about it some more. "And these?"

"Brigitte Bardot. No thanks. Too tragic. Besides, it's too late for me to be a sex kitten. I'd be better off with Hepburn."

Oliver sighed. "It's scary. Nobody's perfect."

Harriet's face lit up. "Of course, there's always Marilyn Monroe. Men stuck to her like flies, but..." she suddenly remembered, "she killed herself. Of course, she's practically a saint now, but... Nah, I'd be miserable all the time. Perhaps I'll settle for Scarlett. She's happy at least, I hear."

A customer looked in and waved to Harriet. "Hello, you still trying to choose?"

"It's tough, Oliver here thinks I should go for Katherine Hepburn."

"Sweet, but didn't she play a nun once? Listen Harriet, you can have my man, but leave me his credit card, OK?"

Harriet laughed as the customer twirled in the dress she was considering buying. Harriet cocked her head to one side and narrowed her eyes.

"Too flashy, Jen. Try the same dress in the blue. Clare, get the blue in size 12."

The woman shook her head. "I'm a fourteen now. I think my bottom is going to end up somewhere behind my knees if I don't exercise soon."

Harriet put an arm around her and steered her back into the shop. "Clare, put the size twelve on her. It's an incentive to diet, Jen. Don't give in, fight it, defy gravity."

Jen sighed, looking over at Oliver. "My husband says *'why can't I dress like I used to?'* So I put on my mini-skirt and then he says, *'Yuk! Cover it up, you're not seventeen anymore.'* You can't win!"

Harriet sympathised. "Maybe you should try changing your hands, too?"

"Listen Harriet, if you want a man in your life, get a man's love-line. The way things are in London now, all they're interested in is each other."

Harriet smiled. "I could get Pierre's hands. Then I'd get it fifty times a week. Of course, it might seem a little shallow."

Jen whistled. "Fifty times a week! If that doesn't make you happy, Harriet, nothing will."

Harriet and Jen laughed together, but Oliver just stared at his Coke, embarrassed. Harriet noticed this and went over to him, hugging him hard.

"You didn't hear that, Oliver. Don't worry. If I can't keep you on the straight and narrow, no one can. I've pledged to Clare and Roxanne that I'll make at least one boy grow up straight in this city. Do you like Clare by the way? She got such cute blue eyes don't you think? I think she likes you."

Oliver immediately went scarlet and for once he was glad his face was buried into her shoulder.

"Now." Harriet said, pushing him away from her and looking at his face.

"What is happening with you? I've been talking and I don't even know why you're here."

"Can I take a look at your phone book?" Oliver asked her.

Harriet seemed surprised, but accepted it easily enough. "Of course, finish your Coke, read the phone book, do what you want. I'd better go see my customer. She usually spends a lot with me. You like the idea of Alton Towers?"

Oliver nodded. "Very much. Harriet? Have you ever heard of Mitch Michaels?"

Oliver immediately noticed a change of expression and mood in Harriet's face. She looked very annoyed he'd asked about him.

"Who's been talking?"

"No one. Is he on TV? Justine says he's on TV. Does he wear a diamond in his nose?"

Harriet must have got the wrong end of the stick. "Don't tell me he's into little boys now. Did you meet him? What did he say to you? You stay away from him Oliver. He's a total bastard. You hear me? The only thing good about him is his dog, JJ and he only got the dog to attract women."

"Harriet?" Clare was calling.

Harriet went into the front of her shop to deal with her customer. Oliver was slightly shaken. She'd really reacted when he'd mentioned the man's name. He'd seen and felt a surge of anger in her voice. But at least she confirmed that he had a dog called JJ. That was important.

Oliver found the phone book, but didn't find his name in it. In his mind he could still see him, still see his apartment, high up, over-looking the city. He was about to give up when he saw Harriet's pink, quilted address book. He knew he was being bad and nosy, but he took a peek at the 'M's. Mitch Michaels's address was the first one there.

Oliver heard Clare's voice and he quickly closed the book and finished off his Coke.

"You coming to Alton Tower's with us? We'll have fun. You made quite a hit with Harriet. I think she wants to adopt you."

"Really?"

Clare laughed. "It's an expression. Don't panic. She's not as crazy as she looks. So, are you coming to Alton Towers?"

"Yep. I've always wanted to go."

"What do you think to the hands? Crazy, huh?"

Oliver looked at the wall and smiled. "I'd be scared."

Clare smiled at him and stroked his nose with her finger. "Who's to say they've got a better future than you? That's what I keep telling her."

Oliver nodded. The killer truck was probably waiting for him someday, somewhere.

"I have to go. See you."

"You take care Oliver."

Clare turned to wave. "We're taking you to Gap on Sunday too."

Oliver nodded, still embarrassed they were making such a fuss of him and went out to where Harriet was closing the deal. He knew he'd have to face at least one more hug, before getting out of there.

Harriet grabbed him by the door and squeezed his hands. She leaned her face into his left ear.

"Whatever that snake wants, don't go near him, alright? He's trouble, Oliver. Mitch Michaels is poison. I'm surprised no one has killed him yet. I'm surprised I haven't killed him myself." She let him go then, calling out a last "Take care!"

But Oliver left Frock Lobster highly disturbed by Harriet's last words. *"I'm surprised I haven't killed him myself."* What had she meant? How did she know him? She couldn't have known that it was his dog that had washed up on the river beach. Then he remembered. She'd left just before he discovered it. How did she know him?

What was he heading towards? Should he go home now? Did Harriet kill him? No, that wasn't right, she didn't know he was dead. No one did, not even Mitch Michaels knew he was dead. That was the weirdest thing of all.

To say Oliver was confused would be to understate things. He knew that going to find Mitch Michaels' home he was doing wrong, but something was compelling him. He told himself that he'd only look, perhaps ask someone if they had seen him and that's all. Nothing more. Then come home, even if nothing happened. That's what he told himself. He ran across the road heading towards the river. The traffic was as dense as ever, the diesel fumes thick in the air.

Oliver was just disappearing from view when Aura went past on the bus. She waved, but he didn't see her. Something in the way he was walking disturbed her. She'd really taken to the kid when he'd come into the library. He seemed quite different to other kids who came in. She looked at her watch. She had time. If she hurried she could get to him before he disappeared.

The bus stopped at the University and Aura ran out quickly. Oliver had looked as though he was going towards the river and she jogged in that direction, keeping an eye out for his green jacket and baseball cap.

But when she reached the dock where the burned out remains of the Cutty Sark were shrouded from view, she couldn't see him at all. Just a few disconsolate tourists were milling around, but no Oliver. She ran on towards the river, thinking perhaps that he was going to look at the water, but nothing. No boys at all. She was disappointed and had no idea why exactly. He was just a kid, but there was something about him that worried her. If she could draw it, it would be a big arrow pointed at his head that meant trouble coming.

"Oh Oliver, where are you?"

She retraced her steps, looked up and suddenly there he was. Getting into the lift that would take him to the under river walkway. She shouted his name, but a riverboat sounded its horn at the exact same time and he didn't hear. The doors closed and Oliver was gone.

For a second Aura thought she'd follow, but remembered she was due at the library. She sighed and turned away. He was just exploring, like any curious boy would. He'd be fine. She was worrying for no reason. He'd be fine. She walked back the way she came. The sun came out and she immediately felt more relaxed.

11. Bad Timing

The lift was free. That was the good part. Walking along the Greenwich Foot Tunnel under the river all by himself was kind of scary, but he liked the echo his footsteps made and terrorising himself with the idea of the roof suddenly caving in and the river flooding it all. Somehow Oliver had expected to find more people using the tunnel between the Isle of Dogs and Greenwich. Maybe everyone was at work. The white glazed bricks were strange. Like this was the secret way in to an underground hospital. He wished he'd brought some blades. It would have been cool to zap along the smooth underground pathway.

Finally Oliver reached the other end and a lift was waiting. The liftman was listening to some play on the radio about ghosts, but it didn't seem to be very realistic. Even though Oliver did consider it to be a great coincidence.

"On your own then?" The liftman asked him.

Oliver nodded.

"Quiet part of the day this. Builds up later. Let's go."

He closed the gates and the old lift began to ascend. Oliver mused on whether he was doing the right thing now. He should go back. Grandma Otis would be mightily upset if he got into trouble. If he was at home, then he would accept that what he'd seen was just a dream, nothing more, that he wasn't psychic. Not like Grandma Otis at all.

"We're here," the liftman declared. "My, you're in a dreamworld, aren't you? Been stood with the doors open for a full minute."

Embarrassed, Oliver hastily walked out of the lift and into the cool, mid-morning air. God, where was he? He had emerged into some sort of little park called Island Gardens. He could see when he turned around, that the whole of Greenwich was on view from here. Straight across the river there was the University and the Royal Observatory up behind it on the hill. He saw movement, the big red ball dropped down the pole on the Observatory roof. It was midday. He knew about that. He'd read about it. An ancient signal to the naval vessels on the river. They always dropped the red ball when it was midday. The tide was quite high now. He turned and was surprised to see a shaft of sunlight had struck the Dome in the distance and it looked quite spectacular. The Dome was bigger than he thought it would be. He would have liked to have stayed and looked at everything, but he had things to do.

Step one, he had to find the signpost to the Docklands Light Railway. That was easy. So was finding the station. You just had to follow the signs and there it was just across the road. It sort of stood to reason that Mitch Michaels would live in Docklands. He was rich, he was on TV, he would be living where rich people lived. Besides, Oliver had always wanted to visit the Canary Wharf towers. These were the tallest buildings in London, or at least, he thought they were. Perhaps the other tower was... Hhhmm, he would have to check that. He hated not remembering important facts like that.

Oliver was crossing the road going towards the station when he heard his name being called. He turned, sure that someone had made a mistake, for who could possibly know who he was? Bullet! He was there, just below the station, walking towards him. Oliver's heart sank. He'd deliberately not gone to the library so as to avoid him, and yet, of all places, here he was.

"It's my man, Oliver." Bullet came over and put an arm around his shoulders. Oliver wrinkled his nose. Bullet stank of aftershave and upon closer inspection appeared to have a huge red bite on his neck with actual teeth marks.

"Shit, what a bloody crap night I've had. This bloke, he said he was a sound designer, whatever that is, anyway, he says he wants to take me back to take some pictures. Well, I said he could do what he likes, but it'll cost him and right then and there he offered £200 for me to pose. So we go back to his place, just over there, right by the river, and next thing I know he's got this vampire costume on, he's making strange noises and he attacks me. There I am, pinned to the floor, he's got his teeth in my neck and I'm thinking I'm gonna be sucked dry when he begins to choke. I mean, he turned blue, and keeled over. Serves him right, I thought. My blood ain't gonna taste so good with all the shit I take and then I thought I'd better call an ambulance. They came really quick, which just shows if you live at a decent address they're just waiting around the fuckin' corner for someone to get sick. Five bloody minutes, that's all, five. When my cousin Lig got sick three years ago, they took forty-five minutes and he died waiting. So anyway, they cart him off on a stretcher.

"They thought I was his son, so they leave me there and when I go to the bathroom to get some TCP for my neck I discover he's taken these little blue pills that make you totally hyper. You should see his place, full of pictures of him as Dracula, he really thinks he's a vampire. Creepy bloke or what? He said he worked on a *Star Wars* film but I didn't believe him. He's got a wife and kids somewhere, too. Bloody rich people all think they can do what they like.

I took his laptop, nothing else worth stealing. So? What are you doing over here?"

Oliver looked at Bullet with a mixture of fascination and disgust. Oliver felt very uncomfortable when Bullet talked about the stuff he was doing. He hadn't known anyone in Louth like this. At least Bullet had called an ambulance, he wasn't entirely heartless. It was pretty scary to think there were vampires living on the Isle of Dogs though. If there were vampires it meant there really could be zombies too and that was terrifying.

"Look," Bullet declared, realising that Oliver was less than pleased to see him. "If you're still upset about the other night, I'm sorry. I had to go. Know anyone who wants a computer? Got everything on it. Worth about two grand, I reckon. You know how to use a computer? You can have it, if I don't shift it."

"You could use it in a coffee shop. My Dad had one. He used to send me emails until..." Oliver suddenly realised that he hadn't heard from his father in so long it hurt.

Bullet pulled a face. "Like they're gonna let me in Starbucks."

Oliver shook his head. "When my Dad had his stolen he paid someone £300 to get it back. Said that he would have paid more, you know, to get back the work he had stored on it. You could sell it back to the man you stole it from, probably. Anyway, laptops are hard to insure. Dad said he couldn't get any insurance at all when he travelled."

Bullet looked at Oliver with surprise. "Fuck, you're a budding criminal after all. I'm going to have to start listening to you now. I bet he'd pay a ransom for it. Brilliant."

Bullet had followed Oliver to the ticket machine below the station now and Oliver felt kind of awkward. How was he going to get rid of Bullet. Oliver followed the instructions and bought a ticket. Swallowed all his money too. Bullet didn't bother.

"Who are you going to see?"

"I'm going to look for someone. That's all."

"Who? Did you hear something about your father? They were talking about you at the library yesterday. That bitch Aura and the old git Joe."

"No."

Bullet caught his arm. "Then where?"

"I'm..." Oliver tried to think of something that would discourage Bullet.

"I'm doing something for Detective Kray. It's important, OK?"

Bullet laughed. "Important police work, huh." He laughed again as he followed Oliver up the steps to the station above them where a train was waiting.

Bullet was mocking him as they climbed the stairs. "Oliver, the great detective. Where's your fingerprint kit? Did you remember to pack a gun? Lots of nasty people out there."

Oliver stopped half way up and turned to face Bullet. "I'm going to find out about a man who died. We found his body under a boat on the shingles and..."

Bullet looked at Oliver strangely, now more curious than ever. "You found the body? Oh, right. You've been watching too much TV. Where did you find it? Shingles? What shingles?"

Oliver turned and began to walk up to where the train waited. How was he going to ditch Bullet? Why didn't he just go away?"

Oliver reached the platform and turned to say goodbye but Bullet unexpectedly ran up to join him. They got on the train together. Two other passengers were waiting on board the train and eyed them both with contempt and suspicion.

Bullet was about to mock Oliver further about the body he'd allegedly found, when he noticed a newspaper one of the passengers was carrying. The headline ran bold across all the columns:

'Body found handcuffed to dinghy'

Bullet snatched the paper from the female passenger who looked as though she was about to protest, but when she looked at Bullet she immediately thought better of it. Oliver wanted to apologise to her, but knew that that would only make Bullet worse. Bullet was reading the front page, oblivious to any mayhem he might have caused.

"This body? This was you? A member of the public? You found it?"

Oliver looked at the headline, but noticed that there was no photograph of the body itself.

"Wonder why they didn't print a photo? They took lots of photos."

Bullet read some more then folded up the paper again and handed it back to the astonished passenger.

"Thanks, sorry, but my friend here has some urgent business to discuss."

The doors closed then and the train gradually pulled away from the station.

"So what was it like?" Bullet asked Oliver.

"What?"

"The body, stupid."

"Detective Kray said it was murder."

Bullet smiled. "No shit. Body found handcuffed to a boat. Could have been suicide. That way you couldn't swim away if you changed your mind."

"He was looking for his dog."

"Didn't you find a dead dog the other day? You definitely said something about a fucking dog." Bullet stuck his face right up close to Oliver's.

"Tell me exactly why you're on this train and where you're going."

Oliver detected the menace in Bullet's voice. He sighed. He knew he'd have to tell the truth to him. No one on this train would help him. It was his own fault for disobeying Grandma Otis. He should have gone to the library, none of this would have happened.

The train pulled into Mudchute, the first station and Oliver contemplated running for it when the doors opened.

"I'm going to see if the man is there or not, in case I dreamt him wrong. I tried calling him, but he's got an answerphone. Besides, that doesn't prove anything. Then I called the TV station and they said he was at home, sick, so if he really is home, then I'm wrong and everything is wrong."

Bullet hadn't exactly followed this. He looked confused. "I don't know what the fuck you're talking about. The newspaper said they didn't know who it was. You telling me you do?"

Oliver wished the train would crash, or something, or at least move. "Kind of." Was his weak reply.

Bullet was enjoying this now, watching Oliver squirm. "And his head talked to you?"

Oliver gave Bullet a look to show that he understood that Bullet was mocking him. "Might have."

The train started off again and Bullet nearly lost his footing. "Might have? You're even weirder than I thought. This is beginning to sound like a two man mission. It's way too dangerous for one bald-headed geek."

Oliver had known he was going to say that, but he had to at least try to shake him off. "It's OK I can go alone. It's going to be stupid anyway."

Bullet nodded. "Oh it sounds stupid alright, but I'm coming. We're talking about the living dead here. Do we get to put a stake through his heart?" Bullet laughed, pleased with his own joke.

Oliver sought desperately to put Bullet off.

"It's at Heritage Wharf. It's a long way to Wapping."

"Heritage Wharf? You're kidding, right. Rich people live there."

The train stopped at Crossharbour Station, then moved off again. No one got on or off.

"I'm just making sure he's there, that's all." Oliver mumbled. "I just want to see if he's really dead, or not."

"Well, what's his name? You're the detective. Do you know his name? You said you called his number."

Two more stops later, the train was finally pulling into Canary Wharf station and Oliver had a strong urge to step out and check out the station. He loved big buildings and the idea of a station running under such a huge building was impressive. He couldn't move, of course. Not with Bullet watching his every move. Maybe on the way back.

Some more people got on. Businessmen with overstuffed briefcases and gossiping secretaries, talking loudly about something that had happened at work.

Bullet still wanted to needle him. "Tell me about the body again Oliver. What did it say? *'Ello, Ollie'*?"

Oliver refused to be riled. He just wished Bullet would go away. The train doors closed again and the train moved off towards the city.

Lena was looking pensive. She'd been all over the library and seen no sign of Oliver, or the old man who brought him the note. Aura was leaving.

"Can I help you? I saw you wandering around."

Lena looked into the face of a beautiful young woman and had an immediate flash of recognition. If Grandma Otis had been there, she would have known what it meant, but all it was was a flash, yet Lena immediately knew that she was looking at someone quite special.

"You know you look like Sara Simmons when she was young. I saw her on the stage, wonderful actress. I often wonder what happened to her."

Aura smiled. "That was my Aunt. I've seen her in a couple of films. She was beautiful. She's got arthritis now, sadly. Can't move."

Lena felt a pang of remorse. "No, really? But she's my age. I was her understudy in *The Rivals* at the National."

"You should look her up. She's quite lonely y'know. She lives in Blackheath."

"Still living by the railway station?"

Aura smiled. "She always says that she never had to walk when she came back from the theatre. She loves that cottage, she won't leave."

"I'll definitely go."

Aura smiled. "But who are you looking for?"

Lena remembered. "A young boy. Wears a hat all the time. Oliver, he's..."

Aura smiled. "I know who you are. Lena, you look after his Grandma. He told me all about you all. Is she OK? She's not ill is she?"

Lena was so surprised to discover she was speaking to someone who knew who she was that she didn't know what to say next.

"He hasn't been here today. In fact, I saw him on my way here. He was going down the lift to the foot tunnel to the Isle of Dogs."

"He said he was coming to the library." Lena remarked, annoyed. "He promised."

"I know he's due to meet Old Joe here tomorrow. Joe's been helping him try to locate his father. Do you think he's alright? Oliver, I mean. Are you worried about him? He does get around. I saw him on Shooters Hill the other night and..."

"Shooters Hill?" Lena asked, astonished. "We wondered where he'd got to. He seems to roam."

"I should have stopped him." Aura declared.

Lena sighed. "His Grandmother is worried about him. He's a bit absent-minded and he's gone through a lot lately."

Aura smiled. "He'll be OK. He's so cute."

"He's too trusting. He's not used to city ways here. He could get into trouble."

Aura conceded that. "Still, he's got to learn. If he comes in I'll leave a message for him to say that you're worried. I have to go to dance class now."

Lena felt she hadn't said it right. She tried again, lowering her voice a little.

"What I mean is, there is a specific warning for him to not go climbing. Definitely no heights."

Aura looked at Lena and saw that she was very concerned. She suddenly had a worry and she went over to an older woman sat by 'book returns'.

"Have you seen Bullet today?"

The woman shook her head. "Not today. He was in yesterday looking for that little boy, the one who wears the hat."

Aura felt a momentary giddy sensation. Bullet. She hadn't liked the way he'd looked at Oliver. But what to do? Who knew where Bullet actually lived – if anywhere. She decided against saying anything to Lena.

"If the little boy comes in, tell him he has to go home. It's important. OK? Tell him his Grandma called."

The woman nodded and Lena got the impression that she would remember.

Aura walked Lena out.

"Perhaps he just went to see what Greenwich looks like from the other side. I know I did that once. The foot tunnel is kind of fun too. You should go that way to look for him."

"I will. But what if he went further? How should I find him then?"

"He'll find his way home. We all like Oliver. Funny, isn't it? We get hundreds of kids in here and he walks in and you immediately notice. Something quite unusual about him."

Lena sighed. "He's shaken our lives up, I can tell you, never mind his cat."

"Oh, his cat. I heard about his cat too."

Lena and Aura laughed together.

Nevertheless, five minutes later when Aura was on her way to dance class she had a returning sense of guilt. She should be out there looking for Oliver. Maybe he was in trouble, and if he was, she somehow knew it would be Bullet behind it.

12. Giddy Heights

Bullet was laughing as he climbed over a wall. A jagged warning sign clearly stated *'Danger of death'*. "See! It's not electrified. They just put the sign up to put people off."

Oliver clambered up the wall and slung his legs over, dropping to the ground beside Bullet. They were standing beside the river again now, on the bend facing south and its forest of buildings beyond. Heritage Wharf lay before them and they now stood in its grounds. The lawns and trees in huge ceramic pots were all new and you could tell from the metal grills in the gravel path that the greenery was built over an underground car park. At least it was better than nothing and it gave good cover to would-be spies and burglars.

"It's bigger than I thought. Must be a lot of people living here."

Bullet was scouting the surroundings. There were warehouses across the river from them, newly converted to flats. It was possible keen-eyed people could see something, but he doubted it. There were a few boats on the river, but they wouldn't be taking much notice of him and the kid. Bullet lit up a cigarette and sat on a bench overlooking the river. The tide was high and a wind was getting up. The sky promised rain.

"Be nice here, when the trees grow a bit taller. Hide all that shit on the other side." Bullet remarked.

Oliver didn't really think trees had any business growing in pots, though he actually liked the view.

"Why did we have to come this way? We could have gone straight to the front door."

Bullet sighed. "'Cause the front entrance won't help you. It'll be full of doormen and security people who'll take one look at us and call the cops. They'll never tell you if that man is there or not. Believe me, this is the best way." He leaned forward looking at how the building overhung the river. "If we'd come by boat we could have climbed up the balconies. That's stupid that is. A real security risk. Anyone could climb into that building if they wanted to."

Oliver knew he was going to get into real trouble now. Bullet would want to do more than just trespassing.

Bullet was looking at him, pointing his cigarette at him for emphasis.

"So you found the body, right? Oh yeah, and the dog, and right away you know it's this guy on the TV. He told you he's got this show on TV."

Oliver sighed. "I just had a dream, that's all. I just heard someone call out his name... Then huge worms crawled out his eyes and..."

Bullet abruptly stood up, flicking his cigarette away. "Shut up about worms, alright? I hate bloody worms, right? Why do worms have to be in heads? People always bloody go on about worms crawling about inside of people's heads. I don't want to know about bloody worms."

Oliver looked at Bullet with some surprise. This was the first time he'd detected any vulnerability. Just the word 'worms' seemed to affect him. Worms were a funny thing to get worked up about, but he guessed it was like himself and spiders.

Bullet suddenly began to cough and he spat. A huge wodge of blood splashed onto the gravel and Oliver looked at it with horror.

Bullet looked at it, then laughed. "Bits of my lung, nice eh? I should see a doctor. Been coughing up blood for days now. I should go to a hospital, least it's warm."

"Just don't eat the food. It can really make you sick, believe me."

Bullet coughed again, then tossed away the cigarette pack. "Bloody things kill you." He spat again, but it wasn't as bloody as the first and he seemed encouraged by that.

"What's his name then?"

"Who?"

"The dead bloke."

"Mitch Michaels."

"I've heard of him. Never seen his show. Is he a singer or something?"

"Does a kind of news show. Exposes people doing bad things."

Bullet looked at Oliver, then laughed. "You said that just like a toff. I bet you turn out to be one of them. Go to University, get to make the bloody rules."

Oliver ignored him.

"So you think the body that washed up was this Mitch? Sure it wasn't a woman? How could you tell? What's a body look like when it's been in the water for hours? Gross I expect."

"It stank."

"Yeah. Bet it did. And then what, it stood up and talked to you?"

Oliver didn't answer. He was wondering how they'd get into the building if they didn't go through the front door. Bullet got up off the bench and began to walk towards the tower.

"Come on then. You know, if I was rich I wouldn't live here. I'd live in Hawaii, or Australia. Live on a remote beach and watch the waves all day. Maybe catch some fish. I've seen 'em do that, catch fish, standing in the waves with a long rod. I like the sound of the sea. This bloody river doesn't make any noise, it's boring. What would you do if you were rich?"

Oliver followed behind him, still anxious about being seen by someone.

"I'd fly to Africa and look for my Dad."

Bullet swore. "Shit, I wouldn't waste a fuckin' penny on mine. I hope he's dead. I hope he's dead twice over."

Bullet put out a hand to halt Oliver. A security car was driving out of the building from the underground car park. An electronic gate rose and fell surprisingly quickly. Bullet pulled Oliver behind a bush and they waited until the BMW had gone by. They didn't notice Oliver and Bullet squatting down close to the road. Anyone looking down from the windows of the apartments above could have seen them, but perhaps no one was. Looking for trouble was security's job.

"Come on, I can see a way in." Bullet whispered, and then he was up and running for the bushes at the base of the tower. Heart in mouth, Oliver followed. He'd been counting the floors. Twenty of them. Oliver joined Bullet as he pressed himself into some evergreens. They were situated below the balcony of a ground floor apartment.

"We wait here." Bullet announced.

"Why? Why don't we go in by the underground car park?"

"Security cameras, can't you see 'em? This place is a fuckin' fortress. I bet this guy is really loaded."

"I didn't come here to steal anything," Oliver hissed. "I just wanted to know if he was really dead."

"You want to find out? You have to catch him by surprise. Of course, if he is dead, he might surprise us." Bullet chuckled at that, but Oliver wasn't in the mood for jokes. "Now shut up, wait. Can you hear the music? What is that racket? There's people up there. She's laying the table for lunch, the balcony door is open. We wait, OK? Wait and listen."

Oliver waited. A rose thorn had caught on his jacket and he struggled to free himself. He could hear some piano music and a voice coming from the apartment above him struggling to be heard. "...I said turn the music down, dear. Your lunch is on the table."

Bullet grinned. Pointing up. Another voice answered her after a few seconds.

"Just a second, dear, I have to wash my hands."

Bullet nodded, tapped Oliver on his arm and signalled that this was it.

"Now, follow me, say nothing and don't lose your nerve. Keep your head low, don't let them see your face."

Bullet jumped up and quickly checked to make sure it was all clear. No one was in the dining room. He scrambled up over the balcony with Oliver nervously following. Oliver was scared now. He knew that this was dumb, but equally he didn't have the nerve to quit on Bullet and run off.

Bullet was being very professional. Quick and silent. He signalled to Oliver to keep absolutely quiet. Fortunately the radio was so loud that it would mask any sound they made, but equally, Oliver was anxious that they couldn't hear the apartment owners either.

Bullet got the patio door to slide open further, and even though it made a grinding sound, he wasn't worried with the music playing. He finally had the door open for both of them to slide through...

A moment later an older man dressed in a sports jacket and immaculately pressed trousers entered the dining room. This was Harry Rose and he stopped as he looked at the dining table. He frowned and looked over towards the kitchen door.

"I thought you said lunch was ready, dear?"

His wife Estelle was abrupt with her reply from the kitchen.

"It's on the table, Harold. Just as you like it. French loaf, paté, potato salad."

Harry did a double take. He could see the table, he could see the plates, but he could not see any food. "Estelle, have you been drinking again? There is no food on the table."

Estelle came storming out of her kitchen, an intensely irritated expression upon her face. "Is this one of your silly jokes, Harry?" She looked at the table in disbelief. "What did you do with your lunch?"

Harry faced Estelle. Estelle faced Harry. Lunch was the issue here, but there were echoes of more fundamental and difficult issues present.

Harry tried to be conciliatory. "Perhaps you'd like us to eat at the club dear?"

The elevator resonated with the sound of laughter. Oliver and Bullet were riding up to the sixth floor and stuffing their faces with French loaf sandwiches, filled with pate and potato salad. Oliver could barely eat he was laughing so much.

"Do you think they'll call the police?"

Bullet laughed and pulled a face as he pretended his sandwich was a phone. "Hello, 999, police? Someone stole our lunch. We paid two million pounds to live here and someone stole our lunch." Bullet laughed again. "Call the cops? Listen, we need lunch more than they do." Then he was suddenly more serious. "You sure it was the sixth floor?"

"Yes. 602."

"I bet there's cameras everywhere."

"What will we do if we set off an alarm?" Oliver asked, his heart racing now.

"We probably will, but they always wait to see if it's a false alarm first. Believe me." Bullet flipped his hood up to cover his head and face. "Pull your hat down. Let the peak cover your face. Alright?"

Oliver lowered his hat and took another bite of his sandwich. They were approaching the sixth floor. The elevator stopped and the door opened. Oliver poked his head out into the corridor to see if it was clear. He looked down and Bullet was on his back on the floor looking out from the bottom of the elevator, checking to see where the cameras were. "One camera right, above the fire escape door, one pointing down the other corridor."

"What do we do?"

"Do what we came to do. Go up to 602 and knock."

"Now?"

"Yes, now, go."

Oliver left the sanctuary of the elevator and walked along the plush green carpeted corridor until he reached the door marked 602. His hands were sweating. He'd never felt so nervous in his whole life, not even when they were going to operate on him. He looked at the white painted door and was impressed to see the name *'M. Michaels'* was actually printed in gold leaf just above the bell. He pressed the bell, it seemed the right thing to do.

"Any answer?" Bullet asked from the safety of the elevator.

"Not yet."

The elevator doors began to close and Bullet rolled out, walking as naturally as he could towards Oliver. Oliver turned to say something to him, but immediately stopped, for Bullet had a Swiss army knife in his hands and a bunch of keys.

"Move over. You sure there's no sound inside? No one moving around?"

Oliver shook his head. "It's quiet. What are you going to do?"

Bullet smiled at him as he tried a key in the door. "All that money he must have paid to live here and they fit a lock as cheap as this. If I was his insurance company I'd refuse to pay out."

The lock clicked and in two seconds Bullet was inside, turning only to pull Oliver in after him. "Come in stupid. You want to pose for the camera all day long?"

It was dark and quiet. All Oliver could hear was the sound of his heart thumping away. He was still in shock about the keys Bullet carried with him. Almost as if he expected to break into homes.

"You've done this before?"

Bullet grinned as he closed the door behind them, sliding a little on the highly polished ash wood floor. "Well, sometimes it's too cold to sleep outside. Vince, he was a neighbour of my mum's, he's doing time now, but he always told me that the reason amateurs get caught is because they break things. If you've got keys, people don't question you if you look as if you live there."

Oliver was about to say something sarcastic about Bullet's appearance, but thought better of it. Bullet switched some lights on. The whole ceiling lit up with powerful little spotlights recessed into the plasterwork. It was as if they had been transported to an art gallery. The walls in the vast semi-circled lobby were lined with framed photos of Mitch Michaels with his arms around celebrities, or playing golf with them. All of them were the same, Mitch Michaels smiling, the person he was with looking awkward or grinning inanely, like you do when posing for a picture you didn't really want.

"Well, kid, here you are. Where's your TV star, eh? Where's your ghost?"

A light was blinking in the security office. The security man was on the phone, bored with his back to the display board. He was struggling to be polite to one of the apartment owners.

"I'm sorry, Mrs Rose, but I'm not authorised to call out the police about a missing sandwich. No... I'm sorry. Mrs Rose, there's a security patrol outside now and they haven't reported anyone in the grounds. The alarms would have gone off. Has anything valuable gone missing? No jewellry? Just your sandwich? Are you sure you actually made a sandwich, Mrs Rose?"

The security man was smirking now. A stolen sandwich, it would have to go down in the daily log sheet. It would be classed as a major incident. An apology would have to be made to the Roses. They were paying enough for security. He stole a glance at the video screens and his eye caught sight of the silent alarm going off in 602. Now he really had something to do.

"I'm sorry, Mrs Rose, we *do* have an intruder. Keep your windows secure. I'm calling Major Pierce now."

His insolent smile had vanished. This was a real alarm. He picked up another phone. "Intruder alert. 602? Michaels. Unauthorised entry."

Bullet had already helped himself to the scotch, drinking it neat from the bottle as he ransacked drawers and cupboards. He didn't care what Oliver was in there for, he'd just known the kid would lead him to something where there would be stuff worth nicking. He was enjoying this.

Oliver was looking at the view. Although it was day, it was the same view as his 'dream'. An apartment right on the river, with a balcony hanging over the water. There was a huge portrait of Mitch Michaels with a naked woman wrapped around him over the gas fireplace. Oliver could see that it had been done in the style of a James Bond poster. The woman, he realised with surprise, was an actress he'd seen on *EastEnders*.

Oliver could see himself reflected in many mirrors and everywhere there were bright colours and weird objects, some of them quite phallic. There was no sign of Mitch Michaels. Oliver closed his eyes. He could remember his dream, entering a room, taking off his jacket, the woman approaching him, the hard slap. He recalled a more detailed moment. Just before the slap, the woman approached from behind a mirror door. Oliver went over to the wall of mirrors and began to try to open them. He could hear Bullet crashing around in the next room, when suddenly he let out a shout.

"Bing-fuckin'-go!"

Oliver went to the open doorway to the living room and was shocked to see the mess Bullet had already made. A beautiful Chinese lacquered bureau lay on its side and Bullet was holding up cash and many plastic self-sealing bags containing something that looked like pills.

"This is big time, Kid. Fuckin' thousands of pounds here. See these? This bloke is a major dealer. Can you fuckin' believe it? He's got a hundred grand's worth of ecstasy here, at least. Who the fuck was this guy?"

"What are you doing?" Oliver complained. "We have to go. Someone will come."

"We got in, didn't we? We'll get out. Got to get me a bag. Find a bag. I'm not leaving all this behind."

"Get it yourself. I'm not a thief"

Bullet got up, grabbed a roll of money from the stash and went over to Oliver. He yanked him close and stuffed the roll of cash down Oliver's shirt.

"Now you are. If you don't take it out, I'll fuckin' throw you into the river. Now get me a bag. We're taking this stuff."

Oliver broke free and Bullet angrily returned to his stash. He took another swig of the scotch and began to stuff some of the cash rolls down his own shirt.

"Stupid fuckin' kid."

Oliver didn't look for a bag. He went back to the mirror wall. He wanted to leave, but he just wanted to see that room first, make sure absolutely that Mitch Michaels wasn't there, or asleep, or... He found the mirror door and pushed it open.

He was in the bedroom. It was a plain room. Huge with a large, unmade bed centre stage. A dog basket and some toys for the dog scattered on the floor. The walls were plain, save for a strange object on the wall that looked very much like a whip, only it had many strands coming from the stem and looked like you could hit numerous parts of a person with it all at once.

All along the twenty foot window ledge there stood rows of old fashioned brightly coloured Japanese tin space toys. Oliver recognised one as Robbie the Robot. He was sure, too, that he'd read that these toys were immensely collectable.

There was, however, no sign of the owner. Oliver walked to a free standing antique plain wooden wardrobe and opened it. Suits. Many suits. Nothing like what Bullet had found. Oliver turned and as he did so snagged a cord. The bedside phone fell to the floor and somehow it triggered the answerphone. Oliver ignored it as he walked back to the door. Only the door had gone. He was faced by a wall of mirrors again and he didn't know which was the exit.

He opened the nearest mirror door and stepped into a small dark room. The door swung closed behind him with a click and his eyes couldn't adjust quickly enough, and he stumbled, bringing something heavy down with him. When he stood up again, he banged his head, which hurt like hell. Trying for the door again his hands found a hanging cord and he pulled on it. A blue light came on and Oliver just stood there and gawped. He was surrounded by pictures of naked women... All of them photographed on Mitch Michaels' bed.

Somewhere in that bedroom there was a secret camera in the ceiling. It was disgusting, but guiltily fascinating. Oliver found himself staring in wonder. He understood now what the whip thing was for that hung on the bedroom wall. What he couldn't comprehend was why people would want to hurt each other like that. What was going on?

The answerphone was playing back the messages now and Oliver dimly became aware of what they were saying on the other side of the door.

> ...Michaels, you can't hide forever. Call me. We have a deal to make, remember?

Oliver certainly registered that one, but had no idea what it meant.

156

📟 *Hey Mitch, the Selma interview. Did you realise we have to shoot it in Mexico? Get back to me, soon.*

Oliver was wondering if Mitch Michaels had heard any of the messages. How long had he been dead exactly?

📟 *Mitch, this is your mother. Remember me? What's this I hear about you with this Paula woman. Didn't I tell you about Catholic girls. Leave her alone, she'll kill you with lawyers and priests.*

Oliver was looking at some other photographs now. Something about one of the women on the bed with Mitch. He couldn't see her face properly. He looked at another and was astonished to discover that he was looking at Harriet! Harriet naked with Mitch. Suddenly he understood her angry reaction when he'd mentioned his name to her. Oliver tore the photo up and threw it on the ground.

Bullet arrived at the door, his eyes lit up when he saw the photographs plastered all over the walls. He looked drunk, or high on something. His eyes were mere slits in his head as he peered through them. He whistled.

"I thought you were keeping quiet. Jesus, will you look at this. He must have had hundreds of women."

Another message came through on the answerphone.

📟 *Mitch? I want those tapes, you bastard. Tomorrow, or else your dog goes fishing. You do miss your dog don't you?*

(A dog barked in the background and then howled when hit)

Oliver looked up at Bullet. That was the message. That was what had happened to Mitch Michaels. They both knew it. That's where he'd ended up. With the fishes.

"Bastard was into everything." Bullet started counting off points with his fingers, "One... He takes sneaky photos of him fucking these women. Two... He's got enough 'E' here to supply a rave. And... Three... He's got some kinda blackmail racket going on." Bullet whistles low, impressed "Wow... this guy, he's a player."

Bullet picked up a photo, pulled a face and threw it down. "He's got a belly on him too. What the fuck did the chicks see in him? Money I bet.

They go for money every time."

"We have to go." Oliver warned Bullet.

"No, I want to see where he put the camera." Bullet said, staggering out into the bedroom and collapsing on the bed. He bounced back up again pretty quick, rubbing his head and pulling the pillow back. There was a gun lying there. Black and cold. Oliver's heart sank. Giving Bullet a gun when he was in this state was asking for trouble.

"Now what have we here?" Bullet picked it up and took aim at Oliver.

"Better hope it ain't loaded, kid. Guns go off just like that, all the time."

"Put it down, Bullet. You don't need it. We're in enough trouble."

"Wonder if it's loaded?" Bullet asked, placing it on his lap and looking for a way to open it up. "Hey, it's a Baretta, 9mm. Real hard case, this Mitch guy. I'm beginning to like him. Seen his ghost yet?" He looked at the gun again with real pleasure. "Shit, I always wanted one of these. You know how much these are worth on the street?"

Oliver was looking for the door Bullet had come in by and found it at last. He turned to say something to Bullet and found he was pointing the gun at him again.

"I could shoot you and no one would ever know. Bet you didn't tell anyone you were coming here, did you? Bet no one knows the name of this dead guy, 'cept you? Nothing to connect him to you or you to this place."

"Bullet, we have to go. Put the gun back." Oliver was very nervous now.

"Wonder why he left without taking the gun? I would have taken the gun if I'd heard that message about the dog. What do you think about your dead bloke now, Oliver? All the cash, the pills, the photos? He was so rich he could keep thousands of pounds in a drawer. He was so sure no one could get to him. Fuck, I bet this bed cost him ten grand."

"Bullet, we have to go now."

Both of them heard it then. Someone was trying keys in the lock to the front door. They could hear the distinctive buzz of someone talking on a two way radio.

Bullet was instantly angry. He was up off the bed and running to the bedroom door behind Oliver in an instant.

"Shit, security. Come on, we have to keep them out."

"What are you going to do?" Oliver asked, his heart thumping loudly.

Outside the apartment four security men were puzzling over the keys. "It says 602, but it's not budging. Someone's got in, broken the lock. I hate bloody locks."

The men looked at each other. The senior man, the Major, sighed. "Well someone is inside, and if they don't open it, we'll have to force it. Knock. Did you knock yet?"

The security man knocked. "Mr Michaels? Is that you? Mr Michaels? Can you hear me? This is building security."

There was no answer. They hadn't expected one.

"I bet it's another false alarm." The Major asserted. "Did you fix the cameras on this floor like I asked you to?"

"They can't fix them till Monday. Parts come from Germany."

"Don't forget the stolen sandwich." The other guard remarked.

The Major looked at the younger security man with pity. "You forget it. We're going to have to force the door. We have to respond to an alarm, it's in the residents' charter."

Inside Bullet had been busy. He'd got the sofa positioned across the entrance lobby directly in line with the front door. He hid himself behind it with the gun aimed and ready should anyone want to come in. He turned to look at Oliver who was standing there looking at him with his pale, vexed face.

"Get out, alright? Get out onto the balcony. You can drop to the floor below. Do it, Oliver. Do it now. No need to get caught."

Oliver did as he was told. He didn't like it, but he desperately didn't want to be caught.

He rolled open the balcony sliding door and stepped out onto the balcony. He was immediately hit by a gust of wind and he saw that the weather had changed completely. It was cold and windy. He stood looking over the side for the balcony below, but he couldn't see it. All he could see was the river, at full tide and on the turn. He felt dizzy. He looked back and Bullet was still behind the sofa, busy stuffing the tubes of ecstasy he'd found into his pockets, keeping one eye on the door. Bullet looked back at Oliver for a moment.

"Don't piss around. Get your fuckin' legs over and drop down. Now!"

Oliver did as he was told, although he was scared and he still couldn't see the balcony below. He swung his legs over and began to lower himself down, hoping he could swing a bit, get some motion so he could drop clean to the ledge below. He closed his eyes, his arms felt heavy and the wind was tugging at his thin body. He daren't look down.

Bullet was aiming at the door again, trying to concentrate as his eyes were going in and out of focus all the time. The pills or the booze, he didn't know- or care which, only that his 'buzz' was being interfered with and he resented that. "They're going to get it," he kept saying to himself.

Oliver thought his foot was connecting to something below him. He'd managed to get his hands down to the last rung of the railings... he called out to Bullet.

"I can't reach."

Bullet took another swig of the scotch, but the bottle slipped out of his hands and in anger he picked it up again and threw it against the front door.

There was an immediate response. The security men outside put the boot in and kicked the door open. Bullet fired twice, missing both times, but scaring himself and the security men so much they immediately pulled back. Glass flew everywhere as some pictures fell to the floor.

"Bastards," Bullet shouted, looking back to where Oliver should have been dangling.

But Oliver had gone.

Bullet knew it was time to go himself. He could hear the security men calling up reserves and just to keep them out he emptied a couple more shots into the hallway. Someone shouted in pain out there. Satisfied, he stashed the gun in his jeans and ran back to the balcony. He legged it over and with a clean swift motion, lowered himself down to the balcony below.

Oliver wasn't there.

"Shit!" Bullet looked over the balcony to the river below, but Oliver wasn't in the water. He'd just vanished. It was just typical, you try to help a kid and he just disappears.

No time to think. He had to get moving. The balcony door was locked, but a swift kick cracked it and another got the flimsy lock broken. He was in and on his way out in under a minute. No one was going to catch Bullet. Of that he was sure.

He remembered flying. He remembered missing a concrete ledge by inches. He remembered hitting the water and being swallowed up. Now it was cold. That's what it was, cold. He wasn't aware of anything else, just the cold and the necessity of breathing. He knew he should be moving, but where was he? How to move? He couldn't feel anything. He was just cold.

He felt something by his head, something hard. He tried to reach for it, but his arms seemed to move in slow motion. He felt water pouring into his mouth and he spluttered as it entered his nose as well. This helped. It was crap, but it helped. His hands found some driftwood. He clung to it, but he was so cold and it was so hard to grip. Now there was the matter of not being able to see anything. Why was it so dark? Dimly he began to grow aware that something was covering his face. He pulled at it, but it was soft and sticky and there was a stink of mud, or oil, he was covered in mud and oil. He wiped at his eyes and slowly light began to flood in, but pain with it, and incredible stinging pain. He momentarily went under the water again, came up coughing, eyes on fire. Think. Think. What happened? Where are you? Why are you so cold? Is this a dream? Is this a dream?

The river was on the move. And it was getting colder.

Bullet emerged from apartment 502 wearing a smart leather jacket and a baseball cap to match. He waited by emergency stairs a moment. There were too many people using the elevator, so much shouting and urgency. An alarm had sounded and people were coming out of their homes, walking down the fire escape to safety. Bullet smiled to himself. He was going to get out of this. No one was going to touch him. They probably thought someone was still in 602. He had no worries. Pity about the kid. Probably drowned, but that's the luck of the draw. Kid would have probably died of cancer anyway. Looked sick. Wouldn't have lasted anyhow.

"The police are here." He heard someone shouting. "Someone's got a gun."

Yes they have, still loaded. Things were going to be different now. No one was going to bullshit Bullet. He was going to run things his way now. Should have got some extra ammunition, but that was always available, if you knew where to look. Place in Clerkenwell. He'd go there.

"Can you open the door?" A woman asked him as she struggled down the hallway with her cat in a box. "Tabby hates all this noise."

Bullet smiled opening the door. Perfect. The woman would get him out past the police. He was home free. "No problem, lady. Let's get you out of here. Probably a false alarm. You know how these things are. I'll take the box. She won't lash out will she?"

"No, no, I've given her a pill," she replied, happy to have someone to hand over the heavy box to. She looked in the box. "It's alright Tabby, this young man is going to take you to safety." Bullet smirked, but patiently carried the box all the way down.

13. The Search Party

Aura left class early. Rehearsals weren't going well and she wasn't really into experimental dance anyway. Too contrived, not enough movement for her. She meant to go home, but the visit to the library from Lena had her worried. Where had Oliver gone? She knew she was being ridiculous to worry about a boy who was probably quite capable of looking after himself, but she did worry. She didn't know why really. There didn't seem to be any rational reason for it.

It was a quarter to three in the afternoon. She'd called the house on her mobile and Grandma Otis had told her that Oliver still hadn't returned. Aura could tell from the old woman's voice that she was in a state about it. Flop, his cat was going mad, apparently, running from room to room crying out for him. Animals can sense trouble and this apparently vexed Grandma Otis most of all.

She went as near to the river as she could, then walked. She was glad she was well wrapped, there was a biting cold wind. She'd started her walk from Park Row by the University grounds and she thought she'd work her way along the river towards Ballast Quay, nearby Oliver's home. If Oliver was around she guessed this would be the place. He must have come back from the other side. There wasn't much to do over there.

The tide was going out and there was a strong smell of diesel in the water. She'd never really liked the smell of the river. She preferred lakes, the rolling mists on lonely lakes.

The Trafalgar pub was quiet, although the street was jammed with cars. She thought of asking the people sat by the windows overlooking the river if they had seen anything, but she felt a bit stupid.

There was another girl standing, watching her. She was wearing the school uniform and Aura vaguely recognised her. Suddenly Lena came out of the pub shaking her head and she stopped by the girl. Lena turned and came face to face with Aura.

"Oh, it's you." She was looking pensive and pale.

"Have you seen him?" Lena asked.

"I was going to ask you the same thing."

Justine couldn't believe it. "You're looking for him too? That boy gets into so much shit. I can't believe it. I still can't believe he knows you."

"You're Justine, right?" Aura said. Justine was impressed she knew her name.

Lena shivered. "Grandma Otis has sent us all out. She's convinced he's in trouble. She keeps on saying. *'The river, the river'* But where? How? The tide's been up, he wouldn't have been looking for anything when the tide's up."

"Did you try the other side?"

Justine nodded. "I already went there. The man on the lift remembers him, but he took a couple of hours off at lunch and Oliver could have come back during his break."

"But why was he over there?"

"He was looking for someone." Justine told Aura. "He left me a note. I couldn't believe it. He just does anything he wants. No idea about the trouble he causes everyone."

Aura was puzzled. "What do you mean?"

Lena sighed. "Oh, it's silly really. Ever since Justine and him found the body by the river he's become obsessed, or so Grandma Otis says."

This was news to Aura. "You found a body? I heard about it on the news. That's horrible."

"We found the dog, too. It's throat had been cut. That's what started it." Justine told her. "Then when we found the man handcuffed to the boat, it seemed to affect him."

Aura looked at Lena with enough scepticism to unnerve her. Lena nodded her head. "It's true. I swear it. He's a magnet for trouble. A magnet. Grandma Otis thinks he's gone looking for Mr Michaels' ghost."

Now Aura was amused. "Looking for a ghost?'

Lena shrugged. "Grandma Otis is..."

"She's a medium. I know. My father knows of her. She's quite a local celebrity. She's worried about Oliver? She thinks he's come to harm?"

Lena nodded. "She thinks it might be too late."

Aura turned away from Lena and Justine a moment and abruptly felt a sharp pain in her head. It was curious. She turned back, looked across the river a moment. Something odd, something directed at her. Suddenly she had it. It was the thing that had been nagging at her for two hours now. She glanced at them both but couldn't find the right words to explain what she felt.

"No. It's not too late. He's here. Your Grandma Otis is right. He's here. I can feel him. Come on, we can get to the river along Crane Street. Come on. He's here."

Lena and Justine watched Aura run and, although they thought it was all a waste of time, they did feel a slight rise in hope. Just having someone else to search with, someone who cared, was something.

"I'm coming!" Lena called, as Justine ran ahead on her young legs. But she ran slowly because she had no doubt that they'd find him, but not alive. Not the bright kid that had been there that morning.

Aura found the wooden floodgates next to the canoe club shut. No time to find someone who had keys. She was agile enough. She leapt up and grabbed the top bar, drawing her legs up and crawled over, dropping to the concrete below with practised ease.

She had absolutely no idea as to why she had said what she did, or why she believed it, but she had experienced the most intense feeling back on the street. Perhaps it was just a romantic thing? She wanted to find him, perhaps she just wanted to believe fantastic things were possible, or...

The high tide had left an incredible amount of scum and deleterious material. Yet nothing so big it resembled a child, or even as much as a... She stumbled and discovered she was looking at a dead fish with a cancerous sore on its side. Gross.

Justine joined her, catching her breath. "You're fit."

"Dance class. Took it up after I was ill, to get myself well again."

"You really think he's out here? He can't last long in the river. It's disgusting."

"I know he's alive. I don't know if he is actually in the river, Justine."

Lena was trapped the other side of the gate and had gone by way of 'The Yacht', a riverside pub adjoining the canoe club, to find a way onto the beach.

"Is there anything there?" Lena asked through an open window.

"No." Aura answered, then added, "...not yet. The tide is picking up speed."

"If he's in the river, he's either dead or washed out to Gravesend and beyond." Lena added unhelpfully, mentally worrying about who would have to look after his cat if he was really gone. Who would tell his cat? That cat seemed to understand things more than most people she knew.

Aura walked to the retreating waters' edge and scoured the water, both ways. She sighed. Nothing. The momentary thrill of sureness had been quickly replaced by despair. How could she have even thought that she would have been able to find him?

"It's useless." Lena was saying from behind her.

Aura was almost inclined to believe her when she spotted some driftwood. It was not in the mainstream, but nosing around a buoy in the river. It was not so far from the water's edge, reachable. She didn't think twice. She wasn't a strong swimmer, but she could swim.

"You're not going in are you?" Justine asked, horrified.

"Have to."

"We could call someone."

"Who? Have to go now. Hold my clothes, Justine. We're going to need blankets. Tell Lena."

"The river's full of poisons, Aura. You shouldn't..."

"Have to. He's out there. Needs help."

Aura shook off her coat and shoes, discarded her sweater and ran into the water and struck out for the buoy. She immediately became aware of the incredibly strong current and the cold, but she thought she could cope with it.

Lena, back in the pub had already run to the phone to call for help. Even if Aura was wrong, she'd need help after going into the river.

Justine felt awful. She should be the one who was in the river saving him. He'd left the message for her, but she was a poor swimmer. Aura had a clean, slick swimming style. She was impressed by her bravery.

Aura began to struggle. It was colder than she thought it would be and the current made her so slow. She began to realise that if she made the buoy at all, she'd be lucky, never mind make it back.

'I'm here.' That's all she heard. *'I'm here. I'm here.'* A voice in her head saying... *'I'm here, I'm here, I'm here.'* A beacon. It was him. The signal that she'd heard on the shore.

Aura swam with a renewed energy. The buoy was within her grasp. The driftwood was still there and as she looked up she could see a hand, blue, a blue hand holding onto the buoy.

'I'm here.' The voice almost shouted in her head.

Aura reached the buoy and the driftwood. Oliver was unconscious, or seemingly so. He was lying across a log in the water, his body half in and half out of the water, his head bloody and his face and hands so blue it was painful to see. Aura was breathless, but her fingers could detect a heartbeat, even though all she could feel of herself was her own heart beating wildly.

"What happened? What happened to you?" She heard herself ask, but Oliver was obviously not going to reply.

She looked back to the shore and knew that she didn't have the strength to make it back. Especially bringing Oliver with her. There was some activity on the beach now. She felt confident that Lena would sort out something.

"You're going to be OK, Oliver. You're going to be OK."

It was something you just said to reassure someone, but who knew what he'd swallowed, or what the injury to his head was?

"Just keep breathing." Aura huddled him close to her as she scrabbled up on the log beside him. Even though she was cold, she was warmer than he was. Something of her body heat would help him. "Just hang on. Hang on."

Lena was on the shore now, waving. A boat was coming out. She'd organised a rescue boat. Aura felt an immense sensation of relief. She looked down at Oliver's face and noticed his puffy eyes and his swollen lips. Suddenly she felt annoyed.

"Boy, you've survived a tumour. Don't you know how precious life is yet? You have to learn to look after yourself. It's all we've got, me and you. Life."

'I'm here. I can hear you.'

His lips hadn't moved, but she heard him in her head. This time she knew she'd heard him.

"And I'm here too, Oliver. I'm here too."

14. In between time

Oliver found himself standing, shivering in what looked like a cellar. There was a smell of coal and a dim, bare light bulb hung from the ceiling illuminating the small musty space. There were empty wooden fruit boxes in the corner and a stack of old beer bottles. He glanced up and saw what looked like meat hanging from a huge hook in the ceiling and there were onions and dried herbs draped from smaller hooks on some shelving. It looked like any cellar he guessed, but it was freezing cold. The coal stank of cat's pee. The cellar window was covered by old newspapers and there were bicycle bits and pieces strewn around the floor, as if someone had started to fix one up and given up.

He wasn't sure how he'd got there and it was only then that he noticed he wasn't wearing any shoes. His feet were freezing on the concrete floor. What had happened to his shoes?

He could hear noises upstairs, scraping chairs and a radio playing. In the distance, outside in the streets, he could hear a siren blaring. It was a distinct noise, like the old fire siren that sounded in Louth in an emergency. He'd gone with the school to see the fire department and they had shown all kinds of sirens, going right back a hundred years.

But what was he doing in this cellar? Whose cellar was it? It wasn't Grandma's, she didn't have a cellar. 'Too damp for cellars when you lived by the river', she'd told him.

He couldn't understand how he'd got there or why. Was this a dream? Was he dead? He could be dead. He was bloody cold and the dead were always cold, right?

He remembered falling. Losing grip, and then a sudden gust of wind whipping him away from the building and plunging him down towards the river. He remembered yelling. He could still feel the impact of the cold water as it took his breath away and how he'd plunged feet first into the riverbed mud. Shoes! That's where his shoes went. They'd become embedded in the sticky goo of the riverbed and he'd frantically had to get his fingers down there into the mud, his lungs desperate for air as he clawed at his Converse trainers. He'd finally wrenched them off before lunging for the surface. That's when he'd hit his head. Something on the surface of the water and he'd collided hard, banged his head, cut it open. He remembered the searing pain as he'd finally reached the surface and sucked in the air.

The current had already taken him right across the river to the other side. He had been so cold, so desperate and he'd shouted for help. The driftwood came just in time and he'd grabbed it to keep him afloat. He couldn't seem to remember how to swim. The current was fast and he was so dizzy. He remembered his eyes were covered in mud or something that stung his eyes. He daren't leave the driftwood and swim for a shore he couldn't see. It was almost dark. Someone would see him, he'd told himself, someone would see him and pull him out.

"That's it? That's all you remember?" A boy's voice asked him, his tone was mocking.

Oliver turned around and at first he couldn't see anyone, but then, after a moment of squinting, he saw him, sat on the bottom step, staring at him. He was dressed in a plain grey shirt, wore grey trousers and scruffy black plimsolls. His fair hair was short, shaved at the sides and it looked quite weird. He looked slightly older than Oliver.

The boy smiled with just the faintest hint of ridicule.

"You're a mess, Oliver. You know that? You really caused a lot of trouble for everyone."

Oliver nodded, a wave of guilt washed over him and he felt his cheeks redden. Clearly people still picked on you, even when you're dead.

"Who are you?" Oliver asked. "Where are we?"

The boy stood up and came into the light. Oliver could see that he was extremely pale and thin with a thin red scar on his forehead.

A man's voice was shouting from upstairs. "Get a lump of coal, Alfie, better hurry up, your bathwater is getting cold."

The boy ignored the voice. He was just studying Oliver.

"You'd better go," Oliver told him. It was puzzling though. If you were dead, why would you still need a bath?

"No need." The boy told him. "It's dirty anyway, my Dad always gets the clean water first."

"I'd better go," Oliver told him, feeling awkward now, unable to comprehend how the boy was reading his thoughts. "I'm sorry. I don't know how I got here, but I'd better go."

The boy smiled again, looking up at the stairs. "He'll be down here soon enough. Come on, we have to go and see your mother."

"My mother?" He suddenly experienced rising panic. "She's dead too?" Why hadn't anyone told him? What exactly was going on here? He was at once excited that he would be seeing his mother and upset that she was dead too. How was it possible? How strange being dead was. All that stuff about going to heaven and instead you end up in someone's cellar. Didn't make any sense at all.

"You don't get it, do you?" The boy said. "There's only one boy dead in this room and it isn't you."

Oliver frowned, gaping at him. "I don't understand," he whispered. "I drowned, didn't I?"

"You don't remember much at all." The boy began to walk to the far end of the cellar towards a door that Oliver could have sworn hadn't existed a moment before.

"You're dead? But you look..." Sick, thin, starved, but definitely not dead, Oliver was thinking.

"I'm not a ghost." The boy declared. "Come, I'll explain."

"But..." Oliver began, suddenly aware that the siren outside had stopped and there was a new sound of the droning of propeller driven planes. Huge planes. He'd never heard such a noise. The air above seemed to vibrate. He could see the boy was growing agitated. What was going on?

Suddenly the cellar door swung open and a half naked man with hairy legs ran down the stairs, grabbing a tin hat on the way down and shouting at the boy to get under the workbench.

Oliver watched with fascination as the boy flung himself under the bench, then worried about what *he* was supposed to do. Standing there seemed utterly foolish. The boy's father grabbed an old great coat off the wall hook and pulled it on, sitting down on the floor with his back to the wall.

"There's more than one this time," he shouted, as the roar of the bombers thundered overhead. Oliver could hear guns going off outside, explosions rang out everywhere, then suddenly the lights went out. The roar of the overhead bombers became unbearable and as Oliver's eyes adjusted to the light, he could see the boy was suddenly standing beside him again, *and* hiding under the workbench. There were two of him!

Even though Oliver only knew the sound from war movies, he knew exactly what was happening. Enemy bombers were flying over London. But... When did war start? Why old fashioned bombers? Didn't they have jets or missiles?

The next sound filled him with dread. The scream of bombs dropping from the air. It was coming down right on top of them. Oliver shook with sheer terror.

The blast obliterated everything in front of him. Oliver saw the flames, the falling bricks, heard the shattering glass, and the terrible scream as the boy tried to cover his eyes, as ordnance exploded right in the middle of the cellar.

Oliver reeled from the blast. This was war. This was hell. Oliver turned away. The boy was standing in the doorway and he walked out through it. Oliver ran after him as the air filled with dust and the smell of blood.

Oliver emerged into a quiet, foggy emptiness. It was almost as big a shock as the cellar before. Everything impossible was happening all at once.

"There were six German bombers." The boy told him matter of factly. "Been coming every night to finish off the docks. We had slept in the cellar five nights in a row, Dad and me. Everyone in Brand Street had done the same. All over Greenwich and Deptford."

Oliver had never seen death so close or so real. This boy had been killed by a bomb, burned alive, just like his dad. Oliver's heart was in his mouth; he was shaking with shock, yet the boy seemed so calm.

Oliver returned to the doorway and looked inside. The room was back exactly to the way it had been, the dim light bulb illuminating the cellar, just as before. No bomb, nothing but an empty cellar in a normal house. How was this possible?

They were shrouded in fog now. Oliver couldn't make out anything at all. Beside him, the boy was tying his shoelace. He looked up at Oliver and could see the shock plain on his face.

"November 3rd, 1941. It was a cold night, just like this. Bath night. Means you have to get the tin bath out, heat up the water and sit in it, in front of the kitchen range. Mum had left us, was in Charlton, at my Gran's. Nerves, Dad said. She hated the sound of the bombers and the ack-ack. Used to scream when the tracers went up in the sky. She'd run for the cellar and cry until the all clear."

"You stayed." Oliver said. "Didn't you want to go? I saw a film, kids were evacuated."

The boy shook his head. "Dad wanted me home. He said the war would be over by Christmas. He was convinced the Germans would win. "Alfie," he would say. "They're organised, they've already got the whole of Europe in their grip. We're next. Be ready. Had me learning German in secret."

"He was wrong."

"Yeah, but he was just looking out for me."

"You're called Alfred?"

"Alfie."

"Alfie, you've been dead for sixty-seven years."

"You never forget the moment you die," Alfie told him. "No one remembers being born, but you always remember dying."

"Unless you don't know you're dead." Oliver remarked, thinking of a certain man and his chocolate dog.

Alfie snatched a look at Oliver. "I've seen them. Wandering. You aren't dead, Oliver. No matter what you think. You aren't dead."

Oliver took a deep breath. "Then where am I?"

Alfie smiled again. "At the moment, you're in hospital. They think you're dying. You're on life-support. There's a young girl with a serious expression sat beside you. She's holding your hand. She thinks you are the stupidest boy that ever existed and yet she likes you."

Justine, Oliver thought immediately, with guilt. He had let everyone down. From the moment he'd arrived in Greenwich, he'd done nothing but let people down.

"But I'm here. Wherever here is." Oliver said. "I don't understand."

"Look more closely, Oliver. You mother is waiting."

The mist seemed to vanish and they were standing in a sunny courtyard. There was a small blossoming cherry tree in one corner, and beneath it, a woman was sitting staring at nothing in particular.

She frowned. She looked up as Oliver nervously approached her. Was she a ghost too? She looked the same as ever, save for her hair being cropped short and there were bandages around her wrists. Oliver snatched a glance back at Alfie who was watching from a distance.

"Is this real, Alfie?" he whispered. "Can she see me?"

"You don't have to whisper," Alfie informed him. "She can't see or hear you."

Oliver was staring at her, looking at her hands that were continually moving against each other, like snakes in a sack. What had she done to her wrists? Had she tried to kill herself? He knew about those bandages. Seen them on other people at the hospital.

He suddenly realised she was looking directly at him. He felt a sudden surge of hope.

"Oliver?" His mother asked, her eyes suddenly clear and alert.

"Ma?"

"You look a mess, Oliver. What have you been doing? Where have you been? What on earth has happened to your head?"

Oliver almost smiled. Hearing her sharp critical voice was so familiar. So typical. Weirdly reassuring. He wanted to hug her, but was that allowed?

Alfie started. This wasn't supposed to happen. He was sure this wasn't supposed to happen. She shouldn't be able to see him at all.

"I'm here now, Ma. Been sick. Been sick a long time."

"Are you dead?" His mother asked.

"No, Ma. My friend, Alfie here," he looked back briefly at Alfie. "He's dead. But I'm not. I'm just visiting."

"Has no one fed you? Look at your head. What happened to your head?"

Oliver felt tears welling. He should be wearing a hat. Why wasn't he wearing a hat? He hadn't had a conversation with his mother in so long it hurt to see her looking so pale and weird with her hair cropped like that.

"I love you, Ma. I nearly drowned. Fell into the river. It was ..."

His mother began to rock from side to side, agitated now. "I'm not surprised. The gypsy said you would."

"The gypsy?" Oliver asked, not sure she was listening really.

"The woman who came to the door. Don't you remember? She said you'd never reach your thirteenth birthday. You'd drown. Nothing I could do to prevent it. You'd drown, no matter what."

This was the first Oliver had heard about this. He remembered the gypsy woman and how his mother had cried for hours, days even, after her visit, but he'd assumed it was news about herself, or Dad.

"It's OK, Ma," he said softly, going closer. "I didn't drown. I think. Aura heard me calling her."

"Aura?" His mother enquired.

"She's my friend."

Suddenly Oliver could see his mother was growing alarmed. "You're fading. Oh my god. OLIVER! You're going. You're going."

An alarmed nurse came out of the building, brushed right past Oliver, as if she couldn't see him and knelt down beside his mother who was sobbing now.

He wasn't aware he was fading, but clearly she couldn't see or hear him now. She looked so distressed. Fat tears rolled down his cheeks.

Alfie appeared beside him. "Come on, we have to find your father now."

Oliver was loathe to leave his mother so soon after he'd got there. Especially as she was so upset. The nurse was giving her pills and he could see his mother was distraught. He'd disturbed her and all he'd wanted to do, all he'd ever wanted to do was love her.

"Oliver was here," his mother was telling the nurse, urgently. "Oliver was here. He just passed over. Right before my eyes. He died right before my eyes."

The nurse looked totally surprised. She dropped some pills and shouted to someone inside. "She just spoke, get the Doctor. Charlotte just spoke."

Alfie was walking along a dusty dirt road. Oliver ran to catch up. All around him the sky was huge and the horizon went on forever, dotted with small stunted trees. It was hot, the sun high up in the washed out blue sky. Now Oliver looked at everything, all the colours seemed faded, except the russet earth. Where were they now?

"Where are we?"

"Africa. Zimbabwe. On the northern border." Alfie informed him.

Oliver did a double take. This was the most brilliant magic. Louth one minute, Africa the next. Could all dead people do this?

"I can only go where you want to go," Alfie told him, reading his thoughts again.

"But how do you know where I want to go?"

"You wanted to see your mother and then you wanted to see your father. It's as simple as that."

"But why do you have to take me? Why can't I get there on my own?"

Alfie turned and looked at Oliver with a curious stare. "Because you aren't dead, Oliver. It isn't magic. I can't go wherever I want. I wouldn't even know where to go."

Oliver noticed some abandoned shoes and a mobile phone. He didn't know why exactly, but he knew that these were his father's and that made his heart jump.

Alfie stared at the shoes. "I just go where you want, I suppose. I'm new at this."

Oliver walked over to a rock and then he noticed an abandoned car, a Toyota, half burned and dug into the sand, about a hundred feet away. He began to walk towards it.

"I don't understand, Alfie. You're new?"

Alfie shrugged, following Oliver through the scrub. "This is my first job. I'm your guide."

Oliver digested this information. "Like Quon? My Grandma's guide. He was from Africa."

"I don't know him. I don't really know anyone. I was just told to wait for you."

Oliver nodded. He'd have to think about this. He turned to Alfie and smiled.

"I'm sorry, Alfie. I'm sorry you died like that. You don't have to stay. I'm sure. I mean, I'm only twelve. I'm not like my Grandmother, I don't help people."

Alfie jumped over a rock and sprinted the last forty feet to the car.

"Well, I have to stay. This is my job now."

Oliver frowned. "Your job? For how long?"

Alfie grinned suddenly, looking back at Oliver. "Until you die. Which might be sooner than you think if you don't pay more attention. I saw you with Bullet. Are you stupid? You must be stupid. Never trust anyone called Bullet. You have to learn judgement. Maybe that's why I was sent to you. To keep you alive. Better get used to it."

Oliver reached the car and stared at it, his attention fixed on the remains now. "You're probably right. I have been stupid and..."

Oliver saw a partially burned briefcase with a Spiderman sticker on it. The coincidence was impossible. He had put that sticker on there. This was his father's briefcase. This had been his father's car. He suddenly felt shaky. Shoes, phone, a burned out car.

"Dad was here." Oliver exclaimed. "This was his car. His briefcase. That was his phone back on the road."

Alfie sat on the car bonnet and looked at the tire tracks and pointed to the bullet holes, sprayed right across the car. "They really wanted to stop him."

Oliver felt tears rolling down his cheeks. Someone had really wanted his father dead. This hadn't been a crash. They'd fired on him on the road and he'd tried to get away, the tracks showed that.

Alfie could see Oliver was upset. "He isn't dead. I checked. He was supposed to be here, but ..."

Oliver studied Alfie through misty eyes. He rubbed away the tears.

"You don't know?"

Alfie thought about it, for what seemed an age, then slowly shook his head.

"No one knows. Sorry."

"Perhaps Quon knows?"

"I just asked, Oliver. No one knows. He's not dead; he's not... Anywhere. This was the last place. He should be here."

Oliver was devastated. Surely if you had a guide they should know everything? Wasn't that the point of guides? Quon would know.

"You mean, he could be here? Should we be looking for him?"

Alfie looked out into the desert. "This happened a year ago, more. No one comes here. He went south. The wind has swept the footprints away."

Oliver moved over to the driver's door, frantically looking for traces of footsteps, noting the bullet hole that had come right through the door. Was that dried blood on the remains of the paintwork? He imagined his father bleeding, injured, stuck out here in the middle of nowhere.

There was no trace, but equally no bones. His father hadn't died here.

Alfie was beside him. "He's alive, somewhere."

"But you found my mother quickly."

"She's in your memory. I had to search a long time to find even this of your father."

"But we just came, you just..." Oliver protested.

"You have been searching for him. Writing letters, remember? I have been looking ever since I knew you would be coming to me."

"You knew I would nearly drown?" Oliver asked.

"Even the gypsy woman knew. It was written in your fate Oliver. But you met Aura and that altered everything. That's how fate works. Everything is set in stone until you stub your toe on it."

Oliver looked at Alfie. "Stub your toe?"

Alfie smiled. "Something my mother used to say."

Oliver had meant to ask. "Did she live? I mean, after the war."

Alfie shook his head. "Broke her heart when she knew Dad and me died. Then there was a flu epidemic and..."

"Sorry." Then, thinking some more. "Did you see her in heaven?"

Alfie walked towards a heap in the sand some distance from the car and stood over it.

"Heaven?"

"You know, where people go when they die."

Alfie squatted down by the heap and beckoned Oliver over. "I don't think there is a heaven, not like people think. It's complicated." Alfie looked up at Oliver as he joined him. "It's like a forest of light. That's what it seems like to me. A forest."

Oliver decided to ask nothing more. It clearly upset Alfie to talk about it. He looked at the heap in the sand. Obviously Alfie wanted him to uncover it. "What do you think it is?"

"We're meant to find it, I think." Alfie replied.

Oliver brushed away the sand and found a rock. He lifted the rock. It was heavy. There was a folder, wrapped in heavy plastic and lined with cloth. Oliver gently lifted it out, shaking any sand off it. It was perfectly preserved in the dry desert sand but he could see some insects had tried to chew the ends.

"What do you think it is?"

Alfie knew, but he preferred not to say. Oliver looked at him as he unwrapped the layers. Finally he extracted the contents. The folder contained photographic images – at least fifty. Dead people. Burned people.

Children shot through the head. Awful, terrifying images, and some, clearly taken in secret, of police and soldiers shooting and beating these same people.

Oliver stared at them for a while, then slowly put them back in the folder. He said nothing. He carefully rewrapped everything and buried the whole thing again, replacing the rock. The sand would cover it next time the wind blew.

"That's why they tried to kill him, isn't it?" Oliver said at length.

Alfie stood up again and started walking back towards the road.

"He buried them, so he might come back to get them, one day." Oliver said. "If he's alive."

"He isn't dead, Oliver. He isn't in the forest."

Oliver frowned. Running after Alfie. "What about the other place? Y'know?"

Alfie stopped and looked at Oliver with a frown. "You think he's there?"

Oliver shook his head. His father had always cared about other people. "No."

"Then we won't think about it. Besides you'd need someone else to take you there and..."

"And?"

"There's no way back."

Oliver was tired now and the sun was burning his back and the top of his head. He'd been told enough times not to get too much sun on his head.

Africa he discovered was so incredibly empty. He'd never thought of a country being so empty. But it was beautiful. So different to England. He wondered why Alfie couldn't find his father. What was blocking it?

"You found this, but you can't..."

Alfie sighed. "You're mother is thinking about you. It was easy to find her. You're father isn't thinking about you. That's all. Maybe he's thinking about the children who got shot. There's always someone who wants to kill children, drop bombs on them. It's not a perfect world, Oliver."

Oliver kicked some dust on the road. "I know it's not perfect. I know that."

Alfie began walking down the road. "We have to go. We can try and look for him again when you're stronger."

"You'll come back?"

"I'm here now. There's no back or forwards. You might not remember anything when you wake up. But you'll know me when we meet again."

"You're going?"

"Doctor's coming to check on you."

"Hey?" Oliver stared as Alfie strode away from him. "Hey? You're leaving me here? In Africa?"

176

"Remember, be good to your friends," Alfie called out. "They'll be good to you."

"Alfie?" Oliver stood still, hot, a pang of loneliness overcoming him. His father's wrecked car lay behind him. Surely Alfie wouldn't just leave him here in the middle of nowhere? What would he eat? What would happen if the men with guns came back? "Alfie?"

He looked at his father's car again. They had shot at him and left him for dead. But he'd buried those pictures. That meant he wasn't dead. He'd want to come back for them, one day. He was still alive, somewhere. But where?

A lizard crawled over his foot and a bird shrieked. He was thirsty.

He turned a full 360 degrees and marvelled at just how big this landscape was.

"How am I going to get home? How am I going to get back?"

But only the lizard was listening. Oliver sighed and began walking south, avoiding sharp pebbles in the dusty dirt road.

15. Guilty as Charged

Perhaps when you are young you are supposed to recover more quickly from any of life's disasters, but it was two days before Oliver was able to hold down food again and breathe normally. The hospital had put him on a intravenous drip and kept a watch on him for the first twenty-four hours. He had a drip in one arm and an oxygen mask on his face. Furthermore, parts of his skin had been covered in some purple stain where it had come into contact with contaminants in the river. His head was bandaged and he looked like a war victim rather than a kid who'd been foolish enough to dive into the River Thames from a sixth floor apartment.

The doctors and nurses had been very worried throughout the first two days because Oliver had not uttered a word. Lena had visited and not gotten even a smile of recognition out of him. He had been oblivious to everything. They had performed tests, but got nothing. Oliver was simply not there. Living, breathing, but deeply traumatised.

It was Old Joe, when he came over on the Sunday, who broke the spell. Oliver had managed breakfast and they'd removed the drip, although it had left a red, raw scar on his arm.

Oliver, who still hadn't said a word, looked up and found Old Joe there, just looking at him from the foot of his bed. Some of the other kids in the ward were making jokes about him, but Old Joe just kept staring at Oliver and Oliver could feel something, could feel a thin shell breaking all around him. He had the sensation of the shell shattering into a thousand pieces all around him. The armour that had protected him, kept him alive from the moment he'd hit the cold, cold, water. All at once he could hear everything, feel everything.

"They told me you were here."

Oliver blinked a moment. His mouth was dry. He commanded himself to speak.

"I'm sorry. I was supposed to meet you."

"She's in the clinic."

"Who?"

"Aura. She went into the river to save you. She's in the clinic. They say she's sick."

"Aura saved me?" Oliver felt tears welling in his eyes. Suddenly, it was as if the floodgates had opened in his mind. Aura had saved him. He'd called out for her. He remembered that. He'd called her name, over and over. Couldn't even say why. But in the water, all he could think of was the shell that protected him and Aura. He'd wanted Aura to come for him. Take him home. He'd not thought about anything right up until the moment Old Joe had appeared, and now, memories exploded in his head. Bullet with the gun, the jump into the water, the cold, the sudden realisation that he was going to die if he didn't will himself warm, and Aura. How he'd just wanted Aura to hold him, make everything better.

Old Joe was holding Oliver's hand now as he sat there, in his hospital bed and let the tears flow down his face. The old gnarled hand was comforting, warm.

"It's alright." Old Joe was telling him. "It's alright. You're alive. God has spared you. She is alive, too. It is good to live through these things. You learn, you never forget. I never forget they killed my family. Sometimes I cry, sometimes I shout, but I never forget. I will always see those faces, laughing as they burn our homes. Sometimes I ask myself, why did I survive? What purpose was served, by keeping me alive, and then I remember, it is for me to remember. To never forget, tell others, never forget.

"Now you. Now you have memories. Something happened? Something bad. Remember why. Remember you survived. Perhaps one day you will speak to your father of these things?"

Oliver heard his father mentioned. "Did you hear?"

"I have a message from an old friend. He will put your father's photo on TV in South Africa. I need a photo. You have one?"

Oliver nodded. He had one picture at home. It was of his father holding him up high over his head when he was eight years old. It was the only photo he had.

"Can I have it back?"

Old Joe smiled, releasing Oliver's hand. "It can be scanned and sent attached to the email. You can have it back almost immediately. When you are better, we will send it."

"Where is Aura? I have to say thank you."

"Somewhere. She knows you are grateful. You will see her when she is better."

Oliver looked up at Old Joe through a cloud of hot tears. "Joe?"

"Ja?"

"I was stupid."

"Ja."

"I let everyone down. My Grandma will hate me now. She'll send me away. I've done something stupid every day I have been here. She'll send me away, I know she will."

Old Joe took Oliver's hand again. "No... She won't. You are family. She loves you. You get better. You come and see me as soon as you can. You know where I will be."

Old Joe released his hand again and left Oliver's bedside. Oliver was aware only of the impression of his large gnarly hand being no longer there. Time had ceased to function in its normal fashion. He had so many things to think about. His father, Aura, Grandma Otis and Bullet. On top of everything, he felt so guilty, so terribly guilty.

Old Joe was leaving the hospital just as Harriet was arriving. Late, flustered and carrying too much with her, and she had other things to do, but Oliver had to be visited. She didn't pay any attention to Old Joe. She marched over to reception to find out where she had to go, worried about the time, the awkward place where she'd left her car and a million other things. She wasn't annoyed to have to visit Oliver in hospital, it was just a bit inconvenient. But visit him she had to do, she had questions that needed to be asked.

Grandma Otis was in her dining room examining her silver collection as she talked to her visitor. She'd dreaded this moment and knew it would come the moment Oliver had been hospitalised. Social services had come to call. The pointy-faced woman wore an oversized man's blue jacket covered with shiny stains, she was probing, professional, but officious and patronising.

"I am old," Grandma Otis conceded, "but since when has that been a crime?"

"I am not saying it's a crime."

"You are saying that someone my age can't manage the 'burden of a difficult child'. Well who says he's difficult? You? You've never met him. You've come here with a set of opinions about a child you've never met."

"I'm merely suggesting that there are care solutions. He's young. He could go into one of our homes and he'd get some discipline."

Grandma Otis looked the woman in the face. Stared really hard at her. "I'm not having Oliver put into care. I know what happens to children in care and care isn't one of the things that happens. They're neglected, molested, taught to be criminals, spend half their time on the streets, and end up in jail.

You think I don't read the papers or talk to people? Your sort just like to crush them, beat them and hide them away. Oliver is a special child. He's intelligent. His father's missing, his mother is sick. This is his home now and this is where he will stay. He's loved here. I've got a housekeeper, who is here all the time. In September he'll start school. He'll make friends, start a new life."

"It's his friends I'm worried about. I've made some enquiries. There's CCTV of him inside private property grounds. Someone broke into a home there. The police report says two children were seen. We've got an injured security guard from a bullet wound. One of the boys was using a gun. You understand, this is a criminal matter now. Your grandson is implicated."

"I've already spoken with the police. They haven't laid a charge and don't intend to and you know he's too young to go to prison."

"But he's not too young to go into care."

"Now you are saying Oliver was the one with the gun? I'd like to see you prove that."

"He was seen there. A gun was used. He's out of control. By your own admission, you let him go out unsupervised."

Grandma Otis swore. "And you're out there persecuting every other mother for letting their child walk the streets? Are you saying that you want all the children locked up? You're one of the reasons there's problems in this town. I see enough women who come to me crying because their kids have been taken from them. Oliver is staying with me and he's likely to have learned a good lesson. When he's speaking again, I'm sure he'll have a perfectly good explanation."

The woman's mouth turned down at the edges. "He can explain all he wants, but I think this boy should be on the 'Child In Danger' list."

"Now you're saying I beat him? First you say I'm not fit to look after him, now you're saying I dragged him to the river, beat him and threw him in."

"I am saying to you that he is mixing with people who might do that. The police tell us that he haunts the river and looks for body parts. This isn't a healthy hobby. It's morbid and sick. He needs counselling."

Grandma Otis slammed her cane down on the table. The social worker flinched.

"He does not 'haunt the river', he lives by the river. This is his home. A boy is entitled to walk by the river if he wants to and if he finds bodies, well it's probably one of your lot who caused it to be there."

"I don't think we are getting anywhere, if I think Oliver is a child in danger, then that's how he will be registered. The courts will enable us to take him from you if he gets into trouble again, or is beaten, or..."

Grandma Otis swore at her again. "Get out of here, you horrible woman. He's staying here and I'll go to court if I have to, to protect him from the likes of you. You're unnatural and perverted, that's what you are. Unnatural. I'd hate to be a child of yours."

The woman rose, closed her briefcase and gave Grandma Otis a professional icy smile.

"I think you will find we have more pull in the courts than you, Mrs Otis. My job is to see that children grow up in a safe and healthy environment. In my judgement this is not such a place. Good day."

Grandma Otis watched her go. She was speechless. She couldn't move, her heart was beating hard in her breast and she was consumed with anger. Take Oliver? Not whilst she was living. She reached down for her bag and brought it up to the table where she slammed it down with a loud clatter. She withdrew her mobile phone and punched in a number. She swore again and muttered.

"...We'll see who has the most pull in the courts... Hello? Judge Parker's chambers please. Yes...it's Mrs Florinda Otis speaking."

Harriet was sat with Oliver huddled in her arms, all her hustle completely forgotten. She stared at nothing in particular as she hugged him hard and Oliver's silent, hot tears dampened her sleeve. Oliver had told her everything. His night in Greenwich with Bullet. The adventure to find Mitch Michaels' place. How Bullet had made them break in and how Bullet had found a gun and Oliver the photographs. The photograph of Harriet in particular, that he'd torn up. He'd spared her nothing and she'd listened with stunned amazement. She hadn't known about the photographs. She'd wished that he'd stolen them and not the money that Bullet had made him take. Not that he'd really stolen anything, as Mitch Michaels was dead. Stealing from the dead wasn't nice, but it wasn't as bad as stealing from the living. Stealing from Mitch Michaels should be completely rewarded in her opinion. (She wondered what had happened to the money? No one had mentioned this to her on the phone.) She'd never met such a creep before, or since. She remembered her night with him, how strange he'd been, how he'd made her flesh crawl. He'd been doing pills, although she didn't know what. All she remembered was him slobbering over her and begging her to beat him. She wished now she had. She didn't know how he'd taken pictures, she just regretted the whole thing, the entire memory. She was glad he was dead.

"It's incredible how you washed up in almost the same place as him."

Oliver raised his head. He'd thought the same once he'd discovered where he'd been found.

"I don't think I'll go to the river again for a while."

Harriet smiled. This was a good sign. A bit of humour. "Teddy, he's a friend of mine, says that you were probably caught by the current which brought you to this side of the river. Something about a scouring action in the water. I favour act of God actually. You think your head is alright now?"

"It was something in the river. Hit my head. Just cut it open. Do you think they'll get Bullet?"

"I don't know. You'd better tell someone. The police have a picture of you outside the building. They don't know who the other boy is. They only found out about you because it was you who were fished out of the river and the hospital reported it." She sighed.

"Are you really going to have your hands done?" Oliver asked.

"Hey, if the only type of man you attracted was Mitch Michaels you'd change your hands, Oliver. I'm going to do it, soon as I choose the right hands."

"Do you believe that people come back from the dead?"

"What, and pay income tax all over again? No way, sweetie. If you're worried that Mitch Michaels is going to come back as a ghost, don't be. That sort of thing is just bad TV. He can't touch you, or hurt you. Believe me." She smiled, just to make him sure.

"I want to see Aura. I want to say thank you."

"We should send her flowers. Can you imagine going into that cold water to save you? She was so brave. We will definitely send her flowers. I will find out which clinic she is in, alright? I'll send them from you."

"I'm sorry I caused so much trouble. I only wanted to see if Mitch Michaels was really dead."

"He is. You nearly were. You'll have to behave now. Lena tells me that social services are going to see Grandma Otis. They can take you away from her, you know? They can do what they like."

Oliver looked at Harriet with astonishment. "Where? Where would they take me?"

"A home. Don't worry. We won't let them. But you mustn't get into any more trouble. They'll think she can't handle you."

Oliver had never thought of this. A home? A home for children? He'd be an orphan. He couldn't believe it. Just because he'd fallen into the river? And what would happen to Flop?

"The thing is to get better quickly. We'd better think of something to say to the police. You'll have to tell them about Bullet. What kind of kid would make you jump off a balcony into the river? He must have known you would drown. I can't believe anyone could be that cruel."

"He scares me."

Harriet nodded. She hugged him again. That was the trouble with life. It was full of scary people, absolutely full of them.

She must have been sitting there for ages. Oliver woke again and saw that someone was reading *The Handmaid's Tale*. He stirred and the hands put the book away.

"I hope you know the story about how curiosity got the cat."

Oliver sat up and stared at Justine. He immediately felt guilty.

'It's alright. I haven't come to criticise."

Oliver sighed. "I'm sorry for making a mess and upsetting everyone."

"You did. Grandma Otis is in a state. Social services want to take you but she's fighting it. They'll probably take me too if they take you. Can't have one kid in danger and not the other."

"Shit. I really messed up."

"Flop misses you. Sleeps on your bed and hisses if we go near."

Oliver smiled. "He's very protective."

"You could say."

"Do you hate me?"

"No. No one hates you. You've been acting stupid, but no one hates you."

"Aura..."

"I went to see her. She got the flowers from you. Don't know how you managed that. She's pretty sick. Pneumonia I think. She was incredible. She chucked off her clothes and ran into the river. She could hear you calling. Don't know how. We couldn't hear anything. She just swam out to save you. School's going to give her a medal. It was in the paper."

"I wish I could see her."

"I wouldn't. She might have saved you, but she's probably pretty angry with you for going off with that boy. I told you anyone called Bullet was bad news."

"I didn't. I went under the river and he was there. Said he'd been attacked by a vampire and..."

"Vampire? Oliver, just listen to yourself. There are no vampires. You really have to separate TV world from your own. Buffy is so over."

"It was nothing to do with Buffy. He was there. I couldn't shake him. He's got a gun now. He'll be big trouble."

"And he'll probably kill someone. It's his destiny most likely."

"My fault."

"No," Justine smiled. "That boy is the one thing that isn't your fault." She stood up and brushed down her skirt. "I have to go. Lena will come later.

Is there anything you want?"

"Tell Flop I'll be back."

Justine nodded. Oliver looked so serious, she felt she better had or Flop would somehow tell him she hadn't. "I will. I promise."

"Thank you for coming."

"Just don't disappear. OK? For all our sakes."

Oliver smiled. He wasn't going anywhere, for sure. He'd had enough trouble for one lifetime already.

"We still friends?" Oliver asked.

Justine looked at him, her eyes narrowing, as if she had just made a decision.

"When you come home, remind me to show you something, OK?" She gave him a brief smile. "...And yes, we're still friends. If you can manage to stay alive from one day to the next, we're still friends."

The boys on the roof were laughing. Someone had produced some beers and there was something of a party developing up above the hotel. Robbie had let them on the roof of a hotel off Tottenham Court Road. Bullet had met Robbie at McDonald's and Robbie had taken him back. People who worked the night shift at big London hotels got bored easily and Robbie got bored more than most. He was working reception, but mostly he was having parties, when a spare room came up, or no one used the Penthouse suite. Bullet thought it was cool to be up there, having fun, sleeping in a big wide bed. Robbie was often busy, so Bullet brought a friend off the street with him, just for company.

"There's nearly a grand in the till and more than that in the bar. You've got a shooter, what are you waiting for?"

Bullet looked at Smiley and shook his head. "I got a shooter, but I've got it good here. This Robbie's mad for me. I'll do it when he craps out on me."

Smiley pulled a face. "Just do it. Do 'im. It's boring. What's the point of having a shooter if you don't use it?"

Bullet shook his head. "Smiley, you're more stupid than you look. This is cool. We've got a hotel to ourselves and hot baths an' everything. Fuckin' grand won't get you much out there. Not this, anyway."

Smiley wasn't listening. He was watching the TV inside. Mitch Michaels was talking.

"Hey, I thought you said he was dead. That's Mitch Michaels ain't it?"

Bullet swung around in time to see Mitch Michaels' head on the TV be replaced by a newsreader. They didn't have the sound up, so Bullet ran inside to look for the remote. He found it on the sofa.

"...The police say that although they have had the remains of Mitch Michaels' body for almost a week now, they weren't able to identify the body as they had been unable to find a match for his teeth. The break in the murder investigation came when Mr Michaels' apartment, in the prestigious Heritage Wharf building in Docklands, was broken into by burglars last week, where it is believed an unregistered gun was stolen. Details have been emerging of a very exotic lifestyle led by the TV investigative reporter, where his probing into the drug underworld may have been compromised by reports of his own drug related problems. A police spokesman has stated that they suspect that the London underworld has executed Mitch Michaels as a warning to others who might want to probe into their illegal affairs.

"The police tonight have issued a photograph of the suspected burglar who broke into Mr Michaels' apartment and say that if anyone sees this young man or have information as to his whereabouts, that they should on no account approach him, but may call Greenwich CID. The police have appealed to this young man to come forward as he may well have information about Mitch Michaels' assailants.

"We repeat. Police tonight have confirmed that television's favourite 'gang buster' Mitch Michaels, has been found murdered, along with his dog. His surviving mother, the former Bluebell dancer, Hilda Michaels, has been rushed to hospital in shock..."

Smiley looked at Bullet with some admiration. "Shit man, you're famous. You were on TV."

Bullet grinned. "I was, wasn't I?"

"You'd better hope Robbie doesn't see it."

"So what if he does? You think he'd call? If they knew he'd been hiding me up here he'd lose his job. Easy. Shit, I think we'll call room service."

Smiley laughed. "He said you couldn't use room service."

Bullet picked up the phone and smiled. "That was before I was on TV. I'm famous. It's better than *Big Brother*. I can call room service."

Oliver was alone in the hospital ward. The other kids had been taken to the baths. He sat there feeling guilty, stupid and angry with himself. He should never have led Bullet to Mitch Michaels' place. It had been a huge mistake. And now he'd damaged his head, just when it was beginning to heal. He just couldn't believe how stupid he'd been. He felt angry that he'd made Aura ill too. Pneumonia was bad. She would be cursing him, he knew. He coughed. His throat was really sore now. Something to do with all the river water he'd swallowed. The antibiotics were working, but slowly. The doctor said he could go home the next day. Although he was keen to get back to Flop, he was scared what Grandma Otis would say. She'd wanted to come to the hospital to see him, but Lena had stopped her. Hospitals were full of germs and she had no business going there and risking her own health.

No one had come to see him after Lena came that night. He'd tried reading, but he hadn't much fancied that. He'd tried thinking, but guilt kept swimming up before his eyes and made him feel uncomfortable. He had resolved to be good, read lots, catch up on all the school he'd missed (a whole year) and not give anyone any grief, but he just didn't know why things kept happening to him. Harriet was right; he had to tell the police about Bullet. But what if Bullet found out he'd told them? He'd come looking for him for sure, and now he had a gun. That was scary. He lay back in his bed and tried to think of nothing again. Life was just so confusing, so complicated. Just how did you live a normal life? How did you avoid trouble if it came looking for you?

The nurse came back with one of the children and saw him lying on his bed, with a mournful expression on his face. She smiled at him. "There was a message for you."

Oliver looked at her with suspicion. Who would be sending him messages? "What?"

"Phone call for you about half an hour ago. Someone called Aura. She said something about you've only got seven lives left. Oh, yes, and she said '*thank you for the flowers*'."

Oliver smiled. Aura. She sent him a message. Harriet was amazing. He would have to thank her for being so cool. Somehow just the thought of Aura phoning him made him feel happy and safe. She'd lived. She could use the phone. He just knew she was OK. It removed a huge weight off his heart and mind. She was safe.

"Are you ready for your bath, or have you had enough water for one lifetime?" The nurse asked him.

Oliver smiled. "As long as it's hot."

"Oh, it's hotter than the river, that I can guarantee."

Oliver climbed out of bed, moving more slowly than normal. He liked this nurse. She was funny. He felt she cared about all the kids in the ward. He remembered how it had been in the Louth hospital. Some nurses had been great, others sour and impatient, always going on about how hard their job was. He also remembered, endlessly staring out of the cold windows across the town, wishing he could run on the hills in the distance. He'd promised himself that he'd never ever return to a hospital once he got out and, yet, here he was. This time he meant it, he was going to make sure he didn't return.

He shuffled down the ward in his borrowed slippers, actually looking forward to his bath. Tomorrow he'd be good. It was a promise.

16. Grounded

Oliver had been home for more than three hours before Grandma Otis could see him. He'd been brought back home by Lena and put to bed straight away, even though he didn't want to. He was sure there was something he could do rather than just lie in his bed. Flop was beside himself. At first he'd been angry that Oliver had been away and given him a lot of miaows that probably weren't very polite; but then he'd jumped upon the bed and curled up right under Oliver's chin, pressing his nose to Oliver's own from time to time, just to make sure Oliver was still there. If Flop's sheer weight could have kept Oliver pinned to the bed, Flop would have willed it. Flop knew Oliver had been sick, he just knew that he'd been in trouble, and quite rightly he objected to having been left behind to fend for himself with Justine, Lena and Grandma Otis. (Even though Justine did slip him the odd slices of bacon and chicken from time to time.)

Oliver calmly let Flop lie there, even though it wasn't at all comfortable. He had to cough from time to time as his throat was scratchy, but Flop just clung there. He accepted it as punishment for neglecting his cat. Cats had a right to punish owners. It was understood.

The moment he'd been dreading finally arrived. Grandma Otis's visitor departed. He knew, any minute now she was going to come into his room and give him hell.

Flop pricked his ears and sat up. He knew. Indeed, the moment the door began to open, Flop was off the bed and under it, just his tail visible, swishing from side to side.

Oliver came face to face with Grandma Otis. She was dressed in black with a large ruby necklace swinging about her chest. Her hair was up and she was wearing make-up. This was not the Grandma Otis he'd come to know. This was an entirely new woman. She looked quite elegant, even if she did have to support herself by holding onto the door.

Outside there was a gale blowing and it was cooler than it should have been for the time of year. Grandma Otis was looking out of his window at the trees that struggled to keep vertical in the breeze. She'd been waiting for this moment, but now it was here, she couldn't quite think of what exactly to say. Oliver looked a mess. Bruises on his face and his head bandaged. If social services saw him now they'd say he'd been beaten. That was the irony of the whole situation. The boy couldn't be more liked and here he was causing himself all the trouble in the world and nearly getting himself killed into the bargain.

"I should have you chained up. I have a weak heart, Oliver. I want you to think about that next time you have a whim to do something."

Oliver saw that she wasn't angry with him. It encouraged him a little.

"It was a stupid, Grandma, I didn't see it coming."

"I know what it was and why. Quon showed me. I saw your fall. I saw it happen before it happened. I even warned you. Didn't even Mr McTeal warn you about heights? Didn't he tell you not to climb? God has spared you twice, Oliver. How many times can you expect him to be looking your way when you do something foolish? There might come a time when he assumes that you don't really want to live after all."

"I just wanted proof, Grandma. I wanted to know what I saw was real."

"You didn't need to get yourself nearly killed to find that out. Quon is never wrong, especially about the dead. He nearly called *you* dead. You would be, if that girl hadn't got the guts to save you. She deserves that medal. A lot of people wouldn't have done what she did. Oliver, stay home, read some books. You leave the dead alone now. They can look after themselves."

Oliver looked at her, reflecting that she was right, but there were still questions he wanted answering.

"Grandma?"

"Yes?"

"Are they going to take me away?"

Grandma Otis shook her head and smiled. "They'd like to. But I spoke to a few people and they'll leave us alone. You're safe. You're safe as long as you don't do anything foolish. I can't protect you if you won't tell me what you're doing. That's got to be the rule now. Be curious Oliver, a boy must be curious about life and its mysteries, but tell me where you are going, tell me who your friends are, bring them home, let me and Quon take a look at them. I'm not going to tell you who you can be friends with and who you can't, but I can tell you who is good and who is bad."

"I didn't want Bullet to be my friend. He just followed me."

Grandma Otis nodded. "There'll be justice for that boy by and by. The devil is his friend right now, but the devil is fickle, and he just leads those who listen to the edge then backs away. He'll fall. He'll fall. If you even as much as get a glimpse of him, you run. You understand? You run."

Oliver nodded. He'd come to the same conclusion.

"Don't even think about getting revenge. He's bigger than you and he's got the Devil on his side. You run and hide. Do we agree?"

Oliver nodded again. "Yes Grandma."

"You have to stay in bed today. You can listen to music, you can read. You'll have to prove to me that you'll keep your word before you can go outside."

Grandma Otis left the room, adding as an afterthought: "You be good this afternoon. I'm having tea with the Standley's."

Oliver looked at the gap where Grandma Otis had stood. He felt that he'd been lucky. If it had been his mother stood there, she would have screamed at him if he'd done something as bad as this. Besides he liked listening to the radio and reading wasn't so bad. His mother's collection of books were waiting for him to read. They looked a bit depressing and fat, but he remembered his father saying *'It's books that connect minds and generations.'* He'd no idea what it meant, but it was something to do with reading old books.

"You can come out now, Flop," he called out, leaning over the bed. Flop didn't answer. He was playing it cautious. Grandma Otis hadn't gone out yet, she might come back.

Oliver kneeled on his bed and inspected the bookshelf. *Catch-22* caught his eye. It looked a very fat paperback indeed, but at least it was about war. *Catcher in the Rye* didn't look very interesting, leastways not the cover, farming had never interested him much really. The Secret Seven books he was definitely going to give a miss too, and all the soppy Mills and Boon books with 'love' stories in them. Yuk.

"It's *Catch-22* Flop. If I'm going to be in bed all week, we're going to need a very fat book to get through it."

He plumped up his pillows, sorted out Radio One on his radio, turned up the volume and opened the book. He was ready. He was going to be 'good' even if it killed him.

Lena was downstairs, helping Grandma Otis put her coat on. There was a healthy smell of baking going on and Grandma Otis was quite calm.

"This coat's getting bigger, I swear."

"You just don't get out much, that's all. The taxi will be here in a minute. Old Mrs Standley will have a nice warm room for you. You'd think she'd have had done with the future by now."

"It's her daughter. She's contemplating divorce."

"But isn't she married to the deputy governor of the Bank of England?"

"She is. Divorce is a big thing in those rarefied circles. Maybe they're hoping Quon can see his way to the other side of it."

There was a toot from the taxi outside. Grandma Otis took Lena's hand.

"Take care of the boy. He's strong. He is stronger than both his mother and father, but he's just too trusting. I just don't think it's all over yet. You know how my knees swell. I don't want him to set foot out of this house for a week."

"That's fine by me. You'll be back by six?"

"Yes. I don't like to stay too long. I get so tired these days."

Lena let her go, watched her walk with her stick towards the waiting taxi, reflecting that she hadn't seen the old woman leave the house of her own free will for months. It would do her good to get out and about.

She sniffed her baking scones. They'd be about ready. Good job Justine wasn't home, she'd eat them straight from the oven.

Outside it began to rain.

At six o'clock there was a knock on the door. Lena answered it and was surprised to find two young attractive girls there, all dressed in black and laden with shopping bags. They walked in, unasked, all smiles. They seemed to be there with a purpose.

"Where's the drowned rat? We've got tons of stuff from the Gap for him. Are you Lena? I'm Clare and this is Roxanne, Harriet sent us."

Lena sighed. "That boy is spoiled rotten. I suppose you'll be wanting coffee and scones as well?"

Clare looked at Roxanne and they laughed. "Yes, of course. Which way to the boy?"

Lena pointed to the back stairs and the two girls made their way noisily up the stairs, laughing and chatting. Lena listened, heard the shrieks as they found Oliver and smiled to herself. It would do the boy good, getting fussed over like that. She heard him protesting, but not very hard.

There was a sudden rush and Flop appeared, his fur all ruffled and panic in his expression. He hid under the table.

"Too rowdy up there for you eh, Flop? Don't blame you. Young girls these days. So much noise."

Old Joe didn't get the photo until the next day. Lena didn't have time to get to the library until then. She'd had to bring it herself as she was sticking to their resolution that Oliver wasn't to set foot out of the house. Joe took it from her in person. Lena still didn't think it was a good idea. Even if they found his father, somehow she knew it was only going to lead to disappointment, or at worst, they'd discover he was dead. Nevertheless, she handed the photo over and waited whilst Joe scanned it. She reflected on how competent the old man was and how it was such a waste no one would take him on for a job. But then again, she knew all about wasted lives.

"I will tell you if we get a reply." Joe told her. "Please, is the boy alright?"

"He's eating, despite his sore throat. He'll be fine. I'll tell him you asked."

Old Joe smiled. "He will find his father. I feel this. Tell him, I have found Greta. Now I must find money for her to come to me."

Lena thought he was going to ask for money from her, but he didn't. She didn't know who Greta was, but obviously she was important to him.

"I want to thank you for helping Oliver." Lena began, but Joe just smiled and shuffled away. He wasn't interested in Lena, or her thank yous. He had some work to do.

Lena left, clutching the all important photograph of Oliver and his father. She looked at it for the first time. His father was tall, handsome, he had a look of a man who knew what he was doing, what he wanted. Oliver looked happy, laughing, swung high over his father's head. All of four years ago. So much could happen to a family. The happy little boy turns into Oliver with a tumour, the father has disappeared, the mother, who must have taken the photo, had disappeared into her own world. Photographs revealed so much, could one predict the future from this photo? Why was this the most important picture to Oliver? Why didn't he have any more recent photographs? Wasn't his father a photographer? Perhaps this was indicative of his withdrawal from his family. The fact that he'd hardly taken any pictures of his son.

Lena looked at her watch. Time enough to visit Harriet's shop, have some coffee with her. She didn't see enough of Harriet. She needed to remedy that. Those girls she'd sent had cheered Oliver up. It was good to hear laughter in the house.

Justine came home early with a cold. She looked awful.

"Can't wait for this term to be over. Can't wait 'till the sun comes out and I stop feeling so cold," she told Oliver. He had immediately gone downstairs to make her a cup of hot lemon and get her some paracetamols from Lena's stash.

He sat at the foot of her bed as Justine sipped her hot drink, looking miserable with Vicks smeared under her nose and a tissue box beside her.

"Colds are horrible. Had one once for a month. Even Flop wouldn't come near me."

Justine looked at Oliver in his new hat and shook her head. "You must be bored."

"No. Actually I've been reading and thinking and Lena made me listen to a play on the radio. I didn't even know they had plays on the radio. It was good too, just like a movie, but it goes on in your head."

Justine was continually surprised by Oliver. How could you *not* know there were plays on the radio. Her own mother was addicted to *The Archers* though quite why she was interested in farming folk was beyond her.

"Here, take these."

Justine looked at the pills Oliver offered her. "What are they?"

"Lena's headache pills."

Justine took them and quickly swallowed them. "I feel like I swallowed cotton wool. My arms feel like lead. I can't believe I got a cold now. I've been well all winter."

"You want a hot water bottle? My mother always put me to bed with a hot water bottle when I had a cold."

Justine tried smiling. She was shivering. "Yes."

Oliver was away in a flash.

Justine finished her hot lemon and set the cup down. She curled up in the bed and hauled the duvet over her. She was really cold now she thought about it. It was exams in a week, she was supposed to be revising and she felt sick from the tension. Why did school have to be so hard all the time, why did they have to learn so much?

Oliver came back with a hot water bottle, carefully wrapped in a tea towel so it wouldn't burn her. Justine was already asleep but he slipped it under the duvet and put it near her tummy, just like his mother did with him, so long ago.

Justine opened her eyes a moment, grabbed the hot water bottle and hugged it. It soothed her. "Thanks." She muttered, but Oliver was long gone.

17. Aura s Return

Another day had passed of confinement. Oliver had managed three whole chapters of *Catch-22* and he was really into it now. It was definitely the best war book he'd ever read (not that he'd read many). He wasn't sure that he was supposed to laugh, but it did make him laugh out loud and instinctively he understood that this was the real truth of war. This was what his father had always said to him, war is stupid, no one ever really wins anything, and everyone loses.

He was sat by the living room radiator. He was dressed in his new Gap sweater and jeans. They had chosen him some really cool stuff to wear. The day before Clare and Roxanne had stayed a whole hour and made him try on everything. Clare promised him a new hat too. She'd said he could never have enough hats. The radio was playing and Flop was sprawled out across the sofa. All was right with the world. Oliver had even removed his bandage and was wearing a strange squashed white cricket cap until he got his new one.

Grandma was upstairs, sleeping, and Lena was out shopping and Justine was grumpy in bed with her cold and didn't want company. Oliver had almost stopped coughing himself and although he did sneak a look outside from time to time, he was content to stay home, and indeed he felt safe there.

An hour later the front door bell rang. Oliver put his book down and raced to the door. He struggled with the ancient lock, but finally got it open.

Aura stood there, she carried an overstuffed red shoulder bag on her back and was dressed in green overalls with blue Converse pumps. She smiled. She looked so beautiful and radiant that Oliver just stared.

"Well, don't just stand there!"

Oliver just wanted to hug her, he could hardly bare to give her the time to come in, set her bag down and close the door.

They hugged. It was like they'd known each other a lifetime. Oliver clung onto her and she kissed the top of his head as she rocked him from side to side. Neither one of them said a word.

Aura held him like this for almost five minutes and Oliver could have hung on for thirty minutes more. He let go eventually and rather sheepishly backed away.

"I don't know how to thank you." He began.

Aura smiled and kicked off her shoes. "That hug will do. Some nice scars you've got there, Oliver. How's your head?"

Oliver removed his hat to show the new wounds. Aura inspected them.

"Nice, looks like the sort of cut they make when they remove your brain."

Oliver laughed and this seemed to melt the distance between them.

"Are you better? I called your home and they said you had new..." Oliver wasn't exactly sure how to say it.

"No, I didn't have pneumonia. But I was sick. Something in the water. God knows what they pour into it. Your skin looked burned when they took you out of the water, so imagine what our insides are like now we've swallowed that stuff."

Oliver acknowledged that well enough. "I had a scratchy throat."

"Tell me about it," Aura agreed. "Still, we're alive."

Oliver smiled. "Come on, come to the kitchen. I'm going to make you some tea. We've got cake too."

Aura laughed and allowed herself to be led towards the kitchen. She was glad to see Oliver in one piece and looking happy. She enjoyed seeing him so excited and anxious to make her feel at home.

"I've got some news about Bullet." Aura told him as they walked into the kitchen.

Oliver was all ears as he poured water into the kettle and switched it on.

"What? Has he been back to the library? Did you know they showed his photo on TV? I didn't see it, but I heard."

Aura sat down at the table and set her bags down.

"He robbed a hotel in town. Got himself on CCTV again. I don't think Bullet is very smart. He used a gun and he left a man tied to a bed in the hotel. Took his keys and looted some rooms. The police were at the library because Audrey called them, told them she recognised his photo on the TV. Anyway, he's wanted everywhere and he's going to be locked away for a long time when they get him."

"Do you think he'll come back here?"

"He'd be stupid to come back here, but you can't rely on him not to do anything stupid. He's banned from the library and Audrey will call the police the moment she spots him. He was with you when you fell into the river, wasn't he?"

"He stole Mitch Michaels' gun. Found it under his pillow. Bullet didn't want me to get caught. He told me to jump down to the balcony below."

Aura looked at him with a bewildered expression. "Harriet told me why you were there. It all sounds so bizarre. I can't believe you survived the fall. I've looked at the building. It was lucky the river was at high tide."

"I was floating in the river, I remember. I kept thinking that I needed to surround myself with something to keep me warm. I remember a big shell, it was right around me and I was thinking about you. About how cross you'd be with me and..."

The kettle boiled and Oliver busied himself with the business of making tea. Aura watched him with a little smile on her face. He looked so confident, so used to looking after himself.

"What have you been doing with yourself?"

Oliver poured the milk and pointed to the sugar. Aura declined.

"I've been reading a book. *Catch-22*. It's about the war. About pilots who have to fly and all they want to do is go home, but they keep saying you have to fly more missions. The only way you can go home is if you are crazy."

"And you have to be crazy to fly, that's *Catch-22*." Aura remembered.

"Maybe it's only crazy people who are interesting to write about? Shakespeare wrote about people who were crazy about killing people, or insanely in love. We're doing *Othello* for our final production next year. I want to play Iago, but no doubt I will end up playing a girl."

"But you are a girl."

Aura narrowed her eyes at him and looked as mean as she could. "Yes, but sometimes I'd like to play a man. Try to understand how a man thinks." She frowned suddenly. "Do you understand *Catch-22*?"

"I like the book. I can't pronounce the names, but I like the book."

Aura grinned at his oh-so-serious expression. He slid the mug of tea over to her and she took it gratefully.

"Do you want any of Lena's cake?"

"Uh-uh. Cake is not what my tummy needs right now. I'm still getting cramps."

"I'm sorry."

"Hey, at least I'm not covered in new scars."

Oliver was looking at her and realised what it was that was different.

"You've changed your wig. Why is it so short?"

"Wig? I'll have you know that this is my real hair. My wig went the same way as your hat. Someone will probably find it on the beach down in Gravesend and think someone else has lost their head, or been scalped."

Oliver smiled, although he was sorry she had lost her wig.

"Here, I've got a present for you. It's in the bag."

Oliver leant right over the table and opened up her shoulder bag. He dragged it over to him and pulled out the Boots bag. He looked at it with some astonishment and then realised it was a joke. "Shampoo?" He laughed and Aura grinned, pleased to see him laugh and not take offence.

"Now if that isn't an incentive for your hair to grow, I don't know what is."

"It'll grow now, for sure." Oliver agreed, laughing again.

"Is your Grandma in? I called first. She said to go up."

"You want to meet Grandma Otis?"

"I've got something to discuss with her, actually. It's something they found whilst I was in hospital."

Oliver immediately knew what she meant. "You're sick again? Is it my fault? Did I make it come back?"

Aura clasped her hands around the hot tea mug and smiled at him. "It's not the same. Actually, I suppose I should thank you. I don't think they would have found it if I hadn't gone into the clinic after being in the river." She shrugged. "It's just a lump on my leg. I'm scared, that's all. This stuff doesn't entirely go away, you know. It likes to turn up in other places. I just wanted to talk to your Grandma... I can't talk to my stepfather."

Oliver knew what she meant. She wanted to talk to Quon. He came around the table and gave her a hug again. "Don't get sick. Please. I ..." There was a lump in Oliver's throat. He realised that he loved Aura. She was the most beautiful person he'd ever known and he just wanted her to be his friend forever. Just looking at her made him feel better. He wished his hugs could do the same for her. Aura hugged him back. It was different this time. It was like they were both drowning again and neither one knew who was supposed to be the rescuer.

"I'd better go and see her," Aura said after a few moments. "I'll take my tea with me. We'll talk after."

Oliver let her loose and Aura placed a finger upon his nose. "Come on, show me to your Grandma. I hear she's quite a dragon lady. She doesn't spare people the truth."

Oliver shrugged. He didn't know about that. He went over to the kitchen door.

"Wait. We'd better take her some tea. She'll be cross if we don't take her some tea. Better make one for Justine too. She's sick with a cold."

"They've got you trained quickly then." Aura commented with a smile.

"It's the only thing we have him trained in," came the comment from the door as Justine shuffled in wearing her pyjamas.

Aura smiled at her. "Hi. You look terrible."

"I feel it." She looked at Oliver. "Where's my tea, Oliver. You promised to look after me."

"Just making it."

Aura looked at Justine and there was a small awkwardness between them. "Thanks for getting my clothes back to me."

"No problem," Justine answered. "You were very brave. I couldn't have done what you did."

"It was weird but..." Aura just shrugged.

"No it was amazing. I heard you were really sick. Did you get the blisters on your skin like him?"

Aura nodded. Justine looked appalled.

"What do they put in the river these days. It's disgusting."

"My doctor thinks it was benzene or something. Some chemical anyway. Frankly I'm surprised Oliver survived at all."

"I did. But only because *you* came for me."

"Got to see his Grandma." Aura told Justine as Oliver had the cups of tea ready.

Justine acknowledged this and let her go. She turned to Oliver. "Boil me an egg, Oliver. I need to eat."

"OK. Just as soon as I've taken this to Grandma Otis."

Aura grinned at Justine. "Keep him busy. That's what he needs."

Grandma Otis was indeed impressed with Oliver when he brought her tea and Aura.

"My goodness, I knew Oliver was smitten, but you are truly beautiful my dear. Just look at you. And to think you hide that lovely figure under those awful men's overalls."

Aura smiled. She didn't mind the insult about the overalls, but she was not used to people thinking she was beautiful, but it had happened more often since she she'd lost the black wig.

"Hello, Mrs Otis. I hope you didn't mind me wanting to talk to you. I know I came to see Oliver, but..."

Grandma Otis dismissed her remarks with a wave of her arm. "My dear, I will speak to you for as long as it takes and as many times as you want. You saved Oliver's life and there's no price on that. It takes a lot of guts to dive into this river. I can remember when I was a girl, several of us going swimming one hot day, two of the girls died a week later; the water was so poisonous. My father wanted to beat me for being so foolish, he would have, too, if I hadn't developed a fever. You are brave and foolish. I hope Oliver has thanked you."

Aura pulled Oliver close to her and squeezed his shoulders. "Oh, he's been a gentleman. Sent me flowers and hugged me. He's alive and that's what counts."

She leaned towards Oliver's left ear and whispered. "Leave me alone with your Grandma for a while. There's something else for you in my bag. It's blue."

Oliver turned to her and smiled. Aura gave him a quick peck on his head and Oliver was out of there. Both Grandma Otis and Aura watched him go.

"He's taken to you." Grandma Otis observed.

"I like him. He's quite different. He's like you, isn't he. I mean, psychic?"

Grandma Otis looked at Aura carefully and invited her to sit beside her.

"He's going to be very strong one day. A mind as clear as a bell. I think that's the problem. People pick up on it and he doesn't know how to shut it down."

"He called me y'know? When he was on the river. He was unconscious, but he was calling me."

Grandma Otis looked at Aura, took her hand and squeezed it. "I heard him talking to his cat the other night. He was talking about you. He's..." Grandma Otis searched for the right words. "I think he loves you. He's never had any love, you understand? His mother, my daughter, was too wrapped up in herself, and his father has left him to grow up wild. I think he sees you as someone special."

Aura felt a little uncomfortable. It was not every day you had to cope with the concept of a boy of twelve being in love with you, but she understood it for what it was. It was this love that had saved him, made him call out to her.

Grandma Otis sipped her tea and flipped Aura's hand over to take a look at it.

"I know your stepmother, you know?"

Aura didn't know.

"She came to me last autumn. Your stepfather. You fight with him a lot?"

Aura nodded, glad they were onto another subject now.

"You know Denis McTeal?"

"I know of him. He's a professional. He's studied and he doesn't exploit people the way others do. But... He doesn't treat his women well. She tells me that he didn't visit you in hospital when you were a child."

Aura found herself surprised. It was something she had forgotten. All those months she'd lain in hospital wanting her stepfather to come and he hadn't. Something about 'bad vibes' in the hospital. How he hadn't wanted his work affected by the negative waves in the wards.

"My stepmother came."

"So did your real mother. You don't like her though, do you?"

Aura shrugged. "It's hard to like someone who abandoned you. She hated my father and my stepfather. I don't pretend I love Denis, either, or that he loves me, but he has never let me down since then. He always keeps his word. My mother treated us both very badly. We never talk about her."

Grandma Otis nodded. That was the truth spoken there. She could work with Aura.

"Aura, I'm going to make contact with my guide Quon. I want you to relax and think of what it is you want to ask him. Be patient and consider your questions well. Quon will tell you the truth, but sometimes we don't want to hear it. I can't take responsibility for what he might say, dear, but he means well. Now relax, wait, be prepared."

Aura watched as Grandma Otis began some deep breathing, settling back into her pillows. She let her eyes wander around the cluttered room. It was just as she had imagined it. A magical place filled with all kinds of strange and mundane objects. Grandma Otis filled her with hope and dread, fear, optimism, every manner of sensation. Just how bad was the lump on her leg? Was this it? Would her life end here? Would Quon really tell her the truth if that was so?

Grandma Otis was looking calmer and Aura began to detect a faint green glow emanating from her. She was entranced. How was this possible? There was no need for fakery. There was just the two of them. What was going on here?

Next door, Mr Ng looked up from his kitchen window. He felt a twinge. He knew what it meant. That woman next door was talking to the dead ones again. He automatically moved to a switch on his wall and flipped it. Immediately, he was surrounded by a hundred illuminated owls, all of them concentrating their power on Grandma Otis' house. He went back to his work carving a small animal object. He was safe. The spirits couldn't get him. Not whilst the owls were alive.

Oliver was looking at the contents of the blue bag with a sense of guilt. It was money. A roll of cash. The roll of cash that Bullet had stuffed down his shirt in Mitch Michaels' apartment. He didn't know how much it was, he didn't dare count. There was a note from Aura enclosed.

**Don't worry he won't miss it. You've earned it.
Start a savings account and think of all the hats you can buy!
Love Aura xx**

Oliver didn't know what to do, but he knew that he couldn't just leave it around. He moved over to his coat and placed the roll in his inside pocket. A savings account made sense. He'd always wanted to have some of his own money.

Justine emerged from the downstairs bathroom. "My egg ready?"

Oliver whipped off a tea-cloth and revealed a boiled egg in an egg cup, two rounds of toast, a mug of tea and a flower from the garden in a little vase.

Justine smiled. "You finally found a career. Waiter. Excellent. I hope the egg is soft. I hate it if it goes hard."

Justine sat down at the table and chopped off the top of the egg. It was perfect.

"I just upgraded you to chef."

"Thanks." Oliver smiled, sipping on his own cup of tea.

They looked up when he heard a sound. Lena was back. She was fiddling with the key outside the back door.

He went to the door. She'd need help with the groceries.

Upstairs Aura was crying. Quon was still talking to her, but hot tears were flowing down her cheeks as he did so. She asked questions, Quon answered. It was much like seeing her doctor, only more honest. Quon told her the truth.

Aura wanted to stop, but Quon had something else to say and she didn't know how to stop him. She didn't want to upset Grandma Otis.

Downstairs, Lena was full of chatter. Pleased to see that Justine was up and eating. She seemed to have emptied Sainsburys of everything they had. Oliver counted over twenty plastic bags. They were heavy too.

"I do this once a month, it saves money and time." Lena explained to him. "The traffic is a nightmare. I was thirty minutes trying to get through Blackheath. I don't know why they don't sort the traffic out around here."

"We should fly," Oliver suggested, but not too seriously. "Y'know, like in *Back To The Future*? Or was it *Bladerunner*? I forget. No, it was both. We should have flying cars."

"Flying cars will bump into each other." Justine remarked. "Won't work."

Lena was putting the cans away when she looked at him with a strange expression on her face.

"You know, you've just broken my dream. I dreamt I was a young girl again and I was flying all over the city. I flew right up to people's faces and they didn't even see me. I was so happy. I just loved flying."

"I don't. You get bruises."

Lena looked at him and shook her head. "I said flying, not crashing. Not diving from tall buildings. You've never had a flying dream?"

Oliver thought about it. "No."

Lena shrugged. "You will, one day. They are always beautiful dreams."

"I had one. I was flying naked across London and dying of embarrassment that someone would see me." Justine commented.

"Typical anxiety dream." Lena told her. "My flying dreams are happy ones."

Oliver made no comment about that. He just handed Lena the tins and packets and she methodically put them away.

"Grandma Otis will want a cup of tea."

"I took her one. She's got a visitor."

Lena looked surprised. "Oh?"

"Aura McTeal."

"Ah. Your knight in shining armour. That's sweet. I'm so glad she called. She must be feeling better. Did you give her some tea?"

Oliver nodded and Lena smiled.

"No wonder you look happy."

Oliver wasn't aware that he looked happy. "She isn't better."

Lena stopped with the food a moment. "What do you mean?"

"She isn't better. She's speaking to Grandma now."

Lena said nothing. She continued to put the things away.

A little while later Oliver heard his name being called. He ran to the hall and Aura was waiting there, putting her shoes back on. He could see her red eyes and the tear stained cheeks, but he didn't say anything about them. Instead, he fetched her shoulder bag, putting on his own shoes and walked with her outside.

Neither one of them spoke as they walked. Oliver took her hand and she squeezed back. Oliver shivered in the cold wind, but he wouldn't have gone back in for his jacket even if it had been snowing.

They sat on a bench in the garden and Aura blew her nose, trying to get back to normal. The mournful sound of cars being crushed in the scrap yard made things worse somehow.

Finally Oliver could stand it no more. "What did Quon tell you?"

Aura smiled and brushed her hair back with both hands. "It's going to be alright. Another operation, but not like before. He doesn't think they'll use chemo. He even thinks I'll marry and live a long life." She was sounding too brave, too strong. She could hear the hollow ring in her voice, she saw Oliver's pale face looking up at her, registering what she was saying, hearing the hope in her voice. "I'll be fine, really. These lumps come all the time. It's just a scare, y'know? It'll be benign, Quon says it will be benign."

Oliver shook his head. He could hardly bear to look at her. "You can't be sick. You just can't be sick. They won't shave your head again, will they? Quon said no chemo." At the back of his mind he was thinking about himself. If someone as beautiful and healthy as Aura could get sick again, what would happen to him?

Aura put a hand out to his own head and gave him a squeeze.

"No chemo. Besides the lump is on my leg. I had one removed last year. See?"

She partially rolled up her right trouser leg and showed Oliver her pale white scar situated below the back of her knee. She placed his fingers on the new lump, only inches from the last. Oliver could feel something hard under the skin. "Listen, if you can survive the river, I can survive this." Aura added.

"I should be thanking you. This might have got a lot worse before they found it. We're always going to be scared, Oliver, you and me. We're always going to have to be watching out for lumps and scars and headaches and you are going to have to watch out for me and I'll watch out for you."

Oliver withdrew his hand and looked at her. "We will stay friends?"

Aura smiled. "We will stay friends. I saved you, one day you might need to save me."

Oliver liked that idea. "I had a dream about you last night. You had a dog. A small sick dog and it ran to me, put its head on my lap. I was scared Flop would see it, but he can't see my dreams."

Oliver suddenly noticed that Aura was looking upset. He'd obviously said something wrong here. "What? What did I say wrong?"

Aura shook her head, trying to stop another tear rolling down her face.

"I'm sorry. I'm just falling to pieces today. It's just that I had a little black dog once. Crapper. No, don't laugh, I called him Crapper because he was always messing up my father's carpet. Nowhere else, just that carpet. When my mother ran off with the tennis player, she missed Crapper and she came back one night and stole him. She claimed Crapper was hers. He always slept with me, but she said he was hers. God, I never missed my mother, but when she took my dog, I think I wanted to die. A week later they discovered I had the brain tumour and..." she sighed. "I suppose it's stupid, but I've always thought that if my mother hadn't taken Crapper I wouldn't have been so sick."

Oliver understood this completely. He took her hand and squeezed it.

"When I got sick and they took Ma away, they tried to take Flop, too. But he hid. No one fed him, he just fended for himself, until one night I had a dream about him. I made my nurse, Susan, go and look for him. She did and she brought him back to the hospital, although he wasn't supposed to be there. I kept him in an old shed. He hated it, he hated the hospital food just as much as me, even though he was really starving. But Flop told me that he knew I was going to get better and that's why he'd waited for me to send for him when I could."

Aura just cried then. Two sad pet stories. Oliver held her hand and she just cried, sat there and sobbed, unable to stop.

Grandma Otis was watching them from her bedroom window, Lena at her side. They could both see that Aura and Oliver were sat still in her car and they both could guess what the conversation was about. Lena was the first to say something.

"It's always the most delicate blooms that die early. Damn weeds go on forever."

"She'll make it. She's got guts. It's good Oliver has her as a friend." Grandma Otis mused. "I wish I'd had a daughter like her. There's not a mean streak in her."

When Oliver came back into the house, he was subdued and didn't feel much like reading. He went up to his room and huddled with Flop. Perhaps he had always known that he was always going to have problems? No one who has ever had a tumour escapes problems, but from the moment he'd seen Aura, and then discovered she'd had the same sickness, he had been inspired. He'd seen in her hope for his future. She was lively, beautiful, strange, in a way he'd never seen before. She had been ill and survived. Now she was sick again. He knew she was being brave, saying it was just another lump... But it was as if a door had opened when he met her and now slammed shut in his face. This was going to be his life. You'd get well, then – wham! – a lump, or headaches, or another tumour. It never completely went away. He'd never actually realised this until Aura had shown him her lump, her scars on her legs and her head. It was as if, yes, you can be all you want to be, but enjoy it, it won't last long.

And about Aura. He realised he was being foolish, but now he knew what it was he was feeling. He loved her. He loved her as much as Flop. Even more. He could look at her and feel stronger. He could look at her and feel as if he could fly. He knew she only saw him as a kid, but it didn't make the feelings go away. He'd had no one to hug for such a long time and Aura was the most huggable person he knew in the world. Well, that wasn't true. Harriet hugged him, but that was embarrassing mostly and she, well, she was Harriet. Aura was Aura. He didn't know exactly how to explain these things. He didn't know why you loved one person more than another, or why some people liked you and others didn't. He just knew that Aura was like, well, like one of Lena's hot scones when it came out of the oven. You had to eat it right then, even if it was too hot, because that's when it tasted and smelled its best.

Flop stirred and yawned in Oliver's face. He gave Oliver a quick lick, then resettled in a different position, happy to have this unscheduled cuddle in the afternoon.

"I'm going to have to be careful, Flop. I don't want to get sick. I just want my hair to grow back and be normal. Do you think I'll ever be normal, Flop?"

Flop opened one eye and stared at him for a second. Oliver knew what he was thinking. Flop wasn't being polite. It wasn't right your own cat could be sarcastic, but that was the way it was between him and Flop. They both knew each other pretty well. Oliver knew that he was never going to be normal, not if he could see a dead person speak. Even if it was in a dream. He just knew that other people would have to be normal.

There was a knock on his door. Lena was there with a cup of tea and someone else.

"Detective Kray is here to see you, Oliver. Can she come in?"

Flop did his usual disappearing act and Oliver sat up, blinking. His heart began to race. The police, in his room. Were they going to arrest him? What about the money in his coat? He suddenly felt a wave of nausea and fell back on his bed, the room spinning.

Detective Kray swam into view, her slim body swaying above him. Lena left them to it. "That's a nasty cut on your head, Oliver. I don't suppose you'll go swimming in the river again in a hurry, eh?"

Oliver struggled to get up, but Detective Kray could see he was a bit distressed. "It's alright. You can lie down. A knock like that on your head? I'm surprised they haven't kept you in hospital longer. I just want to show you a few photographs. You're not in trouble. But someone is and I think you can help us."

Oliver tried deep breathing. It helped a little. The words *'You're not in trouble,'* helped too. "I'll help," he answered at last. "I can't remember much..."

Detective Kray handed Oliver his mug of tea and sipped some of her own. Oliver noticed for the first time that she wasn't wearing a uniform, but an ordinary grey tracksuit. Did Detectives wear tracksuits?

"Well, we have pieced together some information. It doesn't matter if you can't remember everything. We know you were in the gardens outside Heritage Wharf, but just one of you entered Mr Michaels' apartment. Were you supposed to be the look-out?"

Oliver sippped his tea, frantically trying to remember the story he'd discussed with Harriet. "I was just going to see if Mr Michaels was there. I had this dream that it was his body I found and..."

Detective Kray nodded, getting out her notebook. "Yes, your Grandma told us about your dream. It's quite fantastic. In ordinary circumstances I wouldn't pay much attention to that kind of phenomena, but since you did find his dead dog and his body, that makes you very special. Personally I'm surprised you didn't have nightmares."

Oliver nodded. "Grandma said they were nightmares. But they were so real."

"And that's why you went to see where he lived?"

Oliver hesitated. "Yes. I got his address and I was on my way when Bullet..."

Detective Kray showed Oliver a photo. It was of Bullet. It was poor quality, but it showed Bullet with a gun pointed at a man. "That's Bullet. What's he doing?"

"Holding up the Kent Hotel, with the gun he stole from Mr Michaels. How did he get into the building, Oliver?"

"There was a balcony open. I told him we had to go through the front door."

Detective Kray noted this. "We had an intruder reported at a ground floor apartment. So what did you do?"

"He went in and I waited for him."

"So how did you end up in the river?"

Oliver couldn't tell the truth now. He had already lied about not going into the apartment. He wondered if they would catch him out in the lie. Did they have a picture of him there? There were cameras in the corridors in that building, he had seen them. Were they holding it back? Just waiting to prove to him he was a liar? Would this mean they would take him away? Put him into care? The feeling of nausea came back.

"That's what I don't remember. I was standing by the river. Then this..." He indicated his head. "I'm sorry. I didn't take anything. I just wanted to know if Mr Michaels was dead."

Detective Kray sighed and looked up out of the window. "Of course. Mr Michaels had been dead for a week before you went to his apartment. I was just clutching at straws. Hoping you'd seen something."

"Did you catch Bullet yet?"

Detective Kray shook his head. "We will. He's monumentally stupid. Steals a gun, robs a hotel. He's been selling drugs. We've got informants on the street wanting us to get him before he kills someone. He just doesn't seem to live anywhere."

"He doesn't live anywhere." Oliver remembered something. "He's got keys. Lots of keys."

Detective Kray noted that down. "Does he have any place he likes to go to?"

Oliver thought hard about this. Bullet had to be caught, but he didn't want to be the one Bullet blamed for it. What if he came looking for him? With a gun? Bullet would use it. For sure.

Detective Kray smiled. "You wouldn't be holding something back, would you? You know a lot about him. He isn't worth protecting, y'know? He is going to end up killing someone. Boy like that, out of control."

"He doesn't have any real friends. That's why he talked to me. Hasn't he been back to the library?"

Detective Kray shook his head. "He knows he won't be welcome. Besides we think he's got money now from Mr Michaels' apartment. We found a lot of cash there he hadn't had time to take."

Oliver frowned, he had an odd thought. "I want you to catch him. Before he kills someone."

Detective Kray looked at Oliver with surprise. She'd heard the sudden passion in Oliver's voice. She couldn't look at Bullet with the same eyes, but she could see that Bullet had made an impression upon Oliver. Easy enough for an older kid to do.

"We will catch him. I'll make sure he gets put away."

Oliver looked at the Detective with a tired expression and she smiled back at him.

"Now you get some rest and look after your head. It's the only one you've got. If you remember who pushed you into the river, you let me know, alright? Just remember, whoever pushed you in, didn't expect you to come out alive. You absolutely sure it wasn't Bullet?"

Oliver blinked. "Bullet was up in the apartment. I heard shots. That's when I fell in. When there was shooting."

Detective Kray nodded. "You see, you do remember something. Someone pushed you in. You might not have seen them, but someone pushed you in."

Oliver clammed up then. This is where the truth and lies separated.

"Take care, Oliver. Stay out of trouble and stay away from Bullet."

He heard Detective Kray talking to Lena on the way out and he wondered if she'd known he was lying. He knew they could probably charge him with trespass. Why hadn't they? Would he be punished for saying he hadn't gone into the apartment? His fingerprints would be there. He felt this terrible hot flush of guilt. He hated having to lie.

Grandma Otis was calling him.

"Coming, Grandma!" What did she want? She was going to tell him off for lying to the police. He was going to get it now.

"Come into Lena's room, there's a documentary on Africa you might like."

Oliver was once again caught by surprise. She actually wanted him to watch TV.

"Coming now, Grandma."

It was ten o'clock. Everyone was going to bed and Oliver was carrying some hot Lemsip up to Justine to help her sleep, when she emerged ahead of him from the bathroom.

Oliver could see she had been crying. He was surprised. Justine was the strong one in this house, even if she did have a cold.

"What?' Oliver began, but Justine just shouted "Don't look" and ran up her stairs without answering.

Oliver shrugged. He carried her drink up behind her. At the top he was surprised to find Flop curled up on Justine's bed. The traitor found out.

"That's where you've been."

Flop opened one guilty eye but didn't budge. This was where the warmth was and besides it was his job to keep a sick person company, everyone knew that.

Oliver set her drink down and contemplated his cat's disloyalty. Justine looked away a moment. "It's my fault. I kidnapped him. Was feeling shitty and..."

Oliver shook his head. "Should have sent Flop up days ago. He'll make you better. He always makes me better. If he shakes his head a lot it means he wants to go pee. There's no catflap, so he has to tell us."

Justine looked at him a moment. "You're not cross with me?"

Oliver just smiled. "Flop is a house cat. He has to help everyone in the house."

Justine smiled briefly. "See, you are weird, anyone else would have been jealous. Pass me the new tissue box please... And don't look at me, I look like shit."

Oliver reached over and opened it up, raising the tissue a little so she could grab it more easily. He handed her the box and saw that Justine had pulled a letter out from under her pillow. It had a strange stamp on it.

"Can I ask you something?" She blew her nose, upset a little that there was blood in the tissue. "Urgh! Now I'm bleeding. This bloody cold is evil!"

"You need to use the Vicks more and drink the Lemsip, whilst it's hot."

"I'm sore, my throat hurts, I look like shit and I'm supposed to be revising. Life is sooo shit. I just..."

Flop stood up suddenly, stretched and sat down again, curled up the other way.

"I want to be a cat." Justine declared. "No exams, no pressures, you get cuddled..."

Oilver smiled. "Flop's lucky. Some people don't love cats at all."

"That would be me, wouldn't it. I'd be a homeless cat living off scraps and... I got this letter. I can't open it."

Oliver frowned. "Can't?"

"Won't. It scares me. Got it three days ago. I don't..."

"It's from your Dad?'

"Might be. Writing could be his."

"Why won't you open it?"

"I hate him. I hate what he did to us but..." Justine flopped back onto her pillow and buried her head. "I don't know what I think."

Oliver took the letter from her and just held it. Held it for what seemed like ages to Justine but wasn't more than five minutes or so.

"He's in Brazil."

"It says that?"

Oliver smiled. "No, the stamp does though. Look..."

Justine looked at it and saw only the scratchy writing that was most likely her father's, the one who had run away and left her mother to rot in jail and Justine in this cold attic with the madwoman and scary boy.

Oliver put the letter down, still unopened. He looked up at her and put his fingers out to Flop who touched them once and then settled back to sleep again. "You really want to know what he says?"

"No. Yes. No. I don't know."

Oliver handed her another tissue, for her eyes this time. He took a deep breath, abruptly noting that there was an old fading Donnie Darko poster on the wall. "He wants you to forgive him, Justine. He is living in a hotel. He doesn't say where. He's broke. Lawyer took his money and he is unhappy. Not coming back though. He says..." Oliver broke off. Suddenly uncertain.

"Justine? I don't know if I am reading his letter or something else. He thinks he's sick. Not sure he'll ever see you again." Oliver broke off. "Don't think I'll say anymore. "Read it. See if it's true."

Justine took a deep breath, opened the letter and cautiously read it, as if it might burn her. Oliver didn't look at her. Wasn't sure he had read it at all, didn't think he had understood it all. He could feel the heavy emotion of the man who wrote it and the thing he wanted to tell her, but hadn't. About some money. Justine abruptly let the letter drop to the floor. She looked at Oliver and frowned.

"What is Crohn's disease?"

Oliver had no idea but it didn't sound good. Any sort of a disease was bad, right?

"He's got to have his colon removed. People need their colon don't they?"

Oliver took her hand and squeezed it. "He's sick, he's in Brazil and he needs an operation. He wanted you to know. I think..."

"You think he's going to die."

"He wanted to tell you something about money. He didn't. He was afraid someone would read the letter. But if he dies... he has made sure there's something for you."

"You know this?"

Oliver shrugged. "I know nothing, Justine. Nothing. It's just a thought. It's hanging over the letter. I don't know how I can see it, but I see it. When was it sent?"

Justine examined the envelope, giddy with the idea that her father might die, that Oliver could have read that letter so exactly, without opening it. It was an astonishing gift. "Eighteenth of March. That almost two months..."

Oliver felt suddenly overwhelmingly tired. Flop mioued and he knew he had to go to bed and quickly. "Here..." Justine whispered seeing Oliver swaying. She leapt out of bed and unrolled a foam mattress from the corner. Oliver lay down and the last thing he remembered was a blanket being spread over him and Flop looking down, confused, totally unsure which bed to lie on all of a sudden.

"You're the best weirdest boy in the world," Justine whispered in his ears. "Thank you."

18. On Parole

Oliver was a prisoner for another five days. Never once allowed out of the house. Sometimes he thought that they weren't going to let him out until he actually finished *Catch-22*. He was deep into the characters of *Yossarian* and *Major-Majo*r now, but he wasn't sure he'd actually live long enough to finish the whole book. When Lena finally relented and told him that they were going up to town to buy him some school clothes, he had to tell her that they couldn't go straight away as he was finally on the last chapter and he wanted to see how it all turned out. Lena was impressed. It was a long time since she'd read a big fat book herself, and there was Oliver, tackling one of the fattest.

He hadn't realised war was so corrupt. He hadn't understood that there weren't many heroes, just people who got medals for surviving the stupid decisions that Generals made. He knew there'd be many other catches waiting for him in his life. Lots of them.

Grandma Otis was busy seeing clients when they left. He walked to the station with Lena. She was dressed up for the occasion, looked pretty elegant, too. She even smiled when they were sat on the train together.

"We'll have lunch at Café Arista in Covent Garden, then we'll go to John Lewis's on Oxford Street. You'll need a new jacket and some shirts and trousers. The uniform is optional at the school, Grandma Otis says you'll have to look at them, but you can choose."

"You mean you don't have to wear it?" Oliver was puzzled.

"It's that kind of school. Not everyone can afford a uniform, I suppose."

"So if I don't wear one they'll think I'm poor?"

Lena hadn't thought about it that way. "Perhaps we'd better get you a uniform."

Oliver nodded. He didn't want to stick out anymore than he had to. "And lots of hats. They'll steal my hats, I know they will. They'll pick on me because I'm bald."

Lena sighed. *'Yes, they will'* she was thinking and there wasn't a thing she or Grandma Otis could do about that. Bullying was still a big problem in the schools.

"Perhaps your hair will grow by September?" She suggested.

Oliver prayed every night for his hair to grow, but there wasn't anything there yet. September wasn't so very far away. He knew he'd still be bald by the start of term.

The journey was faster than he remembered and in no time at all they were walking out of Charing Cross station and crossing the Strand. "You've never been here before," Lena was telling him as they walked towards Covent Garden, "so don't get lost. If you do, make your way back to Charing Cross and wait for me in the little station café. You understand? Don't let me down, Oliver."

"I won't." He hoped that Bullet wasn't around. The police had to have arrested him by now, surely.

Café Arista was great. Oliver had never really sat in a French restaurant before, with real French waiters. He hadn't even known that Lena spoke French either. (Although she'd been pretty piqued to discover that their waiter was actually a Geordie, a film student from the London International Film School.) Oliver was impressed anyway. Especially when 'jambon anglais avec frites' turned out to be ham and chips. French food wasn't so different to English after all. He sat staring at a huge poster that had been painted onto the wall entitled *La Boheme*, an opera, Lena had informed him, although, the more he stared at the faded scary, misty picture of old rooftops and narrow streets, the more it looked like Greenwich. It seemed to have been signed by someone called G. Puccuni. He drank in the atmosphere. Loved the way the tables were jammed together and there wasn't really room to get between them and the windows which were like patio doors, indeed, some people were drinking coffee outside on the tables. The menu was behind him, chalked up on a huge blackboard. Lena had spent a long time looking at it before ordering and checking her watch. Oliver thought that somehow she was disappointed about something. Then, he heard a voice booming over them as a stranger approached.

"Oh, hello Lena, how delightful to see you. Is this your little boy?"

Oliver looked up and saw someone he knew really well, even though he'd never actually met him before. This was the presenter of 'Wackadoo'. Oliver had watched every show, every day when he was in hospital. It was the stupidest kids' show ever, but he loved it because everyone knew how stupid they were being.

Lena seemed flustered. "Richard. So nice to see you. This is Oliver. I'm his," she searched for the right word, "...guardian."

Oliver smiled. "Like Wackadoo. Watch it all the time."

Richard gave Oliver a smile that Oliver immediately knew meant *'shut up kid'*.

Lena looked at Oliver and he immediately knew what was coming. "Oliver, why don't you have a look around?" She fished out a tenner from her purse and gave it to him. "Go on, and don't get into any trouble. Be back here in an hour, alright?"

Oliver smiled. It was just what he wanted. He'd already guessed that this meeting had been pre-arranged. School uniforms could wait. "Thanks. I'll be back."

Oliver scooted out of there as fast as he could, before they could change their minds. It was impressive to meet someone on TV, but he didn't actually have anything to say to the man and he hadn't looked very interested. At least the mystery of why Lena had dressed up and chosen that particular restaurant had been solved. Oliver was sure that this man had turned up, as if he was expecting to eat with her. Never mind, now he was free for an hour and he could explore what he wanted without being nagged.

It was only as he left the restaurant that he realised they were close to the Opera House. He didn't know much about Opera, but he knew what he didn't like. He turned right and headed towards the crowds on James Street.

Half an hour later he'd completed a big circle, taking in the shops, craft stalls and the Transport Museum and now, a tad bored and wishing he hadn't wasted two pounds on a sickly ice-cream he hadn't really wanted, he found himself on Floral Street. He was staring in a small shop window at some Tin-Tin objects and wishing he could afford the giant red moon-rocket or at least a life-sized stuffed 'Snowy', when he felt a hand upon his shoulder.

"Not a fuckin' ghost after all. Well fuck me, it's that little snitch, Oliver the bald kid."

Oliver turned to face Bullet and got quite a surprise. Bullet had changed completely. He was sporting a razor haircut, wearing a smart suit and Timberland leather boots. This was a completely different Bullet.

"This is my turf now. You need my permission to be here."

Same old Bullet, just a new uniform.

"Leave me alone. I didn't say anything."

"Cops looking for me. Had two walk right past me, just half an hour ago. Couldn't find me if I was to turn myself in and jump right into their arms. Where the fuck did you go, anyway? I checked the library. You haven't been there in weeks."

"I was in hospital."

Bullet sneered. "Got a cold did you? I figured you fell in the river. Arsehole. I told you to get down to the next balcony, not dive into the river. Lucky you didn't break your neck."

"I didn't dive. I fell."

"Yeah? Hurt yourself? Got any scars?" Bullet snatched Oliver's hat off and for a moment there he was actually shocked at the sight of the new scars, but the nanosecond of pity wore off and he flung the hat across the road. Someone passed by, but looked away.

"You have to leave. I don't want you here. Beat it, or pay."

"I haven't got any money."

"Well I have. Stupid kid. I got a lot of money. I got a place to live and I'm going to make me rich. No more fuckin' begging. You'd be surprised what you can get with a gun. Don't have to do anything, just show it. People just cram money into your hand."

"The police have photos of you."

Bullet smiled. "I was on TV. I'm famous. People are real scared of me now. So fuck off, kid. Get off my patch. You come here again, you'll regret it."

Oliver made to get his hat but Bullet shoved him on. "Leave it. Always covering your head. Show it, scare people, show them what a freak you are. Go on, run. RUN!"

Oliver turned and ran. He didn't know where to run, but he ran. He'd been humiliated by Bullet, but if that was all, he was lucky, he was getting away.

Bullet was shouting after him. "Run, freak, run. You fucking tell anyone about me, you're dead. You hear me? Dead. I know where you live."

Oliver ran down Floral Street until it turned onto Garrick Street. He didn't dare look back. He ran across the road and ducked into a Waterstones bookshop. He had to stop. His legs were shaking. He suddenly realised he was scared, truly scared. Bullet was quite capable of killing him. He'd never actually realised this before. He would kill him and laugh about it.

He had to sit, find some stairs, try to get back his breath. He slowly became aware of someone staring at him and he remembered with a burst of hot shame that he wasn't wearing his hat. He couldn't bear being outside without a hat. How could Bullet have been so mean? Why was he so mean? Why did he hate him so?

Oliver realised he could still be seen from the street and he certainly didn't want Bullet to accidentally catch sight of him. He walked up the stairs to the art section and he was still out of breath and shaky. He stopped in front of some prints, trying to make head or tail of them. There were pictures of naked women daubed with blue paint. He didn't understand them, but he'd look at anything to take his mind off what had just happened.

Oliver had been standing there, looking at the paintings for a few minutes now, when he became aware that there was also someone else casually browsing the pictures. Oliver suddenly had this creepy, electric feeling. He knew exactly who this person was standing next to him. He'd know him anywhere, seen his pictures, his strange ears, seen him in the flesh. Never mind how impossible it all was, how unlikely – Mitch Michaels was standing right beside him, studying the paintings.

Oliver forgot Bullet, forgot everything. He retreated to the end of the room and watched him. No mistake. It was him. He was even carrying a dog lead. Suddenly, Mitch Michaels about turned and headed down the stairs. Oliver was aware that he had forgotten to breathe. He took a huge intake of breath and made the decision to follow him. How could everyone have made such a mistake? How could he have thought the man was dead? Here he was, alive, walking around town. What was going on?

Oliver followed him out onto the street. Mitch Michaels walked with the air of a man used to the area, yet, there was something strange about him. Oliver followed. He wasn't concerned about Bullet now. He did think he should stop by a telephone and call Detective Kray, tell her what he was seeing. But he didn't want to lose his quarry.

He didn't have far to go. Mitch Michaels crossed St Martin's Lane and entered Pret-a-Manger. All that stainless steel could only mean fast coffee and pastries. Mitch was going to have coffee. Perhaps there would be time now to call the police.

Oliver followed him into corner coffee bar and took up a position at a tiny table by the door. Mitch Michaels was waiting to get served. The people behind the counter were taking their time about it, too. In fact, they let someone barge right by him and they served him first.

"Excuse me, I believe I was here first. That's my cappuccino."

The counter person completely ignored him and continued to serve the other customer. Mitch Michaels was getting upset now.

"Listen, I demand to be served. Do you know who I am? I want a cappuccino and ham croissant. Are you bloody listening to me? Where's the manager? I want the manager. God, I spend enough here. I want a coffee, dammit!"

Oliver looked around the coffee bar, no one was taking a blind bit of notice of Mitch Michaels, it was almost as if he wasn't there.

Abruptly, Mitch Michaels turned on his heels and began to leave. He saw Oliver looking at him. "I don't know what you're looking at." He snarled at him.

He left the coffee bar and went out into the street again. Oliver followed. He was beginning to think the impossible.

When Mitch Michaels started to hail a taxi and not even empty ones stopped, Oliver knew the truth. He steeled himself for this. He walked up to Mitch Michaels and spoke directly to him.

"They aren't going to stop, y'know."

Mitch Michaels looked at him with annoyance. "Are you following me? Leave me alone. I don't give autographs."

"Why did you take photos of Harriet?" He demanded angrily. "Why did you hurt her?"

Mitch Michaels looked at Oliver without comprehension. "Harriet? Who the fuck's Harriet? Stop hassling me, boy? Don't you know there are laws against stalking?"

He turned and practically stepped out in front of a taxi, only pulling back at the last moment. "Taxi! Goddamn it. Don't they even need a fare these days?"

Oliver had to tell him the truth. He just had to.

"They can't see you. You're dead. You drowned. No one can see you. You washed up on the beach. You've been dead for weeks."

Mitch Michaels looked at Oliver with no sign of comprehension whatsoever.

"Will you go away? I don't know what you are babbling about, but I hate boys and I hate freaky boys most of all, so bug off. You hear me? Taxi!"

"The taxi won't stop. You won't get coffee. No one can see you or hear you."

"You can see me. Stop talking rubbish and go. I have to find my dog."

"You won't find him. JJ is dead too. Don't you understand? You both are."

Mitch Michaels just didn't seem to comprehend.

"He's chocolate brown, a Weimaraner. He got away from me."

"He's dead." Oliver repeated softly and turned away. However, the man wasn't listening. When Mitch Michaels set off again, Oliver followed closely.

Mitch Michaels walked further down the street and went into Browns restaurant. Oliver didn't go inside. He knew what would happen. The same thing all over. He paused outside the glass doors and there was Mitch Michaels sat at a table, remonstrating with the waiters, trying to get served. No one could see him. No one could hear him. Oliver didn't question the fact that he could see him and hear him. He was the one who'd found his body. It made sense to him.

In the end, it was just too sad to watch anymore and Oliver realised that he had to get back to Lena. He didn't know what time it was, but he instinctively knew he was late. He did have a momentary fear that he would run into Bullet, but somehow he'd got over the shock of seeing him now.

Bullet couldn't stop him walking down the street. He wouldn't shoot him. He wasn't that stupid, was he?

Oliver cut through New Row towards Covent Garden once again, his head full of wonder. London had to be the most exotic place on earth. Dead men walking the streets, people like Bullet and Lena, not forgetting Grandma Otis. He wanted to stop and phone Justine, tell her what he'd seen, but he wasn't sure she would believe him. How could he prove it?

Oliver crossed Bedford Street and saw the familiar sight of old Covent Garden market ahead, surrounded by all the tourists. He'd be safe here. He could hear street music in the air.

"Hey you!" A voice shouted on King Street. Oliver's heart skipped a beat. He turned, afraid that he was going to come face to face with Bullet again. A clown reached down from his stilts and gave him a balloon.

"Don't look so serious, kid. You're young, you should be happy. What happened to your head?"

"Hit a tree."

"Is the tree in hospital? Do you visit it? Just what kind of tree was it?"

Oliver smiled. A clown, telling stupid jokes, giving out balloons. Yes, he liked London. He took the balloon. "Someone took the tree. I think they made stilts out of it."

The clown pretended to cry. "Oh, a comedian. I can't stand rivalry. I can't stand these stilts. Do you know how wet the weather is up here?"

Oliver laughed and walked on. The clown called after him. "Go on, leave me with these bruised stilts. You leave the trees alone. Hard head like yours should carry a warning: *'Trees beware – hard head ahead.'* Gee, try saying that with your teeth in. Don't leave me, kid. Come back, don't mistreat that balloon."

Oliver walked on, happy and smiling. He could still hear the clown yelling at people. He crossed the cobbled stones of Covent Garden, unmolested and five minutes later, when he walked back into Café Arista, Lena, all alone again, but in a daze, didn't even notice he was two hours late.

19. Lost and Found?

Two whole weeks had passed since that mad day in London when Lena had met a man and Oliver had seen Mitch Michaels' ghost. Little had happened since. The weather seemed to have improved and people talked of summer finally arriving, which meant they'd soon start complaining about the heat, instead of the cold. Justine had recovered in time to sit her exams, much to her relief. Oliver had started going to the library again, and Old Joe was still helping him getting messages out to South Africa and sometimes to Botswana, getting any messages to Zimbabwe was proving impossible. But Oliver knew now, he didn't exactly remember why, that his father was definitely alive, somewhere in Africa.

There had been no sign of Bullet and more importantly, Oliver hadn't had one bad dream, or seen one ghost. In fact, he seemed to be getting to be the most normal, boring person he could think of. Even Flop wasn't much interested in anything, preferring to lie out in the sun and luxuriate in the heat, catch the odd fly when he could be bothered.

Grandma Otis had announced that she was going to take them all to the sea. Not for her the mundane Torquay or Brighton, she had booked all three of them on the Eurostar. They would be travelling to Paris, then by train to Trouville, where they had been loaned a villa. She hated going by sea, even though one look at the map would indicate that it would be shorter. But, according to timetables, one could leave Waterloo and be in Trouville Station in little over seven hours, should one make the right connections, have God on your side, not lose any luggage, believe the timetable and providing no one was actually on strike on either side of the unlucky tunnel. Even if they did not achieve this, Oliver had already told her that he'd be happy to see Gare Du Nord and with luck, Paris itself. He felt sure Paris would be just the most amazing place, although Lena wasn't sure. She had the idea that Paris smelled of sewage and she'd sooner get to Trouville, which at least smelled of sea or horses, whichever interested one the most.

It was because Oliver was about to depart that Aura had come to take him out to tea. They'd entered the park by Circus Gates and walked all the way up the hill, past the Royal Observatory and out through the far gates, then even further across the barren heath to Blackheath Village. It was here they had scones and cake with her Aunt Sara Simmons, who'd once been an actress and had pictures of herself all over her walls to prove it. Oliver had never heard of most of the actors, but he was sure they were all quite famous. He was impressed by a picture of her with Oliver Reed, who he did recognise from the film *Gladiator*, but she seemed most proud of a film poster framed in the hall which showed her name under someone called Sophia Loren, who Aura assured him was once a huge film star. His query as to whether she had been more famous than *Wallace or Gromit* was met with stony expressions.

She'd been starring in *The Mousetrap* for ten years before her hips gave up the ghost. She wasn't complaining. She had a nice little house with a 'girl' to look after her, who was called Poppy, but Oliver didn't think that was her real name, as she was from Thailand. He'd thought her nice, but she was too shy to stay with them for tea.

It had been Aura's idea to walk. She'd had the new lump removed and it was just as Quon had said, benign. She didn't like the idea of her leg being so scarred, but at least she wasn't ill and to prove it, walked.

They'd left her aunt's at six. The evening was warm and breezy. People were flying kites on the heath and it looked to Oliver that there was a funfair beginning to assemble outside the Royal Gardens wall. That would be something he'd miss, but Trouville sounded alright to him, the villa was right by the sandy beach and there was even a sailing school nearby. He wasn't going to complain.

He was surprised at how sparse the heath was. How dry the grass seemed. The ground was cracked everywhere, as if the previous months' rain hadn't made the slightest difference. He was distressed at the lack of trees. He couldn't understand why no one had ever planted any trees. If it was his heath, he would have planted huge avenues of trees along the roads, at least it would hide the cars.

Aura took his arm. "I'm going to audition for a part in a film. It's about some girl who's a model by day and runs a gang at night and she writes songs which she thinks are going to change the world."

Oliver smiled. "You're sure to get that part. It's perfect for you."

Aura looked down at her legs. "Not if they see the scars."

"A girl in a gang would be proud of her scars."

"Oh yes? This is the boy who never takes his hat off, even in bed?"

"The doctor said I shouldn't get too much sun on it."

"It might stop the hair growing, wearing a hat all the time, did you think of that?"

Oliver hadn't thought of that, actually. Now, there was a dilemma. To wear a hat and be normal, or let the sun help his hair grow.

Aura smiled and put an arm around him, gave him a quick squeeze. "Try leaving it off for a couple of hours a day. Maybe get a tan on it whilst you're in France?"

Oliver nodded. He wasn't going to promise, but he was going to swim in the sea. He was really looking forward to that. Grandma had said they would eat fresh fish, every day, bought from the fish stalls in the harbour.

"Aura?"

Aura looked at him with a sly expression. "What? This sounds like one of those, two part questions coming."

Oliver laughed. "No. I just wanted to ask you something. I didn't discuss it with anyone else yet because they'll laugh at me."

"I never laugh at you. You're the strangest boy in the world, but I'd never laugh at you."

Oliver ignored that remark; he seemed quite serious all of a sudden.

"I don't know if this happened or if it was a dream or... I'm not even sure I should tell you this Aura."

"What? Don't look so serious. I already know you can see dead people. I mean, what could be worse than that. I'm sooo glad I can't. I would be seriously scared."

Oliver took a deep breath. He had to tell someone and Aura was the calmest person and most sensible (other than Justine) that he knew. "I went away whilst I was in hospital."

Aura looked at him more closely, she could tell immediately he *had* to say whatever he was going to say and wanted to be taken seriously. "Away?"

"I met Alfie. I saw him die and he took me to see my Ma and then we went to find my father."

"Alfie?" Aura was immediately thinking of some dud movie she'd given up on showing on TV. "You saw him die? This was in the hospital?"

Oliver shook his head. "Alfie's been dead sixty-seven years, so far. He was killed by a bomb in the war. He showed me it happening. I was never so scared before. I heard it fall, saw it explode. The noise was..." Oliver sought a suitable expression, but couldn't find the right word. "It was like the bomb went off inside my head. It dropped right on top of their house in Brand Street and his father was killed too."

Aura looked up at the sky a moment, following the flight of some geese. She was thinking that Oliver was doomed to a life like this, in and out of reality, the dead had found him and they wouldn't let him go now. She felt sorry for him. This would be his destiny, just like his grandma. Just like Mr McTeal, dependant on the misery of others for his living.

"But he's not a ghost, Aura." Oliver was saying. "He just showed me that, so I'd know how he died. Alfie's my guide. He's been sent to keep me alive."

Aura smiled, taking Oliver's hand and squeezing it. "I'm glad someone will. You are pretty determined to make life difficult for yourself."

"Alfie's my guide. I don't remember much of why now. He's about fifteen, I think. He's really thin and anyway, this is his first job, he said. But he took me to see my mother in the clinic, and she recognised me, just for a moment. And then, suddenly we were in Africa. It was hot, the sky was huge and the road was made of red dust. I thought he was going to show me my Dad, but Alfie couldn't find him. We found his car though."

Aura was listening. This was too fantastic, but it was interesting he had his own spirit guide now. He sorely needed one. "His car?"

"He'd driven it off the road. Dad had been shot at, but he'd tried to drive away from the gunmen, but got stuck. Half the car was burned, but he wasn't there. Alfie says he isn't dead, but he doesn't know where he is. What do you think that means?"

Aura could almost see it. The burned out car abandoned in a remote part of Africa. Perhaps it was his way of adjusting to the fact that his father wasn't ever coming back. She didn't know. She realised that she ought to say something sensible, but she couldn't think of a thing.

"Alfie said I probably wouldn't remember, but I do. Now. Now I've seen the sky." He waved his free hand at the clouds. "You can't see the sky at Grandma's, but this is like it was in Africa. It's empty. That's what I remember. Africa was empty and hot."

Aura smiled. "Well then, you really were there. I was in Kimberley once and that's what Africa looked like, big and empty."

"Kimberley?"

"Mr McTeal had a client there. Very rich client who was afraid he was going to lose everything. He took me, and my mother. My step-mother that is. We drove for miles until we came to this big mansion in the middle of nowhere and there he was, this little man who was so rich he could feed all of Africa for a year or more, if he wanted to. I just remember sitting on a swing in the garden listening to all the insects and then swimming in his gigantic pool." She smiled. "I'd forgotten about it. Thanks. That's a good memory."

Oliver still hadn't made his point. "Does this mean I'm going to end up like Grandma Otis? I mean, will I wake up one day and Alfie will be speaking through me, like her?"

Aura looked at Oliver with some concern. She hadn't actually considered this. It was the weirdest question she'd ever been asked, if only because it was probably true. He was going to develop the same talents as his Grandma.

"I think you have to..." She didn't know what to say. "If it happens, you'll know. At least you know it isn't bad. Your Grandma copes with it alright. Quon is a pretty nice guy. I mean... You might go years before it happens. Did you ask your Alfie what he intends to do? Did you ask your Grandma when it first happened to her?"

"She said it first happened to her when she was married and living in Africa. But I'm already seeing things."

"Oh yes, the famous ghost of St Martin's Lane. Lena told me about that. Actually, I thought it was kind of funny."

"Funny?" Oliver stopped in his tracks and confronted her. "Funny?"

"I mean, the way he was sat in Browns trying to get the waiters' attention. That's what my stepfather used to say all the time when he used to take me to restaurants uptown. "What do I have to do to get served here, die?""

Oliver didn't quite get it. "But that was the point, they didn't serve him because he's a ghost."

"You sure they weren't just ignoring him? Waiters can do that you know. They go to a special school where they learn to look past people without ever seeing them. People from all over Eastern Europe flock to London just to learn how to do it. English waiters are famous for it."

Now Oliver knew she was taking the piss.

"You're mocking me again."

"I am not. I liked your story about Mitch Michaels. I like to think he's wandering all his old haunts looking for his dog and never actually getting served. It's probably karma."

"Karma?"

"Karma's what you get for being who you are. It's a kind of spiritual booby prize. You're bad in this life, you get to be a toad in the next, or worse, a saint. That would be truly karmic."

Aura had lost him again. There was so much to learn. Oliver was wondering where Alfie went when he wasn't with him? Where did Quon go? So many questions.

They resumed walking again, enjoying the warm breeze. The road across the heath was blocked solid with traffic, but they were walking, it didn't affect them. They watched as someone cantered a snorting black horse across the heath. Oliver hadn't seen a horse since leaving Louth and even there, he hadn't seen many. It was a magnificent sight as the hooves beat out a rhythm on the turf.

Aura looked at her watch as they entered the straight avenue to the Royal Observatory. Every parking spot was taken. People loitered in cars, filled with hot, impatient kids and slavering dogs, all waiting for spaces. But it didn't matter, it was summer and the park was an oasis in a stark landscape. Oliver loved the place and all the rustling chestnut trees, and just then, in the distance, he could hear the sound of a military band playing.

"I promised to get you down to Harriet's for six." Aura remembered. "We're going to be late. Your girlfriend will be worried too."

"I haven't got a girlfriend."

"You mean to tell me that Justine isn't your girlfriend? Never seen a girl stare at a boy as much as her. She watches you like a hawk."

Oliver pulled a face. "I like her. Flop likes her and he's picky. But Justine likes older boys. She's never going to like me. No one likes the bald kid."

Aura took his arm and squeezed it. "You might be wrong there. I think Justine likes you a lot more than you think. Harriet is jealous."

Oliver laughed. "Now I know you're being mean. No one has seen Harriet for ages. She said she was busy. Do you think she's met a man?"

"I don't think there are any left this side of the river she hasn't met."

Oliver wasn't sure, but he thought that was a catty remark he'd just heard.

"I hope you get the part in the film. Do you think they'll need any bald kids in it?"

Aura laughed. "If they do, I'll make sure they call you, alright? Come on, let's cut through the park, get away from these fumes."

Aura ran off to the left through the open grassland. Oliver ran after her, watching with amazement as she suddenly cart-wheeled down a slope and ended with a forward roll. Oliver could only manage two forward rolls before getting into a muddle. Aura laughed at him and set off again. Oliver watched her run, then set off in pursuit once more. He laughed. He'd always wanted a friend like this, he hoped it would go on forever.

They'd arrived exhausted after running and fooling around. Somehow, it was nearly seven before they entered the market courtyard and approached Frock Lobster. They could hear the sound of soul music blaring out from the speakers and there appeared to be quite a party going on. Aura stopped a moment outside a shop window. "God, I look a mess! She didn't say she was having a party."

Oliver looked at the crowd of women and a few men crammed into the shop and saw how elegant they were, how loud. He heard the unmistakable 'pop' of a champagne bottle and the accompanying laughter. "Do you think we're welcome?"

"Welcome or not, I need something to drink. I'm really thirsty."

"Me too," Oliver declared. "Do you think she's got Coke?"

"She'll have everything, that's the kind of woman she is."

They entered the shop, squeezed their way to the makeshift bar. Oliver saw Clare and Roxanne serving there, although it looked to him that Roxanne had been serving quite a lot of whatever it was to herself. "It's Oliver!" She squealed, smiling. "Have you seen her?"

"Who?" Oliver asked.

"Harriet. She's holding court in the next room."

Oliver grabbed a can of Coke and squeezed his way through, leaving Aura to fend for herself.

"He's here. Oliver take a look at this."

Harriet swooped down on him and held up both of her hands. They were heavily bandaged with elaborate white crepe. She gave him a hug and indicated that he should sit close to her. The back room was filled with people and they were all studying the palm prints on the walls.

"I did it, Oliver. I went and did it. Keira Knightley's hands. Someone faxed her palm-prints to me from the same clinic she uses and I had Aura's stepfather read them. She's a young woman in control. I like her and men like her. If I don't find a man now, it will never happen."

Oliver looked at her bandaged hands and all he could think was: "Doesn't it hurt?"

Harriet nodded, smiling somewhat crazily. "But I'm numbing it with Krug dear. One more bottle and I'll feel nothing for a very long time, I think."

"How long?"

"One month. Just one month from now I will have a new life. A completely new love life. Eat your hearts out, kids. Harriet's back in town. Did you get a drink? You look so hot? Are you well?"

"Aura and me have been running in the park."

"Aura? She's here? I want to see her. Aura? Come in here. I hope you've got a drink."

Aura appeared with a cold beer in her hands and a mouth full of crisps. She laughed when she saw Harriet's hands. "My God, you did it. I don't believe it." Harriet waved her hands at her and Aura just stared at the bandages. "God, you are so brave. So totally crazy. I really hope it changes your life. I really do."

Harriet smiled, accepting Aura's hopes with grace. Then she remembered.

"Oh, you have to meet Farina. She's here from Turkey and she is the best fortune teller in the world ever."

Aura held up her hand. "No way. I never want to know."

An old woman appeared dressed in what Oliver assumed to be traditional costume.

Harriet pointed to Oliver and Aura, but Farina had already spotted them both. She took Oliver's hand and then grabbed Aura's. She wasn't going to let go of either, even though Aura struggled.

Aura and Oliver looked at each other. Life was hard enough without being confronted with the 'best fortune teller in the world'.

"What can you see? Will I be a detective?"

Farina ignored him and closed his eyes.

"I hate having my fortune told," Aura whispered in Oliver's ear. "I'd rather not know anything. It's always the same anyway, tall dark strangers and red-haired twins, or something like that."

Harriet sipped on her champagne, distracted by others who wanted to talk to her.

Aura didn't know how the old woman could concentrate with old 'Soul to Soul' ballads being played on the stereo, let alone with being jostled by the crowd. Oliver just hated having his hand held so tightly, he could feel her long crimson nails biting into his flesh.

"I don't understand." Farina said at last. "Are you brother and sister?"

Oliver laughed. Aura smiled. They looked at each other as if to express the opinion that she knew nothing.

Aura laughed. "I'm sorry, we're not related. So, what terrible things are going to happen to us?"

Farina suddenly dropped their hands and looked Aura in the eye. "It has already happened," she said, "both of you are supposed to be dead."

The old Turkish woman turned away from them then. She was done.

Oliver looked up at Aura and she reached for him, pulled him close to her. She whispered in his ear. "We've cheated death, Oliver. We don't need fortune tellers. We're going to live a very long time. OK?"

Oliver nodded, suddenly overwhelmed by her sweet body scent and the heat of the room.

"I feel dizzy."

"Come on, it's too hot in here."

Aura quickly pulled him out. She could see his red face and she knew she was overheating too. It was all part of the treatment they had been having, you just couldn't take the heat anymore.

They made their way to the front door where the crowd had spilled out onto the pavement. They stood there, taking in the cooler air, when another fuss began, as new people arrived. Oliver saw them first. "Lena! Justine. Grandma Otis?"

Indeed it was. Grandma Otis came into view, supported by her cane and dressed up for the party in her best flowing party dress. She waved at people she knew and looked really happy to be outside. Lena had her by one arm and she too was impressive in her pastel linen Laura Ashley outfit. Oliver had never seen Grandma Otis outside of the house before, or look so happy, and she seemed fine, smiling and accepting a drink and a chair that was brought out to her.

Justine ran up to them both, relieved to know people. "They insisted I come. You look great Aura. Your hair is beautiful."

Aura gave Justine a hug. "We're fine. Get something to drink and hang out with us. Whatever you do, avoid the fortune-teller."

Justine rolled her eyes. "Not another one." She grabbed Oliver's hand a moment and squeezed it. "Brace yourself. There's news. Mrs Otis has been going mad waiting for you to come back."

Before Oliver could reply he heard Grandma Otis calling him.

"Oliver? Where's that boy?" Grandma Otis was calling.

Aura pulled him over and they stood before her. Grandma Otis looked at him and suddenly gave him a hug. "They think they have found him, boy. You make me very proud Oliver. All your letters and dreams. The International Red Cross has sent a photo to Joe."

Oliver just stared. He could see Old Joe arriving now, wearing his usual faded brown suit with a pink flower in the button hole. He was waving, but Oliver could feel his legs buckling under him. He'd been hit by a tidal wave of emotion.

"It's your father, Oliver. They think he's alive. In Gaberone, of all places. He's been found." Grandma Otis explained.

Oliver spun around into Aura's arms and just sobbed. He couldn't explain why. He just couldn't explain what he was feeling. His father was alive. A million things raced through his mind. He'd just learned to love all these people and now his father had been found, he'd take him away, he'd never see Aura again, or Harriet, or Grandma Otis, or Justine, or anyone and it was all his own fault for trying to find his father...

He just sobbed and Aura wrapped her arms around him and held him tight.

Somewhere in the background, he became aware of Harriet shrieking and yelling about getting Old Joe some champagne, but Oliver just felt so overwhelmed, so suddenly lost.

Lena was talking to Aura as she held Oliver in her arms.

"They say he has been in hospital for two years. He's been temporarily blinded, but they say he'll be able to see if he gets an operation. There's something else. He appears to have lost his memory. It was the photo in the newspapers that found him. A care worker recognised him. Joe has been in touch with them. Joe show him the photo."

Oliver took a deep breath. He couldn't be like this forever. He had to surface for air. Joe was suddenly up close and he produced an email with a photograph attached.

Oliver pulled his wet face away from Aura's T-shirt and wiped his eyes.

"I..." He stared at the photograph a moment, scared to death to look, but in an instant he knew. He looked up at Old Joe and felt a huge weight drop off him, and he immediately felt guilty about that. "It's not him, Joe. I'm sorry, but that's not my Dad."

He could see that he had just disappointed a lot of people, Grandma Otis in particular.

"Are you sure?" Justine asked gently. She'd pressed through the adults and taken up position beside him.

"Dad has fair hair, lots of it. He's got bushy eyebrows and a scar above his eye where he fell in Belize. This man looks a bit like him, but it's not him, Justine. Believe me, I know it."

Everyone fell silent a moment. Joe was a bit embarrassed but Oliver took his hand and shook it. "We don't give up though Joe. He's out there somewhere. I know it, and alive. He wouldn't die without telling me first."

Joe accepted his answer with an embarrassed shrug and Lena suddenly took the old man's arm and steered him away towards the bar. "We all need stiff drinks." She declared, and abruptly conversation started up again everywhere around them. The moment passed.

Justine made Oliver drink some Coke and she found him a place to sit on a cushion as Aura also went to comfort Joe.

Somewhat bemused, Joe sipped champagne and he smiled as Aura gave him a kiss. He could see her eyes were red and glazed with emotion. Joe shrugged.

"Finding people is hard. I thought... I was so sure... I am sorry to do that to him. It's a terrible thing to think you have found someone and lose them all over again."

"You tried, Joe. That's the main thing. Lena tells me you found your niece."

"She wants me to go home. She wants me to go to Hamburg. She's in Hamburg. All this time she thought *I* was dead. Can you believe that?"

Aura was surprised. "Hamburg? Would you like to go and see her? I will get you a ticket. You can go tomorrow. God, I'd take you there myself if I could."

"It's taken care of," Grandma Otis declared, having overheard. "He's coming to Paris with us and we'll send him to Hamburg from there."

Oliver suddenly stood up, determined to make things right. He moved to the bar. "Clare? I want everyone to drink to my Dad, who *will* be found one day and Joe who has found his family at last."

Clare got it organised in no time. She had Roxanne pick him up and plonk him onto the counter top. She pushed a small mug of champagne into his hands. Justine managed to grab some champagne too and stood in front of him in case he fell.

"To Oliver's Dad and Joe!" Everyone shouted in unison. They didn't know who these people were, but a drink's a drink and a toast is a toast.

"To Harriet," Clare and Roxanne shouted. "May she get her perfect man!"

"I'd better, or I want my money back." Harriet declared to everyone.

Oliver was happier now. These people wouldn't be taken from him after all. One day they would find his father. Maybe he'd even go to Africa to find him. He sipped his champagne and laughed at Harriet attempting to dance with Roxanne and making a fool of herself.

Later, Aura and Grandma Otis were watching Oliver closely from outside the shop where most people had gathered to talk and drink. They watched as a very protective Justine stood at his side holding his hand whispering little comments into his ear and making him laugh. Grandma Otis noted this too. "She was the unhappiest girl in the world until he came. He seems to change everyone around him." She had taken Aura's hand and she sensed that Aura was altogether a happier person inside herself. She was glad that she had befriended Oliver. She knew it meant a lot to the boy.

"Of course, he'll break all our hearts." Grandma Otis said, with a sigh.

"That does seem to be what men are for." Aura agreed, opening up some sparking water. It fizzed, she laughed as it cascaded onto the pavement and in that moment realised it was the first time she could remember laughing in an age. She looked around her, at this strange assortment of people gathered to celebrate something quite absurd and realised that she was indeed happy.

Oliver looked over and smiled at her. He was happy too. Weird how it was one found friends in life. Did one chose or was one chosen? she mused.

Grandma Otis chuckled beside her. "I think we'll have everyone back for dinner. What do you think, Aura? I have a sudden urge to keep this moment going. Keep Lena sober girl, we'll need her to do the pasta sauce."

Afterword

If you want to meet Grandma Otis, fancy a walk one evening besides the river in Greenwich to get your fortune told, you will discover that the eccentric crumbling backwards home and it's lush garden has completely vanished. Gone too are the scrap yards and in its place stands a vast ugly red brick apartment tower nudging the power station. The cobbles are new, a rare piece of history has succumbed to the bulldozers. It is hard to see where her home or the yards could have ever stood or believe they were ever there.

The rumour is that Grandma Otis had a sudden realisation that she needed to live far away from the river, others say it was a revelation she had in France that summer, either way she abruptly returned and sold up and the last piece of Dickens' world disappeared from Hoskins Street. Not a trace, not a tree from her wild garden was left in memory. Some say when the fog closes in that you can still hear a car twisting in agony from a crane in the long flattened scrapyard, but I confess I have not heard this myself.

They say Oliver found his way to Africa to search for his father with Justine in tow. We do not know yet if he found him. We do know an old cat called Flop now lives at Trinity Hospital and is often to be found sitting on the laps of those who need the most comforting and still, to this day expects a boy to return to hold him tight and talk for long hours of adventures had and lucky escapes made.

Either way, neither boy nor girl has yet returned. Perhaps one day we shall discover more. I sincerely hope so.

Sam North

Also by Sam North

Another Place to die
ISBN 1-84753-899-1
ISBN 978-1-84753-899-4

Another Place to Die is a vivid account of individuals caught up in a worldwide flu pandemic. Set in Vancouver, Canada, this is a terrifying and realistic scenario of people facing the horror of a killer virus that will kill millions. Everything your Government said would protect you is a lie. Make a choice. Escape to a safe place or tough it out. As martial law is declared and soldiers have orders to shoot anyone breaking curfew, normal life begins to break down. Homeland Security have already closed the U.S. borders. Real estate everywhere is in free fall. Mass burial pits are being dug. Everyone is afraid of each other. The Pandemic is coming. Where will you go? Where exactly is safe? *Another Place to Die* is an essential survival manual everyone should read.

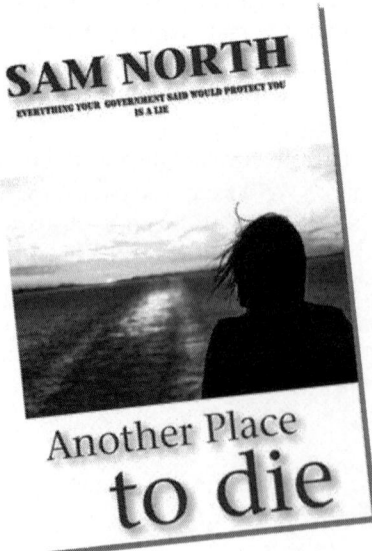

'Beautiful, plausible, and sickeningly addictive, *Another Place to Die* will terrify you, thrill you, and make you petrified of anyone who comes near you...'
Roxy Williams
– Amazon.co.uk

'Fascinating, frightening and compelling, *Another Place to Die* is the ultimate page-turner which I guarantee will result in many late nights under the bedside light with you uttering, 'just one more chapter!!'
Ian Middleton
– Lulu.com

Another Place to die
www.books.lulu.com/content/472938
Available from Amazon.com and direct from the publisher Lulu Press
also Waterstones in the UK

Also by Sam North

Diamonds – The Rush of '72
ISBN 1-4116-1088-1

Diamonds – The Rush of '72 is a true adventure set in the American West. A tale of greed, treachery and bravado. Two prospectors, John Slack and Philip Arnold, arrive penniless and near-starving in San Francisco to deposit raw American diamonds in the Bank of California, it causes quite a stir.

Rumours abound in the city of the biggest diamond find since Kimberley, with fabulous riches to be made. Slack and Arnold try to keep their claim secret. They attract the attention of California's biggest banker, William Ralston and New York's finest investors; including Horace Greeley – only to discover that these fine gentlemen intend to cheat them. But Slack and Arnold are wily men, hardened by years on the mountains. They won't be taken easily. What begins as a trickle in the Colorado mountains would grow into the great rush of '72.

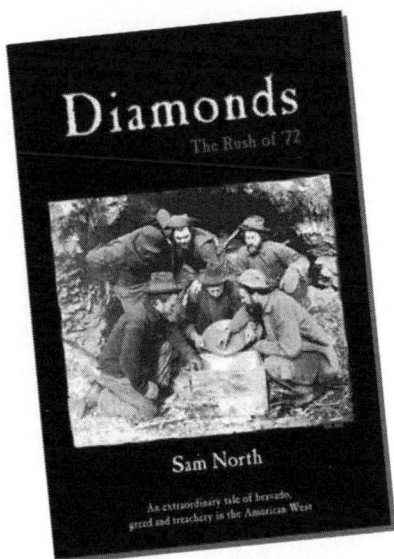

'*Diamonds* took me right inside the people and their dreams... Just when you think you know what's going to happen next, there's another surprise. This book is a marvel.'
Johnny Frem Dixon
– Bolts of Ficton, Vancouver

'This is a terrific piece of storytelling highly recommended for lovers of the Old West and, more importantly, for all those who enjoy a good adventure story well told'.
Chris Lean
– Historical Novel Society Review

Diamonds – The Rush of '72
www.books.lulu.com/content/68464
Distributed by Ingrams and available from Amazon and other online booksellers. Printed in the USA and UK

Also by Sam North

The Curse of the Nibelung – A Sherlock Holmes Mystery
ISBN 1-4116-3748-8

Revealed for the first time the great detective's role in World War II.

It is December 1939. Four British spies have perished in strange circumstances in Nuremberg trying to discover the biggest secret of the Third Reich. Winston Churchill sends Sherlock Holmes on what could be his very last case. Holmes and Watson must enter Germany and solve the mystery. Two ancient men with their beautiful young nurse Cornelia must pretend to be German sympathisers. If captured, England will disown them. Their loyalty and Holmes' skills at deduction will be severly tested. There is no one they can trust and the terrible truth of Nuremberg is far more sinister than even Holmes could imagine. Their chances of ever returning to England, very slim indeed.

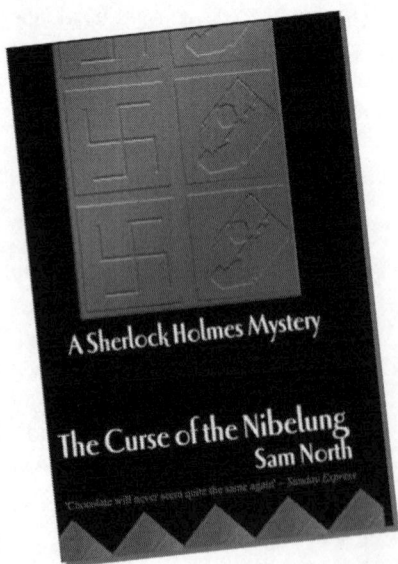

'The triumphant return of Holmes and Watson.'
Eric Hiscok
– The Bookseller

'Chocolate will never be the same again. With an irresistible, high-quality Goon-like zaniness, this dynamically paced thriller follows its own larger-than-life logic. Not to be missed.'
Richard Pearce
– The Sunday Express

The Curse of the Nibelung – A Sherlock Holmes Mystery
www.books.lulu.com/content/132693
Distributed by Ingrams and available from Amazon and other online booksellers. Printed in the USA and UK

1523011R0

Printed in Great Britain by
Amazon.co.uk, Ltd.,
Marston Gate.